... hard SF lovers should flock
to his latest novel ...

—Library Journal on *Leviathans of Jupiter*

"A quick-paced space adventure."
—Publishers Weekly on *Leviathans of Jupiter*

"Bova proves himself equal to the task of
showing how adversity can temper character
in unforeseen ways."
—The New York Times

"Bova gets better and better, combining plausible
science with increasingly complex fiction."
—Daily News (Los Angeles)

"[Bova's] excellence at combining hard science
with believable characters and an attention-grabbing
plot makes him one of the genre's most accessible
and entertaining storytellers."
—Library Journal

FARSIDE

BEN BOVA

A TOM DOHERTY ASSOCIATES BOOK
NEW YORK

This is a work of fiction. All of the characters, organizations, and events portrayed in this novel are either products of the author's imagination or are used fictitiously.

FARSIDE

Copyright © 2013 by Ben Bova

All rights reserved.

A Tor Book
Published by Tom Doherty Associates, LLC
175 Fifth Avenue
New York, NY 10010

www.tor-forge.com

Tor® is a registered trademark of Tom Doherty Associates, LLC.

ISBN 978-0-7653-6359-6

Tor books may be purchased for educational, business, or promotional use. For information on bulk purchases, please contact Macmillan Corporate and Premium Sales Department at 1-800-221-7945, extension 5442, or write specialmarkets@macmillan.com.

First Edition: February 2013
First Mass Market Edition: January 2014

Printed in the United States of America

0 9 8 7 6 5 4 3 2 1

To dearest Rashida,
who is not only a knockout artist
but a lifesaver

My heartfelt thanks to Peter Wehinger,
of the Steward Observatory, University of Arizona,
for his kind and unfailing help

Character determines destiny.

—HERACLITUS OF EPHESUS,
circa 500 B.C.

Yes, we, said Maera. We kill the savage's bulls, and the drunkard's bulls, and the *riau-riau* dancer's bulls. Yes. We kill them. We kill them all right. Yes, yes, yes.

—ERNEST HEMINGWAY

FARSIDE

LOBBER

Trudy Yost was understandably nervous as the ballistic rocket hurtled high above the barren, pockmarked lunar plain.

The liftoff had been a shock. Trudy had dutifully strapped herself into her seat and lowered it back to the full reclining position, as instructed in the safety lecture that played on the screen set into the passenger compartment's overhead paneling.

Then the rocket engines had lit off and the ship hurtled off its launchpad with a deafening roar and bone-rattling vibration. The launch from Earth had been much gentler, and she assumed that a liftoff in the Moon's light gravity would be just as easy.

Something's gone wrong! Trudy thought. The g-force pushed her down into the reclined seat like a ton of cement on her chest. And it wouldn't stop. She thought of the earthquake she'd experienced in Palo Alto, when she'd been a grad student. It went on and on, the whole world shaking and grinding, the dorm building swaying like a ship in a typhoon. Afterward, she was told that the tremor had lasted seventy-eight seconds. But it sure felt like hours.

The rocket engines stopped abruptly, leaving Trudy's ears ringing and her arms floating off the seat's armrests. Her stomach crawled up into her throat. She swallowed bile and swore to herself that she would *not* upchuck.

The pilot's grinning face appeared on the overhead screen. "Well, we're well and truly launched. We'll be at Farside in thirty-two minutes." Almost as an afterthought he added, "You can crank your seats up now and enjoy the view."

Carefully Trudy raised her seat. She swallowed again and told herself that she'd experienced zero gravity on the flight up from Earth and there was absolutely no reason why she should get sick from it now.

Besides, there was this awesome hunk of a guy in the seat across the aisle from her and she'd be damned to hell and back if she was going to make an ass of herself in front of him.

He was smiling at her. "Quite a takeoff, wasn't it?"

Trudy nodded weakly.

"These ballistic flights," he said, "they slam on all the power at liftoff and then let the bird coast the rest of the way. No atmosphere to worry about, we just fly along an arc like an old-time artillery shell."

He's an Adonis! Trudy thought. Handsome, chiseled features; sparkling light brown eyes; thick dark hair long enough to tickle the collar of his expensive-looking jacket. Good broad shoulders, flat midsection. The kind who never looks at mousy little me, she told herself. And here I'm wearing this drab old pullover and jeans. Should have dressed better, should have thought of looks instead of comfort.

It took an effort for her to find her voice. "The ship looks like the Clipperships they use on Earth. Only kind of smaller."

"Most of the Clippers back Earthside are manufactured here on the Moon. At Selene. They use nanomachines to build 'em out of carbon dust. Soot gets turned into diamond structure, thanks to nanotechnology."

Trudy knew that. Everybody knew that, but this hunk of a stud was talking to her as if he were a professor and she a freshman.

"I thought the liftoff would be easier," she said. "Gentler. What with the Moon's lower gravity . . ."

He shook his head. "No, they blast off at four gees. Then coast. Here on the Moon they call these ships 'lobbers.' They just lob them up and out, like artillery shells."

"Yes, you told me that."

He smiled at her, teeth dazzling bright. "So I did." Then he extended a hand across the narrow aisle. "My name's Carter McClintock."

His hand engulfed hers. "Trudy Yost."

He cocked his head. "Trudy? Is that short for Gertrude?"

"No!" Trudy snapped. "Everybody thinks that. My parents named me Trudy. It's on my birth certificate."

"Okay. Okay." He released her hand, then asked, "So what brings you to Farside?"

"I'll be doing my postdoc work there. Under Professor Uhlrich."

"Oh, you're the astronomer," said McClintock, looking impressed. "The professor's new assistant."

"I'll be working with him on the optical interferometer. We're going to image Sirius C."

He nodded uncertainly.

"That's the Earth-sized planet that was discovered about ten years ago," Trudy explained.

"The one they call New Earth, right?"

"Right. It's about two and a half parsecs from us, and it—"

"Parsecs?"

"Three point two six light-years. It's the distance an object would be if it showed a parallax of one arc second. Parallax. Second. Parsec."

"Oh. Yes. I see." He leaned his chair back slightly and turned his attention to the overhead screen.

Stupid, stupid, stupid! Trudy raged at herself. Here you've got this hunk chatting with you and you bury him in jargon. Why do you have to show everybody how smart you are? It's stupid. You just drive them away.

For several moments she sat rigidly in her chair, staring at the display screen, which showed the lunar landscape sliding by far beneath them.

The lobber's passenger compartment was only half full. Six men and women heading for Farside

Consciously refraining from biting her lip, Trudy turned back to McClintock and asked, "And why are you going to Farside?"

"I work there, same as you're going to," he said, brightening slightly.

"You're an astronomer?"

He flashed that knockout smile again. "No. I'm . . . uh, I'm in management. I work with Professor Uhlrich, help him with administrative matters."

"Oh," said Trudy, glowing inside. "I guess we'll see a lot of each other, then."

"I imagine we will."

DATA BANK

By the second half of the twenty-first century astronomers had detected several thousand planets orbiting other stars. Most of these exoplanets were gas giants, bloated spheres of hydrogen and helium, totally unlike Earth. But a few percent of them were small, rocky worlds, more like our own.

One in particular raised hopes of being really Earthlike: Sirius C. It was almost the same size as Earth, and although its parent star was a fiercely blazing blue-white giant, much larger and hotter than the Sun, the planet's orbit lay at the "Goldilocks" distance from Sirius where its surface temperature was not too hot, and not too cold for liquid water to exist.

On Earth, liquid water means life. Beneath the frozen iron sands of Mars, liquid water melting from the permafrost hosts an underground biosphere of microbial life-forms. In the ice-covered seas of Jupiter's major moons, living organisms abound. In the planet-girdling ocean beneath the eternal clouds of giant Jupiter itself, life teems and flourishes.

Sirius C was a challenge to the astrobiologists. It couldn't possibly bear life, Goldilocks notwithstanding, not sandwiched between brilliant Sirius A and its dwarf star companion, Sirius B. The dwarf had erupted in a series of nova explosions eons ago. The death throes of Sirius B must have sterilized any planets in the vicinity. But there it was, a rocky, Earth-sized planet, the *only* planet in the Sirius system, orbiting Sirius A in a nearly perfect circle.

Might there be a chance that the planet did harbor some kind of life forms? The astrobiologists worked overtime concocting theories to support the hope that the Earth-sized planet might indeed host an Earth-type biosphere. The popular media had no such problem. They quickly dubbed Sirius C "New Earth."

Orbiting in a zone where water could be liquid did not necessarily mean that Sirius C actually had liquid water on its surface. Astronomers all across Earth—and on the Moon—strove to discover water, oxygen, other clues to the presence of life on the exoplanet.

Detecting the planet was not the same as imaging it. Sirius C was discovered by the minute gravitational tugs it exerted on its parent star. Then telescopes in orbit measured the tiny dip in light output from Sirius A when the planet transited across its star's shining face. From these data the eager astronomers of Earth deduced the planet's size and surface temperature.

Now the task was to get visual images of the planet, to photograph its surface and measure the constituents of its atmosphere—if it had an atmosphere. No telescope on Earth could produce such imagery at a distance of nearly eighty-four trillion kilometers.

Not even the telescopes in space could reveal much more than a blurry speck of a disc. But calculations showed that a set of very large telescopes, working together as an optical interferometer, might be able to resolve surface features on Sirius C. The telescopes would have to be in space, clear of the Earth's murky, turbulent atmosphere.

Owing to the driving ambition of Anita Halleck, the International Astronautical Authority decided to build such an interferometer in solar orbit. Its segmented mirrors would be placed at opposite locations along the Earth's orbit, producing an instrument with a baseline of two astronomical units: nearly two hundred million kilometers.

The lunar nation of Selene was already constructing a radio telescope facility on the far side of the Moon, where it would be insulated from all the radio chatter of Earth by more than three thousand kilometers of rock. Farside, the side of the Moon that is permanently pointed away from Earth, was the quietest place in the solar system for sensitive radio searches for intelligent life.

The radio telescope, dubbed Cyclops, was to consist of a thousand dish-shaped antennas, each one a hundred meters across, covering a total area ten kilometers wide.

When the IAA announced its plans for the space-based optical interferometer, one of Selene University's distinguished astronomers, Professor Jason Uhlrich, proposed building a more modest optical instrument on the Moon's far side. After all, the surface of the airless Moon was effectively in space. The vacuum at the lunar surface was actually a thousand times thinner than the vacuum in Earth orbit. Lunar materials could be used to build the telescopes, and the Moon offered a firm platform for them.

So the Farside Observatory became the site for an optical interferometer consisting of three interlinked telescopes, each with a main mirror of one hundred meters, slightly larger than an American football field, more than twice the size of any telescope mirror built on Earth. They were to be erected in three giant craters: the longest distance between them would be about eighteen hundred kilometers.

And in the midst of the optical instruments, the Cyclops radio telescope was being erected. Professor Uhlrich was named to head Farside Observatory. He enthusiastically proclaimed that the observatory would be the finest and most important astronomical facility in the solar system.

Yet, even in the gentle gravity of the Moon, building such large and complex structures was a challenge to the skill and knowledge of the men and women who came to Farside.

More than anything else, it was a test of their perseverance and their heart, a challenge that brought out the best in some of them.

In some of them it brought out the worst.

Farside Observatory coming up," announced the cheerful voice of the lobber's pilot. "We'll be down in Mare Moscoviense in five minutes."

Trudy thought that "down" could mean a crash as well as a landing, but she tried to keep the worry off her face as she tightened the straps of her safety harness.

"The Sea of Moscow," McClintock said knowingly. "It's actually just a big crater. Korolev is bigger. So is Mendeleev. Not like the Mare Nubium or Mare Imbrium on the nearside."

"When a crater's that big," Trudy replied, "it's called a ringed plain, not a crater." There, she thought, let him know I'm not a total ignoramus.

Unperturbed, McClintock went on, "Lots of features on the farside are named after Russians, you know. One of their early spacecraft was the first to observe the farside."

Trudy nodded as she stared at the display screen above her head. She saw a curving range of worn-looking rounded mountains, then a flat plain pockmarked with small craters. It looked dusty, bare, utterly barren.

And then, "Look! The Cyclops array!"

Hundreds of round radio dish antennas stood lined up across the floor of the huge crater. The scene reminded Trudy of the segmented eye of an insect. And it looked as if the ship was hurtling down, straight at it.

She glanced across the aisle at McClintock; his handsome features were set in a tight grimace, as if he were trying to steer the ship himself by grim determination. His hands were gripping the seat's armrests tightly.

I'm not the only one who's nervous, she realized.

"Retro burn in thirty seconds," the pilot announced, sounding much more serious than before.

The ground was rushing up to hit them. The array of radio telescopes slid out of the screen's view; there was nothing out there now but empty, barren ground, strewn with boulders and pitted with craterlets. It looked very hard.

A roar and a pressure against her back, like someone slamming a two-by-four along her spine. Then it stopped as abruptly as it had started.

"We're down," said the pilot, cheerful again. "Welcome to the Farside Observatory."

Trudy heard several sighs of relief, and realized that the loudest one was her own. Then everybody started to talk at once, unbuckle their seat harnesses, get to their feet.

We're here, she thought. Now the work begins.

She stood up and reached for the overhead luggage bin. McClintock leaned across and opened the hatch for her, then pulled out her meager travelbag and handed it to her. He was tall as well as handsome: Trudy's plain, lank hair barely rose to the level of his chin.

"Thank you," Trudy said to him.

"You're quite welcome," he replied.

Then he grabbed his own bag and started up the aisle toward the passenger compartment's airlock hatch without another glance at her. Trudy shuffled along after him, walking carefully in the light lunar gravity.

She was ordinary in every way, she knew. Average height for a Canadian woman, with a slim build and dull brown hair. No beauty, although she thought her light green eyes were kind of nice. Men rarely noticed her, especially tall, handsome guys like McClintock. He's got no interest in me, Trudy thought glumly. He made conversation with me during the flight, that's all.

The trouble with living on the Moon, Trudy quickly decided, was that you never saw the Moon. You were indoors all the time. Trudy stepped from the lobber rocket's passenger compartment into an access tube that was sealed to its hatch, then along the spongy-floored, rib-walled tube into a reception area where a young man in a slightly ridiculous-looking pumpkin orange jumpsuit took her travelbag from her and handed it to a gleaming white robot that already had a half-dozen other pieces of luggage draped on its many arms. Then the young man led her through a maze of corridors lined with closed doors.

"Your luggage is being sent to your assigned living quarters," he assured Trudy. "But Professor Uhlrich wanted to see you the instant you arrived."

The kid was kind of cute, she thought. Curly blond hair, light eyes, kind of chubby, but his round face was smiling pleasantly at her. Probably a freshman, drafted from the university to work for the Farside Observatory. Students made a handy pool of slave labor, Trudy remembered from her own undergraduate days.

She glanced at the name tag pinned to his chest: WINSTON.

The observatory's living and working areas were underground, of course, like all the human communities on the Moon, built into the side of the ringwall mountains that surrounded Mare Moscoviense. The lunar surface was airless, and subject to temperature swings from nearly three hundred degrees in sunlight to more than two hundred below zero in shadow. Hard radiation from the Sun and stars drenched the ground, together with a constant infall of dust-mote-sized micrometeorites. It was safer underground. Much safer.

But dismally drab, dreary. The corridors were tunnels, really, narrow, their low ceilings lined with pipes and electrical conduits. Trudy wondered if they would turn her into a claustrophobe.

"Be careful how you walk," her young guide warned. "In one-sixth gravity it's easy to go staggering around like a drunk rabbit."

Trudy had paid strict attention to the orientation lectures

back in the space station before she'd headed out to the Moon. She very deliberately scuffed the weighted boots she had bought during her brief stopover at Selene along the corridor's plastic-tiled floor in a bent-kneed shuffle. It reminded her of videos she'd seen of chimpanzees trying to walk on their hind legs.

Her guide stopped at a door marked:

J. UHLRICH
DIRECTOR
ANGEL OBSERVATORY

"Angel Observatory?" she asked.

"That's the observatory's official name," the guide explained. "Named after Roger Angel, an astronomer who built the largest telescopes on Earth, more'n half a century ago. The name makes for a lot of jokes, you know, about angels and all. We just call it Farside."

He rapped on the door, very gently.

"Enter," a voice called from the other side of the door.

Her guide slid it open and gestured Trudy through.

It was a small office, its ceiling of smoothed rock depressingly low, its four walls blank but glowing slightly. Wall-sized smart screens, Trudy recognized. A desk painted to look like wood stood across from the door, with a conference table joined to it like the stem of a T. Behind the desk sat Jason Uhlrich, director of Farside Observatory.

Professor Uhlrich rose to his feet as Trudy entered, his head cocked slightly. With a hesitant smile he gestured toward one of the conference table's chairs.

"Welcome, Dr. Yost," he said in a nasal, reedy voice. "Please to make yourself comfortable."

Uhlrich was a small man, a bit shorter than Trudy and very slight in build. His face had the prominent cheekbones and high forehead of an ascetic, although his skin looked waxy, almost arti-ficial. His hair was cropped short, as was his trim beard. Both were a soft gray, almost silver. Narrow shoulders, tiny delicate hands. He was wearing a dark blue cardigan jacket over a white turtleneck, neat and precise. Trudy felt shabby in her dull old shirt and baggy jeans.

It was Uhlrich's eyes that caught Trudy's attention. They were as dark as two chips of obsidian. But they seemed blank, unfocused.

She stuck out her hand. "I'm very pleased to meet you, sir."

Uhlrich's smile turned slightly warmer, yet he ignored her proffered hand. "Thank you. I hope we can work well together."

He gestured toward the chair again and sat down behind his desk. Trudy took the chair; it swiveled so that it was easy for her to face Professor Uhlrich.

He turned to the computer screen on his desk and brushed his fingertips across it, frowning slightly. "We should be joined by Mr. McClintock . . . He should be here by now."

Trudy's pulse thumped. He'll be here! I'll see him again. Great!

With a disappointed little sigh, Uhlrich said, "Well, I might as well begin. No sense waiting until—"

A rap on the door stopped him. It slid open and Carter McClintock stepped in, all smiles.

"Professor," said McClintock as he strode toward the desk. Pulling out the chair across the table from Trudy, he added, "It's good to see you again, Trudy."

"I expected you five minutes ago," Uhlrich said. He neither rose from his desk chair nor offered McClintock his hand.

Looking just the tiniest bit embarrassed, McClintock said, "I, uh, I had to answer a call of nature on the way here. Sorry, but it couldn't be helped."

"I see." Uhlrich's tone was frosty. The director swung his gaze from McClintock to Trudy, then said in a resigned tone, "Very well, then, let me describe our observatory and its goals to you, Dr. Yost. Mr. McClintock will fill you in on the observatory's organization and management."

The walls lit up with views of four different lunar craters. Trudy recognized the Cyclops radio telescope assembly, under construction up above them on the surface of the Sea of Moscow.

Uhlrich began, "We are building three one-hundred-meter telescopes at Crater Mendeleev, Crater Korolev, and Crater Gagarin." The frame around each screen lit briefly as the professor mentioned it.

Trudy saw that construction was under way at each crater.

"The hundred-meter main mirrors for each of these sites are being built here, at Moscow. The first of them has been completed, and is now being transported to Mendeleev, where it will be installed—"

The buzz of a phone interrupted him. Frowning at his desktop console annoyedly, Uhlrich said, "Pardon me. That is the emergency line."

He called out, "Answer," and the wall screen in front of Trudy showed the face of a young man, looking grim, troubled. His hair was a thick dark mop, so was his ragged dark beard. He had the saddest eyes Trudy had ever seen, dark and downcast. He looked as if he were carrying the troubles of the world on his shoulders. She saw that he was in a space suit, but he had removed its helmet.

"Professor," he began, then his voice broke.

"What is the emergency? What is it?" Uhlrich demanded.

"The mirror," said the harried-looking man. "Halfway up the ringwall . . . it . . . it slid off the carrier and cracked."

THE LARGE AND THE SMALL

Uhlrich shot to his feet. "Cracked?" he shrieked.

The man on the screen looked as if he'd rather be roasting on a spit. "Yessir. Halfway up the slope the rig slewed off the road and . . . and the mirror slid off and cracked. Too much torsional strain, even in the frame that was holding it."

For an instant Trudy thought that Professor Uhlrich was going to have a stroke. His face went red, then chalk white. His fists clenched at his sides.

"How could it slip off the road?" he demanded. "How could you allow such a stupid, criminal thing to happen? You've ruined everything!"

The man on the screen looked weary, spent. His bearded face was sheened with perspiration, his dark hair matted, plastered over his forehead. But his expression hardened as Uhlrich berated him.

"Look, Professor, I tried to warn you about the risks. *You* try lugging a hundred-meter-wide chunk of glass across those mountains. I *told* you it'd be chancy."

"Don't you understand that we're in a race? A race against time! And you've ruined two years' work! Two years' work!"

In a race? Trudy asked herself. Then she remembered that the IAA was building a humongous interferometer in space. Professor Uhlrich wants to beat them, she realized. He wants to get the Farside Observatory running before the IAA can complete its project. Holy spit, no wonder he's blazing.

Uhlrich slumped back into his chair, then stared at the screen with undisguised contempt. "You built that road, Mr. Simpson. You vouched for it, you told me the mirror could be transported across the ringwall safely. You—"

"Professor, I built the road to the specifications that Nate Oberman set out and you okayed. I told Oberman that we ought to make the grading easier, all those switchbacks were a risk. But you ordered Nate to push it through as fast as possible. You told us you were willing to take the risks. So now you're paying the price."

"Oberman assured me that the road would be perfectly safe!"

"Professor, I warned you it would be a crapshoot."

"I don't remember such a warning," Uhlrich said stubbornly.

"Transporting that mirror isn't like taking a walk in the frigging park, what with those switchbacks and all. If we'd had more time to build the road better—"

"Oberman assured me!"

"And I tried to tell you both we needed more time to make the road better. But neither of you listened to me."

With a shake of his head, Uhlrich moaned, "We'll have to start all over again."

"For what it's worth," said the man on the screen, his voice more conciliatory, "I'm sorry about it."

"Bring it back," Uhlrich told him. "We'll have to remelt the glass and spin it all over again."

The face on the screen nodded tightly.

"And report to me the instant you get back here," Uhlrich added. "I want you and Oberman in my office as soon as you return. The very instant!"

"Yessir," the younger man said. Then his image winked off.

"Two years' work," Uhlrich muttered again, shaking his head in misery.

McClintock spoke up. "Maybe we can repair the mirror."

Uhlrich gave him a withering look. "Repair? The telescope's main mirror? It's ruined! Ruined!"

Smiling easily at the professor, McClintock said, "I understand that the mirror's got to have very exact tolerances, but mightn't it be possible to repair it using nanotechnology?"

"Nanomachines?" Uhlrich gasped.

McClintock replied patiently, "I know nanotech is banned on Earth. But here on the Moon it's used every day. The world's leading nanotechnology expert, Dr. Kristine Cardenas, is over at Selene."

"Nanomachines," Uhlrich repeated. From the dark tone of his voice, Trudy half expected the professor to cross himself or pull out a silver crucifix.

"I could at least meet with Dr. Cardenas and see what she thinks of the possibilities," McClintock urged.

"Nanomachines can be dangerous," Uhlrich murmured. "They have been used to assassinate people."

"That's why they're banned on Earth, of course," McClintock said easily. "But here on the Moon you don't have ten or twelve billion crackpots running loose. Everybody here has been tested, examined for mental stability and technical talent, haven't they? The population of Selene is selected for intelligence and social compatibility. There are no murderers on the Moon, no fanatics or terrorists."

Trudy wondered if that was true. She certainly hoped so.

Uhlrich stared at McClintock in grim silence.

"I really think we should at least look at the possibilities," McClintock repeated.

"Do you?" Uhlrich muttered.

"Yes, I do. I strongly recommend it."

Trudy felt puzzled. There was something going on between the two of them, something more than the words they were uttering.

At last Uhlrich sighed and said, "Very well, Mr. McClintock, go ahead and see what Dr. Cardenas has to say about this problem. I don't suppose it would hurt anything to talk to her."

McClintock rose to his feet, all smiles. "Good. I'll call her right away."

The professor turned back to Trudy. She could see that he

was sizzling, angry. But his eyes were strange; he was looking in her direction, but not directly at her. He made a bitter smile.

"Dr. Yost, I'm afraid I don't feel up to giving you the orientation presentation I had planned."

"I understand, sir," said Trudy. "Maybe somebody else could do it?"

"No. I'll meet with you first thing tomorrow morning. Make it eight A.M. No—seven thirty."

"Seven thirty sharp. Here in your office?"

"Yes. Of course."

"Right."

"In the meantime," Uhlrich said, "I'll get someone from the staff to show you around this facility. So that your day won't be totally wasted."

"That'll be fine," Trudy replied.

She rose and headed for the door, which McClintock was already sliding open.

Turning, Trudy saw Uhlrich sink his head in his hands. He looked as if he were going to cry.

DOSSIER:
TRUDY JOCELYN YOST

Her father was a lawyer and a successful politician in Canada's capital city who married late in life and was already well past fifty when his only daughter was born. He expected Trudy to be a lawyer, too, since he was certain that she had a fine mind and a strong personality. Like himself, he thought.

Her mother died when Trudy was five years old, leaving her feeling lost and alone in a world of loud, uncaring adults who loomed over her and often made her feel small and frightened. But she remembered her mother's oft-repeated advice: "A sunny smile and a positive attitude will carry you far in this world."

Her father, on the other hand, always told her sternly, "Face your challenges, never run away from them. Never back down from your challenges."

So she learned to face her anxieties and by the time she started grammar school she had overcome her fear of her father's overbearing friends. She faced them with a sunny smile and they thought she was precocious, and very clever.

By then, her father had retired from politics and had accepted the chairmanship of the board of Ottawa's Museum of Science and Technology, a board composed mostly of fellow well-heeled citizens.

When Trudy got the best marks in her first-grade class, her father rewarded her by taking her to the museum, grandly explaining the exhibits in words she could not fully understand. He quickly grew tired of her questions.

"Now you're in for a treat," he said as they walked past a big round ball that Trudy recognized as the Earth.

"Where's Canada, Daddy?" she asked.

He paused and turned toward the globe. "Right here, honey. All this region here, from the Atlantic Ocean to the Pacific. The third largest nation on Earth. See? There's the Great Lakes and—"

"Where's Ottawa, Daddy? Where's our house?"

Frowning slightly, her father said, "Never mind that. I'm taking you to a very special place."

Her hand in his, Trudy dutifully went with her father past a long line of people who were standing and waiting for something. They looked impatient and unhappy.

Her father marched right up to a closed door where a young woman in a smart uniform recognized him immediately.

"Your seats are on the wall, Counselor Yost, right beneath the sign that says North," the attendant whispered as she opened the door for them.

It was a round room with thick carpeting and a big gray dome overhead that glowed faintly. The rows of chairs were arranged in a big circle, and it was very quiet, as if the walls absorbed sound. Trudy and her father were the only people in the place. He led her to their seats, which were marked RESERVED. The chairs were comfortably padded and even tilted backwards a little. Trudy leaned as far back as she could, giggling, until her father silenced her with a dour look.

"This is a planetarium, young lady, not a playground."

Just then all the doors opened and the other people started to stream in and fill every seat. Soft music began to play. Then slowly, slowly the room got darker and darker and darker. Trudy couldn't see the dome, or even her father sitting next to her. She felt a little afraid, but she reached for her father's warm hand and that made her feel better. After a few moments, though, her father pulled his hand away.

Then the music stopped, and a man's deep, powerful voice intoned:

"When I consider Thy heavens, the work of Thy fingers,

"The moon and the stars which Thou set in place,

"What is man that Thou should be mindful of him?

"And the son of man, that Thou should care for him?"

At that moment, the darkness was suddenly pierced by stars, thousands of stars, millions of stars. The audience gasped. Trudy felt as if she were falling *up*, up into that cold, remorseless infinite wilderness. She groped for her father's hand but in the darkness she couldn't find it. The stars were like a million million unblinking eyes staring at her, probing into her, making her very, very frightened.

She burst into loud, bawling tears. Her father, embarrassed beyond words, had to take his squalling seven-year-old daughter out of her seat and stumble his way out of the planetarium.

Trudy never forgot that moment, the instant when she first saw the stars as they truly were. Not the soft skies of summer, with clouds drifting by on warm winds. Not the sharp, crystalline dark skies of winter. Even then the stars twinkled at you, distant but friendly. Even then the Moon was generally up there, smiling lopsidedly at her.

But to see the universe as it truly is, vast, cold, infinite, and uncaring—that frightened young Trudy Yost down to the marrow of her bones.

Face your challenges. Never run away from them.

Trudy began to read about astronomy. The unblinking immensity of the universe frightened her at some primal level, so she set out to conquer her fear. She studied the stars *because* they frightened her. When she started college—prelaw—she took a course in introductory astronomy. She was going to learn about that coldly aloof immensity. Knowledge would overcome fear.

Her father thought it a waste of her time. "Remember, you're going to law school," he insisted.

Instead she smiled at her Daddy and switched from prelaw to the astronomy curriculum: a slight, undistinguished young woman with an elfin figure, short-cropped plain brown hair and light green eyes—and a sharp, quick intelligence coupled with a dogged determination.

Trudy persevered with astronomy even over her father's bellowing complaints. Something about the stars lured her, challenged her. The more she learned about them the more fascinated she became, the more she realized that there was still so much to discover. Despite her father's exasperated thundering, she became an astronomer.

Her first sexual encounter came during her sophomore year, with a bearded, slouching assistant professor who smoked a pipe and taught the Introduction to Planetary Astronomy course. He invited Trudy to his apartment off-campus after they had had dinner together, dropped a popular pill into the glass of wine he offered her, and carried her slim semiconscious body to his bed. In the morning she awoke, alone in the bloodstained sheets. He had left a note explaining that he had an early class to teach and she could let herself out.

At first she was devastated, but remembering her mother's advice about a positive attitude, she said to herself, At least *that's* over.

And then the realization hit her: He was afraid I'd say no! The poor dumb jackass drugged me because he was worried that I might turn him down!

She never saw him again. And she didn't care.

She did her graduate studies in California, and then, much to her delighted surprise, was offered a postdoc position by Selene University to work at the new Farside Observatory.

"On the Moon?" her father howled. "No, it's impossible! I won't hear of it."

But Trudy went anyway, leaving her father at the spaceport in Toronto with tears streaming down his cheeks.

For the first time in her life, Trudy realized that her father actually did love her.

MIRROR LAB

rudy slid Professor Uhlrich's door shut quietly. A few paces down the corridor, McClintock was already speaking into his pocketphone.

"Yes, Dr. Cardenas. I appreciate your cooperation. I'll call you back as soon as I get to my quarters here at Farside and we can discuss this problem in detail."

He clicked the phone shut and turned to Trudy. "I've got to run. See you later."

And he actually started to sprint down the corridor, only to bounce and soar in the light lunar gravity. He thumped against a wall, skidded to a halt, and then—throwing an embarrassed grin in Trudy's direction—he started along the corridor again, slower this time, more carefully. Trudy was left alone.

She hadn't the faintest idea of which way to turn. No one else was in sight. Everybody's busy working, she thought. Well, this rabbit's warren can't be all that big. I'll find my way. First thing is to figure out where my quarters are.

Then she saw the same cute blond guy who had met her at the landing site hustling down the corridor toward her in his pumpkin-colored coveralls.

"Professor Uhlrich says I'm supposed to show you around the place," he said, puffing slightly.

"Great," said Trudy. "Maybe you could show me my quarters first."

"Sure."

As Trudy suspected, the underground facility wasn't very

large. One main corridor, with three side corridors branching from it. Trudy's living quarters consisted of a single room, sparsely furnished with a bed, a desk, two chairs—one a recliner that looked like it had been salvaged from a Clipper rocket—and a wide display screen mounted on the wall above the desk. A compact kitchenette took up one corner. Accordion-fold doors opened onto a closet and a lavatory.

She saw that her soft-sided garment carrier and travelbag had been deposited on the bed, which looked big enough for two people.

"All the living spaces are small," her guide explained, almost apologetically.

"This'll do fine," Trudy said. "It'll be like living in a dorm again."

The kid chuckled and nodded. "Not as many parties, though. The prof doesn't like fooling around."

"Nose to the grindstone, huh?"

"And then some," he said fervently.

"Okay, where to now?" Trudy asked.

"The only really interesting thing to show you is the mirror lab. The rest is just offices and workrooms and living spaces."

"So let's see the mirror lab."

As they went to the door, Trudy pointed to the name tag on the guide's coveralls. "Winston, huh? What's your first name?"

He reddened slightly. "Winston. I'm Winston squared." Then he added, "My father's sense of humor."

"Do people call you Winnie?"

Shaking his head, Winston replied, "Not unless they want to fight."

She smiled at him. "Okay, Winston. My name's Trudy, and it isn't short for Gertrude. Just plain Trudy."

"Okay. Trudy it is."

Winston told Trudy that he was an electronics engineer. His nominal job was wiring the hundreds of antennas of the Cyclops facility as they were erected.

"When I'm not running errands for Professor Uhlrich," he said. Then he quickly amended, "Not that I mind showing you around; this is fun."

The mirror lab was the largest space in the underground complex, a natural cave in the ringwall mountain that had been smoothed and filled with the equipment for making hundred-meter-wide telescope mirrors. No frills, Trudy saw. This was a working area. A half-dozen technicians hunched over workstations on a balcony that overlooked a huge, slowly spinning turntable.

"That's the oven where the glass chunks are melted down," Winston explained. "Then the molten glass is spun slowly so it flows over the superstructure and takes on the exact curvature of the mirror. Once that's done, the mirror's allowed to cool, then the final polishing is done."

Trudy stared down from the balcony's railing at the slowly revolving turntable. It looked well used, strictly functional, utterly utilitarian.

"A hundred meters in diameter," she breathed. "Wow."

"You couldn't build a mirror that big on Earth," Winston said. "It'd crack under its own weight."

"Where's the glass come from?"

"From Selene. They scoop silicon from the ground. The regolith has plenty of silicon in it. And oxygen and all the other elements you need to make high-quality optical glass."

"Strictly a local operation," Trudy murmured, still staring down at the turntable as it moved at its stately, unhurried pace.

"Oh, we have to bring in boron and some of the other exotic elements up from Earth," Winston said. "But those're minor ingredients. The bulk of the material comes from the regolith."

One of the technicians got up from her workstation and walked past Trudy and Winston, heading for the dispensing machines at the far end of the balcony.

"Hi, Win," she said as she passed.

He nodded to her. "Lunch break?"

"Kinda."

"You heard they're bringing the Mendeleev mirror back?" Winston asked her.

She stopped and turned toward him. "That's gonna screw up our schedule, for sure. Gotta start all over again, from scratch."

Winston shrugged and the technician headed for the dispensing machines.

Trudy felt her brow knitting as she asked, "When you set up the mirror in its mount, what about the temperature swings between daylight and dark? How's that affect the glass?"

"Doesn't," said Winston. "The mirror's kept inside an insulated tube. Never gets direct sunlight. It's always at a low temperature, so it won't expand or contract very much."

She nodded. "Figures."

There really wasn't much to see, but the mirror lab fascinated Trudy. The biggest telescope mirrors ever made were being manufactured here. The place was quietly spectacular, she thought. The thousand-meter telescopes that the IAA wanted to place in space were composed of smaller segments: None of their sections were as big as the mirrors being built here at Farside.

After nearly an hour of staring at the turntable and talking to the monitoring technicians, Winston led Trudy back out to the central corridor. She left with reluctance, but Winston seemed to have something more to show her.

"Where are we going now?" she asked.

He pointed down the corridor to a closed steel hatch. Above it was a lighted red sign: AIRLOCK.

"Outside," said Winston.

"Outside?" A shiver of alarm flared through Trudy.

"If you're up to it."

OUTSIDE

Winston slid back the corridor door and led Trudy into a locker room, where empty space suits were hanging in a row, like a museum display of medieval armor. A hard plastic bench ran along the front of the lockers. Beyond its end, Trudy could see the heavy steel inner hatch of the airlock.

This is an initiation ritual, Trudy told herself as she slowly wormed her arms through the ribbed sleeves of the thermal undergarment for the space suit that Winston had picked out for her. Like hazing at a sorority or buying a round of beers first day on a new job, she thought. Here they take you out on the bare, airless surface of the Moon to see if you've got the guts to do it. That's how you become one of them.

"You need a small size," Winston said, leading her past several lockers, each containing an empty suit.

You can do this, Trudy told herself, trying to keep her fear from showing. You went outside at Selene and it was okay. Yeah, a sneering voice in her head countered. Outside. In a tour bus. A nice, comfortable, safe bus with twenty-some tourists. And even then you didn't have the nerve to get out of the bus and walk on the surface, you just looked through the glass ceiling and focused on the Earth shining up there nice and bright.

It was dangerous outside, she knew. You could go through four-hundred-degree temperature swings just by stepping from sunlight into shadow. Hard radiation poured out of the sky. And meteors peppered the surface. I could get shot out there!

"Here," said Winston, stopping at one of the lockers, "this one ought to fit you okay."

Reluctant or not, she wriggled into the pants of the space suit and allowed Winston to help her slide the hard-shell torso over her head. Several other Farside employees had mysteriously shown up, grins on their faces, witnesses to the newbie's initiation.

As Winston settled the life-support pack on her back and plugged in its connections to the suit, he asked mildly, "Trudy, are you sure you want to do this?"

"Sure," she snapped, with a certainty that she didn't feel at all. "Why not?"

"Okay."

He pulled down a suit with his own name stenciled on its chest while a couple of the technicians who were standing nearby stepped up to check out Trudy's space suit. Boots and gloves sealed. Backpack connected. One of them started to take the clear glassteel helmet off the shelf atop the locker, but Trudy pulled it out of his hands and lowered it over her own head. I can do that much for myself, she thought.

One of the bystanders, a sturdily built older woman, watched intently as Trudy turned the helmet on its neck ring until it clicked into place.

"Locked and loaded," she murmured with an approving nod.

The woman seemed to be in charge. She carefully checked the suit's radio reception, the servomotors that helped to bend the joints, the air circulation fans and heater. Trudy heard the faint gurgle of water circulating through the undergarment.

"Good to go," the female technician said.

Winston was ready, too. He clumped in his suit's heavy boots to the airlock hatch. Trudy followed a step behind him.

The big heavy hatch swung open and they stepped over its coaming into the airlock itself: a metal-walled chamber scarcely big enough for the two of them in their cumbersome suits. To Trudy it felt comfortably snug, safe, like a protective womb

"Closing the inner hatch," Winston said. Trudy heard his voice in her helmet speakers.

Once the hatch shut, the older woman's voice said, "Pumping down."

A pump started chugging away, but the sound quickly faded as the air was sucked out of the chamber. Trudy felt the vibration of the pump through the soles of her boots. We're in vacuum now, she knew, her breath quickening. They're pumping all the air out.

The vibration stopped and the display pad beside the outer hatch turned from amber to red.

"Ready for excursion," Winston said.

Trudy nodded inside her helmet as she sucked in a deep breath. The air felt cold, dry.

"You're clear for excursion," said the woman's voice.

"Opening outer hatch," Winston said, as he reached a gloved hand to the display pad.

"Copy opening outer hatch."

The hatch swung slowly, noiselessly open. Trudy saw an expanse of open, uneven bare ground. Not a bush or a blade of grass. Nothing can live out there, she told herself. Not unless you're in a suit.

Winston stepped out onto the dusty ground and extended his arm, inviting Trudy to follow him.

Sealed inside the helmet, it was hard for Trudy to see her own booted feet. She tried to bend at the waist, but the suit's joints were stiff, even with the servomotors assisting them. Carefully, she stepped over the hatch's coaming and out onto the lunar regolith.

"You're doing fine," Winston encouraged.

I'm walking on the Moon! Trudy felt excited and scared all at the same time, like the first time she had done a parachute jump, back in California.

She kept her eyes on the ground. It was uneven, pockmarked with little craterlets and strewn with rocks from the size of pebbles to boulders as big as an automobile. Looking up warily, she saw that the horizon seemed strangely close, a hard slash across the ground where the world ended and the infinity of space began. No haze in the distance, she realized. No air.

This isn't so bad, she told herself. Then she saw a structure a couple of dozen meters away. It looked like a shed made of thin honeycomb metal.

"What's that?" she asked.

"The garage. We park the tractors in there. They're both out now, towing the mirror across the mountains."

Looking up cautiously, Trudy asked, "But where are the mountains? I thought we were surrounded by ringwall mountains."

Winston's radio voice answered, "They're over the horizon in the direction you're facing. You can't see them from here—unless you turn around."

She did, a slow full one-eighty turn, and saw the ringwall mountains rising over the airlock hatch. They looked tired, worn, their slopes gentle. Bunny slopes, she thought, if they had any snow on them. There seemed to be a road of sorts carved into the bare rock: switchbacking from the summit to the floor on which they stood.

"Those mountains have been eroded by several billion years of micrometeorite infall," Winston was saying. "Sandpapered by those little dust motes flying in from space."

"Yeah," Trudy replied. No water to erode them. No rain or wind. But if a bullet-sized micrometeorite happened to hit me . . .

She tried to shake off her worries and at last worked up the courage to look up at the stars. There were thousands of them! Millions! Billions! Even through the heavy tinting of her helmet, Trudy could see them spangling the blackness of space, stretching out to infinity, staring down at her with ominous unblinking solemnity. So many stars! Trudy couldn't make out any of the constellations she was so familiar with back on Earth: the profusion of stars blotted them out.

Then it hit her. The sky was empty! No Earth appeared up there, bright and friendly, the way it hung in the sky over Selene. Suddenly she was seven years old again, all alone, very frightened, all alone in the universe, staring at the cold empty sky, feeling as if she were falling *upward* into that unfeeling, remorseless infinite wilderness.

She squeezed her eyes shut and tried to fight down the panic that was surging through her.

RECOVERY

You okay?" Winston's voice made Trudy's eyes snap open. He sounded concerned, worried.

"Me?" she squeaked. "Yeah. I'm okay. I'm fine."

"You sounded like you were puffing, gasping."

"I'm okay," she insisted, concentrating on looking at him, not the sky.

She couldn't see his face through the tinting of his helmet, but she heard him say, "Some people get a jolt when they first come out here. Guys from Selene, they're used to seeing Earth overhead. It bothers them here."

"That's what the farside is all about, isn't it?" Trudy replied, desperately trying to keep her voice from shaking. "I mean, this side of the Moon is always pointed away from Earth. You never see Earth from here."

"Right," said Winston.

"Is that a road?" she asked, pointing with one gloved hand.

"Yeah. Simpson's Highway, we call it. That's where they took the mirror off to Mendeleev."

"And now they're bringing it back."

Winston didn't reply, but Trudy got the sense that he was nodding his head.

"Not much to see, is there?" she said, keeping her eyes on her companion. Not the stars. Not the stars.

"Most of the base is underground. Those are the solar farms, out there." He pointed. "That's how we generate our electricity."

Trudy followed his pointing arm and saw an area of dark solar cells spread across the floor of the plain, silently drinking in sun-light.

"Daylight for fourteen days straight, just about," said Winston.

"And fourteen straight days of night," Trudy added.

"Yeah. We generate twice the power the base needs and store the excess in superconducting coils for the night. We've also got a nuclear generator buried out there, as a backup."

"Just like Selene."

"Uh-huh." Winston hesitated a moment, then said, "Well, that's about it. You want to go in now?"

I passed the test! Trudy exulted. I got through the initiation. As nonchalantly as she could manage, she replied, "I guess."

As they turned toward the airlock hatch, set into the slope of the ringwall mountain, Trudy's eye caught a glint of something halfway up the distant twisting road.

"What's that?"

Winston said, "Oh, that's Simpson's gang toting the mirror back."

An enormous rig was laboriously inching along the winding road, bearing a huge flat load that gleamed in the sunlight.

Trudy stared at it, fascinated. It was like a huge round metal pancake, obviously on wheels of some sort, creeping down the road, painfully slowly.

"Mirror must've cracked at one of the switchback turns," Winston was saying. "It'll take them seven, eight hours to get it back down here."

"Do you have a pair of binoculars on you?" Trudy asked.

"Naw. C'mon, let's go back inside."

A smaller vehicle was speeding down the switchbacks at break-neck speed, kicking up a trail of dust that hung lazily in the vacuum. Lighter gravity, Trudy told herself. Dust doesn't settle as fast as on Earth.

"We'd better get inside," Winston urged.

Whoever's driving that buggy is in an awful hurry, Trudy

thought. He could get himself killed zipping around those curves like that.

"Time to go, Dr. Yost."

Hesitantly, Trudy turned and followed Winston back to the airlock hatch.

"How on Earth do they get the mirror back inside the base?" she asked.

As he pressed the control pad set beside the hatch, Winston replied, "Biggest airlock in the solar system. It forms one entire wall of the mirror lab, over on the far side of the big turntable. Hard to see from this angle, but it's right over there, set into the mountainside."

Trudy nodded inside her helmet. Must be something to see, she thought. An airlock that can take a hundred-meter mirror.

As the hatch slid silently open, Winston went on, "Professor Uhlrich thought about building the mirror lab out here in the open. Vacuum is a lot cleaner than an underground facility filled with air and sweat and all sorts of impurities and contaminants."

"But?" Trudy prompted.

"He decided it'd be easier for the staff to work in air, instead of outside in suits. So they built the big airlock."

Trudy realized that Winston hadn't pointed out the airlock to her when he'd taken her through the mirror lab. He hadn't even mentioned it.

Once back inside, it took nearly an hour to vacuum the dust off their suits and then wriggle out of them. The air in the locker room had an acrid smell to it.

Before she could ask, Winston smilingly explained, "Place smells like gunpowder, doesn't it? That's from the dust."

As she peeled off her thermal undergarment, Trudy realized her blouse and jeans were soaked with perspiration.

"I need a shower," she said, wrinkling her nose at her own odor.

"Yeah. Everybody does after they've been outside."

At that moment the inner hatch of the airlock slid open and a figure in a space suit tromped in. As he unsealed his helmet and pulled it off, Trudy recognized the darkly bearded guy with the sad eyes she'd seen on the screen in Professor Uhlrich's office.

"Hey, Grant," said Winston.

"Hello, Win."

"Uh, this is Trudy Yost. She's going—"

"Hello," said Grant Simpson. And he clomped past Trudy, heading for the corridor that led to Professor Uhlrich's office, without bothering to take off his space suit.

PROFESSOR UHLRICH'S OFFICE

Grant Simpson got as far as the corridor door, then realized he was being asinine. You can't confront Uhlrich in your space suit, he told himself. That'd just confirm all his suspicions about you.

Grimly he turned around and clunked back to his personal locker. The young woman and Win Winston were standing a few lockers up, staring at him.

"Grant, this is Trudy Yost," Winston repeated. "She's a new postdoc."

Grant extended his hand, then realized it was still encased in the heavy glove of his space suit. He ripped the seal open, then pulled off his glove while Winston was saying:

"Dr. Yost, this is Grant Simpson, the assistant chief of the mirror lab's technical staff."

Grant clasped Trudy's hand briefly while he looked at her. Nice face, he thought. Wholesome. Little snub of a nose. Hair cut short. Greenish eyes.

"Good to meet you, Dr. Yost," he said.

She nodded, said nothing.

To Winston, Grant said, "Can you give me a hand with the suit, Win?"

"Sure thing." Winston stepped behind him and began to disconnect Grant's backpack. Once that was done he helped Grant lift the suit's hard-shell torso over his head and rested it in his locker.

"I'm in kind of a hurry," Grant said to Trudy. "Got to see the Ulcer."

Trudy's eyes looked perplexed. "Ulcer?"

Winston laughed shakily. "That's Grant's pet name for the professor. Uhlrich the Ulcer."

"He doesn't get them," said Grant. "He gives them."

"Oh." She looked somewhere between amused and alarmed. "I'm going to be Professor Uhlrich's assistant, you know."

Settling himself on the bench in front of the lockers, Grant replied as he started to undo his dust-covered boots, "Then you'll probably get an ulcer, too, sooner or later."

She glanced at Winston, then said, "I won't tell him that you call him that."

"Doesn't matter," Grant said. "He knows it. Everybody here at Farside calls him the Ulcer."

Trudy seemed unsure of herself. She looked toward Winston again, who merely shrugged. Then she said, almost apologetically, "I've got to get to my quarters. I need a shower."

She started toward the door as if she were fleeing from danger. Over her shoulder she said, "It was nice to meet you, Dr. Simpson."

"*Mr.* Simpson," Grant called after her. "I'm not a Ph.D. I work for a living."

Winston laughed nervously, then started after her. "Her first day," he said.

As if that explains anything, Grant thought. He sat wearily on the bench in front of his locker and unconsciously rubbed at the small of his back. It throbbed with a dull, deep, sullen pain.

The Ulcer was in a grim mood when Grant slid back the door to his office. Carter McClintock was already there; why, Grant could not fathom. The man wasn't an astronomer, not an engineer or even an administrator. He seemed to be nothing more than a visiting playboy, but somehow he was always at the Ulcer's elbow. McClintock was about Grant's own age, but there the similarities ended. Where Grant was a compact middleweight with strong, stubby limbs, McClintock was tall, gracefully good-looking, smiling, and totally at ease. His job wasn't on the line. His neck wasn't in the noose.

"Come in, Simpson," said Professor Uhlrich, his voice as cold and sharp as a dagger's blade. Then he got a whiff of Grant's sweat-soaked clothes.

As Grant took the seat across the table from McClintock, Uhlrich's nose wrinkled. From behind his desk he said stiffly, "And where is Mr. Oberman? I expected him to be here with you."

"Nate's on his way," Grant said. "I phoned him while I was coming here."

As if in response to his words, the office door slid back and Nate Oberman stepped through, looking wary, troubled. He was tall and lean, loose jointed, with a long square jaw and narrow, suspicious eyes.

Although Oberman was Grant's immediate superior, Grant had never warmed to the man. Nate didn't take his job seriously enough, Grant thought. He had a shrunken sense of responsibility: always ready to let Grant do the work while he lazed in the background. He didn't seem to really know very much about engineering; Grant wondered how he had gotten Uhlrich to hire him for Farside in the first place. Probably doctored his résumé, Grant thought. Maybe he even got through college that way. Plenty of hackers ready to improve your record—for a fee.

The thing about engineering, though, is that sooner or later you have to make something work. You can't finesse your way through your entire career. The real world's caught up with Nate, Grant thought.

"Mr. Oberman," said Uhlrich, his voice glacially cold.

Oberman pulled up the chair next to McClintock and eased his lanky frame into it. "I heard about the accident," he said, almost as lightly as if he were talking about the weather.

"The road you laid out was too difficult for the mirror to negotiate," said Uhlrich.

Shaking his head, Oberman countered, "There's nothing

wrong with the road. Grant should've been able to get the mirror across the mountain with no trouble."

Looking as if he'd been forced to swallow a half-dozen lemons, Uhlrich said, "Yet the mirror fell off its carriage at one of the switchbacks that you designed."

"You approved the design," Oberman said.

"After you assured me that it was adequate," Uhlrich retorted.

Jabbing a finger across the table toward Grant, Oberman said, "It's not my fault that he messed up. Probably took that switchback turn too fast, I bet."

The pain in his back flared up again and Grant felt his pulse thundering in his ears. Nate's dumping the blame in my lap, he told himself. And he realized it was nothing less than he'd expected from Oberman. He closed his eyes for a moment, telling himself to relax, don't get angry, be reasonable, rational, calm.

"Well, Mr. Simpson?" Uhlrich's voice cut through his mantra.

Keeping his voice soft, tranquil, Grant said, "I never exceeded the speed limits set by the transport plan. You can check the monitor's record at the excursion control center. I kept to the indicated speed limits."

"Then why did the mirror frame slip off the carriage?" Uhlrich demanded.

"Because the switchback was too tight for the carriage to negotiate," Grant said. Turning to Oberman, he said, "Nate, I told you those curves were too sharp. I warned you we'd have trouble."

"So you're dumping it all on me!" Oberman snapped.

"No, all I'm saying—"

Angrily, Oberman screeched, "My design was fine! Perfect! The professor here okayed it!"

Suddenly Uhlrich looked alarmed. "I approved it only because you assured me it was satisfactory."

McClintock broke in, "Recriminations aren't going to help anything."

"It's not my fault," Oberman insisted. "I did my job right. Grant screwed up."

Grant fought down the urge to lean across the table and smack Oberman in his lying mouth.

"The fact remains," Professor Uhlrich said, his voice quivering slightly with deadly anger, "that the mirror is damaged and it is your responsibility, Mr. Oberman."

"Not mine," Oberman insisted, pointing across the table again at Grant. "His."

"Yours," Uhlrich repeated. He took a deep breath, then said, "I am relieving you of your position, Mr. Oberman."

"You're firing me?"

"Yes."

Oberman smiled maliciously. "You can't fire me. I have a contract. I still have more than a month of employment coming to me. With salary and benefits."

Uhlrich stared at him blankly, then replied, "Mr. McClintock will find some administrative assignment for you for the remainder of your contract. I don't want you involved in any of the technical work here."

Grant felt stunned. He hadn't realized that the Ulcer was so blazingly furious.

Then he heard the professor say, "Mr. Simpson, you will take over the leadership of the technical crew, on a temporary basis."

Oberman hauled himself up from his chair and glared at Uhlrich. "Okay, fine. I don't give a shit. I'll sit around here for another few weeks and twiddle my thumbs—at full salary. Why the fuck not?"

Then he turned back to Grant. "Congratulations, backstabber. You've got what you wanted all along, haven't you?"

JOB DESCRIPTIONS

Grant watched in stunned silence as Oberman slammed furiously out of the professor's office and banged the sliding door loudly shut behind him.

The office fell absolutely still. Grant could hear the whisper of the air blowing softly through the ducts in the stone ceiling.

I'm going to head up the tech team, Grant said to himself. Nate thinks I angled for his job. He's sore as hell. Then he thought, I guess I would be, too, if the Ulcer had bounced me out of my job.

At last Uhlrich asked, in a voice that was low but sharp enough to cut steel, "Where is the damaged mirror now?"

"On its way back here," Grant replied. "It's about halfway down the ringwall road. Should be at the mirror lab airlock in six or seven hours."

"You left it there? You left your crew?"

"You told me to report to you as quickly as possible, didn't you? Well, here I am."

Uhlrich stared blankly at Grant. After several moments, McClintock tried to break the tension. "Couldn't we repair the mirror, instead of recasting it?"

Surprised, Grant asked, "Repair it? How?"

"With nanomachines."

"Nanos . . ." Grant glanced back at Uhlrich, who sat as rigidly as a Chinese mandarin presiding over an execution.

Nanomachines can be dangerous, Grant knew. He had considered suggesting using them to Uhlrich back when he'd first arrived at Farside, but decided against it. Too risky, he'd thought. Especially in a facility as small as Farside. If some rogue nanos got loose they could wipe out the whole place and everybody in it.

Instead, he had followed Uhlrich's decision to spin cast the mirrors. With the Moon's lighter gravity it was possible to spin cast telescope mirrors far larger than anything on Earth.

Yeah, Grant thought. Until you try to get them over the ringwall mountains and they crack on you.

Halfheartedly, Uhlrich said, "If nanomachines can repair the mirror, we will have lost only a few weeks."

Instead of the months it would take to recast the mirror, Grant thought. He looked at McClintock with newfound respect. He might be able to do it. Nanomachines might be the answer, after all. Despite the risks.

Uhlrich dismissed them both with a curt nod of his head. Grant followed McClintock through the door and out into the corridor.

As he slid the door shut, Grant asked McClintock, "Do you really think nanotechnology can save the mirror?"

The taller man made a barely discernible shrug. "I really don't know. Maybe we're grasping at straws."

Starting down the corridor, toward the area where the living quarters were located, McClintock said, "I'm surprised that Professor Uhlrich didn't look into nanotech when he first came to Farside."

"Maybe he should have," Grant replied noncommittally.

"I mean, with Cardenas heading the nanolab over at Selene. She's up for the Nobel, for god's sake."

"Nanomachines can be dangerous, you know," Grant said. "They're banned back on Earth. Worried about murderers or terrorists using them."

"Or the gray goo," said McClintock.

Grant looked at him. The man was not smiling now.

McClintock went on, "Someone could design nanomachines to tear apart carbon-based molecules. There goes all the world's plastics—and people."

"I've heard there are secret nanolabs on Earth," Grant said. "Big corporations have them tucked away here and there."

"Old wives' tales," McClintock muttered.

Grant nodded. "Maybe so."

The corridor was narrow and low-ceilinged. The construction engineers who had cut these tunnels hadn't spent a penny more than necessary. Strictly utilitarian. Bare rock, drab and gray. Pipes and conduits along the ceiling. Overhead lights spaced every twenty meters made the corridor look shadowy. Like a haunted house, Grant thought. He grimaced. I don't need any props or settings to haunt me, he thought. I've got my own demons chasing me.

He felt his hands beginning to tremble, and knew that he needed a fix. Only a few more meters to my door, Grant told himself. I can make it without letting him see how bad off I am. He jammed his hands in his coverall pockets.

Was it my fault the mirror cracked? he asked himself. Nate plotted out the road, and I told him he ought to make it easier, but the Ulcer was in a sweat to get the frigging mirror over to Mendeleev, and Nate didn't have the balls to stand up to him. Maybe I should've tried to help Nate, stiffen his backbone a little. Maybe I could've helped to make the road easier to traverse. I might have saved Nate's job for him. But that would've meant we'd need more time to build the road and Uhlrich—

He realized that McClintock was speaking to him.

". . . my quarters at seventeen hundred, sharp."

Grant blinked, confused. "Your quarters?"

"For my teleconference with Dr. Cardenas," McClintock said.

"You want me in on that?"

"Of course."

They had reached Grant's door. "This is my place," he said.

McClintock stopped and repeated, "Seventeen hundred. Sharp."

"I'll be there," said Grant. Then he realized, "Um, where is your place?"

McClintock broke into an easy smile. "A-twenty-four. That's halfway down the next cross corridor."

"I know. Okay."

His smile fading, McClintock said, "You've something of a reputation, you know."

"Oh?" Grant felt his pulse start to race.

"Fine engineer," said McClintock, "but . . . well, dependent on . . . medications."

"I've got some physical problems, that's true," Grant admitted. "I can't return to Earth. I've got to stay here on the Moon."

McClintock nodded. "I heard that you were bounced out of your job at Selene."

Grant admitted it with a mute nod.

"Fighting. You wrecked the Pelican Bar, they tell me."

His voice low, Grant replied, "I had help. It was a free-for-all."

"So now you're stuck here at Farside."

"That's right, I guess."

"Apparently you've kept your nose clean here," McClintock said.

Grant nodded again, thinking, When is this inquisition going to end?

"Well, you've risen to the top of the tech gang, but that's only temporary. You're on trial, Simpson."

So what else is new? Grant asked silently.

McClintock broke into his sunny smile again and said, "But we'll see what we can do to make your temporary promotion a permanent one."

"I'd appreciate that," Grant mumbled.

"Good." McClintock started down the corridor, but as Grant

tapped out the entry code for his door, he turned back and said, "Oh, and *do* take a shower before you come to my quarters. Right?"

"Right," Grant agreed.

All the living spaces at Farside were the same. Grant thought of it as an engineering-inspired bit of democracy. From the Ulcer down to the lowliest inventory clerk, everybody got identical living spaces. The engineers who designed and built the underground facility had decided it would be cheaper and easier to build that way.

Selene had started out the same way, back decades ago when it had begun as Moonbase. But over the years, as Selene grew larger, the newer living quarters became bigger, more luxurious. Two and three bedrooms. Spacious sitting rooms: well, spacious by the standards of a community where every corridor, every room, every living and working space had to be carved out of the solid lunar rock by plasma torches.

Of course, there was that grotto at Selene's deepest level, a natural cave that zillionaire Martin Humphries had turned into a blooming botanical garden with his own luxurious mansion smack in its middle. Incredibly expensive to maintain, but the Humphries Trust footed the bill and sponsored the fantasy that the area was an ecological research center, dedicated to studying how to establish an Earth-type environment deep underground on the Moon.

Yeah, Grant thought as he hurried down the corridor toward McClintock's quarters. A research facility, with the richest man in the solar system living in splendor smack in the middle of it.

NANOMACHINES

Grant found unit A-24 and tapped on the door. It was precisely 1700 hours.

McClintock's muffled voice called, "It's not locked."

Sliding the door back, Grant saw that McClintock was already speaking with a woman's image on the wall-mounted display screen. She was a good-looking blonde, too young to be Dr. Cardenas, the nanotech guru and a nominee for the Nobel Prize. To Grant she looked more like a California surfer chick: golden curly hair, strong shoulders, and a glowing complexion.

She was saying, "Nanomachines aren't magic wands, Dr. McClintock. You can't say 'abracadabra' and have them work wonders for you."

McClintock was sitting on the small sofa, his long legs stretched out beneath the coffee table, his eyes focused on the woman's face. Still, he waved to Grant, gesturing toward the upholstered chair at one end of the sofa. Grant crossed the room and sat there, thinking that while all the living quarters at Farside were exactly the same size, McClintock's room was furnished much better than the one he himself lived in.

"I understand," McClintock said to the screen. "So tell me what you need to build a mirror with nanos." Before she could reply, he added, "And how quickly you can do it."

It *is* Cardenas, Grant realized. Must be. She must be at least sixty, but she sure doesn't look it.

"First," Kristine Cardenas replied, "I'd need an exact list of the elements that the mirror is made of. Elements and compounds, down to the smallest impurities. Nanomachine assemblers work at the atomic and molecular levels; they take atoms and molecules and put them together to form the macrostructure you want."

McClintock nonchalantly waved one hand in the air. "We can get that information for you."

The woman looked doubtful. "As I understand it, optical glass consists mainly of silicon and oxygen, but there are plenty of minor constituents, too. And they can be critical, isn't that so?"

McClintock turned to Grant. "Is that right?"

Grant said to the screen, "The glass is a borosilicate. About ten percent is boron oxide. And you're right: there're other constituents, as well."

"And you are . . . ?" the woman asked.

Before Grant could reply, McClintock said, "This is Grant Simpson. He's the head of my technical staff."

My technical staff, Grant thought. The Ulcer would pucker his sphincter over that.

"I'm Kris Cardenas," the woman said, with a warm smile.

"I'm very pleased to meet you, Dr. Cardenas," said Grant.

"Call me Kris. And I'll call you Grant."

"Okay."

With just the hint of a frown on his chiseled features, McClintock said, "You can get Dr. Cardenas a detailed list of the ingredients in the optical glass we use for the mirrors, can't you?"

Grant started to answer, but Cardenas interrupted, "If you can simply give me a few samples of the glass, I can program a set of nano disassemblers to take them apart, atom by atom. That'll give us the exact specifications we need."

"Disassemblers?" Grant asked. "You mean gobblers?"

Cardenas's face went cold. "Disassemblers," she said flatly. "I use them in my lab here for analyses. They do *not* get outside of my lab, and even if they did they are programmed to shut themselves down at a fixed time limit. The area can also be bathed in high-intensity ultraviolet light, which deactivates the nanos quite thoroughly. There's no need to worry about gobblers getting loose."

"Okay, okay," Grant said, raising both his hands in a gesture of surrender. "I'm not a nanoluddite. I'm not scared of nanomachines." It wasn't exactly true, he knew, but close enough.

McClintock soothed, "Of course not. That's why we're asking for your help, Dr. Cardenas."

She dipped her chin a notch in acknowledgement.

"Now then," McClintock went on, "once you know exactly what the ingredients are, how soon can you produce a hundred-meter mirror for us?"

"How soon can you gather together all the necessary raw materials?"

McClintock shrugged elaborately and turned to Grant again.

"The glass is actually manufactured in Selene," Grant said. "They ship it here in chunks and we melt it down at our mirror lab."

"Then I should talk with the people at the glass factory," said Cardenas.

"I suppose so," McClintock said. "But once you have the raw materials, how quickly can—"

Cardenas interrupted, "A hundred-meter mirror? To what tolerance?"

Grant answered, "It's got to be curved to within a fraction of the wavelength of visible light."

"Oof! That'll take a bit of doing."

"We spend months polishing the surfaces to the correct figure," Grant said.

With a trace of a smile, Cardenas said, "If you can give me the exact specifications, my little guys ought to be able to do it in a week or so. Maybe ten days, on the outside."

"A week?" McClintock gasped.

"On that order," she replied.

"That . . . that would be fine," McClintock said, grinning at the screen. "Wonderful."

Grant added, "I'll talk to the head of the glass factory, tell him to give you a few samples of the optical glass they make for us."

"And I'll get on this as soon as the samples are in my hands," said Cardenas.

"You'll handle this personally?" McClintock asked.

Cardenas gave him a rueful little smile. "I don't have much of a staff here. Yes, I'll make room in my schedule to handle this myself."

"Fine," McClintock repeated. "Just fine."

"Thank you," Grant said.

Cardenas smiled again, warmer this time, and said, "That's it, then. I'll call you again when I get the glass samples. Good-bye."

McClintock said, "Good-bye for now."

The screen went dark. McClintock turned to Grant. "I want you to get over to Selene and see to it that she gets those samples with the speed of light."

"I don't think that's necessary," Grant said.

McClintock's expression went stony. "It doesn't matter what you think. You get your butt over to Selene. Now."

Grant fought down the flash of anger that surged through him. "I'll have to clear it with Uhlrich."

"I'll take care of Uhlrich. You get yourself moving."

"But—"

"No buts. I know about your work history and I know about your drug habit."

"It's not a drug habit!"

"Medications, then," McClintock amended easily. "I don't care. Can you understand that? I don't give a damn what you swallow or inject into yourself. As long as you perform your job well, you can fill yourself with all the designer drugs you can get your hands on."

Grant glared at him.

McClintock broke into his handsome smile again. "Don't get so tense, Grant. We're going to get along just fine, as long as you do your job." Easing back on the sofa, he added, "You do the work, and I'll take the credit. Deal?"

Grant said to himself, Another one. Just like Nate. At least he admits it openly, though.

To McClintock he grudgingly muttered, "Deal."

DOSSIER:
GRANT PHILIP SIMPSON

For his eighth birthday Grant Simpson received a small Rubik's Cube from his favorite uncle. Fascinated, Grant spent hours doggedly trying to rotate every facet of the wickedly intricate device until he had all the colors properly lined up. He stayed up late for two nights in a row, hiding under his bedcovers with a flashlight, until at last he had solved the puzzle and each side of the cube showed one color only.

Proudly, he brought the cube to school and showed it off to his classmates during their lunch period. One of the boys asked if he could try it. Grant scrambled the facets, then gave the cube to him. Before the next class began the lad handed it back to Grant, grinning broadly. He had solved the cube perfectly.

Grant felt utterly stupid. What had taken him days and nights to do, his classmate had done in less than an hour.

It wasn't until the end of the school term that the boy revealed, with an even bigger grin, that he had simply peeled the colored plastic stickers off the device, then pasted them back on in the proper order.

From that shocked moment onward, Grant Simpson loathed the idea of using trickery instead of earnest hard work. He expected people to do their jobs honestly, the way he did.

Grant always worked hard at whatever he attempted. Sometimes he tried too hard.

He came to the Moon from his home in Johannesburg barely one step ahead of a lynch mob of South African police detectives, lawyers, and media pundits who heartlessly held him responsible for mass murder.

All because he wanted to help the neediest of the needy.

The greenhouse warming had struck suddenly and disastrously all across the Earth. After more than a century of a barely perceptible rise in global temperatures, the Earth's climate reached a tipping point. Within little more than a decade ice caps melted, sea levels rose, coastal cities worldwide were flooded, farmlands parched, and devastating storms stripped millions of families of their homes, their livelihoods, their hopes for the future.

Young Grant Simpson, clasping a brand-new degree in civil engineering, had dreamed of going to the Moon and helping to build lunar habitats for the newly independent nation of Selene. He had applied for a job permit at Selene and been accepted.

"You can build new cities right here," his stepfather had insisted. "God knows we've got enough homeless coolies pouring into South Africa. Blacks, Arabs, even refugees from Israel. Can't keep 'em out. They need shelter almost as much as they need food."

His stepfather was a blustering shopkeeper who bullied Grant's mother and everyone else around him. But although Grant would not be bullied, he still recognized the truth behind the old man's words. He saw the need in the weary, frightened eyes of the helpless, homeless, hopeless immigrants.

Grant tried. He tried very hard. He set aside his dreams of working on the Moon and took on the task of building housing for the desperate, bewildered people who had lost everything. The only challenge in the work was to get the units built faster and cheaper, always faster and cheaper.

Grant warned his superiors that they were taking too many shortcuts. They ignored him. He went to the construction company's management, and all that earned him was their cold disdain and the active hostility of his fellow workers.

"Don't get yourself all lathered up, Grant," his supervisor told him. "We're building for dumbass migrants, not the royal family, for chrissakes."

Offended by his coworkers' slipshod efforts, and incensed even more by their careless attitude, Grant found himself isolated, friendless, alone in his fears that their sloppy work would lead to disaster.

When the company's latest and shoddiest apartment block collapsed, killing seventy-three sleeping men, women, and children, Grant got blamed. Somehow the company's records showed that it was Grant Simpson who drew up the faulty design, Grant Simpson who approved the unreliable reinforcing bars and the fatally weakened concrete mixture.

His stepfather regarded him with ill-concealed contempt. "Don't look to me for help, young man. You made your bed, now you've got to lie in it."

Die in it, Grant thought. The courts are working up an indictment for mass murder. Any moment now the police will come to take me away.

Grant had to run for his life. He fled to the Moon, where the men and women governing Selene at least listened to his side of the story and reluctantly gave him a chance to make good on his never-used job permit.

South Africa tried to have him extradited, but Selene—independent since its short, sharp war against Earth's United Nations—refused to cooperate. Grant immediately applied for citizenship, which was eventually granted. Selene's need for men and women who were willing to work outweighed the tragedy in South Africa.

Grant worked. Very hard. Outside, for the most part, out on the airless lunar surface. Building the solar farms that provided Selene's electrical power. Constructing the second electrical catapult that hurled cargoes of lunar ores off the Moon to the space stations in Earth orbit. Erecting factories on the floor of Crater Alphonsus, factories that produced—among other things—the Clippership rockets that became the backbone of transportation between the Moon and Earth and, in slightly modified form, hypersonic aircraft that brought every place on Earth no more than an hour's flight from any other place on Earth.

Out in the open on Alphonsus's dusty, rock-strewn floor, Grant could look up and see the blue-and-white sphere of the Earth hanging above him. He willed himself to feel no remorse; he told himself that he had cut all his ties with the world of his birth.

He knew he would never again see the dim-witted, know-nothing tyrant who had married his mother, or the mother who allowed the lout to dominate her, or the regimentation of a government that grew more restrictive, more authoritarian, with each new wave of desperate millions migrating into South Africa. He didn't have to deal with the fools and opportunists and out-and-out thieves who grasped at power and money for themselves at the expense of everyone else.

He had left Earth far behind him. Forever. Or so he told himself.

He worked in a space suit, of course. He learned to accept the restrictions imposed by the burdensome, awkward suits: gloves that needed tiny servomotors just to flex the fingers adequately; canned air that chilled his lungs; lunar dust that crept into the suits' joints and made them grind to an arthritic halt if you didn't clean the suits thoroughly every time you used them.

The biggest danger of working outside was the radiation, of course. Invisible, impalpable subatomic bullets rained down from the Sun and stars, blanketing the lunar surface every moment of every day and night.

The suits protected their wearers against radiation, but only up to a point. A person was allowed to spend only so many hours outside on the surface; exceeding that limit meant that even with the suit's protection, the wearer was accumulating a dangerous dose of radiation. Selene's safety department had very strict rules about radiation exposure.

But a hard-working engineer who had jobs to complete could be clever enough to evade the rules. Records could be doctored. Radiation dosage badges could be switched or even lost. Getting the job done was more important than allowing the nitpicking safety prigs to force you off the project.

Grant worked hard, very hard, out on the Moon's radiation-drenched surface. Happily, most of his fellow workers were almost as hard-driving as he was. Most of them. And even the medical staff who monitored the workers' health status were lenient enough to let them get away with bending the safety regulations.

Besides, there were medications to be had that could protect you from the damaging effects of long-term radiation exposure. Grant Simpson got those medications from fellow workers who knew where and how to obtain them. He took steroids, too, to improve his stamina out there in the open.

He worried about taking such medications. Drugs, really, he thought. What am I putting into my body? he asked himself. At first. Once he found that the meds allowed him to work longer, harder, he put such worries behind him. Getting the job done was the important thing.

Within a year Grant was dependent on those medications. They didn't interfere with his work; they enhanced his performance. Steroids could be dangerous, he knew. But he soon realized that he couldn't survive without them. What choice do I have? he asked himself.

He worked hard. He got the job done.

One of the side effects of the steroids, though, was a heightened tendency to anger: 'roid rage. All his life, Grant had kept his emotions bottled inside him. Now, with the steroids coursing through his blood, the anger burst out. He got into fights—real, bloody-knuckled, body-battering fights. He expected the people around him to do their jobs, and most of them did. But the few goof-offs and goldbrickers among his crew infuriated him beyond his self-control.

After a wild brawl that smashed up the bar he and his crew frequented, Grant was brought before Selene's personnel board and expelled from the technical staff.

Devastated, Grant pleaded that he could not return to Earth, where an indictment for mass murder still hung over him. "You'll be killing me," he begged.

After two excruciating days of deliberation, the board informed Grant that he could apply for a position with the technical staff that was building the astronomical facility on the far side of the Moon. He swiftly, gratefully, accepted.

But he could not avoid a routine physical examination when he arrived at Farside, carried out by Farside's resident physician, Dr. Ida Kapstein, a heavyset woman with hard ice-blue eyes.

"Your liver function is deteriorating, you know," she said, coolly unconcerned.

The ache in my back, Grant realized.

"It's from all the shit you've been putting into yourself. Your blood sample looks like a pharmaceutical company's product list, for god's sake."

"I, uh . . . I've been taking . . . medications," he stammered.

"I've heard about your getting into fistfights at Selene. 'Roid rage, isn't it?"

Ohmigod, Grant thought. She's going to redline me. If I can't work here at Farside they'll ship me back to Earth. Back to South Africa.

Sullenly, he muttered, "I can control it."

"Sure you can."

It took Grant several minutes before he understood that Dr. Kapstein wasn't threatening to redline him. She was offering to sell Grant the steroids and anti-radiation medications he had become dependent on. Dr. Kapstein had a thriving little business going, and Grant would swiftly become her steadiest customer.

"I'll take good care of you," Dr. Kapstein told him. "You just put yourself in my care and you'll be okay. The safety department's rules are way too restrictive, anyway."

Grant agreed mutely.

"I'll take good care of you," she repeated.

For a price.

BROKEN MIRROR

Grant felt tired and irritable as he pulled the hard-shell torso of his space suit over his head and slid his arms through the flexible sleeves.

Frigging suit smells like old sweat socks, he grumbled to himself. It's time to requisition a new one. The Ulcer'll hit the ceiling; I bet he hired McClintock to help keep the program's costs down.

It was an hour after his meeting with McClintock. *You do the work, and I'll take the credit,* the man had said. Great, thought Grant. What choice do I have? Well, anyway, I ought to get a new suit out of it.

The woman who was going outside with him was already suited up, helmet and all. She checked out his suit, then Grant checked out hers. The old buddy system. Never go out on the surface alone. Good rule. Except there were times when you had to. Rules are made to be broken, or at least bent.

"Let's make this quick," the woman said as Grant fastened his fishbowl helmet to his suit's neck ring. "I've got a date for dinner."

With their highly tinted helmets over their heads, neither person could make out the face of the other. Together they clomped heavily to the airlock, got the go-ahead from the excursion controller, snug and happy in her booth deep inside, and finally stepped out onto the surface of Mare Moscoviense.

It was still daylight out there, although the Sun was dipping down toward the slumped old ringwall mountains. Long shadows were stretching across the dusty undulating floor of the Sea of Moscow.

Grant took it all in with a glance, then stepped out of the airlock and headed toward the cracked mirror.

"Into the valley of death," muttered his companion, "rode the six hundred."

Grant shook his head inside his helmet. "We're missing five hundred and ninety-eight guys."

"Yeah. I know."

The damned mirror was sitting out there, next to the big airlock of the mirror lab, slightly tilted on the uneven ground. Its delicately figured glass was covered by a thin sheet of metal that was obviously warped.

Grant stared at the damaged mirror inside its protective casing. Not protective enough, he knew.

Why'd you have to crack? he asked the impassive mirror. Why'd you have to ruin all our work?

"How're we gonna get this puppy back into the lab?" his companion asked.

Grant had to concentrate for a moment to remember which of his crew was with him. The bulky space suits removed all traces of individuality; if you weren't close enough to read the name stenciled on the torso, you couldn't recognize who was inside the suit.

She checked you out in your suit, for chrissakes, Grant berated himself. Are you getting early onset Alzheimer's? Then he remembered: Josie Rivera. Smokey Jo. Good-looking Latina, sharp engineer, bosomy and friendly, especially after a couple of drinks. With a pang, Grant realized that it had been months since he'd gotten laid. He hadn't even thought much about sex lately. A side effect of his medications? he wondered.

"It doesn't go back into the lab," Grant replied. "Not yet. Not until we finish the mirror we're working on now."

"So we just leave it out here?"

Shaking his head inside the helmet, Grant said, "We build a

roof over it, protect it from temperature swings and micrometeorite abrasion. I'll have to requisition the honeycomb sheets, then you and Harvey Henderson's gang can put 'em up."

"Hurry-up Harvey." Josie sounded a little resentful, Grant thought. Nobody likes working outside unless they really have to. He knew what was going through her mind: The damned mirror's ruined; what's the sense of putting up a protective roof when we're just going to melt the thing down and start all over again with it?

He said to her, "The Ulcer's thinking about using nanomachines to build a new mirror."

"Nanos? Really?"

"That administrator of his—McClintock—he's talking about it with Dr. Cardenas back at Selene."

"Could it work?" Josie asked.

Grant knew better than to try to shrug inside the bulky suit. "Cardenas seems to think so."

"Well, she would, wouldn't she?"

"Yeah, I guess so." Grant started pacing around the mirror's edge. It was still mounted on the transporter, clamped rigidly in place. Not rigidly enough, he told himself. Otherwise it wouldn't have cracked.

To Josie, he said, "I want you to take snaps of the ground along the perimeter of the mirror, so Henderson and his guys have a full picture of the ground out here. They'll need to build a foundation for the roof."

"I'll have to go in and get a camera," she said.

Shaking his head, Grant said, "I'll tell the controller to get somebody to put a camera in the airlock. All you'll have to do is step in and pick it up."

"Okay."

Still pacing along the edges of the mirror, Grant called in to the controller for a camera. Once the controller told him that the camera had been placed on the airlock's floor, he told Josie to pop in and get it.

She came back with the credit-card-sized camera engulfed in one gloved hand. "You want me to take your picture, boss?" Before Grant could reply, Josie added, "Give the guys inside an idea of the scale."

"Sure," he said. "Why the hell not?"

So he stood beside the mirror while Josie snapped several images of him.

"Better take shots of the transporter's wheels, too," he suggested. "Get close enough to see if any of 'em cracked or bent."

Josie got busy and Grant felt unneeded, but he hesitated to go inside and leave her alone. He knew that subatomic particles from the distant stars were machine-gunning him. His suit protected him from most of them, but there were always some extra-energetic ones that got through and burrowed into the atoms of his body, killing cells or mutating them. He started to feel almost naked beneath their constant, deadly, invisible rain.

"Whattaya think of the Ulcer's assistant?" Josie asked as she made her way slowly around the mirror's perimeter.

"You mean McClintock?"

"Yeah. He's good-looking, don't you think?"

Sourly, Grant answered, "Another layer of management. The Ulcer's enlarging his domain."

"He's supposed to be some kind of efficiency expert, isn't he?"

"Management specialist, I think. He's like a consultant. You know, a guy who doesn't know anything more than you do, but he comes from more than fifty klicks away and carries a briefcase."

She didn't laugh. "Why'd the Ulcer hire him?"

"Somebody else to blame when we hit a problem," Grant snapped. Then he relented a bit. "The Ulcer's hell-bent on getting the first imagery from New Earth. He wants to beat the IAA and get a Nobel Prize."

"You think?"

"What else?"

"Well, I hope the guy knows what he's doing."

"He talked the Ulcer into considering nanotechnology,"

Grant admitted. "McClintock talked to him for five minutes and now we're working with Cardenas and the nanotech lab."

He heard Josie chuckle. "The Ulcer's willing to take any shortcuts he can find, isn't he?"

"Could be," Grant agreed. "Could damned well be."

The excursion controller's voice sounded in his helmet speakers. "Grant, we have an urgent call for you. I'm patching it through. On freak two."

Grant raised his left arm and tapped the keyboard on his wrist for frequency number two. Out of the corner of his eye, he noticed Josie doing the same. She wants to hear what's going on, he realized.

McClintock's voice snapped, "Grant, what are you doing out there?"

Cripes! Grant thought. Has he been listening to our chatter?

"We're checking out the damaged mirror. Have to build a shield over it until we can get it back inside the lab." He suppressed an impulse to add, "Sir."

"Well, I need you to get over to Selene and confer with Dr. Cardenas. A resupply lobber's on its way here and I want you on it when it heads back to Selene."

"Okay. As soon as we're finished here—"

"Now, Simpson. Now. That lobber will be landing in half an hour and it's not going to wait for you."

"But—"

"Get somebody else to finish your little excursion. You get yourself ready for a shot back to Selene."

"Right," said Grant.

SPACEPORT

rant called Hurry-Up Harvey and told him to suit up and join Josie at the mirror. Then he ducked back inside and began to peel out of his space suit. Josie'll be okay out there on her own for a half hour or so, he told himself. By the time he'd showered and changed into a fresh set of coveralls Henderson was suited up and entering the airlock.

The lobber was still offloading its cargo when Grant got to Farside's one-pad spaceport, toting his soft-sided overnight bag. Through the glassteel viewing port, Grant saw the squat, conical spacecraft, its dark diamond structure glittering in the lights that surrounded the blast-blackened concrete landing pad.

To his surprise, the newbie was at the spaceport's pocket-sized waiting area, standing at the viewing port, her nose practically pressed against the glassteel. What's her name? Grant asked himself. Yost, he recalled. Trudy Yost.

"Hello," he said.

She jumped as if somebody had swung an ax at her. Turning, she relaxed and replied, "Oh! Hello . . . Mr. Simpson."

Grant thought he heard a slight stress on the *Mister*. He tried to smile at her. "I guess I was kind of abrupt when we met. I'm sorry."

She immediately brightened. "That's okay. You must have a lot of responsibilities."

"Sort of," he said.

A moment of awkward silence, and then they both said, "What are you doing here?"

Trudy broke into a giggle and Grant laughed with her. Before she could ask again, he hefted his bag and said, "I'm heading back to Selene, once the lobber finishes off-loading."

"You're leaving Farside?"

"Only for a day or so. I'll be back."

"Good," said Trudy.

"And you?"

"Me?"

"Why're you here?"

"Oh!" She seemed genuinely surprised at his question. "The lobber's bringing a new batch of antennas for the Cyclops array. Professor Uhlrich asked me to make sure they get transported to the site okay."

"Asked?" Grant questioned. "The Ulcer *asked* you to?"

Trudy admitted, "Well, it was really more like a command."

"That sounds more like the Ulcer."

"You really shouldn't call him that," she said.

"No, I suppose I shouldn't."

Again a silence settled between them. Feeling uncomfortable, Grant said, "I didn't realize you're a radio astronomer."

"I'm not," Trudy said. "My specialty is optical . . . and infrared." Before he could ask she explained, "I'm just supervising the antenna delivery because the professor asked me . . ." She broke into a halfhearted grin. "Told me to," she amended.

Grant nodded and turned back to the window. The lobber's crew seemed finished with their offloading. Both of Farside's tractors were piled high with cargo containers. The first one of them started trundling slowly away from the launchpad.

In a small voice, Trudy asked, "Does he really give people ulcers?"

"No," said Grant. "Migraines."

"Oh, come on," Trudy objected. "What's he really like? Really."

"You'll find out."

Trudy frowned slightly. "He . . . he's sort of weird, in a way, isn't he?"

"What do you mean?"

Obviously ill at ease, Trudy said, "The way he looks at a person. Staring the way he does. Like he's looking right through me."

"You mean you don't know?"

"Know what?"

"He's blind. Totally blind."

Trudy looked shocked.

"Some accident back Earthside. Burned out his retinas. He can't see at all."

"But he does see!" Trudy insisted. Then she added, "Doesn't he?"

"In a way," said Grant. "They did some fancy brain surgery on him, linked the regions in his brain that handle sound and touch to his visual cortex. He sees through his ears and his fingers."

It was clear from the expression on her face that Trudy didn't understand.

"Look," Grant explained. "His visual cortex—the part of the brain that forms visual images—it wasn't damaged. Only his eyes. So the surgeons rewired his brain so that what he hears, and what he touches, form visual images in his brain."

"Couldn't they grow new retinas for his eyes?" she asked. "You know, with stem cells?"

Grant shook his head. "From what I heard, they tried but it didn't work. That's when they went to the surgery and rewired his brain."

"My gosh."

"Maybe he just got himself into the clutches of a neurosurgeon who needed a guinea pig," Grant said. "It happens."

"The poor man," said Trudy softly. Then she added, "But he does see . . . kind of."

"Whatever he touches or hears forms a visual image for him," Grant said. "I don't think he sees the same image of you, for example, that I see. But he sees something. He sees well enough to function and get around pretty well. But as far as his eyes are concerned, he's blind as a bat."

SELENE

I was a shocked and thoughtful Trudy Yost who left the space-port waiting area and headed toward the control center, where she could monitor the crew that was unloading the latest batch of antennas for the Cyclops radio telescope site.

Grant wondered if he'd been too brutally frank with her about Uhlrich's condition. What the hell, he told himself, she'd find out about it one way or the other. The sooner the better. Help her to deal with the Ulcer.

The lobber was being refueled with powdered aluminum and liquid oxygen propellants, both elements gleaned from the lunar regolith at Selene by specialized nanomachines. Within half an hour Grant was cleared to board the rocket for its return flight to Selene.

After so many months at Farside, Selene felt like a metropolis. There was an automated tractor to whisk passengers through the tunnel that connected the Armstrong spaceport, out on the floor of the giant Crater Alphonsus, to Selene proper, more than a kilo-meter away.

As soon as he cleared the debarkation desk—manned by a smil-ing young woman in a coral red uniform—Grant phoned Dr. Cardenas to tell her he'd arrived.

"Good," she said. In the pocketphone's minuscule screen her face looked somber, almost grim. "Come on over to my lab." And she abruptly clicked off.

Leaving his travelbag at the debarkation center, Grant used

his pocketphone to find his way through Selene's maze of corridors, although there were maps on voice-activated wall screens at every intersection. Dr. Cardenas's nanotechnology laboratory was on the topmost of Selene's four levels of living and working spaces, at the end of a winding side corridor. The corridor walls were blank, bare rock, and the low ceiling was lined with long strips of lights that seemed to be turned off.

Then he saw a sign on the wall up ahead:

**WARNING. THIS AREA MAY BE EXPOSED
TO HIGH-INTENSITY ULTRAVIOLET LIGHT.
LEAVE THE AREA IMMEDIATELY WHEN THE
RED WARNING LIGHTS ARE FLASHING.**

A precaution against nanomachines that might escape from the lab, Grant realized. Even here in Selene they're scared of nanomachines. Down at the end of the corridor he saw a closed door that bore the title NANOTECHNOLOGY LABORATORY.

He raised a fist to knock on the door, but a speaker grill set into the wall beside it said, "Come on in, Grant." Cardenas's voice. Then he noticed the tiny red eye of a minicamera set above the door.

The lab was surprisingly small, but then Grant told himself that machines the size of viruses don't need a lot of room. He threaded his way through a set of workbenches, all of them bearing various pieces of apparatus. Most of the hardware was made of metal, a lot of stainless steel gleaming in the overhead lights, although Grant saw some intricate works of glass tubing, as well.

No one seemed to be in the lab. But then he saw Kris Cardenas sitting at a desk set against the back wall. A big gray tubular object stood man-tall beside the desk. A scanning force microscope, Grant figured. He nodded to himself: that microscope can visualize individual atoms.

"Welcome to the zoo," Cardenas said, her voice flat and hard. She gestured to a sculpted plastic chair in front of the bulky microscope. "Have a seat."

As he sat down, Grant saw a trio of irregularly shaped chunks of optical glass resting on the shelf of a bookcase to one side of the desk. He said, "Mr. McClintock told me to come over. I'm not quite sure—"

"Apparently you're the resident expert on telescope mirrors," Cardenas said, still looking bleak, almost angry. "I need to pick your brain."

"Such as it is," he joked.

Cardenas didn't even crack a smile. Pointing to the glass samples, she said, "The glass factory sent these samples. Is this the raw material you use for the mirrors?"

Grant nodded. "Looks like it."

"Not good enough, Grant. I need to be absolutely certain." She turned and picked up one of the samples, then handed it to Grant.

He turned the lump of glass over in his hand. "Yeah, look at the label etched into it: the serial number starts with an O. O for optical."

"Then this is the type of glass you use to make the mirrors."

"Right."

Cardenas took the sample from Grant and returned it to the bookshelf. "I'll feed it to the disassemblers and get an atom-by-atom breakdown of its composition."

"Good," said Grant.

"I presume you can access all the files I'll need about mirror construction," she said.

"Sure."

"Good. Then let's get to work."

Two hours later Grant felt as if he'd been through a semester's worth of final exams, with a police interrogation thrown in. Cardenas was all business, unsmiling, as if she resented being pressed into this task of mirror manufacture. But she volunteered for the job, Grant remembered. When she talked to McClintock she looked pleased to help. Happy about it. Now, with me, she's pissed as hell.

At last Cardenas seemed satisfied. Her eyes on the wall screen where Grant had forwarded all the data she'd asked for, she finally said, "That should do it, I think."

"That's everything you need?" Grant asked, wondering why McClintock had insisted on his coming to her laboratory. *I could have done this from Farside,* he thought.

"That's the beginning," she said. "The next step is to take apart the samples and get an exact analysis of their composition. Then I'll have to program a set of assemblers to build you a mirror."

Grant said, "Once you've got the raw materials."

"Yes, there is that. I presume you can provide them for me."

"The mirror's supposed to be one hundred meters in diameter. You'll need a place to build something that big."

"That's your department, Grant. You deal with Selene's engineering department. Or maybe it'll be the research department that gets involved in this."

Grant pictured dealing with more bureaucracies. *I'll have to get Uhlrich involved in this. Nobody in Selene is going to stir themselves for me. I'll need the Ulcer's authority to get people here to move.*

Cardenas broke into his thoughts. "It's past seven P.M. Time to call it a day."

She got to her feet and Grant stood up beside her. She was almost his own height, bright blond hair, good trim figure. But her sky-blue eyes seemed troubled, annoyed.

"I'll see you here at eight tomorrow morning," she said.

"Okay." Then Grant realized he had no idea of where his quarters were. He'd left his travelbag with the young woman at the debarkation desk and hustled over to the nanolab before asking about where he was going to sleep.

"Eight o'clock, then," Cardenas repeated. Grant realized he was being dismissed.

DINNER FOR TWO

rant found his way back to the debarkation center. A different person was at the desk, an avuncular middle-aged man with a potbelly and an amiable smile. Grant's travelbag was still there, sitting on the floor beside the desk, and the man looked up the location of the room that McClintock had reserved for him.

Half an hour later Grant phoned McClintock from his one-room quarters. He got an answering machine, made a brief report of his meeting with Cardenas, then quickly unpacked his bag. He realized he was famished; he hadn't eaten anything since leaving Farside in midmorning, and it was now nearly eight P.M.

He knew that Selene's choice of restaurants was limited. There was the Earthview restaurant, which was far too posh for him—and expensive. And the Pelican Bar: the last time he'd been there he'd gotten into the fight that got him expelled from Selene. The cafeteria, he thought. That'll do.

Grant showered quickly and pulled on the only other shirt and slacks he'd brought with him. I'll have to get somebody back at Farside to send me more of my clothes if I have to stay here for more than an overnight, he thought.

He was about to leave his room and head for the cafeteria when the room's phone called out, "Dr. Cardenas calling Grant Simpson."

Cardenas? He felt surprised. Does she intend to work all frigging night?

"Answer," he told the phone.

Cardenas's face filled the screen. Grant realized she was really good-looking: bright blue eyes, strong jaw. She'd be actually beautiful if she'd just smile a little.

"Grant, I just realized that you probably don't have anybody to have dinner with." Before he could reply, she added, "Neither do I."

Blinking with surprise, Grant said, "I was just going to the cafeteria."

She shook her head slightly. "Not the cafeteria. Why don't you meet me at the Pelican Bar in half an hour?"

Happily, he said, "Half an hour. At the Pelican Bar." He wondered if anybody there would remember him.

The place was jammed, as usual. Men and women packed the bar, and all the tables seemed to be already occupied. Cardenas was nowhere in sight, although Grant searched carefully through the crowd for her head of golden hair: it would be easy to miss her in the crush of bodies.

The Pelican Bar had been built in a cave. The bare rock ceiling was raw, unsmoothed, and so low Grant thought he could brush it with his fingertips if he stretched a bit. Pelicans were everywhere: stuffed doll pelicans, pelican statues of wood and metal, paintings and photographs of pelicans on the stone walls. The wide display screen behind the bar showed pelicans gliding just above the wavetops against a background of old Miami Beach hotels—obviously the video had been made before Florida was inundated by the greenhouse floods.

"Hello."

Startled, Grant saw Cardenas standing beside him, a drink already in her hand. She was wearing a soft blue nubby sweater and a darker knee-length skirt. She was smiling slightly, but Grant thought the smile looked forced.

"Hello," he replied.

"You need a drink."

"Yeah."

He followed her as she wormed her way through the crowd at

the bar. The human bartender, an older, heavyset man with pouchy eyes and a receding hairline, hollered over the buzz of the crowd, "What's yours, pal?"

He's new here, Grant realized. He doesn't recognize me.

"Moonjuice," Grant yelled back. Recycled lunar water, infused with carbon dioxide.

The bartender nodded. Cardenas shouted to him, "We need a table, Robbie."

Nodding again, the bartender said, "Ten minutes."

Nine and a half minutes later Cardenas and Grant were perched on stools at a tiny round high-top table in the far corner of the Pelican Bar, studying the menu displayed on the tabletop screen. She picked soysteak, he tapped on eel filets.

It was quieter off in the corner of the crowded, bustling place.

"You must come here pretty often," Grant said.

Cardenas nodded. Then she asked, "You don't drink alcohol?"

"Can't afford it."

"Dinner's on me," she said. "I invited you."

Shaking his head, Grant replied, "I don't want to get into the habit." To himself, he added, I've got enough habits to deal with without adding booze to the list.

A squat little flat-topped robot rolled up to their table, bearing their dinner orders. They picked up the dishes and placed them on the table and the robot trundled off.

"Bon appetit," Cardenas said. Flat, mechanical. Without a smile.

They ate in silence for several minutes. Grant thought the eel was good. Fish and shellfish were a specialty in Selene. Aquaculture produced far more protein per input of energy than meat. Soya was the base for almost everything else, although in-vitro meat—cultured in a bioreactor from animal cells—was available, but expensive.

At last Grant broke their silence. "I appreciate your inviting me to dinner."

"Nothing to it," Cardenas said.

"I don't like to eat alone."

"Neither do I." She looked away from him briefly, then said, "But I'm going to have to get accustomed to it."

"Huh?"

"My husband decided today that he won't come here and live on the Moon. My kids won't even come to visit me. I'll never see my grandchildren again. They'll all stay on Earth." Her voice was flat and hard: not angry, exactly, but bitter, terribly, terribly bitter.

"Well, you can go Earthside, then."

She shook her head. "No, I can't. I'm full of nanomachines. I'm barred from Earth."

"Can't you be flushed clean?" Grant asked.

"And turn into a seventy-year-old hag? No thanks."

"Seventy?"

"Calendar-wise, I was seventy-two last month."

Grant was speechless. Cardenas looked no more than thirty-ish. Maybe forty, on the outside.

"I've used nanomachines to rebuild my cells, to clear plaque out of my arteries, to attack viruses and foreign bacteria that invade my body. Like a super immune system. Without them I'd probably collapse and die."

"And nanotech is forbidden on Earth," Grant murmured.

"It sure as hell is," Cardenas said, with the first hint of fervor Grant had seen from her. "Those stupid luddites are scared to death of nanotechnology. Even if I got a special dispensation from some Earthside government to come and visit my grandchildren, some suicide bomber kook might assassinate me. Blow me away and the grandkids with me."

Another woman would have been in tears by now, Grant thought. But Kris Cardenas's eyes were dry. And hard.

"I've heard there are secret nanotech labs on Earth," he said. "Big corporations run them."

"To what avail?" Cardenas asked. "Do you think some multi-national corporation is going to pay for a nanotech lab when they can't use the products the lab produces?"

"They could use it in secret, I suppose."

She gave him a skeptical frown. "For what? So their executives can stay young? Or their wives?"

"Or mistresses," Grant said, trying to lighten the conversation's tone.

Cardenas did not smile. "I'll stay here on the Moon, and my loving husband and my devoted children and my adorable, innocent grandchildren will never see me again."

Grant told her, "I can't go back to Earth, either."

She nodded. "I know about your legal troubles. I read it in your dossier."

"We're two of a kind then," he said. Then he added, "Sort of."

As if she hadn't heard him, Cardenas muttered, "As far as my family's concerned, I've made a deal with the devil and I'll have to pay the price for it."

Grant heard himself say, "I know what it's like, making a deal with the devil."

Cardenas looked as surprised as he felt. "What do you mean?"

Feeling suddenly flustered, unsure of himself, Grant waved a hand in the air. "Oh . . . I'm taking medications so I can work outside. You know, anti-radiation meds . . . some steroids . . ." Inwardly he fumed, *Why the hell are you telling her this? She doesn't care. Nobody cares.*

Cardenas gave him a long, thoughtful gaze. Then she said so softly that Grant barely heard her over the noise of the crowd, "Maybe there's something I can do about that."

"Something? What?"

"Therapeutic nanomachines," Cardenas said.

Now he fell silent.

"They can help you," said Cardenas, leaning closer to him. "Instead of the drugs you're taking."

"They're medications," Grant snapped.

"Medications."

"Nanotherapy," he mused.

"It could help," Cardenas said, unsmiling, utterly serious.

MARE MOSCOVIENSE

McClintock was on his knees—an unusual position for him—rummaging through his kitchen's mini-sized refrigerator/freezer and the cabinets stocked with packaged foods. No liquor, he saw. Not even wine.

He'd been at Farside for nearly three weeks and he hadn't seen a drop of liquor in all that time. Not even beer.

Straightening up, he wondered if the lack of alcohol was Uhlrich's policy. Has the man banned alcoholic drinks from Farside? If so, McClintock thought, I'll have to find some way around it. After all, rank hath its privileges.

Frowning unhappily, he pulled a prepackaged meal out of the low cabinet and popped it into the microwave oven. Then he returned to his desk and resumed scrolling through the Farside Observatory's personnel files. He paid particular attention to the women: a few of them looked attractive.

"They'll look absolutely gorgeous after a couple more weeks," he muttered.

The microwave pinged and he took his hot meal to the room's only table, sat down, and began to eat absently once he'd told the computer to project the personnel files onto the wall screen.

Engineers, technicians, but precious few astronomers, he saw. Well, Uhlrich's an astronomer, and he really doesn't need any here until the telescopes are finished.

There's the kid I rode in the lobber with, he remembered. He told the computer to display Trudy Yost's file. She's going to be Uhlrich's assistant. Not bad-looking, he thought. But you have to be careful with these young ones; they're quick to holler about sexual harassment.

Then there's this Grant Simpson fellow. Very earnest; apparently capable. Uhlrich's put a lot of responsibility on his shoulders.

McClintock remembered that Simpson had left a message for him. He's at Selene and already working with Dr. Cardenas, the nanotechnology expert. Good. Uhlrich's wary of nanotech, McClintock understood, but he's desperate enough to move in that direction—almost.

Your job, Carter my lad, is to soothe Uhlrich's fears and get those telescope mirrors built with nanomachines. Then you can go back to Pennsylvania with a triumph in your hand. Then you can—

The phone sang out, "Grant Simpson calling."

McClintock put down the forkful of in-vitro chicken he was holding. For a moment he debated refusing the call. Is Simpson going to make a pest of himself, calling at all hours of the night or day? Finally, with a resigned sigh, he ordered, "On screen, please."

Simpson's dark-bearded face appeared on the wall screen, his eyes sorrowful.

"Mr. McClintock," said Grant.

"How's everything in Selene?" McClintock asked. "How's Dr. Cardenas?"

"She's already working to get a complete analysis of the borosilicate glass. Should have it done by tomorrow."

"Fine." McClintock realized that was the first step. "What then?"

"That's why I called. We'll have to get the resources together to produce the raw material she'll need to build a mirror."

"That shouldn't be a problem, should it?"

"I'll work with Selene's mining and manufacturing department," Grant said. "But they'll want some kind of official requisition from Professor Uhlrich."

McClintock nodded. "They'll get it. I'll see to that."

"The big problem is to get a frame for the mirror over here, so the nanobugs have a structure to work with."

McClintock frowned slightly. "You mean like the frame of the mirror that cracked?"

"Or its duplicate."

"Do we have a duplicate?"

"Only the one being used in the mirror lab right now, on the turntable."

"Ah, where the second mirror's being polished."

"Right."

McClintock thought for a moment. One frame sitting out in the open with the ruined mirror, the other on the turntable where the polishing job is going on.

"What do you recommend?" he asked.

"We could build a new frame here in Selene, if Uhlrich will okay the cost."

"And the alternative?"

Grant said without hesitation, "Take the frame from the cracked mirror. It's useless anyway; take it apart and ship the segments here to Selene. We could remelt the broken mirror and use it as raw material for a new one, if the nanos don't work for us."

McClintock rubbed his jaw for a moment. Decisions are what you're here for, Carter my lad, he said to himself.

"All right. We'll break up the cracked mirror, take apart its frame, and ship the pieces to you." Before Grant could reply, McClintock added, "Don't worry about Uhlrich. I'll get his approval. No problem."

U hlrich looked alarmed. "Break up the mirror?"

"You were going to do that anyway, weren't you?" Mc-
Clintock prodded. "It's useless as it is now."

It was morning, although in this underground mole's
nest there's no feeling of day or night, McClintock thought.
He had popped in on the professor to report on how Simpson was getting along with Dr. Cardenas, only to find pert little
Trudy Yost already in conference with Uhlrich.

The professor steepled his fingers in front of his neatly bearded
face and half closed his eyes. McClintock looked across the table
at Trudy, who was staring at Uhlrich, waiting for her boss to make
a decision. But all the man was doing was a half-baked imitation
of a Zen master deep in meditation.

"What do *you* think, Trudy?" McClintock asked.

"Me?"

"Does it make any sense to leave that damaged mirror sitting
out on the crater floor, when Simpson needs its frame to guide
the nanomachines assembling a new mirror?"

She glanced from McClintock to Uhlrich, who had opened
his eyes and dropped his hands into his lap. The professor was
staring blankly at McClintock.

Suppressing an urge to grin, McClintock said silently to the
professor, I'm here to get things done for you, whether you like it
or not. Well, now I'm doing my job, but you don't like it, do you?
You don't like having the decisions taken out of your hands.

Trudy asked, "Does this mean we've given up on trying to repair the mirror?"

Before Uhlrich could reply, McClintock said firmly, "Yes."

Turning to the professor, Trudy said in a hesitant, soft little girl's tone, "Well then, I guess the mirror isn't really of any use to us in its present condition, Professor. And if Grant needs the frame for the nanomachines . . ." Her voice trailed off.

"You agree, then, Dr. Yost?" Uhlrich asked.

Sitting up a little straighter, Trudy replied, "Yes, sir. Yes, I do."

"If this nanotechnology scheme doesn't work," Uhlrich said, "we will have wasted two years of work."

Almost jauntily, McClintock replied, "So what? If the nanomachines don't get the job done, you'll be no worse off than you are now. You have nothing to lose."

Uhlrich began to steeple his fingers again, realized it, and pressed his hands flat on the desktop instead. "Anita Halleck is on her way here, you know."

"I didn't know," McClintock admitted, feeling a pang of alarm.

"Anita Halleck?" Trudy asked.

McClintock knew perfectly well who the woman was. "Director of the IAA's space telescope project," he said to Trudy.

"Space interferometer," Uhlrich corrected.

McClintock dipped his chin in acknowledgement. "Interferometer," he murmured.

Trudy looked halfway between curious and suspicious. "Why is she coming to Farside?" she asked.

"To check on our progress, what else?" Uhlrich said. "To gloat over us."

McClintock said, "She's got nothing to gloat about. They're nowhere near getting any of their mirror segments into space. It'll take them years—"

"And how long will it take us?" Uhlrich asked. His voice was low, but murderously cold.

"We'll be finished before they are," McClintock said, with an assurance he didn't truly feel. "We'll be finished before they get their mirrors put together in space."

Inwardly, he realized that the International Astronautical Authority had the resources of the entire Earth to draw upon. Yes, their project was grandiose, much more complex and demanding than Farside's. But all Farside had—so far—was the resources of the Moon. Selene's governing council was as generous to the Farside project as it could manage, but there were strict limits to how much they could afford.

McClintock could add significantly to those resources, if he chose to. Uhlrich knew it, and McClintock knew that it was the only reason the professor tolerated his presence at Farside.

"We'll be finished and taking data before they get even one of their mirrors assembled," Trudy added bravely.

McClintock thought she really meant it. Well, he mused, it's good to have underlings who believe in what they're doing.

Uhlrich was clearly unhappy, but he agreed to break up the damaged mirror and ship its frame to Selene.

"You've made the right decision, sir," McClintock said.

Trudy looked happy about it, too. As she got up from her chair she said to the professor, "You don't even have to tell Mrs. Halleck about the cracked mirror."

Uhlrich, still seated behind his desk, smiled glumly. "Do you think for one moment that she doesn't already know about it? She knows everything that goes on here."

Trudy's face fell. "Then . . . why is she coming?"

"To gloat over us!" Uhlrich snapped.

McClintock shook his head as he got up from his chair. "I don't believe so, Professor. Anita Halleck doesn't waste her time with emotions like gloating. She's coming here to get something from us."

"And what might that be?" Uhlrich demanded, acidly.

"Nanotechnology!" Trudy blurted. "She wants to use nanomachines, just like we do."

"That's impossible. Nanotechnology is banned on Earth in all its forms."

"But her telescopes won't be on Earth," Trudy pointed out. "They'll be in space."

"But they will be constructed on Earth."

"Or at Selene," Trudy said.

McClintock broke into a knowing grin. "She's not coming to see us here at Farside. She's coming to talk to Cardenas, over at Selene's nanotech lab. Her visit here is merely a cover."

Uhlrich looked plainly unconvinced. But he muttered, "Could the woman be that devious?"

"Does the Pope live in the Vatican?" McClintock quipped.

Once they were outside Uhlrich's office, in the drab rock-walled corridor, Trudy asked McClintock, "Do you really think Mrs. Halleck is after nanotechnology?"

McClintock smiled down at her. "It was your suggestion, remember?"

"I know, but do *you* think that's why she's coming here?"

McClintock started down the corridor and Trudy followed beside him, hurrying slightly to keep pace with his longer strides.

"It's a reasonable assumption," he said. "We'll just have to wait and see."

They walked along in silence for a few moments. McClintock thought the corridor was depressingly gloomy. With the pipes and conduits running along the ceiling it reminded him of the basement in some dreary public building. This entire Farside facility looks more like a prison than a research center, he thought. I may be the warden's special overseer, but I'm still in jail here just like the rest of them.

He noticed that Trudy was looking up at him.

"Where are you heading?" he asked her.

"Oh!" She looked startled. "I . . . I was just following you. I thought . . . I guess I wasn't really thinking." She smiled sheepishly.

With a knowing nod, McClintock said, "Let's take a bite of lunch."

"It's kind of early for lunch," she said.

"I know. I like it better when the cafeteria isn't crowded, don't you?"

"Uh, sure."

Farside's cafeteria was nothing more than another man-made cave, carved into the lunar rock with plasma torches. It was a dismally small, square chamber. McClintock felt as if its low ceiling were squeezing down on him. Two of the cafeteria's walls were lined with food- and drink-dispensing machines; the plastic-tiled floor was covered by three rows of long tables and hard, uncomfortable benches. No one can accuse Uhlrich of wasting money on luxuries, McClintock thought.

The place was empty when they entered it. Good, thought McClintock. Nothing worse than having to eat cheek-by-jowl with a gang of these techie bores.

Trudy followed him like a puppy as he selected a sandwich that purported to be soyburger with lettuce grown in Selene's hydroponics farm. The drink selection was limited to lunar water, fruit juices, and ersatz coffee or tea that McClintock suspected would be miserably weak.

The limited fare didn't seem to bother Trudy at all. She picked a limp salad, a bowl of fresh berries, and a glass of tea.

As they sat side by side at one of the long empty tables, McClintock muttered, "I'll have to take you to a real restaurant one of these days."

She fairly glowed. "Like the Earthview? Over at Selene?"

"Have you been there?"

"No, but I heard about it. Saw it in the orientation vid."

He nodded, then took a bite of his flavorless burger.

"You're not happy here?" Trudy asked, picking at her salad.

Be careful! McClintock warned himself. Choose your words prudently.

He gave her a forlorn look. "I feel as if I'm in some frontier outpost, far from civilization."

"Well, you are!" she said.

With a faint smile he admitted, "I guess I am."

"Why'd you come here if you don't like the place?" Trudy asked.

"Oh . . . family responsibilities."

"Really?"

"You see, in my family one is expected to do some form of public service before one can inherit his share of the family fortune."

Her eyes went wide. "Fortune?"

"The McClintock clan is quite wealthy," he explained. "But very stern. My great-grandfather was apparently afraid that inheriting great wealth would turn his progeny into wastrels. So he made it a provision of his will that every one of us has to work at least two years in public service before we can inherit."

Trudy chewed thoughtfully on her greens for a few heartbeats. Then, "There's a lot of public service to be done, isn't there? I mean, with the greenhouse floods and the droughts and all those monster storms and everything. Lots of people need help."

McClintock got a mental picture of the massive waves of miserable migrants, poor, starving, trekking across the land seeking a job, a living, some hope for the future, a spark of opportunity for their crying, squalling, sick and frail children. He shuddered.

"I decided to do my public service here, on the Moon," he said, stretching the truth considerably. "My goal is to help humankind to extend its habitat beyond the Earth. Quite lofty, don't you think?"

Trudy nodded, wordless.

He failed to mention what his real goal was. Instead, he asked her, "And what brings you to Farside?"

"Sirius C, of course," she said.

"Of course."

Almost quivering with eagerness, Trudy enthused, "I mean, it's the biggest thing to hit astronomy since . . . since, well, glory, since Hubble discovered the red shift."

McClintock suppressed an impulse to ask what she meant by that.

"Y'see," she went on, "the planet shouldn't be there at all. The Pup blew up eons ago and—"

"The Pup?"

She bobbed her head up and down. "Sirius has been called

the Dog Star since ancient times. It's the brightest star in the constellation Canis Major, the Big Dog."

"I see," McClintock said.

"Well, when its dwarf companion was discovered, back in the nineteenth century, naturally people started calling it the Pup."

"And it blew up?"

"Nova," she replied. "Probably blew off its outer shell more than once."

"I see," he repeated.

"Which makes it hard to believe there's an Earthlike planet in the Sirius system. It would've been fried by those nova burps. Boiled down to a cinder. An Earth-sized planet is hard enough to believe, but it can't possibly be Earthlike."

"Yet there it is," McClintock murmured. "And Uhlrich is hell-bent to get imagery of it."

"You know," Trudy went on, "the first extrasolar planets ever discovered were orbiting around a pulsar. That's a star that underwent a supernova explosion. Nothing left of the original star except a tiny core, smaller than Earth. And yet there were a couple of planets around it."

"The planets should have been destroyed in the explosion?"

Nodding again, Trudy said, "But they weren't. Or maybe they formed out of the debris cloud *after* the supernova popped." She jabbed her fork into the salad again. "We've got a lot to learn."

"Yes, I suppose we do." But McClintock's mind wasn't on astronomy. He was wondering if this little waif of a woman might go to bed with him. Without screaming for a lawyer afterward.

DOSSIER:
CARTER NELSON McCLINTOCK

From those to whom much is given, much is expected. Carter McClintock had heard that old saw all his life, and he hated it.

The McClintock clan had made its fortune originally in whaling. During the Civil War, when President Lincoln created the National Academy of Sciences, a McClintock was named to its directing committee. He was clever enough to invest in railroads, and his son was even cleverer: he got the family out of railroads and into chemicals.

McClintock money helped to finance the Spanish-American War, and the family profited greatly from the growth of the munitions industry. World War I was a bonanza. By then, one of the McClintock boys was backing the fledgling aviation industry. While barnstormers and explorers were killing themselves pushing the envelope of aviation technology, McClintock investments financed the fledgling commercial airlines.

One of the McClintocks lost billions when the dot-com bubble burst in the 1990s, but his brothers and cousins bailed him out with money they had made in energy, transportation, and real estate.

In the early years of the twenty-first century, it was a McClintock partnership with the Masterson family that allowed the ill-starred Masterson clan to make commercial spaceflight profitable.

The onset of the catastrophic climate shift that wrecked the lives of hundreds of millions brought new opportunity for the family. Carter McClintock's father quoted Andrew Carnegie's dictum, "It's a valuable citizen who has money during a panic," as he poured billions into nuclear fusion power generation and solar-power satellites.

Young Carter was more interested in fine art than finance. He raised funds to protect the city of Venice from being inundated by the rising Adriatic Sea. He salvaged the Acropolis reclamation projection when the European Union reneged on its commitment because of all the other demands on its resources, stretched to the breaking point by the hordes of refugees fleeing their flooded homelands. Almost singlehandedly, he saved the ancient temples of Cambodia from the mobs of squatters who had moved into them.

Carter had no interest in space. The activities of high-tech nerds in strange and dangerous places bored him—or so he told himself. Actually, those strange and dangerous places frightened him. Floating around in weightlessness? Walking on the dead and deadly surface of the Moon? Spending months in a coffinlike spacecraft heading to Mars? No, thank you. Carter preferred Earth, battered by the greenhouse shift though it may be.

Inevitably, he clashed with his father. "Space is where the action is, boy," the elder McClintock insisted. "It's the frontier now, and the frontier is where new fortunes are made."

Carter was quite content with the family's existing fortune. He had no desire to enlarge it. Let his father and brothers see to that. He wanted to spend the family's money on worthy causes. He wanted to be admired by the people who meant something to him: people of status, of taste, of cultivation.

Yet his father persisted. When Professor Jason Uhlrich, of Selene University, visited Philadelphia as part of his effort to raise money for his cherished Farside Observatory project, the elder McClintock invited the abstemious professor into his home for a quiet little dinner and chat.

At first, Uhlrich struck Carter McClintock as a man of the Old World: cultured, well mannered, obsequious in the presence of enormous wealth. But once the astronomer began to talk about his dream of an observatory on the Moon, Carter saw that the man was just another techie fanatic, so narrowly focused on his arcane goal that nothing else mattered to him.

Yet Carter's father was fascinated by Uhlrich and his hope of beating the IAA to be the first to acquire visual imagery of New Earth. To Carter's stunned consternation, his father suggested that he might help finance the observatory with funds from the McClintock Trust.

"Why?" Carter asked his father, once Professor Uhlrich had finished bowing and scraping and had left their home. "Why on Earth would you—"

"It's not on Earth," his father said, beaming happily from behind his thick gray moustache. "It's on the Moon. The far side of the Moon, at that."

"Ridiculous," Carter groused.

"You won't think so after you've been up there for a while."

"Me!" Carter fairly screeched. "Never!"

"I want you to look out for our interests up there," his father insisted. "See if this observatory the professor wants to build is really worth investing in."

"I won't go."

"You will, if you want to keep receiving your allowance."

Carter had seen his father twist other arms artfully. But this . . . "It's extortion!" he bellowed.

His father smiled and nodded and lit a non-carcinogenic cigar. "Yes, it is a bit of extortion, isn't it?" Then the old man's expression hardened. "But Anita Halleck is heading the IAA's astronomy project."

"You're not still angry at her," McClintock said. But he could see that his father plainly was.

"Her and that bastard Randolph. She's thrown the contract for assembling her telescopes in space to his Astro Manufacturing Corporation."

"I didn't know . . ."

His face hardening brutally, the elder McClintock promised, "I'm going to break that Aussie bitch if it's the last thing I do. And you're going to help me do it!"

ANITA HALLECK

Dutifully, Carter McClintock shuffled down the narrow, low-ceilinged corridor to Farside's reception area, out at the end of the underground facility's central tunnel. He wore the best of the three suits he had brought with him to the Moon: midnight blue jacket and trousers over an off-white turtle-neck shirt. He took special pains to scuff along in the ape-like shamble that substituted for normal walking in the one-sixth gravity of the Moon. He had no intention of stumbling and embarrassing himself in front of Anita Halleck.

Maybe the lobber will crash on landing, he thought. Then Father would finally be rid of her.

But it was too much to hope for. As McClintock sat nervously in the tight little reception chamber, he watched the wall-screen display of the incoming spacecraft falling out of the starry sky like a squat, cone-shaped rock. Then its rocket engines flashed, stuttering, and its descent slowed. It landed squarely on the blast-darkened concrete pad out there on the floor of Mare Moscoviense, all in complete, utter silence.

McClintock got to his feet as the access tube trundled like an oversized caterpillar from the airlock of the reception center to the main hatch of the lobber. The lone clerk got up from behind his desk, checked the readout lights on the control panel set into the stone wall beside the heavy metal hatch, then tapped a square green key set into its bottom row. The hatch sighed open and swung slowly inward.

Peering down the access tube, McClintock saw that only one

person was approaching: Anita Halleck, tall and slim, with a long sweep of chestnut hair draped dramatically over one shoulder. She was wearing a one-piece coverall of metallic golden fabric that seemed to glow slightly as she made her way up the slightly flexing tube. She's the only passenger, he realized. She commandeered a lobber flight just for herself.

He made himself smile for her. "Good to see you again, Anita," he said, stretching a hand in greeting.

She smiled minimally as she stepped through the hatchway and accepted his hand gracefully.

"Hello, Carter," she said. "How's your father?"

She *is* a bitch, McClintock said to himself. Aloud, he replied, "Still pretty sore about you, I'm afraid."

She shrugged. "The course of true love ne'er did run smooth."

Or false love, either, he added silently.

"I was rather surprised to learn you were here," said Anita Halleck. "I didn't realize you were interested in astronomy."

"I'm here to help Professor Uhlrich, sort of an aide to him."

She nodded knowingly. "So your father is going to invest in Uhlrich's project, then?"

McClintock replied casually, "Perhaps. We'll see."

She turned her attention to the clerk, who had slid back behind his desk; he took the data chip Halleck handed him and snapped it into his desktop computer.

Within a few minutes McClintock was leading Anita Halleck down the gloomy corridor toward the cell that would be her quarters during her visit.

"I had expected Professor Uhlrich to greet me," she said. "Not his underling."

Ignoring the barb, McClintock replied, "He'll see you in his office, of course. He thought you'd like to get settled and perhaps freshen up a bit first."

"I see."

She was a handsome woman, McClintock realized all over again as they strode along the corridor. Almost his own height, slim waisted and long legged. Her gold-glowing coverall was modest enough, buttoned at the throat, wrists, and ankles. It wasn't tight, exactly, but somehow it displayed the supple body inside it quite provocatively. Admiring those cheekbones and almond eyes and those pouty lips, McClintock thought she could easily have been a fashion model. Or a vid star. With a toss of her head she swung her long straight hair off her shoulder. It fell halfway down her back.

Yes, he said to himself, it's no wonder that Father went off the deep end over her.

"I'm afraid the accommodations here are rather spartan," McClintock said apologetically.

"I'll only be here overnight," she said. Her voice was low, warmly melodious. Inviting? McClintock asked himself. She can be damnably seductive when she wants to be.

He showed her the room that had been assigned to her. She took it in with a single brief glance.

Turning back to McClintock, she said, "I presume my bag will be brought here."

"Of course."

"All right then. I want to see Professor Uhlrich now."

"Of course," McClintock repeated.

The meeting fascinated McClintock. Uhlrich was stiffly formal with her, never budging from behind his desk. McClintock thought the professor used the desk as a barricade, to protect himself. Even when he stood he kept his fingertips in contact with the desk's gleaming surface. For her part, Halleck sat gracefully on a chair halfway down the adjoining table, swiveling it to face the professor. She never allowed herself to get close enough to shake hands with him.

After politely holding her chair for her, McClintock took the seat next to her, one place farther away from Uhlrich.

"It's good to see you again, Mrs. Halleck," said Uhlrich, with all the sincerity of a headwaiter.

"I'm delighted to be here," she replied, equally hollow.

Brushing a fingertip along his trim silver beard, Uhlrich said, "I was very sorry to learn of your husband's death."

She made a sigh. "He was very old, very frail. It was something of a blessing."

McClintock recalled that she had inherited a massive fortune from the man she had jilted his father for. A blessing indeed, he thought.

Uhlrich called, "Computer: orientation slideshow, please."

Images of the three craters where the telescopes would be sited sprang up on the wall screen opposite the chairs where Halleck and McClintock were sitting.

Uhlrich began, "As you know—"

"Yes, I do know," Halleck interrupted. "You can spare me the orientation, Professor. What I'd like is a progress report."

"Progress report?" Uhlrich asked stiffly.

"I understand your first mirror was damaged before you could get it to its site."

His face paling visibly, Uhlrich admitted, "Yes, that is true."

"So what are you doing about it?"

McClintock saw a blue vein in the professor's forehead begin to throb. This is going to be a lovely meeting, he told himself. Just perfectly lovely.

DINNER

To McClintock's pleasant surprise, Halleck's meeting with Uhlrich was mercifully brief. The professor sputtered a bit but finally admitted to Halleck that he was looking into the possibility of using nanotechnology to make the interferometer's mirrors. Halleck nodded as if she'd known that all along, then got up from her chair.

Surprised, Uhlrich said, "But you haven't told me how your own project is proceeding."

"Oh, we're on schedule," she replied airily.

Uhlrich got to his feet, looking surprised, confused. "On schedule? What schedule? When do you expect—"

"The schedule was published when we began the project. You must have seen it. It's available on our net site, if you need to refresh your memory."

And with that, she turned toward the door. As McClintock stood up, Halleck said, "I suppose I should look in on your mirror laboratory while I'm here." Before Uhlrich could reply, she added, "Although, if you're going to turn to nanotechnology, I imagine your mirror lab will become superfluous."

Uhlrich stood behind his desk, his mouth hanging open but no words coming out of it.

Going to Halleck's side, McClintock said, "I'll show you the mirror lab, if you like."

"Fine," she said.

They left the Ulcer standing there, speechless.

At the mirror lab, McClintock was surprised to see tall, lanky Nate Oberman waiting for them, a bitter little smile on his lean face.

"Professor Uhlrich phoned and told me to show you around the lab," Oberman said, then added, "since I don't have anything else to do."

McClintock heard the acid in his tone; Halleck seemed not to notice.

Oberman showed them the slowly rotating turntable and explained how the spin casting method worked. Halleck took it all in within a few minutes.

"Thank you so much, Mr. Oberman," she said, by way of dismissal.

"My first name's Nate, Mrs. Halleck," said Oberman. "I'll be leaving Farside by the end of the month. I could sure use a recommendation from somebody as important as you are. It'd help me land a decent job."

Halleck eyed him briefly. "Are you returning to Earth?"

"Yes'm. Selene's already turned me down. They claim I don't have enough experience for any of the job openings they've got available."

She glanced at McClintock, then said to the young man, "I'm leaving tomorrow. But call me first thing in the morning, we can talk then."

Oberman's narrow face broke into a triumphant smile. "I'll phone you at seven sharp!"

Smiling back at him, Halleck said, "Make it eight. I'll talk to you then."

"Yes, ma'am!"

As they returned to the corridor, McClintock said, "That was very kind of you, Anita."

She made a vague gesture with one hand. "I'm not the monster you seem to believe I am, Carter."

"I never thought you were a monster."

Halleck cocked an eyebrow at him and changed the subject. "I'm quite famished."

"I'm afraid the eating facility here is rather primitive. Nothing but a cafeteria."

"I suspected as much," said Halleck. "That's why I brought a couple of frozen dinners in my bag."

"Clever lady," McClintock said.

"Would you care to join me for dinner, Carter?"

In his mind's eye, he saw how delightedly happy his father had been when Anita Halleck had been his rousing, laughing, adventurous mistress. It was more than showing off a trophy, McClintock thought. Father was genuinely mad about her. Until she started playing around behind his back.

Now she's coming on to me? he asked himself. Could she be that blatant? What does she want from me?

"I have a dinner engagement," he lied. "One of the astronomers. She's new here."

Halleck's sensuous lips curved slightly. "And you've volunteered to show her the sights?"

Feeling slightly flustered, he answered, "Nothing like that, Anita. She's just a kid."

"So was I . . . once."

McClintock realized that the astronomy office was a few doors down the next cross corridor. Hoping that Trudy was where she should be, he said, "Come on. I'll introduce you to her."

Smiling as enigmatically as the Sphinx, Halleck started along the corridor beside McClintock.

With a surge of relief McClintock saw that Trudy actually was in the astronomy office. It was one of the bigger spaces in the Farside complex, with four desks placed in the four corners of the chamber. Trudy was at the desk in the farthest corner, her eyes fixed on the wall screen to her right; it showed a complex chart of curves and alphanumerics that was incomprehensible to McClintock.

Trudy was staring at the screen so hard she didn't notice McClintock and Halleck until they were halfway to her desk. She shot to her feet like a new recruit suddenly snapping to attention.

The contrast between the two women was extraordinary, he

thought. Trudy was wearing a faded, shapeless blouse that had probably been violet when it was new, over a rumpled pair of beige slacks. Halleck was still in her metallic gold coverall, glowing like a goddess, almost a full head taller than Trudy.

"Trudy," said McClintock, "I'd like you to meet Anita Halleck, head of the IAA's space telescope project."

"I know who Mrs. Halleck is," said Trudy, her eyes on the woman. "I'm very happy to meet you."

Halleck nodded graciously as McClintock finished the introduction. "And this is Dr. Trudy Yost, who has come here to work under Professor Uhlrich."

Smoothly, McClintock continued, "Trudy and I are having dinner together this evening."

Trudy's eyes went wide for an instant, then she said, "If you'd like to join us, Mrs. Halleck . . ."

"Why, thank you, Trudy. I think that would be fine."

McClintock kept his face impassive, but inwardly he wondered if Trudy would be shocked at the idea of a ménage à trois. He knew from his father's boasting that Halleck wouldn't be.

The cafeteria looked even dumpier than usual in McClintock's eyes. They had to sit at one of the long tables, with the two women on either side of him. No decent chairs, he grumbled to himself, just these damned benches. The room was filling up, grubby-looking engineers and technicians lining up at the food and drink dispensers, crowding all the tables, talking and laughing with each other. McClintock imagined that none of them had ever seen the inside of a real restaurant.

And the food selection was pitiful. He had picked what purported to be a soysteak dinner platter. It looked like a pathetic mess on his tray. Trudy had helped herself to fish filets and a reasonably fresh-looking salad. Halleck had gone for the shellfish special. I wonder what she brought with her for dinner, McClintock asked himself. I'll bet she brought champagne with her. Sadly, he concluded, I'll never know.

As they sat shoulder to shoulder with the chatting, gobbling Farside employees, Halleck leaned slightly to speak past Mc-Clintock to Trudy. "So what are you actually doing for Jason?"

"Jason?" Trudy asked.

"Professor Uhlrich."

"Oh! Well, we're using the best imagery that the telescopes in Earth orbit can give us to refine the parameters of Sirius C's density and oblateness. That can tell us a lot about the planet's interior composition. We're looking for indications that there might be a planetary magnetic field, a dipole field, you know, like Earth's, and . . ."

On and on Trudy chattered. With some satisfaction, Mc-Clintock saw Halleck's eyes begin to glaze over. She's no more interested in this technobabble than I am, he realized.

The blare of the speakers set into the cafeteria's stone ceiling interrupted Trudy's increasingly tedious monologue.

"EMERGENCY MEDICAL TEAM TO THE MAIN AIRLOCK," the synthesized voice demanded. "EMERGENCY MEDICAL TEAM TO THE MAIN AIRLOCK."

Half a dozen men and women scrambled from their seats at the long tables and raced out the cafeteria's door.

"A medical emergency?" Halleck asked, looking up at the speakers.

Several other people were heading for the door; others were talking to each other, looking worried, fearful.

Trudy shot to her feet. "Maybe they'll need some volunteers to help them." Without another word she started for the door also.

Frowning at the interruption, McClintock said to Halleck, "I'd better go see what this is all about."

She stood up beside him. "Carter, you're like the man who races to get ahead of the mob because he's supposed to be their leader. But he doesn't know where they're heading."

"They're heading," he said bitingly, "to the main airlock."

He hurried in that direction, Halleck keeping pace beside him. Plenty of others were rushing down the corridor, too.

The main airlock's locker area was crowded. Most of these people are onlookers, rubberneckers, McClintock thought as he shouldered his way through them.

One of the technicians, a chubby-faced redhead, growled belligerently, "Who ya shoving, mister?"

"I'm Professor Uhlrich's deputy," McClintock snapped. "Get out of my way."

The man stepped aside, grudgingly.

Trudy was kneeling beside a man on the floor who was still encased in a space suit, although his helmet had been removed. Several others were gathered around the prostrate body, removing his boots, pressing a breathing mask over his face, clipping a monitor onto one of his bared fingers.

"It's Harvey Henderson," someone beside McClintock whispered.

"What happened?"

"How the hell should I know?"

"He was outside."

"Something went wrong."

"You're a real detective, pal."

Bending over the medics, McClintock demanded, "Who's in charge here?"

Blocky, gray-haired Dr. Kapstein glanced up at him, her squarish face looking somewhere between annoyed and inquisitive. "I am."

"And you are?"

"Ida Kapstein, resident physician. Who the hell are you?"

"Carter McClintock. I'm Professor Uhlrich's number two."

"Since when?" Dr. Kapstein asked as she returned her attention to the injured man on the floor. Others of the medical team were tugging off his space suit trousers now.

"For the past three weeks," McClintock replied, with iron in his voice. Inwardly he realized that he hadn't made much of an effort to make himself known to Farside's rank and file. With more than a hundred people in the facility, he told himself, I can't be expected to keep track of everyone's name.

He saw that the man's right foot was bloody. Another space-suited figure came through the airlock hatch. As she lifted off her helmet Dr. Kapstein asked her, "What happened out there, Josie?"

"We were taking apart the mirror frame," the young woman

said, her olive-skinned face taut, her dark eyes wide with anxiety, focused on the unconscious man.

"And?" the doctor prompted.

"We were breaking it down into segments for shipment to Selene."

"What the hell happened to *him*?" Kapstein snarled.

"He tried to carry one of the segments to the tractor all by himself," the young woman said, her words tumbling out almost breathlessly. "I told him to wait and let one of the robots do it, but he toted it by himself and it slipped out of his gloves and banged his foot."

The doctor puffed out a weary sigh. "Dumb sonofabitch should've known better. Just because things only weigh one-sixth up here they forget they've still got the same mass."

"I tried to tell him. . . ." The young woman seemed on the brink of tears. "He was in a rush to get in for dinner."

A voice in the crowd of onlookers said in a stage whisper, "Hurry-up Harvey ain't gonna hurry for a while."

As if he'd heard the comment, the injured Harvey Henderson stirred slightly and moaned.

"Take it easy," said Dr. Kapstein, placing a gentle hand on Henderson's arm. "You're a lucky man, Harvey. Good thing your boot wasn't penetrated. Then we'd have to suck your body out of the suit with a vacuum cleaner."

Harvey Henderson grinned weakly. "I screwed up, huh?"

Kapstein nodded, then said, "We'll have to ship you back to Selene for stem cell treatment. Get that mangled foot back in shape."

McClintock straightened up and Trudy got up from her knees.

"It can be dangerous out there," Trudy said, her voice low, hollow.

"So I see," said McClintock. The crowd was starting to dissipate as the medical team gently lifted Henderson onto a gurney.

Looking around, McClintock realized that Anita Halleck was nowhere to be seen. She probably went back to the cafeteria, he thought, to pick up some dessert. Coldhearted bitch.

Then he realized that Professor Uhlrich was not there, either.

G lad to be free of Halleck, McClintock walked Trudy back to her quarters. She seemed shaken by the accident, subdued.

"He'll be all right," McClintock assured her. "With stem cell therapy they can rebuild his foot even if it's crushed flat."

"I guess," Trudy said.

They arrived at her quarters. McClintock saw that someone had inserted a plastic tag in the slot on her door: YOST, T.

"Well, it's been an eventful evening," he said.

She nodded. McClintock knew that this was the moment when he should make his move if he wanted the evening to go on.

Before he could make up his mind to say anything, Trudy spoke. "Thanks for taking me to dinner. And introducing me to Mrs. Halleck."

"You're entirely welcome, Trudy," he said.

She looked up at him with the almost-bewildered expression of a lost waif.

"Good night, Trudy," he heard himself say.

"Good night, Carter." Then, impulsively, she stood on tiptoes and pecked at his cheek. Before he could respond she turned, slid her door open, and slipped inside.

Standing suddenly alone in the corridor, McClintock felt slightly ridiculous. Almost angry. But then he laughed at himself. What the hell, he thought. We just met yesterday. I shouldn't rush her.

As he started down the corridor, he told himself, Besides, I haven't had a chance to really look over the available crop here. I might be able to do better.

His pocketphone buzzed.

Yanking it out, he saw Professor Uhlrich's name spelled out on the tiny screen.

McClintock thumbed the REPLY button and lifted the phone to his ear. "Yes, Professor?"

"Did you see the accident?" Uhlrich's voice sounded calm—relaxed, almost.

"I saw them bring in the technician, and the medical team's emergency treatment of him."

"I observed the surveillance camera record of it. Could you come to my quarters, please? We need to discuss this."

Thinking to himself that working with Uhlrich was going to be a twenty-four-hour-a-day job, McClintock said, "Now, Professor? Or in the mor—"

"Now," said Uhlrich. And he clicked off the connection.

With a grim smile, McClintock muttered, "No wonder they call him the Ulcer."

Uhlrich's quarters were exactly the same size as McClintock's own, but his furnishings were much more comfortable. There was a new-looking couch beneath the wide wall screen, with a low metal coffee table in front of it, flanked by two plushly upholstered chairs. Actual paintings in gilt frames hung on the walls: McClintock thought they might have been done by Old Masters. They looked like portraits from centuries ago, stiff white-bearded men in colorfully ornate military uniforms, complete with sashes and swords at their sides.

The professor was sitting at the foldout table in the kitchen area, a stemmed wineglass in his hand, when McClintock stepped in. He got to his feet, a little stiffly, McClintock thought.

"I'm sorry if I interrupted your dinner," Uhlrich said, like reciting a school lesson.

"The accident did that," McClintock said.

Gesturing to the couch, Uhlrich said, "Please, sit down. Would you like a drink? Schnapps, perhaps?"

Surprised at the offer, McClintock answered, "A little whisky, please, if you have it."

"Yes," said Uhlrich. "I think so." He turned back into the minuscule kitchen and delved into one of its cabinets. "Ah! A single-malt scotch," he announced, his fingers fondling the bottle. "Would that be satisfactory?"

"Perfectly. On the rocks, please."

Uhlrich popped a couple of ice cubes into a tumbler and poured a meager splash of whisky over them.

He came over and handed the glass to McClintock, then sat himself on the armchair to his left, holding his wineglass in one hand and smiling mechanically.

McClintock sat on the couch and sipped at the scotch, thinking that although Uhlrich obviously disapproved of allowing liquor at Farside for his staff, he kept a stash for himself. He's not a prig, he's a despot.

After taking a sip, he said to the professor, "Your medical team handled the emergency quite well, I thought."

"It shouldn't have happened," said the professor. "Carelessness, pure and simple."

"All accidents can be prevented," said McClintock, "in hindsight."

Uhlrich nodded unhappily. He took a gulp of his wine, then stared at McClintock for several long, silent moments. McClintock stared back, saying nothing. This is your party, he thought. You make the opening move.

Abruptly, Uhlrich said, "The accident would not have happened if Simpson had been there, where he should have been."

So that's what this is all about, McClintock said to himself. A test of wills. "I'm afraid I'm responsible for sending Simpson off to Selene. I want him to work closely with Dr. Cardenas on this nanotechnology effort."

"I see," said Uhlrich.

"The man can't be two places at the same time," McClintock said.

The professor nodded, then lapsed back into silence. At last he offered, "The past two days have been very—eventful."

"Yes. Very."

"Trying."

"Yes."

"Two accidents," said the professor. "Perhaps you are a Jonah?"

Feeling suddenly nettled, McClintock shot back, "Me? You've never had any accidents here before I arrived?"

Uhlrich replied, "Of course. Of course. I was merely joking with you."

McClintock made himself smile.

"How long will Anita Halleck stay here?" the professor asked.

Aha, thought McClintock. So that's what this is about. "She's leaving tomorrow, I believe," he said.

With a slight shake of his head, Uhlrich replied, "There is no lobber scheduled to arrive tomorrow."

"She can requisition a vehicle whenever she wants one," said McClintock. "Rank hath its privileges."

"She saw the accident."

"Only if the surveillance camera views are shown in the cafeteria."

"She didn't go to the airlock?"

"She started to, but actually I don't think she was the slightest bit interested."

Uhlrich rubbed his trim little beard absently. Then, "She came here to spy on us."

"I think her real reason for coming here is to meet with Dr. Cardenas in Selene and recruit her help in using nanotech to build her telescope mirrors."

"But why is this set of telescopes so important to her?" Uhlrich wondered. "Why is she so interested in Sirius C? She's not an astronomer."

McClintock knew his father's explanation: Halleck was using

the New Earth program to throw lucrative contracts to Dan Randolph's Astro Manufacturing Corporation. But he said nothing. No sense telling the professor that she cuckolded my father with Randolph.

To McClintock's surprise, Uhlrich answered his own question, "She wishes to defeat me."

"Defeat you?"

"To prevent me from getting the Nobel. That's her motivation."

McClintock started to tell him that he was being silly, but hesitated. Be careful here, he told himself. If you say that he's not important enough for her to be bothered with, he'll hate you for it.

"Perhaps that's it," he said. But he still thought his father was closer to the truth.

Uhlrich straightened in his chair and asked, "What will be your recommendation to the board of the McClintock Trust? Will you support my work here?"

Slightly surprised at his direct thrust, McClintock temporized, "Professor, I've only been here for a couple of weeks. I can't make up my mind so quickly." Inwardly he reasoned that his father expected him to stay exiled at Farside for at least a month before making a recommendation.

"Time is of the essence."

"Still . . . give me a chance to get a firm impression of the work you're doing here."

"Selene's funding only allows us to proceed at a snail's pace. I need your help."

"I understand," said McClintock.

"Time is of the essence," Professor Uhlrich repeated.

UHLRICH'S QUARTERS

Professor Uhlrich looked in McClintock's direction, seeking some clue, some hint of hope, that the man understood how important, how crucially vital, the work of the Farside Observatory was.

It was like gazing at a frosted window: he could discern nothing but the opaque surface. Uhlrich knew from the level of McClintock's voice how tall the man was, and the information from his dossier and various net sites said he was a strikingly handsome man in his early thirties. Uhlrich's visual cortex drew a picture that vaguely suggested a vid star from many years earlier.

McClintock knows how to keep his thoughts hidden, Uhlrich realized. The man just sits there saying nothing, knowing that he has the power of life and death over the Farside Observatory, over me, myself.

At last he asked McClintock, "Is it absolutely necessary to keep Simpson at Selene?"

McClintock started to reply, hesitated, then answered, "He'll only be there a day or so. If you want Cardenas to help you, we should keep Simpson reasonably close to her."

The man understands nothing, Uhlrich thought. Patiently, he tried to explain, "With Mr. Henderson incapacitated, I need Simpson here to direct the technical crew. They must take apart the mirror frame so it can be shipped to Dr. Cardenas's laboratory. I need Simpson here to direct them."

"Couldn't one of the other—"

"No," Uhlrich said flatly. "Simpson. He's the only one who can get the job done. The others are not equal to the task. Believe me, I know them well."

"None of them?"

Struggling to remain calm despite McClintock's obtuseness, Uhlrich replied, "You saw how lacking the man Oberman is. I've tried others before him: None of them were competent enough to head the technical team. Simpson is my last hope—unless I could hire someone else from Selene. Or perhaps even from Earth. But that would be expensive."

McClintock said, "You know, Simpson has his own problems."

"It's rumored that he's a drug user, I know."

"And that doesn't bother you?"

"Of course it bothers me!" Uhlrich snapped. "But what choice do I have?"

"There's no one else among your entire technical team that can handle the work?"

Dolt! thought Uhlrich. I've told the man twice that I need Simpson here and he still doesn't understand.

"Mr. McClintock," he said, very slowly, as if speaking to a child, "you don't seem to realize how limited we are here. I have a mere fifty-some engineers and technicians—even less than that now, with Henderson out of action. They must run the mirror laboratory, do all the construction work out on the surface, and all the other technical tasks that are necessary. There are another eighteen specialists struggling to construct the Cyclops radio telescope array. Eighteen people! Eight dozen would be barely enough."

McClintock shifted in his chair but said nothing.

"Selene's governing council has given us only the barest minimum of funding," said Uhlrich.

"Which is why you need help from the trust," McClintock said, finally understanding.

"Which is why I need help from the McClintock Trust," Uhlrich echoed. "Yes."

"Well . . . as I said, Simpson can't be in two places at the same time."

"He is needed here. He can maintain contact with Dr. Cardenas over phone links."

"I suppose so," McClintock said doubtfully.

"Then it is settled," said Uhlrich. "Simpson returns here at once."

Sounding reluctant, McClintock said, "I'll tell him so."

"Good."

McClintock seemed to understand that he was being dismissed. Uhlrich sensed him taking a final sip of his scotch, then getting up from the couch. The professor stood up beside him, barely as tall as McClintock's shoulder.

The two men walked to the door and shook hands.

"Thanks for the drink," McClintock said unenthusiastically.

"You are entirely welcome," said Uhlrich, with equal warmth. "I hope we can work together fruitfully."

"So do I, Professor."

McClintock left and Uhlrich slid his door shut, leaned against it for a moment, then threaded his way back to the chair he'd been sitting in. He found his wineglass, drained it, then brushed his fingers along the tabletop until he found McClintock's tumbler. The professor carried both glasses to the dishwasher in the kitchenette.

As he slipped the glasses into the half-full machine, Uhlrich thought, Simpson is the key to everything. He's the only one who can get those technicians to do their jobs properly. He may be dependent on the medications he takes, but as long as he gets the job done I don't care if he eats dogs and drinks vinegar. I need him!

The professor went to his desk and sat wearily in its little wheeled chair. He called up the latest data on the Sirius system and told the computer to display it in the audio mode.

"Sirius C will begin transit number thirty-eight in thirty-two hours, seven minutes, and fourteen seconds," the synthesized voice began.

The planet will pass across the blazing face of the Dog Star,

Uhlrich understood. From the minuscule dip in the star's brightness, the planet's size could be calculated to a finer precision. My new assistant, this young woman, Dr. Yost, will do that, he thought. Then he remembered that he had ordered her to report to his office again at 0730 hours.

I'd better get to bed, he told himself.

Simpson, he repeated silently. He's the key to getting the work done. And McClintock: he's the key to getting the funding to carry out the work.

Uhlrich shook his head as he began to get undressed. A drug user and a spoiled rich brat. He sighed, thinking that it was almost criminal that the great things he wanted to achieve depended upon such people.

DOSSIER:
JASON MAXIMILLIAN UHLRICH

He was born to genteely impoverished nobility in the Austrian city of Linz, which was famous for the pastry called Linzertorte and for being the childhood home of Adolf Hitler.

Tales of the family's bygone splendor filled his childhood, and his father still had enough influence to place young Jason in good schools. Because he was bookish and got better grades than his classmates, and because he was pompously proud of his family heritage, but most of all because he was slightly built and physically frail, Jason became a favorite target for the bigger and more rugged boys. He got his revenge against them by consistently being first in his classes, despite occasional swollen lips or bruised ribs.

It was at the prestigious University of Vienna that Jason Uhlrich turned to the study of astronomy. He had won a full scholarship and started in the physics curriculum, inspired by one of the university's most illustrious alumni, the Nobel laureate Erwin Schrödinger. But astronomy lured him away from theoretical physics: Uhlrich fell in love with the study of the stars. Nobel Prizes rarely went to astronomers, he knew, but Uhlrich burned with an ambition to be among the rare few who achieved that lofty goal.

Alas, reality was very different from his dreams. Uhlrich was a gifted teacher, but only an ordinary researcher. A generation of students adored him, some of them going on to outstanding careers in astronomy. Uhlrich himself remained virtually anonymous: a slim gray figure in the background, not the forefront, of astronomical research. He was the person to whom his students dedicated the books that made them famous.

Then came the accident. He was working with a graduate student, a pretty young Hungarian woman with thick honey-blond hair who was specializing in infrared astronomy—at Uhlrich's suggestion. She was building a sensitive IR detector and—again at Uhlrich's suggestion—using liquid hydrogen for its coolant rather than liquid helium. When she worried about the dangers of the highly flammable hydrogen, Uhlrich assured her that the increase in the instrument's sensitivity would be well worth the risk.

It wasn't. One fine spring afternoon, as he worked alongside the student, inhaling her lovely perfume, the hydrogen exploded in a searing fireball that burned the student to death and destroyed both Uhlrich's retinas.

Stem cell therapy could rebuild his burned face but could not repair the completely destroyed retinas. Neurosurgeons made Uhlrich see, after a fashion, by rewiring his visual cortex so that it could be stimulated by the auditory and tactile centers of his brain.

He saw through his ears and his fingertips. He was hailed as a living miracle of medical science. He returned to an almost normal life. The miracle was not perfect, of course: the images his visual cortex drew in his mind were not perfect reproductions of the people and things about him.

But he did see that lovely young graduate student in his mind's eye. Saw her afire, heard her screams, every time he closed his sightless eyes.

Uhlrich exiled himself to the Moon. The newly independent lunar nation of Selene was starting a university and looking for top-flight people to fill its faculty. Through old associates (he had very few friends) Uhlrich received an invitation to head the astronomy department of the fledgling University of Selene.

"We need good men like you, Professor," said one of his former students, who now headed Selene University's selection committee.

"Dependable, reliable, the kind of man who can turn out top-notch students."

Thus Uhlrich traveled to the Moon, learned to live underground in the strangely light gravity, walked and talked and existed almost like a normal, sighted man, and tried to forget his previous life and sorrows.

Then another of his former students, now a leading astronomer at the University of Arizona, discovered Sirius C, an Earth-sized planet orbiting a star that was less than nine light-years away, so close that the International Astronautical Authority launched a plan to get visual imagery of the world that the popular news media dubbed New Earth.

Suddenly Uhlrich was seized by a frenzy. Selene was already constructing a radio telescope facility on the far side of the Moon. Why not build an optical interferometer that could image Sirius C—before the IAA's grandiose plan for space-borne telescopes could be completed?

Insisting that Selene could gain enormous prestige from the project, Uhlrich faced the lunar nation's governing council in a white fury of ambition. They decided to study his proposal, which Uhlrich took as a polite way of refusing him. Just as when a father tells his importuning child, "We'll see," what he really means is no, but he doesn't want to have an argument about it.

Desperate, Uhlrich sought an audience with Douglas Stavenger, the retired leader of Selene, the man who had directed the community during its earliest years, who had led Selene's brief, almost bloodless fight for independence, who had chosen the very name for the lunar nation.

Stavenger, still Selene's éminence grise despite his apparent youth, smiled at Uhlrich's enthusiasm and agreed with him. Selene should be the first to obtain visual imagery of New Earth.

Selene's governing council agreed to support the project—minimally. Which led Uhlrich to seek additional funding from the McClintock Trust. He had not expected the scion of the Mc-

Clintock clan would actually come to the Farside Observatory and interfere with his operation.

But Uhlrich was determined to do whatever was necessary to make Farside Observatory succeed. His one chance for a Nobel Prize was at his fingertips.

Almost.

The room felt strangely crowded to Uhlrich, stuffy and hot, even though there were only three people in it.

The professor had been informed that Grant Simpson had returned to Farside the morning after Uhlrich had ordered McClintock to bring him back. But when Uhlrich tried to reach Simpson on the phone, to discuss the engineer's meeting with Dr. Cardenas, he received a recorded statement:

"I'm unable to speak with you at the moment. Please leave your name and a brief message and I'll get back to you as soon as I can."

Unable to speak with *me*? Uhlrich fulminated. The nerve of the man!

He asked the people monitoring the surveillance cameras that watched over every public space in the facility to locate Simpson. Within a minute they reported that Simpson was in the teleoperations center.

For all of three minutes Uhlrich drummed his fingers on his desktop. Too busy to answer my call, is he? His first impulse was to go down to the teleoperations center and let Simpson know in no uncertain terms that when he's called by the chief of the Farside Observatory, he'd better answer right then and there.

But then he thought that it would be beneath him to go searching for one of his employees. Simpson should come to me; I'm his superior, he works for me. But I need him, the professor admitted to himself; he's the only man around here who seems to be able to get things done. At any rate, Uhlrich felt safer in his own office, behind his own familiar desk. Why go traipsing through the corridors if you don't have to? he asked himself. Why risk blundering into an embarrassing wrong turn?

Finally, though, he decided to sacrifice his dignity a little and go to the teleoperations center. Show them that I can go anywhere I decide to go, he thought. That I'm not a prisoner of my own office. I want to talk with Simpson, I want to talk with him *now*. I'll make him understand that when I call, he comes. Or else.

He got up from his desk and started for the teleoperations center, his face set in a grim mask of determination, his fingers brushing along the wall of the corridor as he walked.

But as he strode down the narrow rock-walled corridor his irritation eased somewhat. No sense making a scene, he told himself. Go to the teleoperations center as if you're checking on how the work is going. A good leader looks in on his people from time to time. Talk to Simpson from a position of authority, not like a helpless blind man or an angry fishwife.

So when he slid open the door to the teleoperations center, Uhlrich was quite composed and ready to speak to Simpson in a reasonable manner.

For several heartbeats Uhlrich stood just inside the door, feeling tense and sweaty in the small, poorly ventilated room. He knew there were four consoles standing against the far wall. Simpson had to be at one of them.

Then he heard Simpson's voice: "Almost there, Josie."

Josie. Uhlrich mentally riffled through his personnel file: Josefina Rivera, one of the technicians. Hispanic American, age twenty-six, degrees in electronics and software engineering.

Uhlrich coughed softly to get their attention. He sensed the woman turning to look over her shoulder at him. Simpson remained with his back to him.

The woman half whispered, "Grant . . ."

"Not now," Simpson snapped.

She lapsed into silence.

Stiffening, Uhlrich called, "Mr. Simpson."

"Not now," he repeated, louder.

Uhlrich felt a blaze of anger surge through him.

"He's working one of the tractors," Josefina Rivera explained. "Loading the last section of the mirror frame onto a flatbed."

"Almost finished," Simpson called out, still without turning away from the screen.

Seething, Uhlrich debated storming out of the room. But what would that accomplish? he asked himself. I've come this far, I'd look foolish if I left now.

So he stood there, folding his arms across his chest, and waited as Simpson operated the tractor outside. From what Uhlrich could gather, the task of disassembling the mirror frame was almost completed. He pictured the doughty little tractor trundling around the perimeter of the mirror and taking the last remaining section of the frame in its metal grippers. Slowly, carefully, it was tugging the frame loose from the mirror, then lifting it and stowing it in the trailer with the rest of the disconnected sections.

All in response to the motions Simpson made on the console's joystick and dials. Uhlrich admitted to himself that none of his staff could work the teleoperations consoles as well as Simpson could.

To the young woman, Simpson said, "That's the way it's done, Josie. If Harvey had kept his butt in here and done the job right he wouldn't have gotten himself hurt."

Uhlrich pictured the young woman's face, outlined against the glow of the console's screen.

"Harvey can't handle the controls the way you can, Grant," she said, her voice brimming with admiration.

"Then he ought to learn."

"Mr. Simpson," Uhlrich called, steel in his voice.

Simpson turned in his squeaking chair, then got slowly to his feet. "Professor," he said, by way of acknowledgment. Nothing more.

"I expected you to report to my office this morning," said Uhlrich, "to tell me about your meeting with Dr. Cardenas."

Sounding almost embarrassed, Simpson said, "I filed a report last night, soon as I arrived back here. Didn't you get it?"

"I want a personal report," Uhlrich snapped.

"Oh." A heartbeat's hesitation, then Simpson said, "I thought it was important to get the mirror frame taken apart and get it ready for shipment over to Selene."

"That is important, yes," Uhlrich conceded, "but your report to me should come first."

He sensed Simpson's shoulders slumping slightly. "I thought my written report would do. And I wanted to get the frame off to Selene as soon as possible."

The woman said, "I'll call the transportation people and schedule a lobber flight for the frame, Grant."

"Thanks, Josie," Simpson replied.

"Come with me," said Uhlrich, reasserting his authority. "You can tell me about your meeting with Dr. Cardenas on the way back to my office."

"But there's more to do here," Simpson objected.

"You can do it when you come back from my office," Uhlrich insisted.

"Yessir," said Grant Simpson. Very reluctantly, Uhlrich thought.

IN THE CORRIDOR

There's not all that much to tell," Simpson said as he walked alongside Uhlrich down the corridor.

The professor knew from tactile representations of his staff's personnel dossiers that Simpson was just about his own height. Much broader in the body, wide shoulders and a solid frame, but the man's arms and legs were short and thick. They made him appear squat.

"Dr. Cardenas is willing to help us?" Uhlrich asked.

"Almost eager," Simpson replied. "That's why I wanted to get the mirror frame to her as soon as possible. She's already analyzing samples of optical glass that Selene's glass factory gave her."

"That's good," Uhlrich conceded. Then a new worry struck him. "But how is she to be paid for her work? We can't afford a big addition to our budget."

"From what I could make out," Simpson answered, "she's got a pretty good discretionary budget of her own, from Selene. She won't be a drain on our finances."

"For now," Uhlrich said. "When it comes to actually building the mirrors . . ."

"That should cost less than spin casting them. And it'll go a lot faster than spin casting, too."

"And how will we transport the mirrors from Selene?" Uhlrich demanded. "You couldn't get one of them across the ringwall without cracking it."

If the remark stung Simpson, Uhlrich couldn't tell. The man's normal tone of voice was a downcast image of worry. Yet he speaks to me like an equal, almost. A strange man. Talented, but tainted.

"Dr. Cardenas thinks it would be best to build the mirrors in situ. I agree with her," Simpson replied.

Startled, Uhlrich asked, "You mean, build the mirrors at the craters where they are to be sited?"

"That's right."

"But that would mean—"

Simpson interrupted, "It'll be a lot easier carrying a batch of nanos and the associated equipment on site than to try transporting the mirrors from here to the craters."

Uhlrich fell silent, trying to sort out the possibilities.

Simpson kept on. "We've learned that transporting the mirrors is risky. From what Kris tells me, the nanos can work perfectly fine out on the surface. They don't need air. All we'd have to do is build a temporary roof over the site to protect everything from radiation and micrometeors. The rest can be done remotely, from the teleoperations center, with a minimum of human oversight at the craters."

"You have this all figured out," Uhlrich murmured.

"We can build all three mirrors at the same time, get the job done in less than a year."

"Less than a year?"

"Once the foundations are built, and the frames. And the raw materials are delivered," Simpson said matter-of-factly.

Uhlrich's head was spinning. Less than a year! We'd be taking data even before Halleck and her IAA team can assemble their mirror segments in space. Let alone align and test them. But can I trust Simpson's judgment? Is this scheme of his an actual possibility or merely some drug-induced fantasy?

The professor realized they had stopped walking. He had lost count of their paces, but figured they must be at his office door.

"It's all in my report," Simpson was saying. "Dr. Cardenas agrees with my conclusions. You can check it out with her."

Drawing himself up to his full height, Uhlrich said, "That is exactly what I intend to do, Mr. Simpson."

The engineer replied sadly, as if he'd expected such treatment, "That's what I thought. Now I'll get back to the teleop center. There's still a lot of work to do."

"And I will read your report," said Uhlrich, "then contact Dr. Cardenas and discuss it with her."

"Fine," said Simpson. Without another word he turned and started back down the corridor.

As he listened to the audio of Simpson's report, Professor Uhlrich had to admit that the man was thorough. It was all there, each step necessary to build all three mirrors simultaneously at their sites, using nanomachines.

He must have stayed up all night to produce such a detailed report, Uhlrich thought. When does the man sleep? Of course the cost estimates are very rough; I'll have to get the accounting staff at the university to make a refined cost estimate. Still, if Simpson's figures are anywhere close to accurate, it should cost us a fraction of what spin casting the mirrors would cost.

Can I trust Simpson's judgment? Uhlrich wondered. The man uses drugs. Medications, he claims, but whatever they are they could cloud his judgment seriously. His work has been impeccable, so far. But how far can I trust him?

Uhlrich decided to make two phone calls. One to Dr. Cardenas, at Selene's nanotechnology laboratory. The other to Farside's resident physician, the woman who was overseeing Simpson's medications.

MEDICAL REPORT

D r. Ida Kapstein sat at the table abutting Uhlrich's desk. He could fairly *feel* her radiating displeasure. He pictured her in a white medical smock, gleaming and crisp.

Diplomatically, Uhlrich began, "I'm sorry to call you away from your duties, Doctor."

Her voice almost growling, Kapstein answered, "I figured it must be important if you wanted me to come to your office."

"It's about Grant Simpson."

"Ah. I should have guessed."

Uhlrich steepled his fingers. "This is a rather delicate matter." He waited for her to respond, but she just sat there like a block of cement, silently staring at him.

At last he said, "I need to know about his drug use."

Kapstein's tone turned even more nettled. "There is a certain expectation of doctor-patient confidentiality, Professor."

Smiling thinly, Uhlrich said, "Even when the safety of the entire Farside staff is at stake?"

The doctor hesitated. Then, "I don't think that's at issue."

"Would the technician Henderson have been injured if Simpson had been at his job, where he should have been?"

Sounding surprised, she said, "It was my understanding that *you* sent him over to Selene."

"Why he was away from his position is not the question here. The question is, would that technician have been injured if Simpson was where he should have been?"

"That's got nothing to do with the medications he's taking."

Uhlrich realized she was being loyal to Simpson, not to himself.

"Doctor," he said, as amicably as he could manage, "my task is to ensure that my staff works in the safest environment possible."

"Grant Simpson isn't a threat to anybody's safety," she said flatly.

"He's not taking narcotics?"

"Not that I know of."

"What medications have you prescribed for him?"

"That's on record. You can look it up in the medical files."

"Please enlighten me."

He sensed Dr. Kapstein tugging her phone from the breast pocket of her coverall. She said to it, "Simpson, Grant, medications prescribed. Audio presentation."

She held the phone up so that Uhlrich could hear its tinny voice. It was a long list, mostly incomprehensible.

"I'm afraid I'm not up on the pharmaceutical terminology," the professor said.

"Most of it's pretty standard for somebody who works out on the surface a lot. Anti-radiation meds, a couple of stem cell injections to repair damage caused by radiation exposure."

"You said 'most of it,'" Uhlrich said.

"He's taking some steroids, too," the doctor admitted grudgingly.

"Steroids? Why?"

"They improve physical performance. Stamina. Strength." Her voice went strangely gentle as she added, "Some men use them in place of aphrodisiacs."

Uhlrich felt his face flush.

The doctor quickly continued, "But Grant isn't using them that way, I'm sure. He's taking steroids to help him do his work outside. It isn't easy, you know, out on the surface stuffed inside one of those hard-shell suits."

Steepling his fingers again, Uhlrich asked, "If he didn't have to work on the surface, could he stop taking these medications?"

She thought a moment before replying, "Yes, I suppose so."

"What kind of an answer is that?"

Sounding uncomfortable, Dr. Kapstein said, "Well, some of those steroids can be habit-forming. It could be hard to shake loose of them."

"Like withdrawing from narcotics?"

"Different symptoms, but—yes, sort of like narcotics withdrawal."

"I see."

"Trouble is," the doctor continued, "he's going to have to stop the steroids, sooner or later."

"Why is that?"

"Side effects build up. Liver deterioration, for one thing. His liver function is already in decline."

"It is?"

"Nothing serious. Not yet. But . . ." She left the conclusion unspoken.

Abruptly, Uhlrich got to his feet. "Thank you, Dr. Kapstein. You've been most helpful."

She pushed her bulk up from the chair, making Uhlrich wonder how she would fare if she ever went back Earthside.

He walked her to the door, then slid it shut again and returned to his desk. *I should prohibit Simpson from working outside,* Uhlrich told himself. *Yet I'm going to need him to direct building the mirrors at their crater sites.*

His decision was clear. *Work Simpson as hard as possible. Get those mirrors built. Monitor the man's medical condition, of course, but by all means get him to build those mirrors!*

Smiling to himself, Uhlrich asked his phone when he could expect Dr. Cardenas to return his call.

The phone replayed Cardenas's response to his earlier call: "I'm going to be in conference with Anita Halleck for most of the morning, Professor Uhlrich. I'll call you back after lunch."

Anita Halleck! Uhlrich trembled with sudden anger. *That woman is going to usurp Cardenas's time and effort, steal her away from me, ruin my chance to be the first to image Sirius C.*

He saw his Nobel Prize crumbling before his eyes.

NANOTECHNOLOGY LABORATORY

t took all of her self-control for Anita Halleck to suppress the shudder of outright fear she felt. Since she'd been a child, earning a living by salvage diving through the flooded ruins of downtown Sydney, nanotechnology had been dreaded by everyone she knew.

Not that she believed the religious nonsense that nanomachines were inventions of the devil, evil in its purest form. That rot was for the brainwashed fools who substituted religious dogma for thinking. Still, nanomachines had been used to murder people, she'd been told, and the threat of nanos going wild, devouring everything in their path like a blindly hungry swarm of unstoppable mechanical ants, had given her terrifying nightmares for years.

But here on the Moon, in this underground wombat's den called Selene, nanotech was used quite openly. And Anita Halleck was sitting face-to-face with the leading nanotech expert, in her laboratory where she produced nanomachines as routinely as chickens produce eggs.

They were sitting next to each other at a small round table in a corner of Kristine Cardenas's nanotechnology lab. An assistant had carried in a tea tray, complete with a small platter of scones. Now, as they sipped from the thin ceramic cups, Cardenas looked quite normal, ordinary: except that she appeared decades younger than the age given for her in the bionets. Young, healthy—and teeming with virus-sized machines crawling through her body.

Again Halleck fought down the urge to shudder.

"Are you all right?" Cardenas asked her.

Halleck blinked at the woman. "Yes. Of course. Why do you ask?"

Cardenas looked concerned. "You seemed to drift out of the conversation . . . as if your mind was wandering."

"Sorry," said Halleck. "I was merely thinking about how different things are here from the way they are on Earth."

Her expression hardening, Cardenas said, "Yes, they are, aren't they?"

"I understand that you're not allowed back to Earth."

"Not unless I flush my body of the nanos in it."

Halleck's breath caught in her throat. "Then it's true. You're filled with them."

Smiling bitterly, Cardenas replied, "You don't have to be worried. They won't come out and infect you."

"I didn't think . . . that is, I mean . . ."

"I know," said Cardenas. "All your life you've been told that nanomachines are dangerous—"

"Well, aren't they?" Halleck challenged.

"So is a rock," Cardenas snapped. "You can use a rock to smash someone's skull, can't you? So is penicillin dangerous, if you put too much of it into your veins. So is water dangerous, if you fill your lungs with it."

Halleck lowered her eyes. "I understand. It's just . . . well, please give me a little time to get used to it."

With an expression that was almost contemptuous, Cardenas said, "You're frightened of nanomachines, yet you're here to see if nanotechnology can help you."

Halleck nodded.

"Isn't that just the tiniest bit contradictory?" Cardenas asked.

Now Halleck allowed herself a minimal smile. "There's an old legend about the great moguls of Hollywood, back when movies were still flat, two-dimensional. Every one of those studio heads is alleged to have told his assistants, 'Never let that bastard back on this lot again—unless we need him!'"

Cardenas eased back in her chair and broke into a chuckle. "You need nanotech."

"I believe I do."

"Tell me about it."

Half an hour later Cardenas didn't seem as hostile as she'd been earlier.

"Yes," she was saying, "we can build your mirror segments in space. The nanos are machines, they don't need air or gravity. They'll work perfectly well in space."

"We'll have to bring the raw materials up from the ground," said Halleck.

"Get the raw materials from Selene. That's what Uhlrich is doing, over at Farside. It's more than twenty times cheaper launching cargo into space from here than from Earth."

"The lower gravity, of course," Halleck murmured.

"And the Moon's surface is airless. We launch cargo with an electric catapult. Much cheaper than rockets."

"Then you can do it?"

Cardenas hesitated a fraction of a heartbeat. "We're already committed to producing mirrors for Farside."

"Ah. Professor Uhlrich."

"Yes."

"Couldn't you take on my project as well? I can finance whatever expansion you'd have to make in your lab, your staff. Whatever. Within reason, of course."

Cardenas reached for her cup of cooling tea and sipped at it, obviously thinking about what she should answer. At last she said, "It won't take much of an expansion here, actually. I can produce the nanos for you once you get your specifications for the mirror segments to me. The rest of the project is up to you."

It was Halleck's turn to do some thinking. "I'd need to have a sample built and tested before we start building the actual segments in space."

"That's reasonable."

"Can you start on that right away?"

"In a few weeks," Cardenas answered.

"A few weeks?"

"Uhlrich's in line ahead of you."

"Oh," said Halleck. "Of course. I see."

Looking slightly puzzled, Cardenas said, "I got the impression that you and the professor were in competition. A race."

"Oh, he's in a race. I'm not. But he doesn't believe me when I tell him so. He's hell-bent to get imagery of New Earth before anyone else does. He's slavering for the Nobel Prize."

"Aren't you?"

"The Nobel Prize?" Halleck laughed. "I'm not a scientist. I'm not eligible. I'm just a poor little girl from Sydney."

DOSSIER:
ANITA MARIE HALLECK

She was born in the Outback, the only child of a sheep rancher and his schoolmistress wife. Anita Marie was barely three when the abrupt greenhouse climate shift struck Australia, flooding the coastal cities while parching the arid Outback worse than ever. One of her earliest memories was of her father's fields littered with scruffy, bone-thin sheep dead and dying of thirst in the brittle brown grass while the merciless wind blew gray dust over their bodies.

The little family moved to Sydney, which was also dying—of too much water. Together with nearly a million other refugees, they lived in one of the tent cities that dotted the hills above Sydney's flooded downtown. By the time she was ten, Anita Marie was contributing to the family's finances by scuba diving among the city's drowned high-rise towers, fetching souvenirs for tourists who cooed over the fearless little girl who swam like a dolphin.

By the time she was sixteen she was orphaned, her mother killed in one of the horrific tropical cyclones that blew in from the Tasman Sea and tore the refugees' tents to tatters, her father slain soon afterward in a drunken fight. Anita quickly learned that she could obtain protection, and even kindness, by using her hard, lively intelligence and her lithe, very feminine body.

She climbed through a succession of lovers, adroitly avoiding the pitfalls of other girls who fell in love too easily or succumbed to the need for drugs or other palliatives. She stayed clean and sober, and rose to a comfortable and almost secure life.

Then she met Morgan McClintock. He was a generation older

than she, incredibly wealthy, and attracted to her from the moment they met—at a party celebrating his fiftieth birthday. Within a week Anita dumped the hard-muscled construction engineer she'd been living with and moved into the McClintock mansion.

Morgan McClintock gave her everything: sophistication, luxury, education, social contacts, even employment in one of the corporations he controlled, McClintock Securities Ltd. Everything except marriage. After living as a widower for years, the thought of marrying this slim young mistress of his never entered his mind. And Anita never pressed him on the subject. She knew that Morgan did not truly love her, not in the starry-eyed way of romantic fantasy. She didn't care. She had fallen truly in love with Morgan McClintock.

She became an astute businesswoman and an accepted part of his international social set. Eventually he wangled a position for her on the governing board of the International Astronautical Authority. She had to resign from McClintock Securities, but Morgan was delighted with her new situation, expecting her influence to send lucrative IAA projects to his web of interconnecting corporations.

When she began to show some independence, and failed to follow his demands for contract favors, a rift began to grow between them. She begged him to consider her obligation: "I can't throw contracts your way, Morgan, I simply can't. It wouldn't be fair. It wouldn't be ethical."

"Ethics be damned," he growled. "This is business."

Gradually Anita realized that security, even love, were not enough for her. She wanted to be somebody. On her own, of herself. She wanted to be Anita Marie, not Morgan McClintock's mistress, not a woman who was known by the man she slept with, not even a woman who was known by her job or career. Herself. For herself and by herself.

The IAA's work was interesting, in a cerebral, non-visceral way. But directing that work, making decisions that influenced giant corporations, decisions that moved stock markets around the world and affected thousands of men and women, agreeing to fund *this* project and withholding support from *that* one: that was power, and Anita enjoyed wielding it.

Morgan McClintock grew increasingly unhappy with her increasing independence. They argued, more and more heatedly. The end came when he angrily accused her of sleeping with Dan Randolph, the womanizing founder of Astro Manufacturing, and handing juicy deals to Astro. Furious, Morgan accused her of stabbing him in the back and slapped her face. Then he threw her out, actually emptying her closets and hurling her clothing out the window onto the lawn below.

It wasn't the slap: she'd been hit much harder by other men. It wasn't even the humiliation of her expulsion from his home. It was the realization that his industrial empire meant more to Morgan McClintock than she did. And that she'd been foolish not to have gotten a signed financial arrangement with him in the first place.

They parted bitterly, for she truly had loved him—for a time. But the love had withered into a painful husk of resentment and regret. While they were together Anita had never looked at another man, not even Morgan's handsome young son.

Morgan McClintock immediately found another mistress. A younger one.

Anita found an even richer man, an older one: Brian Halleck. And this time she married him.

THE EARTHVIEW RESTAURANT

Her last night in Selene, before she returned to Earth, Anita was invited to dinner at the Earthview restaurant by Douglas Stavenger and his wife.

Anita was delighted by the invitation, and pleasantly surprised by the restaurant. Most of Selene reminded Anita of Coober Pedy, the opal-mining town in South Australia that had been carved out of the multihued veins of opal, underground where the residents could escape the summer's blistering heat. But where the opal-rich stone of Coober Pedy was bright and colorful, Selene was drab: the lunar rock was mostly shades of gray, and the endless corridors and chambers were dismally narrow, their ceilings depressingly low.

The Earthview restaurant was very different. It had started as a huge natural cave, but the residents of Selene had enlarged and improved it in every way. There were five tiers of tables, with winding rampways connecting them. The plastic tablecloths, manufactured from lunar raw materials, looked and felt like crisp white linen. Selene-made tableware and wineglasses sparkled on every table in the light of lamps designed to flicker like candles.

Human waiters in dark suits and squat little robot aides moved up and down the ramps with quiet efficiency. The smoothed rock walls supported sweeping flat screens that showed the view outside, on the floor of the giant ringwalled plain of Alphonsus: the stark barren grandeur of the pitted, dusty lunar surface with the gorgeous blue and white beauty of Earth hanging in the utterly black sky.

A dark-clad waiter led Anita to the table where Douglas Stavenger and his wife were already seated. Stavenger rose and introduced, "This is my wife, Edith. Edith, meet Anita Halleck."

As Halleck took the chair the waiter was holding for her, she stared at blond, smiling Mrs. Stavenger and asked, "Aren't you Edie Elgin, the newscaster?"

Edith's smile brightened. "I used to be. Haven't done much lately. I'm sort of retired. But it's good to be recognized."

"I've enjoyed the newscasts you've done from Selene."

Douglas Stavenger asked, "How do you like the restaurant, Mrs. Halleck?"

"Please call me Anita."

"Fine. And I'm Doug." Pointing to his wife, Stavenger added, "But she'd prefer Edith. Edie is just for the news nets."

"Very well, then," said Anita. "Edith."

"So what do you think of this place?" he asked again, full of youthful eagerness.

"It's spectacular! I didn't expect anything so . . . so . . . opulent."

"It's our one luxury here in Selene," Stavenger said, grinning. Then he added, "Well, this and the swimming pool up in the Main Plaza."

"I can see why people want to come up here after they've retired," Halleck said.

"Too many of them," Stavenger said, sobering. "More than we can handle."

Edith said, "We're building new living spaces for them, but there's still lots more applying for residency than we can make room for."

"They're running away from the disasters back Earthside," Stavenger muttered.

A human waiter took their orders, and their food and drinks were delivered by one of the little flat-topped robots that trundled nimbly among the tables.

"I understand you've been talking with Dr. Cardenas," Stavenger prompted, between bites of his catfish filets.

"Yes," said Halleck. "We're going to see if her nanomachines can build the mirror segments we need."

"For the big telescopes you're gonna hang out in space," Edith said.

Interferometer, Halleck corrected silently as she nodded at Mrs. Stavenger. But then she thought, Well, they actually are telescopes, aren't they? We'll simply be using them differently.

"Kris's bugs will build your mirror," said Stavenger. "She's a wonder with nanotechnology."

Halleck heard herself ask, "Doesn't it worry you? Just a bit?"

"Worry? About nanomachines?"

"Yes. You're a completely enclosed community here. If some of those nanobugs got loose, they could destroy everything, couldn't they? Wipe you out. Kill everyone."

Stavenger glanced at his wife before answering. Then, in very measured tones, he replied, "That is a possibility, of course. That's why we're very careful with nanomachines. We have very strict safeguards in place. The only time we've had any problems was when someone deliberately tried to kill people with nanomachines."

"Your father was murdered by them, wasn't he?" Halleck asked.

"My father was murdered by a madman who used nanomachines as the murder weapon, yes," Stavenger said tightly.

Edith chimed in. "You might's well say that guns kill people on Earth."

"Well, they do, don't they?"

"Only if some killer uses them to commit murder."

Halleck pointed out, "That's why so many nations on Earth have banned gun ownership."

"You think nanotech should be banned here in Selene, the way it is on Earth?" Stavenger challenged.

Halleck sidestepped with, "If it were, I wouldn't be able to get my mirrors built by nanomachines."

Hunching over the table toward her, Stavenger said earnestly, "We need nanotechnology here. Nanomachines pull the oxygen we breathe out of the regolith. They manufacture water for us—"

"But you were refining oxygen from the regolith and manufacturing water before you started using nanotechnology, weren't you?"

"Yes," he admitted. "But it was much more expensive and limited. We could never have expanded Selene to the size it is today without nanotechnology."

"Yes, I see."

"Nanotechnology saves lives, too, you know," Stavenger went on. "Nanomachines have saved my life. More than once."

"I see," Halleck repeated. So it's true, she thought; his body's filled with nanomachines, too.

Edith made a bright smile and said, "We've made a deal with the little bugs, Anita. They help us and we keep 'em under control."

"It's worked very well for us," Stavenger added.

Trying to make her voice light, pleasant, Halleck said, "I understand. You've done very well with nanotechnology."

And she thought that nanotechnology was going to be very useful to her, as well.

While they waited for Cardenas to confirm that she could build Farside's mirrors with nanomachines, for nearly a week Grant found himself buried in paperwork. There was little work going on outside, but now that he was head of the tech staff, Grant found that there was plenty of record-keeping, schedule fixing, workshift adjusting to be done. Once he had dismissed such tasks as nothing more than paper shuffling. Not that they used paper; everything was done digitally. But Grant began to understand that without the paperwork, the *real* work could not be done.

And then there were the personnel problems. Personality problems, really. Harvey Henderson returned from Selene but his foot was still on the mend; he couldn't work outside. Josie Rivera was flirting with several guys at the same time, causing lots of resentment. Grant remembered the days when he had first started taking hefty doses of steroids, and his chemically induced aggression had led him into roaring arguments and even battering brawls.

And while he sweated over records and schedules, the damned cracked mirror just lay there on the dusty ground, absorbing hard radiation from the Sun and stars, and being slowly abraded by the constant hail of dust-mote-sized micrometeorites falling to the Moon's surface.

The Sun was touching the ringwall mountains of Mare Moscoviense; Grant knew that once the two-week-long lunar night settled across the giant crater's floor, the mirror's glass would begin to contract in the cold and its crack would worsen. He tried to get

Uhlrich to okay building a roof over the mirror to protect it from the meteoroid infall, but the professor kept delaying that decision.

When Grant complained to McClintock that nothing was being done, he told Grant to be patient.

"Your job here is safe as long as you keep your nose clean," McClintock said daily. "Don't antagonize Uhlrich. And follow my orders."

Grant said nothing, but he thought that it was more important to get the job done, and done right, than to pussyfoot around the Ulcer or wait for this playboy to make decisions that were clearly beyond his understanding.

He spoke several times with Kristine Cardenas, back at Selene, checking on the progress of her effort to build the telescope mirror with nanomachines. He had another motive for keeping in touch with her: he desperately wanted Dr. Cardenas to inject him with a set of nanomachines tailored to repair his damaged liver and protect him from radiation effects once he began working out on the surface again.

He was growing more impatient, more apprehensive, with each passing day. The dull ache in the small of his back seemed to be getting worse. Grant knew he faced an increasingly desperate conundrum: he needed the steroids he'd been taking so that he could work out on the surface, but those steroids were damaging his liver, perhaps permanently. And god knows what else, he thought.

He pressed McClintock for permission to fly back to Selene, but McClintock evaded the issue with a brittle smile and a vague, "Not yet. Soon, but not just right now."

So Grant was pleasantly surprised one morning when McClintock woke him with a phone call.

"Grant, there's a resupply lobber coming in later this morning. I want some of your people to help the crew offload its cargo and then you ride back to Selene with them."

Sitting up in his wrinkled bed, Grant said eagerly, "I'll call Kris Cardenas, tell her I'm coming."

In the phone's small display screen, McClintock's face took on a pensive expression. "Yes, I suppose you might as well touch base with her while you're in Selene, but the reason I want you there is to meet a Dr. Frederic Palmquist, who's visiting from Earth. He's asked for a tour of Farside."

Frowning with puzzlement, Grant said, "There's nothing much here to show a visitor."

Almost smirking, McClintock replied, "You know that and I know that, but Professor Uhlrich's in a sweat to get this fellow here and impress him. Woke me up at five this morning, all excited about Palmquist."

"What's so damned exciting about the man?"

"He's from Stockholm."

"A Swede?" Then it hit Grant. "The Nobel committee?"

McClintock nodded solemnly. "It's nothing official. Palmquist isn't even on the committee. But Uhlrich's in a lather. You'd think Jesus Christ and all twelve Apostles were coming to town."

Grant couldn't help grinning. "Yeah, I'll bet the Ulcer is salivating."

"Like Pavlov's dogs."

"Okay," Grant said, pulling his legs free of the tangled sheets. "What time's the lobber due to land?"

"Between ten thirty and eleven."

"I'll have a crew there, suited up and ready to help."

As soon as McClintock hung up, Grant put in a call to Dr. Cardenas.

It took more than an hour to unload the supplies that the lobber carried: mostly food, with some replacements for pieces of laboratory equipment. Grant worked with the lobber's crew and two of his regular Farside team.

He was worming his arms out of his space suit, feeling tired and smelly, when he saw Trudy Yost step into the locker area.

Surprised, Grant asked her, "What brings you down here?"

She wrinkled her nose slightly, caught herself, and put on a smile instead. "Professor Uhlrich wants me to go to Selene to meet this Swedish visitor and bring him here."

"That's what I'm supposed to be doing," Grant blurted.

"The professor thought it would be best if an astronomer met the man."

Leaning over to unfasten his boots, Grant muttered, "Instead of a lousy engineer, huh?"

Trudy looked confused. "What do you mean?"

"McClintock told me to go pick up the Swede."

"The professor told me," said Trudy.

Grant thought it over for all of six seconds. "Looks like we're both going."

"I don't think the professor would want both of us to go."

Standing up in his thick-stockinged feet, Grant said, "McClintock told me to go. Nobody's told me not to."

"But the professor . . ." Trudy's voice tailed off.

With a shake of his head, Grant said, "McClintock and the Ulcer screwed up. The left hand doesn't know what the right hand is doing."

"I'll phone Professor Uhlrich," Trudy said.

"No!" Grant snapped. "We'll both go. Why not?"

"Because the professor will pop his cork when he finds out, that's why not."

"Let him," said Grant. "He can argue it out with McClintock. In the meantime, you and I can go visit Selene together."

Trudy looked apprehensive, but slowly a mischievous grin dimpled her cheeks. At last she said, "Sounds good to me." Then she added, "But there'll be hell to pay when we get back."

"We'll be bringing the Swede with us. The Ulcer won't dare show his temper in front of him."

Besides, Grant thought, I'll get my chance to see Cardenas and get injected with her nanomachines while Trudy's making nice-nice to our Swedish visitor.

DR. FREDERIC PALMQUIST

Grant and Trudy were the only passengers aboard the lobber on its return flight to Selene. The vehicle was configured for carrying cargo, not passengers, so they sat in a pair of fold-out seats up in the cramped cockpit, shoehorned in behind the pilot and copilot.

Grant saw that once they had lifted off, the pilots had nothing to do during the forty-five-minute flight except watch the control panel instruments. The ballistic flight followed Newton's Laws faithfully.

Then he noticed that Trudy looked . . . not frightened, exactly, but concerned, almost worried, her face a little taut.

"It's okay," he said, trying to reassure her. "Everything's going smoothly."

Trudy looked startled. "I know. I just feel kind of like a sardine, cooped up in here."

"It's not first-class accommodations, that's for sure," he admitted.

"Can't see the ground at all."

Pointing between the pilots' shoulders, Grant said, "We'll see it on their display screen when we start to descend."

Trudy nodded uncertainly.

"The flight's on trajectory," Grant said. "No worries."

With a smile that looked forced, Trudy said, "Fliers claim that flying is the second most exciting thing a man can do."

"And what's first most exciting, sex?"

"No," she said, her expression quite serious. "The first most exciting thing a man can do is landing."

She is worried, Grant realized. He wondered what he could say to make her feel better.

"It'll be okay, don't worry about it."

Grant thought it sounded pretty lame, but Trudy smiled again at him. It was a pretty smile, he thought.

The lobber's landing was fully automated, although the two pilots hunched over their instruments, ready to assume manual control if necessary, as the rocket plummeted toward Selene's blast-blackened landing pads.

Despite his reassurances, Grant felt a wave of relief once they touched down. He grinned at Trudy.

"Piece of cake."

"Sure," she said. "Now."

As soon as they cleared the debarkation desk and got aboard one of the automated trams that ran through the kilometer-long tunnel to Selene proper, Grant phoned Dr. Palmquist.

The Swede was in a tour bus, taking in the tourist sites out on the floor of Alphonsus's broad ringed plain.

"We are approaching the *Ranger* 9 site," Palmquist said, in English slightly accented with a reedy Swedish intonation.

The phone's reception was weak in the tunnel, its video image grainy. In the miniature screen, Palmquist looked to Grant like bleached white flour: his thinning dead white hair was combed straight back from his high forehead, his complexion was pale, his face roundish.

Grant nodded and asked, "When is your tour scheduled to return?"

Palmquist's pallid face took on a slightly puzzled expression. "They told me it was a three-hour tour," he replied, "and we left promptly at eleven o'clock."

"So you'll be back at fourteen hundred," Grant prompted.

"I suppose so," Palmquist said, looking uncertain about it.

"We'll meet you when your bus arrives."

"Fine. Very good. We can have tea together."

Grant suppressed a chuckle. "We'll go to the cafeteria."

"Good," said Palmquist.

Clicking his pocketphone shut, Grant turned to Trudy, sitting beside him on the tram. "He thinks he's still in Stockholm. Tea in the afternoon."

She shrugged. "We can do a tea, I betcha. The cafeteria's got cookies and buns. We'll make do."

Glancing at his wristwatch, Grant said, "I've got to see Dr. Cardenas."

"Fine," said Trudy. "I'll go over to the university and chat up the people in the astronomy department, see what they're up to."

The tram stopped at the end of the tunnel and Trudy agreed to meet Grant at the main garage, where the tour busses came in, a few minutes before 1400 hours. Then she started off for the university's underground classrooms and offices. Grant headed straight for the nanotechnology lab.

Kris Cardenas was in a pensive mood when Grant reached her desk.

"You realize what you're letting yourself in for, don't you?" she asked Grant as soon as he settled himself in the chair by her desk.

"Letting myself in for?" he asked.

"Once people know you've ingested nanomachines, they'll treat you differently. They'll be wary of you, scared, even."

"Not here," Grant scoffed. "We use nanomachines all the time."

"People are still scared of them."

"You think so?"

Cardenas's bright blue eyes fixed Grant with a hard stare. "Take it from me. I've gone through it. I lost a lot of friends once they realized my body's full of nanos."

Grant puffed out a little grunt. "I don't have that many friends."

"You'll have fewer, once they know. You'll become a pariah."

"Even at Farside?"

"Even at Farside," Cardenas said, utterly serious.

Grant thought about it for a few silent moments, then said, "Maybe it'd be better if nobody knew about it, then."

She pursed her lips, then murmured, "I think you're right. Keep it to yourself."

Nodding, Grant said, "Okay. That's what I'll do."

"It's nobody else's business, really."

"Yeah. I suppose so."

Cardenas brightened slightly and pulled a desk drawer open. She picked a small plastic vial out of it.

"Here's your first dose." She handed the vial to Grant.

He held it up and peered at it. "Looks like orange juice."

"That's what it is. Orange juice—with a few million nanomachines suspended in it."

"That many?"

"They're programmed to the blood sample you gave me. You drink them down and they'll start repairing your liver."

"What about radiation protection?"

"That's the next batch. I want you to let these little fellows work on your liver. You come back here in two weeks. I'll set up a medical exam for you. If everything's working right, we'll go on to phase two and build up your cellular repair mechanisms."

Grant asked, "So what do I do, drink this stuff?"

"That's right."

He unscrewed the vial's top and drank its contents in one long swig.

Cardenas gave him a wry smile. "Welcome to the club."

Grant knew it was psychosomatic, but as he walked from Cardenas's nanotech lab to Selene's main garage, he thought that the dull ache in the small of his back was lessening.

They can't act that fast, he told himself. But he actually did feel better.

Trudy was already in the garage's nearly empty waiting room, looking like an anxious little waif in her plain tan coveralls. There were three other people—two men and one woman—also waiting for the tour bus to return.

"Been here long?" he asked Trudy.

"Less than two minutes," she replied, gazing through the window that looked out on the busy, clanging garage. Busses and tractors were parked in rows, while maintenance crews worked on them. Beyond that stood the big dulled metal hatch of the huge airlock.

Grant was just about to say that Palmquist was late when the airlock hatch swung inward and the bus rolled through, a gleaming silver cylinder on spindly little wheels, its lower flanks coated with gray lunar dust.

The passengers got out of the bus and filed into the waiting room. Grant easily recognized Dr. Palmquist: ghostly pale, wearing a business suit of soft pastel blue, walking very carefully in the unaccustomedly light gravity. He entered the waiting room and looked around uncertainly.

"Dr. Palmquist," said Grant, going up to him and extending his hand. "I'm Grant Simpson—"

"Ah! The fellow who called me on the phone," said Palmquist in his soft voice.

"—and this is Dr. Yost, Professor Uhlrich's assistant," Grant finished.

Trudy took Palmquist's hand. "I'm very pleased to meet you, sir. Professor Uhlrich is so looking forward to your visit to the Farside Observatory."

"So am I, my dear," said Dr. Palmquist.

As Grant walked them out of the garage area and down the corridor that led to the cafeteria, Palmquist asked Trudy, "You are an astronomer?"

"Yes, I am. Are you?"

Palmquist shook his head self-effacingly. "No, no. I am an economist. But certain, er . . . certain acquaintances of mine asked me to look in on Professor Uhlrich while I was here visiting Selene University's economics faculty."

"I see," Trudy replied.

The Nobel committee, Grant thought. Those were Palmquist's "acquaintances."

As they walked to the cafeteria, Grant thought about the afternoon's agenda. He knew that Uhlrich had laid on a special flight back to Farside at 1800 hours. Not enough time to ask Trudy to have dinner with me, he told himself. We'll do this silly tea business with the Swede and then head back to Farside. Maybe Trudy and I can have dinner there, after we drop Palmquist off with the Ulcer.

But all through their brief repast in Selene's noisy, bustling cafeteria Palmquist spoke only to Trudy, ignoring Grant as if he weren't there. Grant never got the opportunity to ask her about dinner.

RETURN TO FARSIDE

hlrich was practically quivering with anticipation in the tiny reception area of Farside's one-pad spaceport when the lobber landed. McClintock stood beside him, much cooler.

"Dr. Palmquist," Uhlrich gushed as the Swede stepped through the access tube's hatch, "how kind of you to visit our facility."

Palmquist smiled genially. "I look forward to seeing the work you are doing, Professor Uhlrich."

As Grant walked with Trudy and the other three men along the corridor to Uhlrich's office he was amused to see the Ulcer fawning all over the Swede. But when they reached his office door, Uhlrich turned to Grant and said, "Thank you for escorting Dr. Palmquist here, Mr. Simpson. You can return to your regular duties now."

Then the rest of them went into the office. Trudy glanced over her shoulder at Grant, looking surprised and concerned, but Uhlrich slid the door shut, leaving him standing alone in the empty corridor.

Nodding to himself, Grant thought, Right. I'll get back to work while you try to impress Palmquist. I'll build what you need built and you work on getting your fucking Nobel.

Feeling justifiably resentful, Grant headed toward the teleoperations center, which was where he did most of his work. There, and in his one-room quarters. Uhlrich had not assigned him a private office of his own.

The teleoperations center was dim, shadowy, the only light in the chamber coming from the display screens of the consoles set against the far wall. A soft Cuban samba was purring from the overhead speakers. Josie Rivera was at one of the consoles, with narrow-eyed Nate Oberman sitting beside her.

What's he doing here? Grant asked silently, bristling at Oberman's presence. He's not on the tech staff anymore, we're carrying him in administration until his contract's up.

What annoyed Grant most about Oberman was the guy's snotty attitude. Nate could always get under Grant's skin with just a few pointed barbs. Back in his 'roid rage days, Grant would have pounded Oberman's face in. I would've sent him to the hospital, Grant thought. Or to the morgue.

Dr. Kapstein was feeding Grant extra medications to control his steroid-induced fury, but nonetheless he had tried to keep as much distance from Oberman as possible. So it was only natural that when Uhlrich fired him, Oberman concluded that Grant had been angling for his job.

"What're you doing here, Nate?" he asked, trying to make his tone casual, noncombative.

"Just visiting," Oberman replied easily. "Got nothing much else to do."

Turning to Rivera, Grant asked, "What's up, Josie?" as he slid the corridor door shut.

Rivera swiveled her chair toward him and gave Grant a flashing smile. "Nothing much, boss," she said. "It's been pretty quiet around here lately."

"How'd your joyride to Selene go?" Oberman asked.

Trying to ignore his snide tone, Grant replied, "I did what McClintock wanted; picked up this Swedish guy and brought him to Uhlrich. No sweat."

"You and Trudy Yost," said Josie Rivera.

"Yeah, that's right."

"Must be nice, taking a day off with a good-looking chick," Oberman said.

Before Grant could bristle, Rivera quickly asked, "Anything between you two?"

Grant felt astounded. "Between . . . what're you talking about?"

With a knowing look, Rivera said, "Boy meets girl. It happens all the time."

"Come on, Josie," Grant sputtered.

Oberman asked Rivera, "He ever come on to you, Josie?"

She shook her head, turning down the corners of her mouth in mock regret.

"Maybe he's gay," said Oberman, with a malicious smirk.

"I could straighten him out, I bet," said Rivera.

Grant remembered that he'd been attracted to Josie Rivera, with her friendly ways and generous figure. But he had made a decision not to get involved with any of the women at Farside. The place was too small, too inbred. A serious relationship, even a non-serious fling, could cause emotional fracture lines among the staff. Better to stay celibate, or go over to Selene for fun and games, Grant reminded himself. But it had been a long time since he'd had any fun and games.

He didn't know how to handle their bantering, so he decided to ignore it. "Now look, we've got a lot of serious work ahead of us."

But Oberman wouldn't quit. "Work on who?"

Grant gave him a withering look. "When's your contract up, Nate? It can't be soon enough."

Josie said, "Now boys . . ."

But Oberman pointed a skinny finger at Grant and replied, "I'm leaving at the end of the month. And I'm getting a position in the IAA office at Selene. Whattaya think of that?"

"Good," said Grant, thinking, Anyplace but here.

"Anita Halleck herself recommended me," Oberman added, sneering.

"And I thought she was supposed to be smart," Grant said.

"You think you're better than me, don't you?" Oberman growled.

For the first time since Dr. Kapstein had started controlling his steroid dosage, Grant felt the urge to start punching.

But he fought it down. "Forget it. We've got work to do."

WORK AGENDA

Serious work?" Josie asked, her teasing grin fading away.

Pulling up one of the little wheeled chairs from the next console, Grant said, "We've got to lay out roads between here and Korolev and Gagarin."

"And improve the road to Mendeleev?" Rivera asked.

"No, that won't be necessary," said Grant.

Oberman huffed. "Hell, you couldn't even get that mirror over the ringwall."

Again Grant fought the urge to smack the nasty little snot. Keeping his voice even, he told them, "We won't be transporting mirrors. We'll be hauling construction materials in regular tractors. No need to tow big mirror rigs."

"The mirrors are going to be built at the craters, then?" Rivera asked.

"Right," Grant replied. "By nanomachines."

Oberman whistled softly. "So you'll be hauling nanobugs out to the three craters."

Grant nodded. "It'll be easy to get the loads over the ringwall mountains and onto the sites for the telescopes." Then he added, "Nanos are tiny little things."

"I just hope you don't spill any of 'em," Oberman said.

"That won't be a problem. If they're exposed to ultraviolet light they're disabled, and there's plenty of UV in sunlight."

"Yeah, but if you're moving them at night . . ."

Rivera suggested, "Maybe we should schedule moving the nanos only during daylight hours."

Grant thought about it for a few seconds. "Makes sense, Josie. Probably unnecessary, but an extra safety precaution wouldn't hurt."

"So how're the bugs going to work once you've got 'em at the sites?" Oberman asked.

"We build temporary roofs over each site. No big deal, just lightweight honeycomb metal sheets. That'll protect the sites against incoming micrometeoroids as well as solar UV."

"And once the 'scopes are completed we can take down the coverings, right?"

"Right," said Grant. "The nanomachines' work will be finished by then. They'll be deactivated."

Oberman rubbed his long jaw as he asked, "You're claiming that those nanobugs'll produce mirrors shaped to the tolerances you need?"

"Probably not. We might have to do some final polishing."

"That means hauling the measuring equipment to the craters," Rivera said.

"To Selene first," Grant said. "We'll have to check the demo mirror that Cardenas is building there."

"Yeah, but sooner or later you'll have to lug the polishing equipment out to each one of the craters," said Oberman. "Christ, you'll have to haul the whole turntable from here to there. Three theres!"

"Maybe," Grant conceded. "But the turntable's a lot more robust than the damned mirrors. Should be no sweat to haul it back and forth."

Oberman looked totally unconvinced.

"That's a lot of outdoor work," Rivera said.

"I know," said Grant. "That's why we've got to automate the work as much as possible. We need to adapt the robots to do as much of the job as they can."

"Robots," Oberman muttered. "You'll wind up spending more time maintaining the damned robots than anything else."

"I'm going to put Harvey in charge of robot maintenance,"

Grant told them. "His foot ought to be fine by the time we get started on this."

Josie nodded, accepting Grant's decision. Oberman looked cynically doubtful.

"Okay then," Grant said. "Now, the first thing we need to do is get those roads scraped out."

Once Grant had finished with Josie, he walked down to Farside's little cafeteria. The place was nearly empty; dinner hour had long passed.

As he stood before one of the food-dispensing machines, wondering which of the meager packaged meals he wanted to select, Trudy Yost came up beside him.

"Hi," he said, happily surprised. "I didn't see you come in."

She gave him a grin. "You were studying the machine's display as if your life depended on it."

He shrugged. "Well, it does, sort of. Don't you think so?"

"I guess so, if you put it that way."

"The Ulcer let you go?" Grant asked.

"No way. I'm here to pick up meals for the four of us and bring them back to the prof's office. We're eating in there."

"Oh."

"The professor's burying Dr. Palmquist with facts and figures," Trudy said. "The poor guy's eyes glazed over an hour ago but the prof is just plowing ahead, telling him how we're gonna produce images of New Earth before anybody else can."

Grant banged one of the buttons at random and stooped down to grab the package that slid into the tray at the bottom of the machine.

Her voice softening, Trudy said, "I'm sorry he cut you off like that."

He straightened up and looked into her gentle green eyes. "That's okay. I'm used to it. I'm just a crummy engineer, far as he's concerned. Dirt under my fingernails."

Trudy said, "You're much more important than that, Grant."

"It's nice of you to say so."

For a moment they stood facing each other, close enough to touch. Feeling awkward, almost like a teenager on his first date, Grant shifted his dinner package from one hand to the other.

"Maybe we could have dinner together some time," he heard himself say.

Trudy smiled at him. "That'd be great."

"Uh, my quarters aren't all that much, but I could microwave a meal for you. It'd be more private than the cafeteria here."

"I guess," she said, a trifle uncertainly.

"I've got some old movies, Hollywood classics. Or we could watch video from Selene."

"Sure," said Trudy. "But right now I've got to get dinners for the professor, Mr. McClintock, and Dr. Palmquist."

"And yourself," Grant added.

She laughed. "Yep. And myself." After a heartbeat's pause, she said, "But I'll look forward to dinner with you. Real soon."

"Sure," he said. "Real soon."

CRATER MENDELEEV

The weeks zipped past before Grant realized it. Palmquist returned to Selene, with Uhlrich falling all over himself to please the Swede and promising to send him the first images of New Earth that the Farside Observatory obtained.

Grant's days were long and busy, juggling the road-building work with planning the construction jobs that were needed at the three crater sites and coordinating Cardenas's work on the sample mirror that her nanomachines were making at Selene.

One of the tasks facing his team of engineers and technicians was to transport the materials for a protective roof to the Crater Mendeleev, 750 kilometers from the Farside facility. The load was too much for one of the short-range rocket hoppers that Farside kept on hand, and not big enough to warrant calling for a lobber mission from Selene. So Grant decided to send a tractor out to Mendeleev. And he decided to make the run himself.

He was driving the tractor up the slumped, gentle slope of the mountains ringing Mendeleev crater, with one of his team, Sherrod Phillips, sitting beside him. They had driven continuously for more than twenty-six hours, taking turns sleeping in their space suits inside the tractor's cramped cab.

The road they had built here at Mendeleev had only a few switchbacks in it because the area Grant had picked to cross the ringwall was relatively low with an easy grade. We could have gotten that damned mirror up this mountain with no sweat, Grant told himself as he steered the tractor slowly along the smoothed road. If it hadn't slid off the road back at Farside we could've gotten it up here and into Mendeleev okay.

Yeah, a mocking voice in his head sneered. And if you'd put wings on the mirror you could've flown it here, wiseass.

The two men were in their space suits even though the tractor's cab was pressurized. It was enclosed with a thin metal roof and glassteel sides that gave them a layer of protection against the radiation out there in the lunar vacuum. Safety regulations insisted that they wear the protective suits, even though they could have ridden inside the cab in their shirtsleeves—in theory.

It was still night, and would be for another week. The universe hung up in the dark sky, uncountable myriads of stars, hard cold points of light, unblinking. No Earth up there, no warmth or familiar comfort. The horizon was brutally near, a slash where the hard familiar world of lunar rock and dust ended like the edge of a cliff plunging into the infinite uncaring expanse of stars.

Grant topped the ringwall mountain and started down the interior slope. In the distance, almost at the horizon, he could see the square, flat concrete foundation that had been laid out for the telescope mirror. It was his imagination, he knew, but the low slabs already looked old, worn, covered with lunar dust.

Sherry Phillips was sitting in the tractor's right-hand seat, encased in a bulky space suit. Grant couldn't see his face through the tinted glassteel of his bubble helmet, but he heard the engineer say:

"So whattaya think of this new kid?"

"New kid?" Grant asked.

"Yeah. The Ulcer's new assistant. Trudy."

"She's an astronomer."

"She's a good-looker. Cute."

Grant knew that Phillips was married, but his wife was back Earthside with their two children. Phillips was a sharp engineer, a reliable man in the field, but possessed of a roving eye. Farside gossip claimed that he and Josie Rivera had had a fling several months back.

"Forget it," he told Phillips. "The Ulcer would have a stroke if you came on to her."

In his helmet speakers, he heard Phillips chuckle. "Hell, Grant, I wouldn't tell the Ulcer about it. Or ask his permission, for that matter."

Grant shook his head. "Better stay clear of her. Don't cause problems."

"Yeah. Maybe you're right." But Phillips didn't sound convinced.

Grant drove the tractor across the crater's wide floor to the telescope site, then he and Phillips stepped out onto the dusty, rock-strewn ground. The tractor was carrying sheets of honeycomb metal that they would erect to form a roof over the foundation. It also carried a pair of slim, cylindrical-shaped robots that were supposed to do the actual construction work.

"I'll activate Mike and Ike," said Phillips, walking around to the rear of the tractor. He was the robotics expert on Grant's little team of engineers and technicians. Like almost all humans, he anthropomorphized the machines he worked with.

Mike and Ike, Grant thought. What'll he call the other pair, the ones we're going to bring to Korolev? Punch and Judy?

Using a handheld remote controller, Phillips stirred the robots to life and began checking them out while Grant set up the ramp they would roll down once they were ready to go to work.

"Got a bad fuse on Ike," Phillips muttered.

Grant looked up at the tractor bed, where Phillips stood between the two shoulder-tall robots.

"Dammit, those machines were checked out at Farside. How can they have a bad fuse?"

He sensed Phillips trying to shrug inside his bulky space suit. "It happens, Grant. Murphy's Law."

"Who did the checkout?" Grant demanded.

"Dunno. You want to call back and get the file?"

"Might as well."

While Phillips replaced the faulty fuse from the supply of

spares they had carried with them, Grant called up the documentation on the robots' checkout. The checkout had been done by Nate Oberman, filling in for the injured Harvey Henderson. Grant seethed. Who the hell let him do the checkout? That dumbass can't even do a simple job without screwing it up. He just doesn't care. He could get somebody killed and he just doesn't give a damn about it. He can't leave Farside soon enough.

Phillips got both robots working and they rolled on their sturdy little trunions down the ramp, kicking up lazy clouds of dust as they moved to the tractor's side and began unloading the honeycomb sheets with their long, spindly, many-jointed arms.

Grant walked over to the concrete slabs of the foundation and began examining them with a handheld radar probe. Looks okay, he thought as he peered at the tiny screen's display. No major cracks, everything within tolerances.

"I'm putting them on their own," Phillips reported.

"Wait a minute," said Grant. "Let me set up the linkage."

Using the keypad on the left wrist of his suit, Grant contacted Josie, back at Farside's teleoperations center.

"We've activated the robots," he reported. "Putting them on autonomous mode now."

There was a barely noticeable half-second's delay while his message was relayed from one of the communications satellites in low orbit.

"Gotcha," said Josie. "Signal's coming in loud and clear."

Grant nodded inside his bubble helmet. "Okay, Jo. They're your responsibility now. Anything exceeds nominal limits—"

"I'll shut them down and initiate the failure analysis program," Josie said. "Don't worry about it, boss. I've got 'em on my screen."

"Good."

The two men stepped away from the tractor and watched the robots methodically unload the honeycomb sheets and supporting aluminum beams. Then they began to assemble them into a gracefully curving roof that covered the foundation.

"Ol' man river . . ." Phillips began to sing, in a wavering baritone. Despite himself, Grant laughed at the guy's sense of humor. Slave labor.

But while they watched the robots patiently, efficiently, erect the roof, Grant's thoughts wandered to the radiation invisibly sleeting down from all those distant stars. How much damage is it doing to us? he wondered. Phillips hadn't been outside in two weeks, he knew. Safety regulations. You were only allowed so much time out on the surface per month. Grant regularly bent those rules, while Dr. Kapstein sold him the medications he needed to keep going.

Well, he said to himself, we'll see if Cardenas's little bugs do their job. Just like Mike and Ike: do your work and don't complain.

What if the nanos don't work? Grant asked himself.

The answer came to him immediately. If they don't work I'm a dead man.

ON THE ROAD

We oughtta start back," Phillips said.

Grant lifted his arm and peered at the watch set into the pad on his wrist. Christ, we've been out here more than six hours, he realized. The roof was half finished and the robots were working away industriously.

"Yeah," he agreed. "Looks like the 'bots are working okay."

"Josie's keeping an eye on them," said Phillips as he headed for the tractor.

Josie's off-shift now, Grant knew. He tried to remember who was next on the duty roster for the monitoring task. Not Oberman, he told himself. I don't care how shorthanded we are, I won't let Nate get his hands on anything important. Keep him on the administrative side; let him do a clerk's job.

"You coming, or you gonna stay out here permanently?" Phillips called

"I'm coming."

Grant turned away from the busy robots. From here on they would be operated remotely, from the teleoperations center. Once the roof was finished their next task would be to erect a shelter for humans who visited the site and then construct a frame for the mirror that the nanos would build. There would be no need for humans to come to Mendeleev for many weeks. Unless something went wrong.

Phillips was in the driver's seat as Grant climbed into the tractor's cab and scaled its hatch. Together they went through the tractor's abbreviated checklist, then Phillips leaned a gloved finger on the start button. Grant heard nothing in the lunar vacuum, of course, but he felt the vibration of the tractor's electric motor starting up.

"We should've flown out here on a hopper," Phillips said as the vehicle lurched into motion. "Make it in less than an hour instead of a frickin' two-day trip, one way."

Grant knew that the flimsy little rocket hoppers couldn't carry the cargo that they'd just delivered to the site, and he knew that Phillips knew. He was just griping for the sake of something to gripe about.

Over the ringwall they trundled, then out onto the pockmarked plain, heading back to the Sea of Moscow and the Farside facility. After four days out in the open, Farside's bare-bones accommodations would look like a five-star hotel, Grant thought.

They followed the smoothed road across the barren plain. Grant thought the undulating ground looked like the waves of an ocean, only frozen solid. It was liquid once, he reminded himself. Molten lava, a few billion years ago. Now it was an empty expanse of dust-covered rock, pockmarked by craters of all sizes, from fingerpokes to depressions so deep and rugged that you didn't dare drive a tractor into them.

Half dozing, Grant recalled that some of those deeper craters were partially filled with dust. Drive into one of them and you sink into the dust, like a ship sinking in the sea. He remembered reading a story once about a place in India where a guy got himself stuck in a dust-covered depression and couldn't crawl out. Was it by Kipling? he asked himself.

Phillips's voice jarred him into wakefulness.

"Yeah, we're moving along, no sweat," Phillips was saying. Grant realized he was talking to the excursion monitor, back at Farside. "Gonna stop for a meal in a few minutes."

"Copy you stopping for meal," came the voice of one of the technicians. Grant recognized Harvey Henderson's sweet, almost girlish tenor.

"What're you doing on the monitor console, Harvey?" Grant asked.

"Just filling in for a few minutes while Rava takes a leak, boss."

"How's the foot?"

"Just fine. I'm gonna take the new kid out dancing later tonight."

Grant knew Harvey was joking, but he also knew that "the new kid" he mentioned was Trudy Yost and his brows knitted at the idea.

"Time to stop and get something to eat," Phillips said, tapping a gloved finger on the mission schedule displayed on the control console's central screen.

Grant nodded, then realized that Phillips couldn't see it inside his helmet and said, "Right."

Phillips actually pulled the tractor over to one side of the road. Grant smiled inwardly. Sherry doesn't want to block traffic, he thought.

They double-checked the seals of the cab's hatches before removing their helmets. Grant's nose wrinkled at the body odors. God, we smell like a couple of cesspools, he thought. But he said nothing as he turned awkwardly in his seat and reached into the storage bin at the back of the cab. They ate prepackaged sandwiches, chilled and soggy from refrigeration, and drank an energy-enriched fruit drink.

Then Phillips said, "I've gotta take a crap."

Grant dreaded using the toilets built into the cab's seats. In their space suits, it was a laborious and degrading ordeal: sealing the suit's bottom to the toilet hatch, opening both, checking the readouts to make certain the connection was secure, and then finally doing your business. With your crewmate sitting beside you. Grant took the diphenoxylate pills that Kapstein offered and tried to avoid the whole ugly business. The pills made him thirsty as hell, but using the relief tube was a lot easier and much less humiliating than working the trapdoor.

Once he was finished and buttoned up again, Phillips said,

"I'm gonna flake out, Grant." He started to crank his seat back as far as it would go.

"Change your air tank first and then put the helmet back on," Grant said.

"I got enough air—"

"Do it now," Grant said.

Phillips looked unhappy about it, but he gave in without a complaint. It was awkward sitting in the tractor's seats, but they helped each other to replace the air tanks on their backpacks, then fastened their helmets back in place.

"Now you can sleep in peace and the safety police will be happy with us," Grant said.

"By the book," Phillips grumbled.

"By the book," Grant echoed. It's always best to go by the book, he thought. But then he added, Almost always.

Phillips slept like a dead man for more than five hours while Grant drove the tractor across the empty lunar wasteland. Rocks, rocks, and more rocks, some as big as a house, most of them the size of pebbles. Sinuous rilles snaking across the dusty ground. Craters. He thought about putting the tractor on autopilot and taking a quick nap, but fought off his drowsiness and doggedly kept control of the vehicle. Phillips woke up at last, popped his helmet to take a few sips from the thermos of coffee they'd brought with them, then took over the driving and allowed Grant to nod off.

He slept well enough, although he dreamed of being a little boy in South Africa once again and sailing a raft out into the tossing waves of the ocean. The raft capsized and he was floundering in the freezing water when he suddenly woke up.

Phillips was muttering as he bent over the tractor's control panel, his thumb jammed against the starter button.

"Sonofabitch died on me," he said to Grant.

FAILURE MODE

D ied?" Grant mumbled, still thick-headed with sleep.

"Motor just crapped out, pooey, just like that."

Grant couldn't see Phillips's face inside his helmet but the tone of his voice had an edge of fear in it.

"Is it the motor or the generator?" Grant asked.

The tractor's electric motor drew its power from a miniaturized nuclear generator, buried inside heavy lead shielding in the belly of the vehicle.

"How the hell should I know?" Phillips snapped. "It just happened."

"Check the diagnostics."

Together they ran through the diagnostics program.

"Engineer's hell," Phillips muttered as they stared at the display screens. "Everything checks but nothing works."

"Life support's still working," Grant muttered. "Radio's still powered up. The batteries aren't discharging."

"So the generator's still putting out kilowatts. It's not the generator."

"Must be the motor."

"Better call Farside, get 'em to send a hopper out for us."

"Not yet," said Grant. "I'll go out and open her up, see what's going on."

"We're gonna need a hopper," Phillips insisted.

"Just tell Farside we've got a problem and we're trying to fix it."

"But—"

"Keep cool, Sherry. No need to panic." But Grant added silently, Not yet.

As his partner sent a message to the excursion monitor, Grant opened the hatch on his side of the cab and jumped down in lunar slow motion to the ground. Like most of the Moon's surface, it was covered with several centimeters of soft, talc-like dust. Almost like a sandy beach, back Earthside. Grant walked to the rear of the tractor and as he opened the motor's hatch he glanced back at the bootprints he'd left in the dust. They were bright and new-looking compared to the dust-gray surface of the ground.

The motor looked all right to his eyes. But it wasn't working. Grant couldn't see any obvious damage. We haven't been hit by a micrometeor, he thought, remembering that last year a hopper had been crippled while sitting at the edge of Farside's spaceport by a chip-sized meteor that had hit its control computer as accurately as a sniper's bullet.

It's got to be *something*, Grant said to himself as he bent over in his unwieldy space suit to examine the motor's magnet coils more closely. They were superconductors, encased in metal dewars that held liquid nitrogen.

The pressure gage on the stator coil's dewar read zero. Grant blinked with surprise. All the nitrogen's gone? How could that happen? He could see no obvious damage to the dewar, no puncture or leaking seal.

Without the nitrogen coolant the magnet loses its superconductivity. Then it shuts down. Either that or it dumps all its energy into an explosion. We're damned lucky the magnet didn't blow up.

The nuke was still generating electricity, that's why the life-support equipment and the radio were still working.

Okay, Grant said to himself as he plodded back to the cab. We know what's wrong. Now we've got to fix it. And then figure out why it went wrong.

Phillips was still on the radio, chattering nervously with the excursion monitor back at Farside, when Grant climbed back into the cabin.

"Yeah, the motor's dead," Phillips was saying. "How many times do I have to tell you guys?"

Sherry sounds scared, Grant thought. Normal reaction. I guess I am too, a little.

"This is Grant," he said as he settled into his seat. "Nitrogen coolant on the motor's main coil is gone. We'll need a replacement dewar."

He sensed Phillips staring at him from inside his bubble helmet.

"Replacement dewar, yes," the monitor's voice replied. Grant recognized Rava Sudarthee, the Hindu computer analyst, taking her turn at the excursion center. "We'll send it out on a hopper. It should get to you in one hour or less."

"Send a replacement crew with it," said Phillips.

"Negative," Grant snapped. "Once we get the motor running we can drive this buggy back home."

Phillips said nothing, but Grant could feel the fear-driven anger radiating from him.

Once he cut the connection to Rava, Grant said, "There's no need for a replacement crew, Sherry. We can drive back home once we get the dewar replaced."

"Says you," Phillips muttered.

Grant drew in a breath and thought it over. Sherry's scared. He wants out. Maybe I should be scared too, but it's my responsibility. I can't leave this to somebody else. It's my responsibility.

"Tell you what, Sherry," he said. "You go back with the hopper. I'll drive back to Farside."

"You know damned well you can't go alone; the safety regs require two people."

Pursing his lips before replying, Grant said, "Okay, tell Rava to send Harvey along on the hopper. You can go back and Harvey'll keep me company on the drive home."

Phillips hesitated only a heartbeat. "Okay, fine." Then he added, "Uh . . . thanks, Grant."

McClintock was waiting for Grant at the airlock. The instant Grant stepped through the inner hatch and began unfastening his helmet McClintock demanded, "What the hell happened out there?"

Before Grant could begin to explain, McClintock's expression went to disgust. "Good god! Go take a shower, for pity's sake."

Grant saw that even though McClintock was wearing ordinary gray coveralls, like almost everyone at Farside, on him the coveralls looked somehow a cut above anyone else's: crisper, newer, finer.

Tightly, Grant replied, "Shower. Right."

"Then come straight to my office," McClintock said to Grant's retreating back.

He's just as bad as the Ulcer, Grant thought. Another pain in the ass.

After showering and changing, though, Grant went not to McClintock's office but to the maintenance center. It was little more than a scruffy workshop where technicians labored over various pieces of equipment, trying to keep them all in working order. Most of them knew that their work meant the difference between life and death outside on the Moon's harsh surface.

Grant went to the workbench where two of the technicians were bending over the dewar from his tractor's motor.

"So why'd it go dry?" he asked.

Toshio Aichi looked up from the dewar. He was the best maintenance tech among Grant's people, unsmilingly serious. His face was lean, sallow, with hollow cheeks and an unruly mop of straight black hair going every which way. Despite his scarecrow frame, Toshio could out-eat any of the technicians, and often won bets against newcomers about who could stow away the most chow in the least time.

The dewar rested on the workbench, its cylindrical body split down its middle, its inner layers of insulation open to inspection.

"Pinhole leak," Toshio said. "Microscopic."

Grant looked down at the dewar.

"You can't see it with the naked eye," Toshio told him. "We had to scan it with the laser probe to find the sucker."

"That small?"

"Nanometer sized," said the other technician, Delos Zacharias. He was physically Toshio's opposite: a chubby, apple-cheeked kid, with an eternally sunny disposition.

"That small," Grant repeated.

"Plenty big enough for nitrogen molecules to sneak through," said Toshio. "The pinhole must have looked like the main gate of the Imperial Palace, to them."

"How come the coil didn't explode?" Grant asked.

Zacharias jumped in. "The enn-two escaped slowly enough so that the coil shut down. It wasn't a rapid loss. The coil didn't develop a hot spot. The whole assembly warmed up gradually and once it passed its critical temperature it stopped being superconducting and just shut itself down."

Grant looked from the empty dewar to the two technicians. "I guess we were pretty lucky, then."

Almost cheerfully, Zacharias said, "Actually, the system worked the way it was designed to, even in failure mode."

Toshio was more restrained. "You were indeed pretty damned lucky, Grant. A slightly bigger leak, a more rapid loss of coolant, and the coil could have gone off like a bomb."

Zacharias disagreed. "There's not that much energy in the coil—"

"There's enough to blow off the rear end of the tractor, rupture the cab, and shred the drivers with shrapnel," Toshio insisted.

Zacharias's round face looked more like a disappointed little boy's than a serious technician's. "Oh, well, yeah," he admitted. "Maybe so."

ow long does it take you to shower?" McClintock demanded as Grant stepped into his office.

Uhlrich had given McClintock the office next to his own. Or, Grant wondered, did McClintock arrange things this way for himself? Grant still didn't understand what McClintock was doing at Farside, or why Uhlrich tolerated the man. He wasn't an astronomer, wasn't a scientist or engineer of any stripe. All he seemed to be doing was getting in the way of the real work, adding another layer of bullshit to Uhlrich's little empire.

McClintock sat behind his standard-issue metal desk without asking Grant to take one of the curved plastic chairs in front of it.

Staying on his feet, Grant said, "I stopped off at the maintenance center to see what they'd found out about the failed dewar."

"And?"

"Pinhole leak. The nitrogen drained out and the coil went normal."

"Normal?"

"Lost its superconductivity. We were lucky it didn't explode."

McClintock leaned back in his swivel chair and fell silent. Grant thought he was a handsome guy, video-star looks, but there wasn't much going on inside his head.

"How could the dingus get a pinhole leak?" he asked at last.

Grant shrugged. "Beats me."

"Maybe you should check all the other dewars, make certain they haven't developed any leaks."

Grant's estimation of the man went up a notch. "Good idea," he said. "I'll get right on it."

"Do that," said McClintock.

Grant turned and left the office, not bothering to tell Mc-Clintock that he already had four technicians checking out all the other dewars on the tractors and hoppers.

Two weeks later, satisfied that the robots were working as specified at Mendeleev, under the remote direction of Farside's controllers, and the transport vehicles were all in operable condition, Grant scheduled himself for a ride back to Selene on the next resupply flight.

The cause of the dewar's leak still bothered him; Grant did not like unsolved mysteries, especially when they involved equipment that human lives depended upon. But the press of everyday business drove the dewar mystery to the back of his mind.

Physically, he felt better than he had in months. Dr. Kapstein confirmed that his liver function seemed to be improving, which puzzled her. Grant didn't tell her about the nanomachines he'd ingested.

"I'm tapering off on the steroids," he lied. It actually wasn't that much of a lie; he intended to stop using the steroids altogether if Cardenas would give him nanos that would take their place.

He had dinner with Trudy Yost a few times. She was pleasant, intelligent, good company. Much more than cute, he thought. But he told himself there was no sense getting involved emotionally with someone you work with. Farside's way too small for that.

Still, he felt strangely disappointed whenever Trudy mentioned Carter McClintock's name, which she did often.

"He's really handsome, don't you think?" she asked.

And I'm not, Grant said to himself.

Then Dr. Cardenas called from Selene to tell him that her nanomachines had finished building the sample mirror.

"You can come over and take a look any time," she said, a bright smile on her youthful face.

"I'm already scheduled for tomorrow's lobber," he said.

"Fine," said Cardenas.

"I'll have to bring the measuring equipment," Grant said, "to see how close to our specs your bugs have come."

"Sure," said Cardenas. "I'm anxious to see how well they did, too."

"By the way," Grant added, "my latest physical was pretty good."

Cardenas's expression sobered. "We'll talk about that when you get here."

MIRROR, MIRROR

And there it is, Grant said to himself as he gazed down at the sample mirror. He was standing on a metal catwalk one floor above the mirror, leaning on his forearms over the railing to get a better look at it, Dr. Cardenas beside him.

It looks no different from the mirror we built at Farside, he thought. Wide as a football field, the mirror gleamed in the overhead lights. A pair of technicians were trundling a handcart around its perimeter. Grant could see the mirror's underlying honeycomb structure as it sat in the frame he had sent from Farside to Selene.

The chamber they were in had originally been used to build components of the rocket vehicles that Selene used for transportation across the surface of the Moon: lobbers and hoppers. When Selene shifted its large manufacturing programs to outdoor facilities, to take advantage of the cleanliness of the vacuum environment, this spacious volume had been turned into a storage area. Cardenas had commandeered it for constructing the mirror—with the help of Douglas Stavenger's influence on Selene's governing council.

"So what do you think of it?" Kris Cardenas asked. She looked pleased, satisfied that her nanomachines had done their job, eager to hear his assessment of her work.

"It looks okay to me," said Grant. "Now we'll have to set up the measuring lasers and see how much polishing it needs."

Cardenas nodded. "It'll be interesting to see how close to your tolerances my little guys came."

Straightening up, Grant said to her, "You take a personal interest in your little bugs, don't you?"

"Of course. Don't you take a personal interest in your work?"

With a shrug, Grant acknowledged, "Sure."

"Besides," Cardenas added, "it looks like the Nobel committee is serious about me."

"That's what Palmquist was here for!" Grant realized. "Not Uhlrich. You."

"It looks that way." Cardenas could not disguise her delight.

"You'll be going to Stockholm then, for the ceremony."

Her expression darkened. "Not likely. Sweden won't accept a person who's carrying nanomachines in her body. Neither will any other nation Earthside, just about."

"But they'll make an exception for the Nobel Prize, won't they?"

"And have the ceremony bombed by some fanatic?" Cardenas shook her head.

"That's bloody rotten," said Grant.

"Yes, it is," Cardenas agreed.

She started toward the door, Grant following her.

"The measuring equipment's waiting out at the spaceport. I'll need a tractor or something to carry it over here."

"I've already told my technicians to bring your equipment over. That's what they were doing downstairs with the cart."

A little surprised, Grant said, "You're a jump ahead of me."

She made a thin smile.

As they stepped through the door and out into the corridor, Grant said, "My latest physical's pretty good. Dr. Kapstein was surprised that my liver function's improved."

"You haven't told her about the nanos?"

"I haven't told anybody."

"Good."

Walking along the corridor beside her, Grant said, "So when can you give me the next set?"

Cardenas did not meet his eyes. Looking straight ahead as

they walked, she said in a lowered voice, "Fixing your liver is one thing. Providing you with cell-rebuilding nanos is another."

Startled at her response, Grant demanded, "What do you mean?"

She turned her head to look at him briefly, then said, "Come to the lab tonight. Pick me up there and we'll have dinner together."

"Okay."

Grant spent the rest of the day helping Cardenas's technicians to unpack the lasers and optical gear that would measure the mirror's curvature down to a fraction of the six-hundred-nanometer wavelength of orange-colored light. Yet he couldn't help worrying about Cardenas's attitude toward giving him the nanomachines he needed to protect him against radiation.

Why's that any different from the bugs she's already given me? he wondered. She gave me the nanos for my liver easily enough. Now she's balking? What's wrong? What's going on?

Although he felt physically tired by the time he and the technicians got the measuring equipment set up, Grant wanted to start the measurements as soon as the lasers were in place above the mirror and the optics equipment was checked out. But he saw the technicians glancing at their wristwatches and then at each other. It was well past 1900; he understood that their regular working hours were over and they wanted to leave for the day.

If I push them I'll alienate them, he thought. They work for Kris, not me, and they'll get sore. Besides, we'll all work better tomorrow morning, when we're fresh.

"Okay, guys," he said. "And gals," he added, nodding toward the two women among the half-dozen of them. "Let's call it a day. See you here at eight tomorrow morning."

They broke into satisfied grins and swiftly left the chamber.

Grant headed toward Dr. Cardenas's office.

"I thought you were going to stand me up," Cardenas called to him as Grant threaded his way through the workbenches of the nanotech lab.

"We just finished setting up the measuring equipment," he replied. "Hope I haven't kept you waiting too long."

Getting up from her desk chair, Cardenas said, "No, I'm only moderately famished."

She breezed past Grant, heading for the door.

"About those nanos . . ." Grant began.

"Let's get some food first. Then we can talk."

ONE-WAY STREET

Feeling distinctly nervous, apprehensive, Grant followed Dr. Cardenas to the cafeteria. The place was crowded with diners, long lines at all the counters.

Cardenas loaded her tray with a bowl of soup, a plate of soyburger, a salad, and a steaming mug of tea. Grant took fish filets, creamed corn, and a cola. They both avoided the dessert counter.

She found a table for two in a corner of the bustling, clattering cafeteria.

"Hard to carry on a quiet conversation," Grant said as they sat down, raising his voice over the noise of the crowd.

"Good," said Cardenas. "Less chance of being overheard."

Grant blinked at her. She's acting as if we're hatching some kind of a conspiracy, he thought.

Leaning slightly across the table, Grant asked, "So what about my nanos?"

Cardenas spooned up some soup and drank it before raising her cornflower blue eyes to meet Grant's.

"Fixing your liver was one thing, Grant. Easy. A one-shot proposition."

"And?" he prompted.

"Putting nanomachines into your body that will repair cellular damage from radiation or other causes is an entirely different thing."

He waited for the other shoe to drop.

Her face utterly serious, Cardenas continued, "That kind of

nanotherapy is continuous, ongoing. Once you put that type of nano into your body, you've started down a one-way street."

"I don't understand."

Patiently, Cardenas explained, "Look, you'll be ingesting nanomachines that will fill your body. They'll invade your cells and repair any damage they find. You'll be carrying billions of little repair kits inside you."

"So that's good, isn't it?"

"Yes, certainly. But they're so good at what they do that your body's natural repair systems will begin to shut down. As far as your natural immune system is concerned, you'll be in such good health that they can slack off."

"Great," said Grant.

Cardenas shook her head. "Your body's production of leukocytes—white blood cells—T-cells, all your body's defenses against infection and cellular damage will decline. Steeply."

"But if I've got the nanos in me I won't need them, will I?"

"That's right," she said, so faintly Grant could barely hear her. "You won't."

"So what's the problem?"

"You'll be chained to those nanomachines, Grant. Like I said, you'll be heading along a one-way street. Once you start taking nanotherapy you'll have to stay with it for life."

Grant thought it over for all of five seconds. "Okay by me," he said.

Cardenas smiled sadly. "Easy enough for you to say, Grant. But the nanomachines have finite lifetimes. They break down, eventually. You'll need to replenish them from time to time."

"I see."

"You'll be hooked on them, just as you might become hooked on narcotics or alcohol."

Grant saw that she was trying to give him the whole picture before he made a decision that he'd have to live with for the rest of his life.

"You're living with them, aren't you?" he asked.

"Yes, I am."

"And you seem to be doing okay. Fine, in fact."

"But I can never go back to Earth. Never go home. I'm an exile, Grant."

"I'm not going back to Earth, either," he said. "I've got nothing to lose."

She looked surprised. "I remember you told me that before. But are you certain? Absolutely certain? It's a decision that you'll have to live with for the rest of your life."

"Which could be centuries long, from what I've heard."

Cardenas almost smiled. "Yes, you could live for a long time, with nanos protecting you."

Grant reached out and clutched her hand. "I'll take the chance."

"You're sure?"

"I'm sure. And thanks for the warning. I appreciate how much you care."

Cardenas seemed to brighten, as if a weight had been taken off her shoulders.

"All right, Grant," she said. "Come down to my lab tomorrow evening and I'll have the nanos waiting for you."

Y ou'll be all right, Trudy told herself as she stepped out of the airlock and onto the open floor of the Sea of Moscow. Just don't look up; keep your eyes straight ahead and don't look at the stars.

She was following Winston Squared out to one of the spindly little hoppers standing near the blast pad where the bigger, more powerful lobbers landed and lifted off.

"The nanobots have finished the mirror at Mendeleev crater," she said. She knew that Winston knew that, everybody at Farside knew it, but Trudy needed something to chatter about. "Now Grant's getting them started on the mirror at Korolev. At this rate we'll have all three telescopes working before the end of the year."

"Yeah, that's good," Winston said. "And Cyclops is starting to get data from the antennas we've already put up. The prof's a happy camper."

"You're looking for intelligent signals?" Trudy asked.

With a cynical little chuckle, Winston said, "The great and wonderful search for extraterrestrial intelligence. The more we look the less we find."

"I thought SETI—"

"Trudy, radio telescopes have been searching for intelligent signals for more than a century. With nothing to show for it."

"You're not using Cyclops for SETI?"

"Oh, sure. We're scanning for intelligent signals. But it's strictly routine, nobody expects to find anything."

"But you said you were getting data," Trudy said, keeping her eyes focused on his space-suited back, a few paces ahead of her.

"We sure are," he replied, brightening. "We're looking at the afterglow from gamma-ray bursters. Exploded superstars, three, four megaparsecs out."

"Hypernovas?" Trudy asked.

"You know about them?"

"Only a little," she said.

The hopper was about a hundred paces ahead of them, a flimsy-looking craft, little more than a platform resting on spidery legs. Trudy knew that Crater Mendeleev was nearly eight hundred kilometers away, and Winston had been ordered by Professor Uhlrich to fly her there.

"Sounds like interesting work," she said.

"Not as glamorous as talking to ETs," Winston replied. "But it sure as hell interests me. And the rest of the Cyclops crew."

She nodded inside her fishbowl helmet. The Cyclops assembly would be the biggest and most sensitive radio telescope facility in the solar system, she knew, capable of picking up intelligent radio signals from thousands of light-years' distance.

If there are any intelligent signals out there, she added silently.

They reached the hopper and Winston put a booted foot on its frail-looking ladder, then stopped and turned toward her.

"Ladies first," he said, with a stiff little bow.

Thinking that there were advantages to being one of the few women at this lonely outpost, Trudy grabbed a rung and started up the ladder. She felt the rung sag slightly as she put her weight on it but ignored that and clambered laboriously in her bulky space suit up to the open platform.

Following right behind her, Winston went to the control console, nothing more than a slender podium at one edge of the platform. She stood beside him and clutched the slim railing with both her gloved hands.

"Better slip your boots into the loops on the deck," Winston told her. "These little buggies don't generate many g's, but still you want to be anchored down good and tight."

"How long will it take to get to Mendeleev?" she asked.

"We're scheduled for forty-five minutes. Could go faster but that'd burn up too much of our fuel."

Trudy felt her pulse thumping in her ears as Winston went through the brief checkout procedure and then asked the flight controller, safe and snug back in Farside's underground shelter, for permission to lift off.

"You are cleared for liftoff," she heard in the speakers built into her helmet.

Winston said, "Okay. Here we go."

The sudden surge of acceleration made Trudy's knees buckle, but she held tight to the railing and straightened up immediately. The ground fell away and all at once they were soaring up, higher and higher, as if they were riding a magic carpet. No sound, no feeling of wind rushing by; it was almost as if she were watching a 3-D video.

"Fun, isn't it?" Winston asked, his voice light and carefree.

"Sort of," Trudy replied cautiously.

She could see the barren, pitted ground sliding past them far below, pockmarked with craters, studded with rocks. I'm flying across the Moon, she told herself. She felt light-headed and her insides began to churn.

"We'll be weightless most of the flight," Winston said cheerily. "Feels great, doesn't it?"

"Sort of," was all that Trudy could say.

Her stomach was crawling up toward her throat and she felt that if she let go of the railing she would float off into infinity. Squeezing her eyes shut, she commanded herself to ignore the queasiness. Forget about it. Forget the cosmic emptiness out there. Think of something else. Something pleasant.

She thought back to her date with Carter McClintock.

They had bumped into each other in the cafeteria. Over the months since she'd arrived at Farside they saw each other daily, of course. But two days ago, there in the cafeteria, Carter had asked her to have dinner with him, in his quarters.

"I'm afraid I'm not much of a cook," he had said, a rueful expression on his handsome face. "But then, there's not much available here except prepackaged meals."

"That's okay," Trudy had said brightly. "I can perform miracles with a microwave."

"Can you? How wonderful."

McClintock's quarters were somehow more luxurious than Trudy's. The place was the same size as hers, and had the same standard-issue sofa and chairs, desk and wall screens. The same kind of kitchenette. The same-sized bed. But McClintock had a real carpet on the floor, a red-patterned oriental. And the coffee table in front of the sofa was a handsome curved piece of glass, not the more practical boxy type that Trudy had in her room. An additional flat screen was mounted on the wall over the sofa; it showed an image of some famous painting of a woman and her little boy on a green summery hilltop.

"It's not much," he'd said as he showed her in, "but it's home. For now."

Trudy had worn her best dress, a sleeveless short-skirted thing of buttercup yellow, and she'd spent nearly an hour trying to make her hair look decent. McClintock was wearing a casual sweater, coppery red, and neatly pressed slacks.

With a wily grin he said, "I smuggled some wine from California in with the latest supply delivery. Would you like some?"

Dinner was wonderful. The food was quite ordinary, but Carter was a good conversationalist and kept her laughing with stories about his family Earthside. She wound up in his arms on the sofa, her heart pounding so strongly she thought he'd hear it or maybe even feel it as he held her close.

"I . . ." she had to take a breath before she could continue, "I haven't had much experience, Carter. With men, I mean."

"Neither have I," he whispered. "With men, that is."

She giggled and he began to undress her.

Yes, Trudy thought, there really is an advantage to being one of the few women at Farside.

"Starting retroburn in ten seconds."

Winston's voice broke into her reverie. Trudy blinked away the happy memory of her night with Carter McClintock and looked down past the edge of the hopper's gridwork decking.

And there was the telescope, a big fat tube standing slightly tilted in the middle of Crater Mendeleev like the stumpy old-fashioned smokestack of an ocean freighter. At its base Trudy could see the hump of rubble where the robots had built the underground shelter for visiting humans.

The flight controller's voice from Farside said crisply, "Copy retroburn."

Suddenly weight returned as the hopper's rocket engine fired silently. Trudy swallowed, then held her breath as the ground came rushing up to meet them. Miraculously their descent slowed, became almost dreamlike, until she felt the landing pads touch down with a gentle thump.

"We're down," Winston said.

"Copy your landing," said the flight controller, a heartbeat later. "Right on time. Good job."

"Thank Isaac Newton," Winston wisecracked.

Then he turned to Trudy. "Come on, girl. Time to go to work."

They spent the rest of the day checking out the telescope's controls and the electronic links back to Farside. We could have done this remotely, Trudy thought as she ran through the diagnostics on the console inside the cramped underground shelter that the robots had built. No need for a person to come out here. After all, what's important is how the controls work at Farside.

But Professor Uhlrich had insisted that an astronomer should go to the telescope site and check out everything in situ. Since Uhlrich could not go himself and Trudy was the only other optical astronomer at Farside as yet, she got elected.

"It's a shame we had to drag you out there," she said to Winston as she bent over the console, her eyes on the display screens.

Both of them were still in their cumbersome space suits, although they had both removed their helmets inside the pressurized safety of the underground shelter.

"Glad to help out," Winston said. "They can get along without me at Cyclops for a day."

It was strictly routine work, but Trudy felt excited to be doing it. This is the first time the telescope's been operated. I'm at the cutting edge, she told herself. This is something I'll be able to tell my grandchildren about. Then she laughed inwardly. Yeah, tell them how boring the cutting edge can be.

But when she put the telescope's imagery on the console's center screen her breath caught in her throat.

"That's Andromeda, isn't it?" she heard Winston ask, in an awed whisper.

"M31, the Andromeda Galaxy," Trudy confirmed.

It was magnificent, a giant spiral of billions of stars, its gracefully sweeping arms aglow with the bluish light of newborn stars.

"I've never seen it so clear," said Winston.

The telescope's "first light" image was truly beautiful, Trudy thought. This ought to please the professor.

"Let's zoom in," she murmured, turning a dial on the console.

"Holy god, I can see individual stars!" Winston sounded awed, and Trudy felt thrilled at his reaction.

"Good resolution," she said. "That's sort of what our own Milky Way looks like, if we could see it from outside."

"Maybe we will someday," said Winston.

"Maybe we will," Trudy agreed. "Someday."

The controls worked perfectly. The telescope moved ponderously in response to Trudy's computerized commands. She knew the "first light" views the telescope was seeing were being relayed back to Farside. Uhlrich had already made a connection with Selene University's public relations department to broadcast the images all across Earth.

The cutting edge isn't boring after all, she told herself. My grandkids will be just as excited about this as I am.

It took a real effort for her to shut down the console and turn control of the telescope over to Uhlrich, at his Farside office.

"Time to go," Winston said as he put his bubble helmet on.

Trudy twisted her helmet in its neck ring until it clicked shut and, with some reluctance, followed Winston out through the shelter's airlock and onto the surface where the hopper waited.

After a dozen paces, though, Winston suddenly began to stagger.

Trudy grabbed for his shoulder. "What's wrong?"

"Can't . . . breathe . . ."

In her helmet speakers she could hear Winston gasping. "Can't . . ."

He collapsed. Trudy couldn't hold him and he sank slowly to his knees, then fell facedown onto the dusty bare ground.

COLLAPSE

Her gloved hands shaking, Trudy punched the Farside frequency on the keypad built into her suit's left forearm and yelled, "Emergency! Emergency!"

It took two heartbeats—an eternity—before the flight controller's voice snapped, "What's wrong?"

"Win . . . he's down! Collapsed!"

The woman's voice took on an edge of tension. "Where are you? What happened?"

"We're outside, between the shelter and the hopper. I don't think he's breathing!"

"Can you get him back inside the shelter?"

"I'll try."

It wasn't easy dragging Winston's inert body across the dusty ground to the airlock set into the mound of rubble that served as shielding for the shelter. Trudy was awash with perspiration as she tugged him inside the airlock, then banged the control panel to close the outer hatch. It slid shut with painful slowness.

As the airlock cycled, pumping air into the steel-walled chamber, Grant Simpson's voice came through Trudy's speakers:

"What happened, Trudy?"

"I don't know! We were going back to the hopper when Win said he couldn't breathe and then he keeled over. I think he's dead!"

His voice calm and even, Grant instructed her, "Get him inside the shelter, then take off his helmet. It might be a glitch in his suit's air supply."

"Okay," she said.

"I'll come out in a hopper, with Dr. Kapstein. You just sit tight."

"Okay."

The airlock's inner hatch sighed open and Trudy hauled Winston's body inside the low-ceilinged, narrow shelter. Fumbling in the suit's gloves, she tried to remove his helmet, then ripped her gloves off and finally got the helmet unlatched. Winston's eyes gazed sightlessly at her.

"He's dead," Trudy sobbed. "He's dead."

No reply from Farside. Suddenly Trudy felt totally alone, impossibly far from help, abandoned in the middle of a stark airless nowhere.

"Are you all right?" the flight controller's voice asked sharply.

"Yes. I think so," Trudy replied, glad to have someone to talk to.

"Grant's gone out to the hopper. He'll be with you in less than an hour."

Nodding inside her helmet, Trudy said, "That's good." In a frightened little girl's voice.

Then she noticed that it was getting difficult for her to breathe. Nonsense! she snapped at herself. It's your imagination.

Still, she unfastened her helmet and lifted it off her head. Then she took a deep breath. The canned air of the shelter felt wonderfully good.

It was the longest forty minutes of Trudy's life, alone in the cramped shelter with Winston's dead body. His eyes kept staring, and when she touched his face it felt cold. She sat on the springy little wheeled chair by the console, awkward in the space suit, and tried to avoid looking at Winston's body—but she couldn't help herself.

You can't be dead, she pleaded with him. We've got good air in here, take a breath, move your arms—stop staring at me!

But Winston did not move, did not breathe, did not blink his unfocused eyes.

Stay calm, Trudy told herself. Stay calm, calm, calm.

"I'm on my way, Trudy." Grant's voice crackled from the shelter's console. "Hang on, I'll be there in half an hour."

Trudy had never been so grateful for the sound of a human voice in her life.

"How's Win?" Grant asked.

"He's dead."

"You're sure?"

There was no doubt of it in Trudy's mind. "I'm sure."

"I've got Dr. Kapstein with me. She's upchucking in her helmet."

Trudy supposed that Grant said that to lighten her tension, but it didn't make her feel any better.

"The doctor's coming out here for nothing," she said to Grant. "There's nothing anybody can do for him."

"We'll see."

Grant kept talking to her and she felt enormously grateful for it. Something to do, someone to talk with, so she didn't have to sit in this coffin of a buried shelter and stare at Winston's dead body.

"We're entering descent mode," Grant said.

Trudy glanced at the clock on the console. Less than forty-five minutes had elapsed.

"You made it quick."

"High-g burn. But the doc still got the heaves when we went weightless."

"She really threw up?"

"Inside her helmet, yeah. Pretty messy."

Trudy couldn't see outside the shelter and the hopper's landing was soundless in the lunar vacuum, but suddenly she heard the airlock pumps chugging. They're here! She jumped to her feet.

The airlock hatch slid open and two space-suited figures clomped in. One of them pushed past Trudy and staggered to the shelter's minuscule lavatory, nearly tripping over Winston's body.

As the lav door slid shut with a heavy thump, Trudy turned and saw Grant Simpson lifting the tinted bubble helmet from his head. His hair and beard looked matted with perspiration, but his sad, dark eyes seemed filled with concern.

"Are you okay?" he asked.

Trudy nodded tightly. "I'm okay. But Win . . ."

Grant dropped to his knees beside the lifeless body. "His suit hasn't decompressed. But he's dead all right."

A retching, gargling noise came from the lav, followed by heartfelt cursing.

Grant broke into a grim smile. "The doc isn't much of a flier."

Thinking how her own stomach had gone queasy on the flight to Mendeleev, Trudy said, "Zero g can get to you."

"Yeah. You'd think that a doctor would've popped an anti-nausea pill—"

The lavatory door slid open and a very unhappy Ida Kapstein stepped into the room, still encased in her bulky space suit, minus the helmet. She looked slightly green. The shelter suddenly felt unbearably crowded.

Glancing down at Winston's body, Dr. Kapstein said, "So now we've got to fly him back to Farside. Just what I need, another good bout of vomiting."

INQUEST

But what did he die of?" Professor Uhlrich demanded.

He was sitting behind his desk, as usual, his fingertips brushing against the desktop. Grant and Dr. Kapstein sat side by side at the table abutting his desk; Trudy sat opposite Grant, wondering where Carter McClintock might be.

"Asphyxiation," said Dr. Kapstein.

Uhlrich's brows knitted in a puzzled frown. "Asphyxiation? You mean he had no air to breathe?"

"That's right."

"But he was in a space suit, wasn't he?"

Grant said, "I checked him out before he left with Dr. Yost. His suit was working fine."

"Then how could he die of asphyxiation?" Uhlrich demanded.

Trudy volunteered, "He said he was having difficulty breathing when we left the shelter and headed back to the hopper."

"His suit's air tank was about half full when I got to him," Grant said. "The suit didn't decompress, there was air in it."

"This makes no sense," said Uhlrich.

"I've got Aichi and Zacharias checking out his suit," Grant said. "There weren't any obvious signs of a defect, but if anything's wrong with the suit, they'll find it."

"And if they find anything wrong it will be your fault that he died. You checked his suit, you say."

Grant's darkly bearded face settled into a scowl. "The suit checked out fine," he repeated sullenly.

"I don't like mysteries," Uhlrich muttered. "Especially when they involve the death of one of my staff."

Trudy thought the professor looked as if he felt personally betrayed. By whom? she wondered. Grant?

"You must find out what happened," Uhlrich went on. "We cannot have an unsolved death on our hands. The university is going to demand an investigation."

Dr. Kapstein said, "I've conferred with the top people at Selene's hospital. They've examined the body by video link and agreed with my finding of asphyxiation, tentatively."

"Tentatively? What do you mean—"

"They want to do an autopsy, of course," said Kapstein. "I'm having the body shipped to Selene on the next lobber flight."

Uhlrich turned from the doctor to Grant, but said nothing.

Grant abruptly pushed his chair back and got to his feet. "Well, we're not going to learn any more sitting here and talking. I'm going down to the maintenance center and see what Zach and Toshio have found."

He headed for the door. Uhlrich started to say something, but snapped his mouth shut, staring at Grant's back. He sure doesn't look like he's blind, Trudy thought.

Dr. Kapstein rose ponderously from her chair, as well. "If there's nothing more . . ." she murmured.

Uhlrich waved a hand at her. Trudy watched them both leave the office, then started to stand up, too.

"Please wait, Dr. Yost," said Uhlrich. "Sit down, please."

She waited for several moments. Uhlrich said nothing, merely stared blankly ahead.

Trying to break the silence, she asked, "Um, shouldn't Mr. Mc-Clintock be involved in this? I mean, he's your assistant, after all, and—"

"Mr. McClintock," said Uhlrich, "is here in an advisory position only. He is *not* involved in the administration of this facility."

"Oh," Trudy said, confused. "I thought . . . that is . . ."

Uhlrich glared at her, but then his expression softened.

"Have you given any thought," the professor asked, in a calmer, softer voice, "to putting the Mendeleev telescope to use?"

"Put it to use?"

Uhlrich called out, "Computer, Mendeleev imagery on screen." The smart screen facing Trudy lit up with the telescope's view of the Andromeda spiral, covering the entire wall.

"The 'first light' images you obtained were very good," Uhlrich said, obviously pleased. "Excellent, in fact."

"How can you . . ." Trudy caught herself before she went any farther.

"How can I see the images with my blind eyes?" Uhlrich actually smiled. "I had some of the computer specialists at Selene develop a program that transfers visual data into tactile. I see with my fingertips, Dr. Yost. I brush my fingertips across my special tactile screen and pictures form in my visual cortex."

"That's . . ." Trudy searched for a word. "That's wonderful."

"It serves its purpose."

Trudy didn't know what to say.

But Uhlrich did. "Now. We have the Mendeleev telescope up and running. There is no sense letting it sit there doing nothing. I want you to develop a research agenda for it. How can we best use it while we are waiting for the other two telescopes to be completed?"

"It's a very powerful instrument," Trudy said.

"Yes. I think we should begin imaging Sirius C as swiftly as we can. That could produce favorable publicity for Farside and get the media's attention off this unfortunate accident."

"I suppose," Trudy said hesitantly.

"The single telescope won't be able to yield much detail about the planet," Uhlrich went on, "but we can refine the estimates of its size and perhaps even get some rough spectroscopic data. Finding water on the planet would be a significant step. Or free oxygen."

Uhlrich hunched forward, clasping his hands together and talking earnestly, eagerly about how they might use the Mendeleev telescope.

He isn't concerned about Winston's death, Trudy realized. Except for how it affects his plans. He doesn't really care a rat's ass about Win.

MAINTENANCE CENTER

Grant was mildly surprised to see Carter McClintock at the maintenance center. He looked out of place, dressed in a carefully tailored white long-sleeved shirt and neatly pressed gray slacks. Toshio Aichi and Delos Zacharias were wearing their usual tan coveralls, rumpled and faded. Grant himself was in a comfortable pullover and large-pocketed cargo pants.

Zach and Toshio were sitting on stools at a workbench; McClintock stood between them with a puzzled frown creasing his chiseled features. Aichi looked glum, Zach's usual pleasant smile was nowhere in sight.

Winston's space suit was stretched out atop the bench like a corpse in a morgue, its hard-shell torso and flexible leggings smeared with gray dust. Grant smelled the faint odor of gunpowder, typical of lunar dust.

"Do you mean to tell me you can't find anything wrong with his suit?" McClintock was saying.

"Not yet," Aichi replied, almost hissing the words.

Zach added, "We've only been at it for a few hours, man. Give us some time."

Grant came up to the workbench. "Having a problem?"

Zach shrugged good-naturedly. "Mr. McCee here wants us to find some failure in Win's suit."

"And there is none," Aichi said. Grant could tell from the tone of his voice that Toshio was bristling with suppressed fury.

"Give them some time, Carter," Grant said easily, smiling as he spoke. "They—"

"We don't have time," McClintock snapped. "Selene's news service has put in six calls about this accident in the past two hours. Earthside news nets are sniffing around, as well. We have to have something to tell them."

In a small voice, Zacharias said, "No news is good news."

McClintock glowered at him.

"Look," said Grant, "if there're no defects in the suit that's good news, isn't it?"

"Good news for you, maybe," McClintock shot back. "You'll be off the hook for letting the man go out in a defective suit."

Grant looked into McClintock's tawny eyes and said evenly, "The suit checked out fine."

"But we've got a dead man on our hands and the newshounds yapping at our heels."

"Give the guys some time to check the suit in more detail," Grant said. "You can't force results in something like this."

McClintock turned from Grant to the two technicians. "I want you to call me the minute you find anything. Do you understand me?"

"And if we find nothing?" Aichi countered.

"There's got to be *something*!" McClintock insisted. "Find it!"

He brushed past Grant and strode out of the workshop. Neither of the technicians said a word until the door slid shut behind him.

Then Zacharias muttered, "Asshole."

"Take it easy on him, guys," said Grant. "He's right, you know: There's got to be some reason why Win died, and we've got to find what it is."

Aichi's stern expression did not waver by a millimeter. "If this suit was the cause of death, we will find the defect. But if that reflects poorly on you, Grant . . ."

"Find the defect, guys," Grant told them. "We can't sort out the responsibilities until we know what the hell happened—and why."

Grant went back to the teleoperations center and slumped into a chair next to Josie Rivera.

"How's it going, Grant?" she asked, without taking her eyes from her console screen.

"Don't ask," Grant muttered.

"That bad, huh?"

Grant saw that Josie was monitoring a team of space-suited technicians and gleaming white robots working out at Korolev crater, building the foundation and shelter for the mirror that the nanomachines would create there. Four humans, four robots. They could form teams and play tennis, Grant thought wryly. Doubles.

Turning to face Grant, Rivera asked, "What happened to Win?"

"Damned if I know," Grant said.

"Damned shame."

"Yeah." Jabbing a finger at the console screen, Grant asked, "So how's the work at Korolev going?"

"No problems," said Rivera. "They're getting the job done. Nanomachines arrive from Selene tomorrow."

Grant nodded. But he was thinking, Nanomachines. Could they have anything to do with Win's accident? My body's carrying a shitload of nanobugs. Will they attack me, somehow? He decided to call Kris Cardenas and check out the possibilities.

As he got up from the little wheeled chair he patted Rivera's shoulder. "Keep up the good work, Josie."

"Thanks." As Grant headed for the door, Rivera called out, "Hey, Grant, whatcha doing for dinner tonight? Want to come over to my place?"

"I can't," he heard himself say, before he even thought about the consequences. "Until we figure out what happened to Win, I'm not going to be very social."

"Your loss," Josie teased.

"Raincheck," said Grant.

"Sure, boss. Anytime."

NANODEATH

Grant hurried to his quarters and put in a call to Dr. Cardenas. Her answering vid came up on the phone screen, smiling perfunctorily as she said, "I'm not available at this—"

Abruptly, the image was replaced by another view of Cardenas, her face serious, grave.

"I heard about the accident, Grant," she said. "I've been expecting your call."

"Could it be me?" Grant blurted. "Did the nanos in my body somehow cause Win's death?"

"No way," said Cardenas. "No way on God's green Earth."

We're not on God's green Earth, Grant thought. But he said to Cardenas's unsmiling face, "How can you be so sure?"

She held up a hand and ticked off on her fingers, "One: the nanos in your body are tuned to your metabolism, nobody else's. Two: they're designed to attack microbes and viruses; they are not random disassemblers."

"Gobblers," muttered Grant.

Cardenas frowned at the word, but continued, "Three: the only way the nanomachines in your body could get into anyone else is by direct physical contact with your blood. They don't fly through the air, Grant. They're not evil spirits."

"Okay. Thanks." He hesitated a beat, then added, "I had to ask, Kris. I had to know for certain."

She smiled minimally. "I know. I understand. Don't take it personally if I come down too hard."

"That's okay. I guess you get a lot of damn-fool questions."

Cardenas's smile turned bitter. "That I do, mister. That I do."

Grant fought the itch to return to the maintenance center and lean on Toshio and Zach. Let them do their work, he told himself. They're not going to get results any faster with you breathing down their necks.

He went to the engineering office and plunged into the problems of scheduling the construction of the telescopes at the Korolev and Gagarin craters. Coordinating the crews who would construct the foundations, shelters, protective roofs; scheduling the arrival of the nanomachines; checking the maintenance of the robots, the duty shifts at the teleoperations center: there was plenty of work to be done.

His phone buzzed. Annoyed at the interruption, he yanked it from his coverall pocket and saw that it was Trudy Yost calling. His annoyance dwindled away.

"What's up, Trudy?" he asked.

In the phone's tiny screen, Trudy's snub-nosed face looked troubled.

"I need your help," she said.

"What's the problem?"

"Can we talk? Face-to-face, I mean."

His first impulse was to suggest meeting at the cafeteria, but then he remembered that he had turned down Josie Rivera's invitation to dinner. If Josie sees me with Trudy she'll get the wrong idea, he thought.

"Can you come to my quarters?" he asked Trudy. "In half an hour?"

"Sure," she said, without the slightest hesitation.

Thirty-two minutes later Grant was straightening up his messy room when he heard a tap on the door. Sliding it open, he saw Trudy standing there, looking a little like a lost urchin.

"Come on in," Grant said.

"I appreciate your taking the time to see me," Trudy said as she stepped into the room.

"What's the problem?" he asked again. Looking at the place through her eyes, Grant thought that his quarters were shabby, strictly utilitarian. This is where I sleep, he apologized silently. Where I sleep and work.

Trudy seemed oblivious to the meager furnishings, though. She went straight to the sofa and perched herself on its front few centimeters.

"Professor Uhlrich wants me to come up with a plan for using the Mendeleev telescope. He doesn't want it to sit idle while the other 'scopes are being built."

"Makes sense," Grant said, heading for the kitchenette in the corner. "Can I get you something to drink? Juice? Tea?" He glanced at the half-full coffeepot next to the two-burner stove. "The coffee's a couple days old, I'm afraid."

"Juice will be fine," Trudy said.

As he bent down and yanked open the little refrigerator Grant called to her, "So you have to come up with a plan for Mendeleev."

"The professor wants to start taking spectra of Sirius C right away," she said.

"Is that doable?" Grant found a half-empty bottle of grapefruit juice, shook it vigorously, and poured a glass for her.

"Yes. The planet's too small for us to image with any decent resolution, but we should be able to get a spectrum, see if it has an atmosphere."

"I thought that was settled," said Grant.

With a curt nod, Trudy replied, "The planet gives a fuzzy edge in the imagery that telescopes in Earth orbit have gotten. Not a sharp edge. That indicates an atmosphere of some sort."

"That's what I'd heard."

"But it shouldn't have an atmosphere, not really," Trudy went on. "When Sirius B went through its nova phase, the burps of hot plasma should have boiled away any atmosphere the planet might've had."

"But you said it looks fuzzy-edged."

"Yeah," said Trudy, almost wistfully. "It shouldn't. But it does."

As he handed the glass to her, Grant asked, "So can you measure the atmosphere's constituents?"

"If it really has an atmosphere—and the absorption lines are strong enough."

Sitting beside her on the sofa, Grant said, "So there's your research program."

She nodded uncertainly. "I suppose so."

"Measuring the components of an exoplanet's atmosphere," said Grant. "That would be an accomplishment, wouldn't it?"

"If I can do it."

"Sure you can," he encouraged. "It'll give you a solid reputation."

"But what if I fail?"

Grant looked at her. She's really worried, he realized. Uhlrich's given her this responsibility and she's scared of it.

"Behold the lowly turtle," Grant quoted. "She only makes progress when she sticks her neck out."

Trudy looked surprised, then puzzled. Then she broke into a grin, all within the span of a second.

"You're telling me I should get to work and stop worrying about it," she said.

"I'm telling you that you can do the job. Uhlrich wouldn't have hired you if you couldn't."

For several heartbeats Trudy said nothing. Then, in a low voice, "Thanks, Grant."

"I didn't do anything."

"Yes you did. And you kept me from falling apart when Win died. You came out and saved me."

He didn't know what to say, how to answer her.

Trudy got up from the sofa. "Thank you, Grant. You're very kind."

Standing beside her, Grant replied, "De nada."

He followed her to the door, then leaned past her and slid it open. "Any time you need to talk, I'll be here."

Trudy gazed at him in silence with her light green eyes. Pretty eyes, he thought. There's flecks of amber in them.

Abruptly, Trudy stood on her tiptoes and gave Grant a peck on the lips. Then she turned and hurried down the corridor.

Grant stood there, somewhere between bemused and astonished. Women, he thought. Studying the mysteries of the cosmos is simple. Figuring out women is the real challenge.

His phone buzzed again as Grant slid his door shut.

"On wall screen," he commanded the phone.

Toshio Aichi's face filled the screen: ascetically lean, unsmiling. Talk about inscrutable, Grant thought. Tosh doesn't let anything show.

"Grant, we've found a defect in Winston's suit," Aichi said without preamble.

Grant's chest tightened.

"A defect?"

"Relax," Aichi said, his expression unchanged. "You couldn't have seen it when you checked Winston's suit. Nobody could have, not without a laser probe."

"What do you mean?"

"It's a pinhole leak in the suit's collar ring. Too small to see with the naked eye, but big enough to slowly leak air out of his helmet. Not enough of a leak for decompression, but enough to asphyxiate him."

"A pinhole leak?" Grant asked.

Nodding a millimeter or so, Aichi said, "Pinhole. Like the leak that knocked out your superconducting coil."

DENIAL

rofessor Uhlrich sat behind his desk, staring in Grant Simpson's direction.

"A pinhole leak in his suit's collar ring?" Uhlrich asked, unbelieving.

"That's what Aichi and Zacharias found," said Grant, his voice heavy, morose.

Uhlrich saw an image of Simpson's darkly bearded face, an image triggered by the sound of his voice. Simpson was the stubborn kind: very capable, but dependent on medications. I can't run this facility without him, Uhlrich knew, but he can't function without his drugs. I should find a replacement for him; I shouldn't be forced into such a dependent position.

McClintock was sitting across the table from Simpson. Uhlrich heard a tinge of sarcasm as the man asked, "And how did a pinhole leak happen?"

For a long moment Simpson did not reply. Uhlrich could visualize the sullenness etched into his brooding face. At last the engineer said, "It might have been produced by nanomachines."

"Nanomachines?" Uhlrich snapped, instantly alarmed.

"That's impossible," said McClintock.

"Is it?" Simpson retorted. "The Mendeleev mirror was built by nanos. The accident happened at Mendeleev."

A bit more subdued, McClintock said, "Then we'll have to get Dr. Cardenas here to examine the situation."

"Damned right," said Simpson.

"Wait," Uhlrich said. "We mustn't jump to wild conclusions. Just because an accident occurred—"

"A man died," Simpson snapped. "We've got to find out why before anybody else is put at risk. We've got to halt the mirror construction jobs at Korolev and Gagarin. We've got to—"

Uhlrich's temper flared. "Stop the construction at Korolev and Gagarin! We haven't even started building the mirrors there!"

"And we shouldn't start," Simpson insisted. "Not until we know what's going on."

McClintock's voice took on a more conciliatory tone. "I agree that we ought to investigate the possibility. But we shouldn't screw up the construction schedules unless we absolutely have to."

"How many deaths will it take?" Simpson growled.

Uhlrich could picture McClintock's frosty smile. The man doesn't confront you, he told himself. He simply sits on top of his money and smiles condescendingly until he gets his way.

McClintock was saying, "You're getting all worked up over what might be just a maintenance failure."

"Winston's death wasn't the first failure," Simpson said.

"What do you mean?"

"The tractor problem we had several weeks ago," said Simpson. "Superconducting motor went dead because the main coil lost its coolant. Through a pinhole leak."

"Coincidence," McClintock scoffed.

"Are you willing to bet your life on that?" Simpson replied heatedly. "The lives of everybody in this facility?"

McClintock didn't reply.

"We're a closed little community here," Simpson went on. "If we have some rogue nanos eating into metals we could all be killed in a few days."

"I can't believe that," said Uhlrich. But he knew that he wasn't speaking the truth. His insides were trembling.

"Famous last words," Simpson muttered.

"All right, let's get Dr. Cardenas here," said McClintock, trying to sound reasonable. "Let her make a determination."

Simpson said nothing for several moments. At last he agreed, "That's a start."

"Very well, then," said Uhlrich. "I will call her myself."

"In the meantime, we should stop delivery of the nanos for Korolev and Gagarin."

"No!" Uhlrich snapped. "That would throw off our schedule."

His voice hard and unrelenting, Simpson replied, "Professor, we're months ahead of our original schedule. We've got the Mendeleev 'scope up and running already. For god's sake, don't put the damned schedule ahead of safety, ahead of people's lives! We can make up whatever time we lose."

Uhlrich heard the earnestness in the engineer's voice, visualized the intensity of his sad-eyed expression. What does he care? the professor asked himself. He's young, he has a life, a career ahead of him. I've only got this one chance, this one last chance.

"I will not upset our schedule," he said flatly. "If we suspend construction of the mirrors Selene will wonder what's gone wrong. The university will send people here to pry into our situation. There will be an investigation. The news media will learn of it! It will be a disaster!"

McClintock said, "Perhaps we could distract the news media."

"Distract?"

"Trudy Yost is going to use the Mendeleev telescope to get imagery of New Earth, isn't she?"

"Spectra," Uhlrich corrected. "Not imagery."

"Besides, Sirius C has already been photographed," Simpson pointed out.

"I've seen those pictures. New Earth is just a little dot, a blob," McClintock countered. "We can produce much better stuff, can't we?"

Uhlrich saw a glimmer of opportunity. "If Dr. Yost can detect oxygen in Sirius C's atmosphere. Or water vapor . . . perhaps chlorophyll . . ."

"Whatever," said McClintock. "We can feed her results to the media. The first close-up imagery from New Earth! They'll lap it up and ignore whatever else is going on here."

"Including a death," Simpson said.

"Accidents happen," McClintock said. Uhlrich could picture him shrugging. "It's not the end of the world."

"Isn't it?"

McClintock didn't answer. Instead, he pushed his chair back from the table and started to get to his feet.

Before either of the men could leave his office, Uhlrich said firmly, "There will be no word of a possible nanotechnology problem. Absolutely none. Not to anyone outside this room. Do you understand that? Neither of you is to say a word about this."

"How will you explain Dr. Cardenas coming here?" Simpson asked.

McClintock replied, "Simple. We're using her nanomachines to build the mirrors. She's dropped in to see how they're working."

"Excellent," said Uhlrich. "No mention of a possible problem. Not a word!"

He could feel resentment radiating from Simpson. But the engineer said grudgingly, "Probably a good idea. Don't want to start a panic."

"Exactly," Uhlrich said.

They left the office. Uhlrich sat behind his desk, thinking that McClintock had hit on the perfect strategy. Distract the media with the first spectra from Sirius C. It would even gain credit for Farside in the public's eyes. And from the committee in Stockholm. This could all end up as a positive step for me.

Now to get results from Dr. Yost, he said to himself. And quickly.

ARGUMENT

Trudy sat dutifully in Professor Uhlrich's office, with handsome Carter McClintock sitting across the table, smiling pleasantly at her.

He hasn't called me since the night we spent together, Trudy thought. Maybe I disappointed him? Wasn't hot enough in bed for him?

Professor Uhlrich's voice broke into her self-recrimination. "How soon can you produce spectra of Sirius C's atmosphere?"

Trudy snapped her attention to the professor. She heard the anxiety in his voice, saw the tension etching his lean, austere face. Those sightless eyes of his unnerved her; they seemed to be peering straight at her, penetrating her like X-rays.

"The spectrometer's ready to be packed up and delivered to Mendeleev," she replied. "I'll have to go out there with a technician to install it on the telescope. Maybe two technicians."

"Why do you have to go?" McClintock asked. "Can't the technicians do the installation work, under your supervision? Remotely, from here at Farside?"

Trudy caught a note of apprehension in Carter's voice.

"It'll be a lot easier if I'm there," she replied.

"What about the robots?" McClintock pressed. "Why can't they—"

"Nonsense!" Professor Uhlrich snapped. "We cannot trust such valuable equipment to robots."

"I don't mind going to Mendeleev," Trudy told them. It was

a stretch of the truth, and she knew it. "It'd only be for a day or so. I can spend a night in the shelter. It'll be okay."

Carter looked decidedly uneasy, she thought. He's worried about me! How sweet.

But the professor said, "How soon can you do the installation?"

"I could leave tomorrow."

"Very well," said Uhlrich. Turning to McClintock, he ordered, "Make the necessary arrangements for a hopper and tell Simpson to assign two of his best technicians."

McClintock nodded unhappily.

"Is there anything else?" Trudy asked. "If not, I'll get started on packing the spectrometer."

"By all means," said the professor.

She got up from her chair, flashed a warm smile at Carter, and left the professor's office.

McClintock watched her go, then turned back to Uhlrich.

"Do you think it's safe to let her go to Mendeleev?"

The professor frowned at him. "How can we get spectra from Sirius C unless she installs the spectrometer?"

"But if . . ." McClintock hesitated, sorting out his thoughts. "If Mendeleev is dangerous, if there's a problem with the nanomachines . . ."

"Nonsense," Uhlrich snapped.

"Simpson doesn't think it's nonsense."

"Simpson is an engineer," the professor replied. "They're all overly cautious."

"Perhaps."

"Dr. Cardenas is due to arrive here this afternoon. Have you prepared quarters for her?"

McClintock resented being treated like a servant, but he thought, It's just his way. He doesn't mean anything by it. He's just a wannabe aristocrat. Then he corrected himself: No, he's a wannabe Nobel laureate.

And he wondered how insufferable Professor Uhlrich would become if he actually did get a Nobel.

That afternoon, when the lobber from Selene settled on Farside's lone landing pad, McClintock waited at the airlock hatch to greet Dr. Cardenas.

The heavy steel hatch sighed open; a pair of technicians in sky-blue coveralls stepped through and walked right past him. For a moment McClintock worried that Cardenas wasn't aboard the rocket, but then she strode into the tiny reception area, tall and graceful, blond curls and china blue eyes, looking radiant and youthful and altogether delightful.

She was not smiling, though. She looked quite serious, almost grim, in fact.

"It's good of you to come," McClintock said as he shook her hand. It felt warm and strong and he realized that she was a very desirable woman.

"You think you might have a problem," she said. "Let's find out what's going on."

"I'll take you to Professor Uhlrich's office," McClintock said. "Your bag will be sent to your quarters."

Cardenas nodded curtly, but said, "Let's go to the lab where they examined the space suit that failed. Professor Uhlrich can meet us there."

McClintock said, "Good idea," grinning inwardly at the thought of rousting Uhlrich from his office and making him go to Cardenas, rather than the other way around.

Two Nobel candidates, he said to himself. There ought to be sparks flying.

Trudy was surprised when Grant Simpson popped into the storage area where she was packing up the spectrometer and its associated gear.

"You're going to Mendeleev?" Grant asked, without preamble.

"Yes," Trudy said. "Tomorrow morning."

"Can't you let the techs do the installation? You could monitor their work from here."

Trudy felt her brows knit. First Carter and now Grant, she
thought. All of a sudden everybody's worried about me going to
Mendeleev.

Tell the truth now, she said to herself. You don't like the
idea yourself: flying out there in the open, it's kinda scary, admit it.

But to Grant she said, "What's the big deal about me going to
Mendeleev?"

Grant looked determined, almost grim. "It's foolish to go out
there if you don't have to."

Pointing to the crate that held the spectroscope, Trudy said,
"I'm the only one who can put that rig on the telescope properly.
That's why I have to go."

"You're not indispensable," Grant said.

"Indispensable? When did I say I was indispensable?"

"Just now. You're not the only person here who could put that
dingus on the 'scope."

"Oh no?" Trudy felt her blood beginning to seethe. "Who
else around here could do it?"

"I could."

"You?"

"Me," Grant said. "You're staying here. You can direct me remotely. I'll go out to the telescope and attach the equipment to it."

She planted her fists on her hips and glared at him. "You
don't have the authority to keep me here."

"Then I'll get the Ulcer to give you a direct order. Is that what
you want?"

Trudy stared into Grant's dark, brooding eyes. He doesn't
look angry, she thought. He looks . . . worried, fearful.

More gently she asked, "What's going on, Grant? Why don't
you want me to go out to Mendeleev?"

"There's no need for you to go," he said, lowering his voice a
notch. "I'll go. You direct me from here."

"And if you louse up the installation, the professor will blame me."

"No he won't. I'll take the responsibility. I'm used to working outside. I've got plenty of experience. You don't."

"Well, I'm not going to get any experience sitting in here while you go out and do my work for me," she said.

"That's the way it's going to be, Trudy."

"No it's not! This is *my* responsibility and I'm going to do it, whether you like it or not!"

"Look, you went out there once and a man got killed. I don't—"

"You're blaming me for Winston?" Trudy screeched, her temper boiling now.

"That's not what I meant."

"The hell it wasn't!"

"It's dangerous out there, Trudy."

"I'm going and you can't stop me," she said hotly.

"I'll get Uhlrich to stop you."

"The hell you will!"

"I don't want you going out to Mendeleev," Grant repeated stubbornly.

"Why not?"

Grant started to reply, but hesitated. "You're not going," he said, his voice low, hard, final. "That's all there is to it. You're not going."

McCLINTOCK'S QUARTERS

Make yourself comfortable, Dr. Cardenas," said Mc-Clintock as he ushered her into his room. "Can I offer you some wine?"

Cardenas stood by the door and surveyed the room in a single swift glance.

"No thanks," she said. "I'm here to work. I thought we were going to the lab where the damaged space suit was examined."

Smoothly, McClintock replied, "Professor Uhlrich thought it would be best if you weren't seen examining the space suit by anyone else. We have some very bright people here; if they see the nanotech expert examining the suit they might realize that we have a potential problem on our hands."

"Nanofear," Cardenas said.

"No sense starting rumors," said McClintock. "This is a very small, tightly knit little community, you know."

"I understand."

Gesturing to the sofa, he said, "I can show you all the test results on the wall screen. Any information that you need."

"And Professor Uhlrich?"

"He'll meet us here shortly."

Cardenas seemed to think it over for a moment, then she said, "All right, let's look at the data."

Half an hour later she was peering at a photomicrograph of the pinhole in the metal collar of Winston's space suit.

"What do you think?" McClintock asked.

Her face set in a tight frown, Cardenas said, "Can you pull up an image of the pinhole in the superconductor's dewar?"

McClintock ordered the computer to find the image.

Cardenas nodded, then said, "Put them side by side on the screen, please."

She stared at the two images for a long, hard minute. McClintock noticed that the data bar running along the bottom of the screen showed both holes were exactly the same diameter.

"Identical," Cardenas murmured at last.

"Which means?"

She turned to McClintock, her expression bleak. "Which means that both holes were drilled by nanomachines. The same batch of nanomachines."

"How can you tell?"

"Characteristic microgrooves. Like the rifling of a bullet." She sat in tense silence for a moment, then added, "You're infected."

"I am?" McClintock yelped.

Shaking her head impatiently, Cardenas said, "Not you personally. Your base is. This facility is. Or at least that spot out there where the telescope is sitting."

"Mendeleev crater."

"You'd better isolate the site and send a team of robots in to sweep the facility with high-intensity ultraviolet light."

"That will kill the nanomachines?" he asked.

"It should."

Feeling somewhat relieved, McClintock said, "I'll tell Uhlrich. We'll get started on this right away."

"Where is Professor Uhlrich?" Cardenas asked. "I thought he was going to meet us here."

Professor Uhlrich was still in his office, caught squarely between Trudy Yost and Grant Simpson, who sat on opposite sides of his conference table, obviously glaring at each other.

"I still don't see why I can't go out to Mendeleev," she was insisting. "It doesn't make any sense to try to do the installation remotely."

Before the professor could reply, Simpson said, "There's no need for you to go. I'll do it, with you directing me from here."

"That's ridiculous!" she snapped.

"No it's not!"

Uhlrich felt torn. On the one hand, he agreed with Simpson that allowing Dr. Yost to go to Mendeleev might be dangerous. *One man's already been killed there; why risk the life of the only astronomer on my staff? On the other hand, it is perfectly true that Dr. Yost is the only one really capable of installing the spectrometer, and I need to get spectra from Sirius C as quickly as possible.*

His phone buzzed and announced that Carter McClintock was calling. *He's with Dr. Cardenas,* Uhlrich knew.

Instead of putting the call on one of the wall screens, Uhlrich picked up the handset. Yost and Simpson fell silent, but Uhlrich could feel the heat of their anger toward each other.

"Yes," he said quietly into the phone.

"Professor, I'm in my quarters with Dr. Cardenas. We were expecting you to join us."

"In a few minutes," said Uhlrich. "I'm tied up with something at the moment."

"Oh."

Lowering his voice to a whisper, Uhlrich asked, "What has she found?"

A heartbeat's hesitation. Then McClintock said, "It's nanomachines. The Mendeleev site is infested with them, somehow."

The professor squeezed his sightless eyes shut. "Mendeleev, you say? Not Farside?"

"Apparently not."

Letting out his breath in a long, weary sigh, Uhlrich said, "Very well. I will join you in a few minutes."

He hung up the phone and sat there in silence, wondering what he should do, how he should proceed.

Simpson said impatiently, "Well, Professor? Do you agree that Dr. Yost can direct the job from here? There's no need for her—"

"Yes, yes, I agree."

Trudy Yost immediately began to complain. "Now wait a minute, this is my responsibility and I—"

"Dr. Yost," said Uhlrich, with a firmness he did not really feel, "you will remain here at Farside and direct Mr. Simpson, who will install the spectrometer—under your guidance."

"That . . . that's . . . it's wrong!" Yost sputtered. "It's stupid!"

"That is my decision and you will abide by it."

From the other side of the table, Simpson said, "Trudy, it's for your own good. Believe me. I'll do the job right. You tell me what to do and I'll do it."

Uhlrich could sense the young woman sitting there, awash in anger and even shame. *She thinks I don't trust her to install the spectrometer. She thinks I'm belittling her. So be it. I can't tell her that we have a nanomachine problem. That would start a panic here that could destroy everything I'm trying to accomplish.*

Simpson can handle the job. He's quite capable. With a pang of alarm, Uhlrich asked himself, *What if the nanomachines attack him? What if he's killed out there? It will mean the Mendeleev site is useless, I'll be unable to get spectral data on Sirius C.*

Then a new thought struck him: *What if the nanomachines destroy the spectrometer? That would be a disaster! An utter disaster!*

CONFESSIONS

A s they left the Ulcer's office and started down the corridor, Grant could see how depressed Trudy felt. What can I say that'll make her feel better? he wondered.

"Look," he said to her, "nobody doubts your ability. You'll still be directing the installation, it'll just be that you're directing it remotely instead of being out there."

"Where I should be," she said, her voice heavy with resentment.

"Come on, cheer up. I'll buy you dinner, okay?"

She stopped in the middle of the corridor, eyeing him suspiciously. "Grant, what's going on? Why's everybody so set on keeping me away from Mendeleev?"

He wanted to tell her. He wanted to put his arm around her shoulders and explain to her that Mendeleev was too dangerous for her, too risky.

Instead, he merely shrugged and said, "You're going to have to run the 'scope from here, remotely, aren't you? So why're you getting spooled up over directing the installation remotely? It's no big deal."

Trudy looked totally unconvinced.

"Besides, you don't have the experience to work outside. I do. It's that simple."

"I don't believe you," Trudy said, her eyes narrowed with suspicion.

Grant heard himself say, "All right, I'll tell you the truth. I don't want you taking any risks that you don't absolutely have to take. You're the only astronomer here, outside of the Ulcer, and . . ." Suddenly he ran out of words.

"And?" she prompted.

"And you're too important to be sent on jobs that a technician can do."

"Or an engineer?"

"Yeah," he said. "Engineers are expendable. Astronomers aren't."

Trudy's expression softened. Her voice gentler, she said, "So what about dinner, Grant?"

"You're sending someone out there before the site's decontaminated?" Kris Cardenas couldn't believe what Professor Uhlrich had just told her.

The professor was sitting bolt upright in the shiny new recliner that McClintock had somehow acquired and added to his room's décor.

"Decontaminated?" he asked.

McClintock intervened. "Dr. Cardenas believes we should bathe the Mendeleev facility in high-intensity ultraviolet light. That would kill any nanomachines present there, wouldn't it?"

"It will deactivate them, yes," Cardenas agreed, with a tight nod. She was sitting on the sofa, facing Uhlrich across the low coffee table, fists clenched on her lap. McClintock was beside her. He had brought out one of the bottles of wine he had managed to bring in from Selene and three stemmed glasses, but no one had touched their drinks.

Uhlrich looked directly at Cardenas, and McClintock marveled at how the man could disguise his blindness.

"The Mendeleev telescope is bathed in ultraviolet light constantly," he said. "Solar UV and background radiation from the stars."

Before Cardenas could reply, McClintock said, "But the shelter, Professor. The underground shelter. That must be where the nanomachines are lurking."

"Ah, I see," said Uhlrich.

"The man who died was leaving the shelter and heading for the hopper when he collapsed," McClintock pointed out.

Uhlrich began to nod, but then asked, "How is it that the person with him was not affected by the nanomachines?"

"That's a good question," said Cardenas. "We should examine the space suit she wore, too."

"I have another question," said the professor. "How did the nanomachines get there in the first place?"

"From the nanos that built the telescope mirror," said McClintock. "They somehow got into the shelter and—"

"No," Cardenas said flatly. "That's not possible."

"You don't think they could have gotten into the shelter?" McClintock asked.

"The nanos that built the mirror are entirely different from the nanos that damaged the space suit," Cardenas said. "They couldn't have damaged the suit, not in a million years. In fact, if you examine the mirror, you'll find that all the nanomachines that constructed it are completely deactivated."

"I don't understand," said Uhlrich.

Patiently, Cardenas explained, "The nanomachines that constructed the mirror are deactivated by now. Dead, if you want to use that term. The nanomachines that damaged the space suit are an entirely different type of nano. Not the same as those that built the mirror. Not the same at all."

Uhlrich looked confused. "Then . . . where did they come from?"

"I wish I knew," Cardenas said.

Dinner was awkward. Trudy knows I'm not telling her the whole story, Grant realized. I can't. I promised the Ulcer that I wouldn't. He's right: if the staff found out we've got a problem with nanomachines they'd fly out of here like air escaping from a popped balloon.

A contradictory voice in his head argued, But don't they have the right to know? If they're in danger, shouldn't they be told about it?

"You're awfully quiet," Trudy said.

Grant snapped his attention to her, sitting across the table from him. The cafeteria was practically empty this early in the evening, but still its stone walls rang with the clatter of dinnerware, the buzz of conversations.

"Sorry," he said. "Got a lot to think about."

Trudy looked squarely at him, her green eyes unwavering. "Grant, you're not telling me the whole story, are you?"

He almost smiled at her. "The whole story is, I don't want you to take any risks that you don't have to take."

"But you're willing to take those risks."

"That's right," he said, picking up a fork and jabbing it into his salad.

"How come?"

"It's my job. It's what I get paid to do."

For a moment Trudy said nothing. She too picked up her fork, but she held it like a fencing saber and pointed it directly at Grant.

"Installing that spectrometer is *my* job, Grant. It's what *I* get paid to do."

"You'll be doing your job."

"And you'll be taking the risks of working out in the open."

He shrugged. "I've had plenty of experience. You haven't."

Trudy shook her head, like a stubborn little girl. "There's more to it, Grant. I know there's more."

She's like a bull terrier, Grant thought. What in hell can I tell her to get her off this business?

He looked into her green eyes and saw that she was waiting patiently, expectantly, for him to tell her the truth.

"I can work outside without as much risk as you or anybody else would face," he said.

She put the fork down and folded both hands beneath her chin, waiting for more.

Leaning over the table so close that their heads nearly touched, Grant told her, "My body's full of nanomachines. They protect me from radiation damage and any other physical trauma."

"Nanomachines?" Trudy whispered.

"I don't want anybody to know," he whispered back.

She nodded. "I guess not."

"I'm trusting you, Trudy. Please, *please* keep it to yourself."

"Of course. Certainly." A flash of confusion showed on her face. "But . . . I still don't see why you don't want me to go out to Mendeleev with you."

He blurted, "Because I think too much of you to let you take unnecessary risks."

Trudy's mouth fell open. Then slowly a smile curved her lips. "You do?"

"Yeah, I do." And Grant said to himself, Holy god, that might even be the truth.

TO MENDELEEV CRATER

Grant was surprised to see Nate Oberman suiting up in the locker area next to Farside's main airlock.

"What're you doing?" he demanded. "Where's Harvey?"

"Hung over," Oberman said, smirking. "He and Josie had a big night, celebrating his return to . . . uh, active duty."

Before Grant could respond, Oberman added, "Harvey asked me to fill in for him."

How the hell did he finagle his way into this assignment? Grant wondered. And why? All the way out to Mendeleev and back with this clown, Grant fumed. It'd be easier to do the job alone.

But Oberman's long-jawed face grew serious. "Hey, Grant, I know you don't like me—"

"We've had our differences, that's sure enough."

"Yep."

"Nate, I never tried to take your job away from you. When Uhlrich bounced you I was just as surprised as you were."

"I know," Oberman said. "I was pretty sore about it at the time, but I know you didn't undercut me."

Grant didn't see any anger in Oberman's eyes. But there was something, some hint of knowledge that Nate was not sharing with him.

"I've only got 'til the end of the month and then I'm out of here," Nate said. "I figured I'd do Harvey a favor and finish on a good note."

Grant rubbed his beard, thinking, It'd be better if we're at least civil to each other on this trip. No sense getting him sore at me. If we start pounding on each other out there at Mendeleev it could be big trouble.

"All right," he said, sitting on the bench beside Oberman. "You stay focused. That'd be good."

Oberman stuck out his hand and Grant clasped it in his.

But he couldn't help thinking that Oberman's real motivation was to get a decent job appraisal to show to his next prospective employer. Then he remembered that Oberman claimed he already had a job lined up at Selene, courtesy of Anita Halleck, no less.

McClintock stepped into the locker area, smiling like an insurance salesman. Grant thought he looked completely out of place. This is where the working stiffs suit up, he said to himself. What's this playboy doing here? The man was wearing a long-sleeved white pullover and sharply creased pearl gray slacks. The shirt looked like cashmere, for cripes' sakes, Grant thought. The space suits hanging in their lockers had been white once, but now they were gray from hard use. No matter how hard you vacuumed them after a job outside, it was impossible to get rid of all the lunar dust that clung to the suits.

"Grant, could I speak with you a moment?" McClintock asked, pointedly polite. Noblesse oblige, Grant thought.

"Go right ahead," said Grant, as he pulled his thick-soled boots from his locker.

McClintock's smile dimmed. "In private, if you please."

Grant glanced at Oberman, then got to his feet. He followed McClintock to the door of the locker area and out into the low-ceilinged corridor beyond.

Lowering his voice, McClintock said, "Dr. Cardenas recommends we decontaminate the shelter at Mendeleev. So Professor Uhlrich wants you to take a couple of high-intensity ultraviolet lamps out with you and kill any nanobugs in there."

With a nod, Grant said, "Makes sense."

"Good. I've already called the storeroom. Two lamps are on their way here."

Glancing back into the locker area, Grant asked, "What about Oberman? This'll tip him off that we're worried about nanos."

McClintock's phony smile returned. "I already thought of that. Tell him you're sterilizing the shelter, getting rid of any bacteria in the air, biofilms on the surfaces of the equipment, that sort of thing."

Grant said, "Yeah, he might believe that."

"No mention of nanomachines to him," McClintock commanded.

"He's not altogether stupid, you know."

"No mention of nanomachines."

McClintock turned and headed down the corridor, looking to Grant as if he were eager to get back to his office and away from the grimy workers' area. Can't say I blame him, Grant thought. This place smells of sweat and machine oil and lunar dust.

As he returned to his locker Grant saw that Oberman was industriously wiping the metal neck ring of his suit with a heavy cloth.

"What're you doing?" Grant asked.

"Cleaning my suit," said Oberman without looking up from his work. "I want to do this job perfectly, Grant. I want to show you I can do things right."

Grant sat on the bench beside Oberman, impressed with the man's eagerness.

"Great," he said.

By the time Grant was about to lift the hard-shell torso of his space suit over his head, two clerks from the storeroom arrived, pushing a cart that carried a pair of ultraviolet lamps. Grant signed for them and they left the cart and departed.

"What's that for?" Oberman asked. He was almost fully suited up, only his gloves and helmet remained to be put on.

"Routine health procedure," Grant lied. "We're going to disinfect the shelter while we're out at Mendeleev. UV kills bugs in the air, biofilms, stuff like that."

"Huh," said Oberman.

Grant let it go at that and picked up his suit's torso.

Oberman eyed him intently as Grant lifted the hard shell

over his head and wormed his arms through the fabric sleeves. When his head popped through the neck ring, he saw that Oberman was grinning at him.

"What's funny?"

"Your beard. I was wondering how you'd keep it inside the collar."

Grant said, "I keep it trimmed short enough so it's not a problem."

"So I see," said Oberman, still grinning. "So I see."

They checked each other's suit connections and seals, Grant hoping that Oberman was as conscientious and thorough as he should be. My life is in his hands, he thought.

Satisfied that the suits were in working order, Grant flicked the comm frequency and announced, "We're ready to go outside."

"You're cleared for outside," came the voice of the excursion controller.

Grant recognized the voice. "Harvey? Is that you?"

"Yup."

"I thought you were too hung over to work."

A moment's hesitation, then Henderson answered, "I don't feel all that great, to tell you the truth. And Nate offered to fill in for me, so we switched assignments."

"Without asking me." Grant felt nettled.

"Hope you don't mind, boss."

Harvey only called Grant "boss" when he wanted to divert Grant's displeasure.

Grant glanced at Oberman. He could see enough through Nate's bubble helmet to recognize that the technician looked worried, apprehensive. What the hell, he thought. Nate wants to make a good impression on me, and Harvey's helping him along.

"Okay," he said. "We're entering the airlock."

"Copy entering airlock."

To Oberman, Grant said, "You pick up one of the UV lamps and I'll pick up the other. No sense trying to push that dumb cart across the regolith to the hopper."

INSTALLATION

O kay," Trudy's voice said in Grant's helmet speakers, "now plug in the connector cord from the backup computer. . . ."

Grant was standing on the spider-work platform built halfway up the telescope, where its secondary mirror had been placed. It was dark inside the hundred-meter-wide tube, and he was glad that it was nighttime again out on the floor of the crater. He was sweating enough inside his insulated suit. Cooling water gurgled through the tubes of his thermal undergarment, yet still he was perspiring. I should've remembered to bring a headband, he berated himself, blinking sweat away from his eyes, wishing he could snake a hand past the suit's neck ring and rub his eyes, scratch his itching nose.

"You're doing swell, Grant," Trudy encouraged. "Almost finished."

Grant saw her snub-nosed gamine's face on half the display screen he had set up on the work platform's grilled floor. The other half showed a schematic of the spectrometer's mount. Trudy's right, he saw: we're damned near finished.

Nate Oberman was way over on the other side of the big tube, carrying out a routine check of the telescope's steering motors. Grant plugged the computer cord into its socket and the schematic flickered briefly, then its edges turned bright green.

"That's it," said Trudy happily. "All finished."

Grant felt good about it, too. "See?" he said to Trudy. "You did it remotely. You didn't have to come out here after all."

"*You* did it, Grant," she said. "I just looked over your shoulder."

He huffed, then told her, "Well, you owe me a steak dinner when I get back."

"You're on! And no soy product, either. We'll have cultured steak."

Trudy seemed to be glowing happily, but Grant felt strangely glum, let down. He said a reluctant good-bye to her and cut the communications link. Then, on the suit-to-suit frequency, he hailed Oberman.

"I'm finished here, Nate. How're you coming along?"

Oberman replied, "I've been finished for half an hour, buddy. I've just been stoogin' around, waiting for you before I headed in for the shelter."

"Okay, I'm coming down." Grant glanced at the digital time display on his wristband. Fifteen forty-three. We can jump on the hopper and get back to Farside in time for dinner, he thought.

Then he remembered that he had to decontaminate the shelter. Don't rush that job, he told himself. Take plenty of time, shine UV in every nook and cranny.

It was well past 1900 hours when Grant finally clicked off the ultraviolet lamp he'd been holding for nearly four hours. He and Oberman had taken off their space suits and stored them by the shelter's airlock—and then irradiated them with UV, inside and out.

Standing in the middle of the narrow shelter, in his sweat-damp gray coveralls, Grant looked around, then nodded, satisfied. "That's it, I think."

Oberman lowered his lamp to the steel mesh floor. "Jesus, Grant, we've shined these damned lamps everywhere in this dump except up our respective assholes."

With a chuckle, Grant said, "Thoroughness is next to godliness."

Oberman forced an exaggerated sigh. "Okay. Pull your pants down."

Grant laughed, but he thought that if Oberman knew his body was filled with nanomachines the guy wouldn't be so nonchalant about it. They're therapeutic nanobugs, Grant reminded himself. They can't hurt anything. They can't get out of your body. Even if they did, Kris engineered them to go inert once they no longer had my body heat to power them.

He wished he really believed that.

"So whattaya think," Oberman asked, breaking into Grant's thoughts. "You want to bunk in here or fly back to Farside now?"

Grant mulled it over for a few moments. "Safety regs recommend we sleep here. No sense flying the hopper when we're tired."

"Unless we have to," said Oberman.

"No reason for us to go now."

"I thought you wanted to get Trudy Yost to buy you a steak dinner," Oberman said, grinning. "If we start out now we can make it back to Farside by midnight. Nice romantic midnight dinner, buddy."

The sonofabitch has been tapping into my comm link back to Farside! Grant realized.

"You could even have dinner in bed, I bet."

Suddenly Grant wanted to smack him in his leering face. Instead, he took a deep breath.

"We'll sleep here," he said tightly. "You can use the lav first. Just be sure to clean up after yourself."

DINNER FOR TWO

McClintock was examining the bottle of wine that he had offered Uhlrich and Kristine Cardenas the previous day. It had cost him a fair amount of effort—persuasion, cajoling, and finally an actual bribe—to get a few bottles of wine carried to Farside, tucked in with a regular shipment of food supplies. Uhlrich didn't waste his funds on luxuries such as wine, but McClintock agreed with the Italians: a meal without wine is like a day without sunshine. Even on the Moon.

None of them had touched the wine when he'd opened it for them. Well, McClintock thought as he pulled out the stopper and sniffed the wine's aroma, all the better. We'll have it all for ourselves; I only spilled a few drops when I poured it back into the bottle.

Kris Cardenas had agreed to have dinner with him, and McClintock intended to make the most of his opportunity. Cardenas was far better-looking, and much more sophisticated, than any of the women on the Farside staff. Trudy Yost had been amusing, almost pitifully pleased that McClintock had deigned to notice her. But why settle for an inexperienced kid when a beautiful, intelligent, and altogether pleasurable woman was available?

How available is she, really? McClintock asked himself as he bent down to select a pair of prepackaged dinners from his small but well-stocked freezer. Well, we'll soon find out.

That's the excitement of it all, he thought. Men are hunters by nature, and the thrill of the chase is almost as exciting as the reward at the end. He laughed to himself. Almost.

Precisely on time he heard her knock at the door. McClintock straightened up, kneed the freezer door shut, and started across the room. Take your time, he told himself. Don't rush. Don't make her think you're anxious or overly eager. But he was.

He slid the door open and there stood Kristine Cardenas, smiling at him, looking fresh and tempting in a coppery red frock that complemented her thick curly hair and cornflower blue eyes.

"Right on time," said McClintock, ushering her into the room with a sweeping gesture. "Punctuality: the pride of princes."

Her smile widening, she replied, "I'm on time because I'm hungry."

McClintock showed her to the sofa, then went to the kitchenette to pick up the wine bottle and a pair of glasses.

"I'm afraid this is all I have to drink," he apologized as he sat beside her. "Professor Uhlrich doesn't encourage alcohol consumption here." Except in his own quarters, McClintock added silently.

"Doesn't matter," said Cardenas. "I never get drunk, anyway."

"Never?" he asked, pouring the wine.

"My nanomachines take apart the alcohol molecules before my digestive system can get them into my bloodstream."

"Really?"

"One of the unexpected side effects," she said.

They clinked glasses and sipped. McClintock thought that the wine tasted slightly tart. California chardonnay? he asked himself. I'll bet this stuff was cooked up in a lab at Selene. I overpaid.

Cardenas asked, "Have you decontaminated the shelter at Mendeleev?"

McClintock nodded. "I've got two men out there now, with ultraviolet lamps."

"Good. That should take care of the problem."

He studied her face as he took another swallow of wine.

"May I ask you a personal question, Kris? Um . . . you don't mind me calling you Kris, do you?"

"Not at all," she said. "And I think I know what your question is. Yes, my body is filled with nanomachines. Has been, for years."

"They protect you against disease."

"And keep me young."

"But there are side effects."

"Only one that's harmful: I can't return to Earth."

"That's political," he said.

Her face going somber, Cardenas replied, "No, it's emotional. Irrational. The product of ignorance and fear."

"I suppose so," McClintock said. He had no intention of getting into an argument with her.

Cardenas put her wineglass down on the coffee table, practically untouched. "Do you have any idea of how the nanos got into that space suit?"

McClintock shook his head. "Not the faintest. But once the shelter out at Mendeleev is decontaminated the problem should be solved. Right?"

"Maybe."

"Maybe? What do you mean?"

"Carter . . . those nanomachines didn't get into that space suit by themselves. Or the dewar in the tractor's motor. Somebody put them there, whether by accident or on purpose."

McClintock felt his face creasing into a frown.

"You've got to find out how they got there," Cardenas went on. "Otherwise, you could be attacked again."

"Attacked? You think someone deliberately sabotaged the space suit? Murdered the man who was wearing it?"

"Perhaps not deliberately. But somebody, somehow, put destructive nanomachines into that man's suit. And the tractor's motor, earlier."

"My god!" McClintock exclaimed. "How on earth do we go about finding out who did it?"

"Good question," said Cardenas.

Dinner was far more somber than McClintock had planned.

They talked about nothing but nanomachines; he couldn't get her off the subject.

"There couldn't have been more than a milligram's worth of them," Cardenas said. She was eating automatically, paying no attention to the food. Just as well, McClintock thought, the meal was bland and undercooked.

"They were gobblers?" he asked.

She scowled at the word. "Disassemblers, yes. Programmed to take apart a specific metal alloy: the metal that both the dewar and the space suit's collar are made of."

"Could they be an offshoot of the nanos that built the telescope mirror?"

"No way. That's like expecting a flower to turn into a hand grenade."

"But still—"

The phone buzzed. Annoyed, McClintock looked across the room at the phone console on his desk.

"Who'd be calling at this hour?" he grumbled.

Trudy Yost's eager young face appeared on the phone's screen. "Carter, I just got a call from Grant, out at Mendeleev. They've finished the spectrometer installation! I'm going to take some test spectra tonight! Right now!"

"Aren't you going to answer?" Cardenas asked.

"No," said McClintock. "Not at this hour."

"She seems very excited."

"Scientists," McClintock growled. Then he remembered that Kris Cardenas was one of them.

"Go ahead and call her back," Cardenas urged. "Let her know you approve of what she's doing."

Thoroughly disgusted with the way the evening was going, McClintock called out, "Phone: reply to latest incoming call."

Trudy babbled enthusiastically for nearly half an hour while McClintock watched his dinner cool. By the time he got her off the phone, Cardenas pushed her chair from the table and stood up.

"Thank you for a lovely meal, Carter." She said it mechanically, like a child repeating a lesson learned by rote.

"You're not leaving?" he blurted, trying to keep the disappointment out of his voice. "You haven't had dessert yet."

"No dessert for me, thanks. It's not good for my figure."

Annoyed, McClintock said, "I thought your nanos took care of that."

She grinned at him. "I don't want to overwork them." Heading for the door, she said, "Thanks for dinner. And you'd better start thinking about how to find who planted those disassemblers."

Reluctantly, he slid the door open. Cardenas patted his cheek as she went past. "Thanks again, Carter."

"You're welcome," he said dully.

He slid the door shut behind her, then turned and surveyed his empty quarters. He had taken special pains to make up the bed neatly. All for nothing, McClintock thought. All for goddamned nothing.

He went back to the coffee table and carefully worked the artificial cork back into the wine bottle. No sense throwing it out, he thought, we only had one glass apiece and Kris hardly touched hers.

There's always tomorrow, he said to himself as he tucked the bottle back into his refrigerator.

RETURN TO FARSIDE

Grant was listening to Trudy's excited voice as he fastened the two ultraviolet lamps to the metal floor of the hopper.

". . . swung the 'scope over to the Orion constellation and took spectra of Betelgeuse." Even in the small speakers of his helmet he could hear the exhilaration in her voice. "Beautiful! You should see 'em! I got emission lines nobody's ever seen before. Not from old Beetlejuice! I could write a paper about it!"

"That's great," he said. "You didn't stay up all night, did you?"

"Oh no. I got to bed around three, three thirty, somewhere in there. Maybe four."

Glancing at the digital readout on his wrist, Grant said, "So you got maybe four hours' sleep?"

"Something like that. I'm going to set up the 'scope to look at Sirius C today. Get spectra from its atmosphere."

"Assuming it has an atmosphere."

Trudy replied, "We know it's got something of an atmosphere, Grant. Now I'm going to find out how thick it is and what it's made of."

"Good," he said. "I'm about ready to haul my butt back to Farside. As soon as Nate comes out of the shelter."

"Great! Call me when you get back. I owe you a steak dinner."

"I'll do that," said Grant. Steak grown out of a culture in a laboratory was nowhere near as satisfying as the real thing, but there weren't any beef cattle closer than half a million klicks, and dinner with Trudy would be fun no matter what was on the platter, he thought.

Straightening up stiffly in the cumbersome space suit, he looked at the mound of rubble that marked the shelter as he called Oberman on the suit-to-suit frequency. "Nate, I'm ready to get going. How about you?"

A moment's hesitation. Then, "Be with you in a minute, Grant. Just tidying up my bunk."

Housekeeping, Grant thought. Nate's paying attention to the finer points. Housekeeping was important. You made the place neat and clean for the next guys to come out here. And they did the same for you. Grant wondered if cowhands in America's Old West did the same with their frontier shacks.

Turning, he looked at the big tube of the telescope. It rose like some ancient tower, canted over slightly, the huge mirror and frame at its base serving as an anchor to keep it from tipping too far. The Leaning Tower of Mendeleev, he thought.

"I'm getting into my suit now," Oberman called. Grant sighed to himself, then said, "Okay, I'll come in to check you out as soon as I finish preflight on the hopper."

"You haven't checked out the bird yet?"

"Not yet. Just starting."

"Jeez, you said you were ready to haul ass."

"I am. Preflight only takes a couple of minutes," Grant said, starting to feel irritated.

"Unless you find something wrong," Oberman added.

Yeah, Grant replied silently. Unless I find something wrong.

Professor Uhlrich got up from his chair, went around his desk, and brushed the fingertips of both his hands against his special tactile wall screen, which displayed the spectrum of the red giant star Betelgeuse.

"Impressive resolution," he murmured.

"That's the carbon monoxide line," Trudy said, barely able to stay in her chair at the conference table.

"And this," Uhlrich said as his fingers moved across the glow of colors and dark absorption lines, "this is . . . ?"

"Formaldehyde!" Trudy burst.

"No! It can't be. Not in Betelgeuse's photosphere."

"I checked the reference spectrum twice last night and again this morning," Trudy said. "It's formaldehyde, all right."

"Incredible. A complex organic in the photosphere of Betelgeuse."

She had never seen the professor look so pleased. He gazed right at her, smiling, absently stroking his trim silver-gray beard.

"We must write a paper on this," Uhlrich said. "And we must send an online message to *International Astrophysics Letters* with the raw data, to establish precedence. Then we will write a full paper for the journal."

Agreeing eagerly, Trudy added, "I think we can detect Sirius C's atmosphere directly and get spectra on it."

"Yes! Of course!"

Uhlrich returned to his desk, as sure-footed and confident as if he were sighted, his face beaming.

As he sat at his desk again, the professor recited, "First results from the Farside Observatory's hundred-meter optical telescope. That will be the title of our message to *IAL*."

Our message, Trudy thought. I'll write the paper and he'll put his name on it. In front of mine. Doesn't matter. He's in charge here, he's got the prerogative. Everybody'll know I did the work.

"I'll send out the tweet right away," she said.

"And mention Sirius C, as well," Uhlrich commanded. "Spectroscopic analysis of the atmosphere around the planet will be a spectacular feather in our cap."

Trudy nodded happily. "You bet!" She pushed her chair back from the conference table, then hesitated.

"Is there something else?" Uhlrich asked.

"Something . . ." Trudy started. "Something I've been wanting to ask you."

"What is it?"

"It's . . . personal," she warned.

"Yes?"

Trudy bit her lip, then finally said, "It's about how you perceive the world around you. I mean . . . I know your sight is gone, but . . . you get around so well, you don't let your blindness stop you in any way. I think you're very courageous, sir."

Uhlrich looked mildly surprised. "Why, thank you, Trudy. I do the best I can."

"Can I ask you . . . how do you see me? I mean, do you actually know what I look like?"

He smiled slightly. "How do you know that one sighted person sees the same image of you as another one does? That's why we describe spectra in terms of wavelength, rather than color, isn't it?"

"I suppose," said Trudy.

"Your impression of the color red might not be the same as, say, Mr. McClintock's. There's no way for another person to know what it looks like inside your head, is there?"

"No, I guess not."

Steepling his fingertips, Uhlrich went on, "But, to get back to your original question, I have a distinct image of your face in my mind. Your dossier includes a verbal description, which the auditory center of my brain sends to my visual cortex. I know that you have green eyes, light brown hair, a roundish facial structure. My visual cortex has created a picture of that face for me."

"But how much detail do you see?" Trudy asked, hoping she wasn't intruding too far.

"Enough to tell me that you are quite a lovely young woman," said Uhlrich, his voice strangely hushed.

Suddenly Trudy felt embarrassed. "Oh! Thank you. I guess I should get out of your hair and go write that message to the *IAL*."

She hurried out of the professor's office, leaving Uhlrich smiling benignly from behind his desk.

Grant realized that he half expected a problem with the hopper, another glitch caused by nanomachines. But the bird checked out almost perfectly: a slightly lower voltage than normal from the fuel cells was the only anomaly and even that was too trivial to worry about.

He climbed down from the hopper and trudged toward the shelter's airlock.

Could the nanos have come from me? he asked himself for the thousandth time. I don't remember touching the tractor's dewar. But I did check out Winston's suit before he left for Mendeleev. Could I have infected him with rogue nanos? Kris says it's impossible, but the nanobugs got into his suit *somehow*. How?

He cycled through the airlock and saw that Oberman had already donned the lower half of his space suit and was holding the hard-shell torso in his hands, ready to lift it over his head.

"Almost ready, Grant," said Oberman.

"Let me give you a hand," Grant said, as he took off his helmet.

"I can do it myself."

Oberman slid the shell down his torso. Once his head came through the collar he wriggled his arms through the sleeves. Grant picked up the life-support pack and attached it to the fittings on the suit's back.

"Hopper check out okay?" Oberman asked as he pulled on his gloves.

"Fuel cell's voltage is a tad low. Nothing to worry about."

"Batteries okay?"

Grant nodded, then realized Nate couldn't see him because he was still behind the man, checking the connections between the backpack and the suit.

"The batteries are fully charged. We could make it back to Selene, almost, if we had to."

"Not on a lousy hopper," Oberman said.

"I said almost."

Once Oberman sealed his helmet to the suit's neck ring, Grant insisted on a radio test.

Looking sour, Oberman asked, "You want to go outside to check the stupid radio?"

Grant reached for his helmet. "Not a bad idea. I'll go out and call you."

"Whatever," said Oberman.

Ten minutes later the two men were standing on the hopper's open platform, hurtling across the barren lunar landscape, heading back to Farside.

And Grant was still wondering if somehow he was responsible for Winston's death.

ALTERNATIVES

B ut how could the nanomachines have gotten into the man's space suit?" Professor Uhlrich demanded.

McClintock answered with another question. "And into the motor of that tractor?"

Uhlrich sat rigidly erect behind his desk. His brain's visual cortex created a picture of McClintock based on the smoothly urbane sound of his voice: tall, handsome, slim, and self-assured. The image reminded Uhlrich of a video star he had seen years ago, a smiling rogue of a lady's man.

"Dr. Cardenas believes they were planted deliberately," Uhlrich muttered.

"Actually, she said they *might have* been planted deliberately. She didn't rule out an accidental situation."

Uhlrich drummed his fingers on his desktop. "Deliberate or accident, someone planted those nanomachines. Who? And why?"

He sensed McClintock's shrug. "Damned if I know."

"We must find out."

"How?"

"We must enlist Dr. Cardenas's help. After all, she is the leading expert on nanotechnology."

"But she's leaving to return to Selene on the next lobber flight."

Shaking his head forcefully, Uhlrich said, "She mustn't leave! You must convince her to stay here."

McClintock thought about the disappointing dinner he'd had with Cardenas the previous night. Getting her to stay might not be altogether a bad idea, he said to himself. It could give me another chance at her.

He asked Uhlrich, "And just how do I do that? If she wants to go I can't stop her. Unless you want me to kidnap her."

"Don't be ridiculous," Uhlrich snapped. "You must convince her of the seriousness of our problem. I'm sure she'll agree to stay and help us once she understands."

Sounding utterly unconvinced, McClintock said, "She understands the seriousness, all right. That's why she's flying back to Selene."

Uhlrich's temper seethed. But he kept it under control. *I can't afford to alienate this dilettante. He holds the purse strings.*

So Uhlrich changed the subject. "Have you made a decision about investing your trust's funds in the Farside Observatory?"

A long hesitation. Then, in a slippery, evasive tone, McClintock said, "It's my father's trust. He controls the money."

"But he will base his decision on your recommendation, no?"

With a nod, McClintock answered, "I don't see how I can make that decision until we discover the source of the nanomachines."

Before Uhlrich could respond, McClintock went on, "I mean, you might have an actual saboteur in the facility. It wouldn't be prudent to sink the trust's funds into a facility that might be destroyed by—"

"Destroyed?" Uhlrich thundered.

"It's a possibility, isn't it? If you have someone here who deliberately infected that tractor and the space suit with destructive nanos, what's to stop him from wiping out your whole facility and killing everyone here?"

"My god, man," Uhlrich breathed.

"I've got to tell you, Professor, if there's another incident with nanobugs, I intend to leave Farside and return home."

Without granting me any of your trust's funding, Uhlrich added silently. *I'll be ruined. All my dreams will turn to dust and ashes.*

"You can't do that," the professor said, his voice pleading.

His tone flat and sure, McClintock replied, "It would be the prudent thing to do, Professor. In fact, I think you should have your staff prepare an evacuation plan. Just in case."

"No!" Uhlrich snapped. "That would start a panic."

"Better a panic than a catastrophe," said McClintock.

CAFETERIA

reshly showered, his hair and beard neatly combed, Grant walked briskly through Farside's central corridor from his quarters toward the cafeteria.

He had thought about knocking on Trudy's door on the way, but decided against it. Trudy had said she'd meet him in the cafeteria and he was content to leave things that way. This dinner is her idea, don't push it. We're just having a friendly dinner together, don't make more of it than is really there.

The cafeteria was crowded with people lining up at the dispensing machines and staking out territorial claims at the long tables.

And there was Trudy, sitting at the far end of the farthest table, chatting with Josie Rivera and Harvey Henderson. The place opposite Trudy was empty. Obviously she was saving it for him.

She jumped to her feet when she spotted Grant approaching. He said hello to Harvey and Josie, who gave him a sidelong glance and a smile that Grant thought was damned close to being a smirk.

As he sat opposite Trudy, Grant asked, "Am I late?" over the buzz of two dozen conversations.

"No, I got here early to make sure we'd get seats together," said Trudy.

"You look all slicked up, Grant," Josie said, her voice purring. "You clean up nice."

He forced a grin. "Yeah, I take a shower every month, whether I need it or not."

They all laughed, and then the four of them went through

the lines at the dispensing machines together. Trudy pulled an in-vitro steak dinner for herself and Grant did the same. Harvey complained that it was the last steak dinner in the machine but Josie told him the next machine still had plenty of soysteaks.

"That's okay, I'll take the soy veal cutlet, instead," Harvey said good-naturedly.

"They all taste pretty much the same," said Josie.

Trudy dominated their dinner conversation, bubbling about Sirius C and its atmosphere.

"The team at the Southern Hemisphere Observatory, in the Andes, made an indirect observation of the planet's atmosphere," she told them. "When Sirius C transited across the star's disc they saw that the planet's edge was fuzzy, not sharp the way it would be if it was airless."

Grant watched the animation of her childlike face, the excitement and sheer delight she took in her work. Harvey nodded in the right places, but put most of his attention into shoveling food into his mouth. Josie's eyes flicked back and forth from Trudy to Grant, and she smiled knowingly.

She thinks Trudy and I are involved, Grant realized. And with an inner jolt he thought, Maybe we are. Or will be.

"But with the 'scope out at Mendeleev I detected the planet's atmosphere directly," Trudy announced proudly. "First shot out of the box, I got it!"

"You saw clouds or something?" Josie asked, hunching toward her.

"No, not imagery," Trudy said. "We'll need the other two 'scopes working together before we can produce imagery."

"Then what?"

Speaking slowly, deliberately, as if she were making a case before a judge and jury, Trudy said, "I got absorption spectra of water vapor . . . and oxygen! Very strong oxygen lines. The planet's atmosphere must be like eighteen, twenty percent oxygen. Just like Earth!"

Even Harvey looked up from his plate. "Just like Earth?"

"Within spitting distance of each other," said Trudy. "Sirius C is really just like Earth! The news media are right. It's New Earth!"

"Wow," Josie said.

"And there's more to it than that," Trudy went on eagerly. "That much oxygen in the planet's atmosphere means the atmosphere is way out of chemical equilibrium."

Henderson looked at her quizzically.

"On Earth the oxygen in our atmosphere comes from green plants. Without living plants the oxygen would disappear from the atmosphere in less than a millennium, an eyeblink, geologically speaking."

Grant broke in. "That means that there must be photosynthetic plant life on New Earth."

Bobbing her head up and down, Trudy agreed. "There must be at least some plant life on Sirius C. Or something like it that's continuously pumping oxygen into the atmosphere."

"Hot damn," said Josie.

Grant smiled at Trudy. "Congratulations. Uhlrich must be delirious."

"He's pretty damned happy," Trudy agreed.

Once they finished dinner, Grant walked Trudy back to her quarters and she invited him in.

"I'm too excited to sleep," she said happily as Grant stepped into her room. It was tidy and clean, the bed made up neatly, nothing out of place.

"I, uh . . . I can't stay long," Grant heard himself say. "Lots to do tomorrow."

"Me too," said Trudy. She crossed the room and went to the kitchenette. "You want something to drink, Grant? Coffee, tea, fruit juice?"

"Juice, I guess," he said, heading for the sofa.

She poured two glasses of orange juice. "Fresh from Selene's hydroponics farm," she said as she carried them to the coffee table and sat beside Grant.

He smiled at her, but her face went serious. "All right now, what's the real reason why you didn't want me to go out to Mendeleev?"

Grant blinked with surprise. She's like a Gila monster: she won't let go.

A pretty nice-looking Gila monster, he told himself as he looked at her.

"It's like I told you, Trudy. I can work outside. I've got the experience; you don't. It's that simple."

"And you've got nanobugs in your body to protect you," she said, almost whispering.

Nodding solemnly, he said, "Yep. They're allowing me to cut down on the steroids and the anti-radiation meds."

"Steroids are harmful in the long run, aren't they?"

"They can be, yeah."

"I'm glad you're getting off them."

"Me too," Grant replied. "The side effects can be pretty bad."

"Like 'roid rage?"

"You heard about that too, eh?"

Trudy nodded solemnly. "You had quite a reputation. I heard you got into a fight once with three other guys and beat up all three of them."

"And spent a week in the infirmary getting my ribs to heal up," he said, trying to make it sound light.

Trudy didn't smile.

"That was when I first got here," Grant said, as if that explained anything. "When I was young and foolish."

"And now?" she prompted.

"Now I take aromatase inhibitors," he said. "They cut down on the aggressive feelings that the steroids cause. I'm not a victim of 'roid rage anymore."

"And the nanobugs," she said.

Grant laughed uneasily. "And the nanobugs," he admitted.

"But why?" Trudy asked. "Why endanger yourself?"

"Kris Cardenas says the nanomachines won't cause any

harmful side effects. I'll just have to keep on taking them, that's all."

"But why?" she repeated.

"So that I can work outside, work better and longer than anybody else. That's what counts. That's how I got the job here at Farside. The Ulcer doesn't have the budget for a big staff; he needed somebody who could ride herd on a small team of techie types. Once he found out about the meds I was taking he wasn't pleased. Looked like he wanted to puke. I thought he was going to fire me. But I get the work done and that's what counts. He needs me and he hasn't regretted keeping me on."

"But he doesn't know about your nanos."

"Not yet," Grant said. And he wondered all over again if somehow the nanomachines in his body were the cause of Winston's death.

In a very small voice Trudy said, "I'm glad the professor's kept you on."

"Really?"

"You came out and rescued me, remember? You're officially a hero, as far as I'm concerned."

For a long moment Grant stared into her cool green eyes, unsure of what was going on behind them. Then he broke the spell by reaching for his glass of juice. Trudy picked up hers and they clinked glasses.

"*Ad astra*," Grant said.

"To the stars," Trudy translated.

They sipped, then Grant put his glass down and got up from the sofa.

"Big day tomorrow," he muttered.

Trudy stood up beside him. She's no taller than my shoulder, he realized. A little elf. A kid.

"Do you have to go so soon?" she asked.

"If I stay I'll probably make a fool of myself and get you angry with me."

"I won't be angry, Grant," she whispered.

He didn't know what to say, what to do. He stood there mute, paralyzed, awash in conflicting emotions. Don't get yourself involved, a voice in his head warned. This is too small a facility for personal relationships. Yet the visceral need was there, he could feel it surging through his body.

"After all," Trudy said, sliding her arms around his neck, "you're not going to go berserk, are you? You've got the 'roid rage under control, haven't you?"

"I . . . think so."

She giggled. "Maybe not under total control?"

He grasped her about the waist and pulled her slim body to him. "Maybe not. We'll see."

It was in bed, when they were both pleasantly drained and weary, that Trudy asked him, "With the nanos, you'll be able to stop the steroids altogether?"

"That's what Kris Cardenas says."

"That's good, Grant," she said sleepily. "I'm happy for you."

And Grant felt happy, too. For the first time since he'd fled from Earth, he felt happy.

INVESTIGATION

've got to *what*?" Grant blurted.

McClintock had welcomed Grant into his office and, instead of going back to his desk, sat Grant down at the little round table in the corner of the room and pulled up a chair beside him.

"You've got to find out who infected the Mendeleev site with those nanomachines," McClintock said smoothly.

Grant studied the man's amiably smiling face.

"*I've* got to find out?" Grant asked. "Why me? I'm no detective."

His smile fixed in place, McClintock ticked off points on his fingers as he explained, "One: the nanomachines didn't get there by themselves. Someone planted them at Mendeleev, whether by accident or design. Two: the only people who've been at the site are *your* people, engineers and technicians. Three: you know them better than Professor Uhlrich or I do; you work with them every day."

McClintock leaned back in his chair and spread his arms as if he'd proven his case. "That makes you the logical person to find out who brought the nanos to Mendeleev."

Grant started to snap off a reply, but hesitated, thinking, Whenever they have a dirty job they stick me with it. He looked around the room, at the softly glowing wall screens, all of them blank except for the one behind McClintock's desk, which displayed a pastel painting of a leafy green glen half a million kilometers away. The desk itself was a standard-issue metal one but so new there wasn't a scuff mark on it. Its top was clear, bare. No work being done there, Grant thought.

Focusing back on McClintock, Grant countered, "One: if the person who carried the nanomachines to Mendeleev did it unknowingly, he—"

"Or she," McClintock interjected.

"Or she," Grant conceded. "Whoever it was, he or she won't be able to tell us anything if he or she didn't know he or she did it."

Before McClintock could reply, Grant went on, "And two: if the person did it deliberately he—or she—certainly isn't going to admit it."

"I suppose not," McClintock agreed.

"So how in hell am I supposed to find out anything?"

His face growing serious, McClintock said, "I'm not a detective, either, Grant. But we've got to find out who's responsible for your technician's death, and you're the man who knows your crew best. It's up to you."

"Why don't you ask Selene to send some—"

"No!" McClintock snapped. "The professor has absolutely forbidden us to ask for help from Selene. This is our problem and we've got to solve it for ourselves."

"I don't understand why."

"Because he doesn't want Selene shutting down Farside, that's why."

Grant muttered, "Better to shut down this facility than to have more people killed."

Pointing a finger in Grant's face, McClintock said sternly, "This is your responsibility, Grant. The fate of this facility and everybody here depends on you."

Terrific, Grant thought. Now they want me to be Sherlock Holmes.

Aloud, though, he said to McClintock. "I'll see what I can do. But I'm not promising anything."

McClintock beamed at him, pleased. "Just do your best, Grant. I'm sure you'll be able to crack this problem."

Grant got to his feet and McClintock did likewise.

Putting out his hand, McClintock said, "We're depending on you, Grant. All of us."

Grant took the proffered hand reluctantly. "I'll try," he said.

Where to start? Grant asked himself as he headed back to the teleoperations center. Most of the Farside staff were members of his crew, forty-eight engineers and technicians, plus another dozen and a half working on Cyclops. The rest were clerks, paper shufflers, maintenance personnel, and other workmen. There was Dr. Kapstein, Farside's one-person medical staff. And Trudy Yost, the only astronomer on-site, except for Uhlrich himself. And McClintock.

Sitting at an unused console in the dimly lit chamber, Grant scrolled through the names. Not Uhlrich and not McClintock, he said to himself. I can scratch them off right away.

Whoever did it had to have been at Mendeleev at one time or another, Grant realized. How many of my people have even been out there?

But then he thought, Suppose somebody planted the nanos on one of the guys going out to Mendeleev? It could've been anybody on my crew!

It could've been me, he thought. No matter what Kris says, I might have planted the nanos on Win when I checked out his suit.

He decided to call Kris Cardenas.

Kristine Cardenas was in her quarters, her travelbag on the bed, packed and almost ready to be zipped up for the return flight to Selene. Carter McClintock had phoned and asked to see her before she left.

As soon as McClintock stepped into her room, he took one glance at the travelbag and said, "I've come to ask you to stay, Kris."

"Stay? I can't stay, Carter," she said.

He tried to smile but it looked forced. "We have a crisis on our hands here. A real crisis. We need your help."

She shook her head. "I can't stay away from my lab indefinitely. I've got a big design conference with Anita Halleck's people tomorrow."

"It won't be indefinitely," he countered. "Probably just a few more days."

Cardenas started zipping up her bag. "I've got to be back at Selene tomorrow morning. I'll be available on the phone and by computer link. I can answer your questions from Selene just as well as I can from here."

McClintock frowned slightly. "Look . . . Kris. It's not me. It's Professor Uhlrich. The poor man's in a panic. He needs you to stay here and help us find out what's going on."

"Nothing's going on," she said. "You've decontaminated that shelter, haven't you? That's the end of your problem."

"But how did the nanos get there? Who planted them there? *That's* our problem."

"What do you expect me to do about it?"

Waving a hand in the air, McClintock replied, "I don't know. But you're the expert on nanotech and this is a nanotech problem."

Hefting the bag, Cardenas said, "No, Carter. It's a human problem. Either a fool or a madman planted disassemblers in that shelter. The nanomachines were merely his weapon of choice. It's exactly the same as if he'd planted a land mine."

"But—"

She brushed past him, heading for the door. "I'm going back to Selene, Carter. You can talk to me anytime you want to—from there."

G rant sat at one of the consoles and put in a call to Dr. Cardenas. The teleoperations center was quietly busy with two teams of techs monitoring the robots' construction work at Korolev and Gagarin, while a third team huddled around Trudy Yost, who was happily operating the Mendeleev telescope.

In the bud-sized microphone he had wormed into his ear, Grant heard the phone say, "Dr. Cardenas is unavailable."

"Is she in her quarters?" Grant asked, keeping his voice low enough so that he wouldn't disturb the others.

The phone's softly feminine voice replied, "Dr. Cardenas is unavailable."

Privacy protocol, Grant realized. There're no surveillance cameras in the rooms, only out in the corridors and workplaces. He asked for the surveillance command system and quickly scanned through the camera views.

And there was Kristine Cardenas, marching determinedly along the main corridor with her travelbag in one hand, looking taut, almost angry. McClintock was striding along beside her, talking nonstop, gesticulating with both hands.

She's heading for the landing pad, Grant realized. He called up the transportation program and saw that a lobber was due in from Selene in twenty minutes. Kris is heading back to Selene and McClintock's trying to talk her out of it.

Grant pulled his earbud out, got up from the console, and

headed for the reception area. The three teleoperations teams sitting at the other consoles barely noticed him leaving.

I can't talk to her while McClintock's yammering away at her, Grant told himself. I've got to see her alone.

He hustled down the corridor, actually passing Cardenas and McClintock along the way. He nodded a hello to them as he went by. Kris gave him a tight smile, McClintock didn't even blink, he was so intensely pleading with her.

Nate Oberman was at the desk in the reception area, looking bored, his chair tipped back and his soft-booted feet on the desktop. Watching a video. When he saw Grant enter the little room Oberman scrambled to his feet, looking surprised and a little guilty.

"Relax, Nate," said Grant. "I've got to get into that lobber as soon as it sits down on the pad. Before they begin unloading."

"Okay," Oberman said uncertainly.

"Let me use your phone, please."

"Sure." Oberman cleared his screen, then stepped away from the desk. "Be my guest."

Grant called the flight monitor and asked her to patch him through to the pilot of the incoming lobber. Grant recognized the pilot once his beefy face showed on the phone screen.

"Hey, Grant, how're they hangin', buddy?"

"Fine, Derek. And you?"

"Gonna be busy landing this bird in a coupla minutes."

"I understand. Look, I need to come aboard as soon as you land. Before you start unloading cargo."

"You goin' back with us?"

"No, I just need a few minutes with your outbound passenger."

The pilot frowned with puzzlement. "She's right there at your facility, isn't she? Whyn't you talk to her there?"

Making himself smile, Grant replied, "Long story. I'll chat with her aboard your ship while you're unloading, if it's okay with you. I won't delay your departure."

"Okay by me, long's we get out on time. My boss is a stickler for keeping to schedule."

Clicking off, Grant turned back to Oberman. "I'll run the access tube, Nate. You can stay at the desk."

Oberman's lean face looked curious, but he said only, "You're the boss."

Grant went to the airlock hatch and quickly scanned the controls for the tube that would connect the airlock to the hatch of the lobber, once it landed. Behind him, he heard Cardenas and McClintock enter the area. Actually, he only heard McClintock talking nonstop, more and more frantic with each sentence. He was talking to Kris, Grant knew, but she wasn't saying a word back to him.

On the control console's minuscule screen Grant saw the lobber settle down on the blast-blackened landing pad, silently blowing a spray of dust and pebbles across the barren, pitted ground. He worked the access tube out to the ship, watched it groping its way like a blind giant caterpillar and finally connecting to the lobber's main airlock hatch.

As soon as the console's lights flashed green, Grant opened the airlock hatch and sprinted along the tube to the ship. The man at the other end, in the sky-blue uniform of Selene's transportation department, eyed him curiously.

"What's the rush?" he asked.

"I don't want to get in your way," Grant said, heading for the empty passenger compartment.

He saw the ship's pilot clambering down the ladder from the cockpit and got an idea. "Hello, Derek."

The pilot's face was fleshier and ruddier than it had looked in the comm screen. "Welcome aboard, Grant," he said.

"Dr. Cardenas is your only passenger on the flight out, right?" Grant asked.

With a curt nod, the pilot said, "Unless you people make a last-minute addition."

Shaking his head, Grant said, "No, no additions. In fact,

there's a guy with Dr. Cardenas who'll probably try to come aboard with her. She doesn't want him to."

"Oh?"

"He's trying to sell her something she doesn't want. I'd appreciate it if you didn't let him come aboard. Dr. Cardenas would appreciate it, too."

The pilot shrugged his heavy shoulders. "Okay, I'll stop him at the hatch."

"Great. Thanks." Grant climbed up into the passenger compartment while the pilot went to the airlock hatch.

Fidgeting along the thinly carpeted aisle between the empty passenger seats, Grant heard bangs and thumps as Farside's technicians began unloading the lobber's cargo. Food, mostly, Grant knew. And supplies for sixteen different kinds of equipment, from tractors to computer screens.

Kris Cardenas stepped into the passenger compartment, her eyes going wide with surprise when she recognized Grant.

"Are you going to Selene, too?" she asked as she dropped her travelbag onto one of the empty seats.

Grant hurried to her. "No. I need to talk to you for a few minutes, that's all."

Her expression hardened. "Don't tell me you're trying to get me to stay here, too. I told Carter and—"

"No, not that," Grant interrupted. "I just need to ask you . . . is there *any* way that the nanos inside me could have caused the problems out at Mendeleev? Any way at all?"

"Absolutely none," Cardenas said firmly. "You can't blame yourself for what happened, Grant. It's not your fault."

"You're certain?"

"Completely."

Somehow her reassurance didn't make Grant feel any better. He said, "Suppose somebody, somehow, mixed some gobblers in with the nanos you gave me?"

Now Cardenas scowled at him. "Grant, you're getting paranoid."

"But just suppose. Is it possible?"

"No one in my lab would do such a thing."

He agreed with her. He knew she was right. But deep in his gut he was unconvinced.

"Is there some way to check out the possibility?" he asked.

Cardenas huffed impatiently. "I could take a blood sample and examine it."

"Could you do it now? Here?"

"Does your clinic have an atomic force microscope?"

"No, but the maintenance center has a laser probe that can do nanometer resolution."

Looking decidedly unhappy, almost disgusted, Cardenas glanced at her wristwatch.

"You've got an hour before they lift off," Grant coaxed. "You could check my blood and still make it in time."

Cardenas sighed heavily. "I doubt it." But she studied Grant's face for a long moment, then picked up her travelbag and said, "What the hell. Let's see if we can make it."

Grant knew that there wouldn't be another flight in from Selene for three days. We'd better get this done before that lobber takes off, he thought. Otherwise Kris is going to be damned unhappy with me.

eading Cardenas out of the lobber and down the access tube, Grant was relieved to see that McClintock had left the reception area. Derek got rid of him, he thought gratefully as he hurried with Cardenas along the narrow tunnel toward Farside's minuscule infirmary.

Grant phoned the maintenance center as they entered the infirmary and told Toshio Aichi to be ready to test a sample in the laser probe, then he explained what he wanted to a surprised Dr. Kapstein while he rolled up his coverall sleeve. As he sat down for the blood drawing, Cardenas asked:

"If I miss today's flight, when's the next one out?"

Grant swallowed hard, then admitted, "Um . . . three days from now."

"Three days?" she yelped.

"I'm afraid so."

Glaring at him, Cardenas said, "Well, we'd damned well better get this done quickly. I can't miss today's flight. Anita Halleck's people expect me to be in my lab for a design conference about their mirrors."

Wielding a needle, Dr. Kapstein said, "This will only take a moment."

"Three days," Cardenas muttered while Grant flinched at the needle's prick. "We'd better make today's flight. I can't hang around here for another three days."

"I appreciate this very much," Grant said, by way of an apology.

Clutching the vial of his dark red blood, Grant hustled Cardenas down to the maintenance center and introduced her to Aichi and Zacharias.

He explained what they needed and the two techs walked them down to the far corner of the center, where the laser probe was already humming. Grant saw from the digital clock on the probe's readout screen that they had forty-seven minutes before the lobber was set to lift off.

As Aichi and Zacharias adjusted the laser, Toshio asked, "We are looking for nanomachines?" His face was impassive but his tone clearly uneasy.

"That's right," said Grant, his eyes on the bead of bright red blood that Cardenas had smeared onto the probe's specimen stage.

Zacharias's butterball face suddenly went somber. "Grant, you've got nanomachines inside you?"

He nodded tightly.

"Cheez," said Zach, with awe in his voice. "I didn't know." He edged slightly away from Grant.

"It's only been a month or so," Grant said.

Toshio said, "Am I correct in believing that you also carry nanomachines within you, Dr. Cardenas?"

"That's no secret," Cardenas replied.

"Cheez," Zacharias repeated.

The wall screen to the right of the workbench lit up and Grant stared at the sight of dozens of little blobs racing back and forth.

"Not the sharpest resolution," Cardenas murmured.

"It's the best we can do," said Aichi.

"Those are nanos?" Zacharias asked.

"Yes," said Cardenas. "They are programmed to disassemble molecules that don't carry Grant's specific genetic markers."

"Any molecules?" Grant asked.

"Only organics," answered Cardenas. "And only within the specific environment of your body. If any of those nanos get outside your body they will automatically deactivate themselves. They're tailored to your body, Grant. They'll switch themselves off in any other environment."

Grant glanced at his wristwatch. Twenty-four minutes to liftoff.

"How can you tell if there are any other types of nanomachines in my blood?" Grant asked.

Frowning at the display screen, Cardenas replied, "I can't. Not at this resolution. But . . ."

Standing beside her, Grant peered at the screen. He could feel Toshio and Zach behind him, literally breathing down his neck.

"What am I supposed to be seeing?" he asked.

Cardenas murmured, "Wait . . . just a minute or so more. . . ."

The frantic little specks on the screen were slowing down. As Grant watched, the blobs that were nanomachines moved more and more sluggishly. Finally they stopped altogether.

Nodding as if satisfied, Cardenas said, "That's it. They're deactivated."

"They're dead?" Zach asked.

"Deactivated," Cardenas corrected. Turning to Grant she said, "You see? Once the nanos are outside your body, no longer powered by your body heat, they shut down."

Grant was still staring at the screen. The specks that were nanomachines were totally inert now, unmoving.

"Are you satisfied, Grant?" Cardenas asked. "Do you feel better now?"

He broke into a guarded smile. "Yeah, I guess I do."

"All right, then," Cardenas said. "Let's get to that rocket!"

Grabbing her by the wrist, Grant raced out of the maintenance center, leaving Aichi and Zacharias staring at them, dumbfounded.

As they sprinted along the corridor, Grant flicked his pocketphone open and called the flight control monitor.

"They're on schedule," Josie Rivera said.

"Find a reason to delay their liftoff for a few minutes, will you, Jo?"

"A reason? You mean, like make up some excuse for delaying them? I can't do that, Grant. You know I can't do that. The Ulcer would fry my butt if he found out. Flight control at Selene would go ballistic!"

"Just a couple of minutes," Grant pleaded, puffing as he ran. "Dr. Cardenas doesn't want to miss the flight."

Josie's dark-eyed face looked stubborn in the phone's tiny screen. "I'll see what I can do," she said, in a tone that Grant knew meant that she would do nothing.

They skidded into the reception area, startling Nate Oberman so badly he dropped the mug of juice he'd been sipping. It spilled across the desk.

". . . eight . . . seven . . ." The automated countdown sounded in the speakers set into the stone ceiling.

Grant stood by Oberman's desk, chest heaving, Cardenas panting beside him. Ten seconds too late, he thought. Ten frigging seconds.

"Dammit," Cardenas muttered.

". . . two . . . one . . . liftoff."

The wall screen showed the lobber hurtling off the launchpad in a silent blast of dust and pebbles. The pilot's voice confirmed, "Liftoff on schedule. Bye-bye, Farside."

"Confirm liftoff," Josie Rivera said. "Have a good flight, Derek."

"See you in three days, kiddo."

"I'll be waiting for you."

The automated camera out by the landing pad was tracking the lobber as it climbed higher and higher into the star-filled black sky.

"Pressure drop!" the copilot's voice yelled.

In the wall screen's display the lobber suddenly blossomed into a glaring ball of white-hot flame. Grant could see pieces of the rocket hurtling across the sky, falling slowly, gently, spinning lazily like children's toys.

One of the pieces was the body of a man, Derek or his copilot. Frozen in horror, Grant watched the guy's arms and legs flailing as he screamed in the utter silence of the lunar vacuum all the way down to the hard, barren ground.

A PLAGUE OF NANOMACHINES

G rant couldn't move. He stared at the display screen as the fireball that had been a lobber dissipated and pieces of the rocket fell bouncing to the ground.

"It . . . it . . ." Cardenas's voice was choked, gasping.

"It blew up," Nate Oberman said, his voice a hollow whisper.

"Oh, my god." Cardenas began to sob.

Turning toward her, Grant took both of her hands in his. It took him three tries before he found his voice. "Are you okay?"

Her eyes filled with tears, Cardenas nodded as she pulled in a deep, shuddering breath. "I might have been on it," she whispered. "I might have . . ."

"You weren't on it," Grant said firmly, "and you're alive. You're okay."

She said nothing, simply stared at him.

Josie Rivera's voice came through the overhead speakers. "It's gone. It . . . it . . ."

Raising his voice, Grant said, "Better call Selene, Josie, tell them what happened."

"Yeah, right." Her voice sounded weak, dazed. "But how did it happen? How did it happen?"

That's what we've got to find out, Grant told himself. But first I've got to tell Uhlrich about it.

.   .   .

Grant walked Cardenas back to the quarters that had been assigned to her.

"Will you be okay by yourself? I can get somebody to stay with you."

Her eyes red but dry now, Cardenas said calmly, "I'm all right. It was . . . a shock. But I'm all right now."

"Good. I'll look in on you in a while. Right now, I've got a lot to do."

"I understand. Go ahead."

Grant left her and started sprinting down the corridor toward Professor Uhlrich's office. As he ran he called Harvey Henderson on his pocketphone.

"Get a crew suited up and go out to pick up the bodies," Grant ordered.

"What's left of 'em," Henderson said grimly.

"Don't touch the debris," Grant continued. "Leave it where it fell. We might be able to establish an idea of the force of the explosion from the debris pattern on the ground."

"Yeah. Right."

He reached Uhlrich's office, rapped on the door once, and slid it open.

The professor was at his desk, as usual, with Trudy Yost sitting at the conference table. One of the wall screens was filled with spectrographic data.

Uhlrich looked annoyed at Grant's interruption; Trudy seemed surprised.

"What do you want, Mr. Simpson?"

"There's been an accident, Professor."

"An accident?"

"The lobber from Selene. It exploded on liftoff."

"What?" Uhlrich shot to his feet.

"The two men in the crew were killed. Dr. Cardenas wasn't aboard it, though. She's okay."

"It exploded? How? Why?"

"That's what we'll have to find out," said Grant. "The flight monitoring people have all the telemetered data from the vehicle. I think the copilot said something about a pressure drop just before she blew up."

Uhlrich slumped back into his chair and stared sightlessly at Grant.

"It blew up?" he asked, his voice a thin, pitiful whine.

Grant looked at Trudy. She seemed shocked, distraught.

"I'll get down to the flight control center and see what the telemeter record can tell us," Grant said.

Uhlrich shook his head in misery. "Selene will send investigators. They'll get in our way, poking and probing everywhere. Just when we're starting to get results from the first telescope, they'll ruin everything."

"Professor, two men were killed. Of course Selene will want to investigate."

"They'll ruin everything, everything," Uhlrich moaned.

Trudy suggested, "Maybe I could go out to Mendeleev and work the telescope from there, out of their way."

"No!" Grant snapped.

She turned toward him. "Why not?"

"You'll be safer here."

"Safer?" Uhlrich demanded. "Safe from what?"

"Nanomachines," said Grant. As he spoke the word he realized that his deepest fear was looming before him. "I think this place is infested with destructive nanomachines."

"That's insane!" Uhlrich roared. "You're insane!"

"Face the facts, Professor. Winston was killed at Mendeleev. Now the lobber blows up."

"There is no evidence that nanomachines destroyed the lobber," Uhlrich insisted. "None at all!"

"They killed Winston and now they've blown up the lobber," Grant countered stubbornly.

Leveling a finger at Grant, Uhlrich seethed, "If you mention nanomachines to anyone outside this room I'll fire you! I'll send you packing, Simpson!"

"Send me where? Do you think Selene or anyplace else will take somebody from a site that might be infested with a plague of nanomachines?"

QUARANTINED

Trudy watched Grant leave the office, sliding the door shut with a heavy thud. She turned to Professor Uhlrich and saw him seated at his desk, his head in his hands.

"I'm ruined," Uhlrich moaned. "Utterly ruined."

Without thinking about it, Trudy got up from her chair, went around the professor's desk, and knelt at his side.

"It might not be that bad, Professor," she said, her voice soft, tender.

"They'll stop our work, I know they will," Uhlrich said. "Just when we were starting to get significant results . . ." His voice trailed off.

Trying to make him feel better, Trudy said, "I can write up our spectrographic results. We can publish that. First spectra from Sirius C. Oxygen and water vapor in the planet's atmosphere. That'll put Farside's name on the map!"

Uhlrich seemed inconsolable. "What good will that do? We won't be able to make any progress beyond that."

"But it's a breakthrough!" Trudy insisted. "I'll bet it'll impress those guys in Stockholm."

He looked up at her. "The Nobel committee? Do you think so?"

"Certainly. And we won't be shut down for long, I bet. Selene'll send some accident investigators here and soon's they figure out what caused the explosion we'll be back in business."

Uhlrich began to nod. But then he said, "What if Simpson is

right? What if this facility is infected with nanomachines? They'll shut us down, perhaps permanently."

Trudy had no reply for that.

Dog tired after hours of poring over telemeter data, Grant made his way to the cafeteria and blindly punched buttons for a late supper. The cafeteria was almost empty at this time of the night; only a pair of technicians at one of the tables and a lone administrator bent over a digital reader as he sipped at a mug of tea.

Grant carried his tray to the farther end of the table and plunked himself down.

"Mind if I join you?"

He looked up to see Kris Cardenas standing there, holding a dinner tray.

"I didn't see you come in," said Grant.

Cardenas nodded as she sat beside him. "You seemed totally wrapped up in your own thoughts."

Grant said, "Yeah."

"Tough day."

"Yeah."

"I've made arrangements to meet with Halleck's engineers from here," she said. "We'll do the conference electronically instead of in the flesh."

"Good." Grant stuck a fork in the plate before him. He had forgotten what it was supposed to be. Some soy derivative or another, masquerading as real food.

"Have you found anything?" Cardenas asked quietly.

With a halfhearted shrug, Grant answered, "Looks like the oxygen feed line to the rocket engine gave out. Pure oxygen dumped into the hot exhaust. Boom."

"And what caused the line to fail?"

Grant looked at her. Cardenas seemed wary, as if she expected an answer she didn't really want to hear.

"Don't know yet," he said.

Before she could reply, Grant added, "But the coupling that

connected the feed line to the rocket's combustion chamber was made of the same alloy that our space suit collars are made of."

"The same alloy?"

"Yeah. Some coincidence, eh?"

"What are you saying, Grant?"

He ran a weary hand across his saddened eyes. "The same kind of nanobugs that ate through Winston's space suit collar could have eaten through the oxygen line's coupling."

Cardenas took the news without flinching. "But how could they get there? It's just not likely. It's pretty close to impossible."

"Close only counts in horseshoes," Grant said. "Maybe it is unlikely, but that's what happened, I'm certain of it."

"You're jumping to a conclusion that—"

"Here's another conclusion I've jumped to," he interrupted. "It's not just the shelter at Mendeleev that's been hit by the nanos. We're infected here, right here, at Farside."

"You don't have any evidence for that!"

"Tell that to Derek and his copilot. For chrissakes, Kris, you came within ten seconds of getting killed yourself!"

The two technicians at the other table looked up at the sound of Grant's raised voice. The administrator kept on reading peacefully.

Cardenas stared at Grant for several moments, silent, looking almost resentful.

"We're going to have to quarantine this facility, Kris," Grant said, his voice lower. "Nobody in, nobody out. Not until we find out how those bugs got here. And who brought them."

NANOFEAR

This teleconference is a farce, Cardenas thought. Instead of discussing the design of the space-based telescope mirrors, Halleck's engineers wanted to talk about nothing except the accident.

She was sitting in the recliner in her quarters, facing the wall screen, which showed the three engineers side by side at a table in one of Selene's conference rooms. Two of them were good-looking young men, the third an older woman, portly, matronly, wearing a scarlet red scoop-necked blouse that showed plenty of fatty cleavage. The men had the sense to wear ordinary business attire: dark cardigan jackets over turtleneck shirts.

"There are all sorts of rumors flying around Selene," said one of the young men. He was blond, with pale blue eyes.

"I'm sure there are," Cardenas said, eager to get back to the subject for their meeting.

The other guy, his dark hair shaved down to a fuzz, added, "Selene's sending an accident investigation team to Farside."

Before Cardenas could reply, the woman asked, "Do you think nanomachines could have had anything to do with the accident?"

"That's what everybody's wondering about," said the blond.

Cardenas bit back the sharp denial that was her first instinctive reply. Measuredly, she answered, "That's a possibility that must be investigated, of course. I think it's a remote possibility, but still, the investigators will have to look into it."

The blond went on, "I mean, Farside's using nanos to build their mirrors, after all."

"That," said Cardenas, "is like saying that since Farside is using plasma torches in the construction of the underground facilities here, plasma torches might have caused the rocket's explosion."

"Not really the same, though, is it?" the woman engineer said, with a knowing smile that was almost a sneer.

Cardenas admitted, "Not quite the same, I suppose."

The data bar across the bottom of the wall screen started blinking red, then displayed: ADDITIONAL CALLER, MRS. ANITA HALLECK.

The screen split to show Halleck, looking elegant in a crisply tailored pale chartreuse blouse and with a long fall of chestnut hair draped artfully down one shoulder.

"I'm sorry to interrupt," she said, a slight smile curving her full lips. "I just arrived here at Selene, only to find that you're at Farside, Dr. Cardenas."

Somewhat flustered, Cardenas replied, "I didn't realize you intended to join this conference in person, Mrs. Halleck."

"Oh, yes," Halleck said coolly. "My staff must have failed to make that clear to you."

The three engineers on the other half of the screen looked just as surprised as Cardenas felt.

"Well," Cardenas temporized, "I should be back at Selene in a few days, at most."

Halleck seemed to consider that information for a moment. Then, "I doubt that I can wait that long. But I do want to personally inform you that despite this unfortunate accident at Farside, I intend to press ahead with our construction of the mirrors using nanomachines. I want to make that perfectly clear."

Cardenas sat up straighter. "I'm delighted to hear that, Mrs. Halleck."

"Just because there's been an accident at Farside, there's no reason to delay our own work."

The woman engineer's head bobbed up and down. "Yes, of course." The two male engineers glanced at each other, then they began to nod, too.

Cardenas suppressed a grin. At least Halleck has her head screwed on right, she thought. Now maybe we can get back to work.

Grant was just getting into bed when Trudy called. He started to tell the phone to answer, but hesitated as he realized that he was naked. Hell, she's seen me naked, he thought. Still, he ordered the phone, "Reply audio only."

Trudy's face filled the wall screen. She looked tired, concerned, almost frightened.

"Grant? I'm sorry to call so late. . . ."

"It's all right," he said, sitting on his bed and pulling the sheet up to his waist.

"I'm worried about Professor Uhlrich," she said.

"The Ulcer?"

"Grant, he's terribly concerned," she said earnestly. "He tries not to show it in front of you, but he's worried that this team of investigators coming in from Selene is going to shut us down completely."

"He's worried he won't get the Nobel Prize," Grant replied sourly. "That's the only thing he gives a damn about."

"That's not fair!"

"Isn't it?"

Trudy bit her lip for a moment, then asked, "Can I come over to your place? We need to talk—"

"No!" he snapped.

She looked surprised, hurt.

Agonized, Grant explained, "Look, Trudy, my body's filled with nanomachines. All this trouble might be my fault. I'm not going to risk hurting you. I can't."

"But you said Dr. Cardenas told you it couldn't be your fault."

"Who else? I get injected with nanos at Selene. I come back

here and the tractor engine dies, then Win gets killed, and now the lobber blows up—everything I touch!"

"It's not you, Grant. I know it's not."

He knew he should feel touched at her reaction. Instead he felt almost angry. "And how do you know it's not?" he challenged.

Her face dimpling into a grin, Trudy said, "You've touched me, haven't you? I haven't fallen apart."

Grant shook his head wearily. "Trudy, this isn't a joke."

"But it's true, isn't it?"

"You're not made of metal," Grant said.

"So there's no problem then, is there?" She looked absolutely impish now.

"You can't—"

"I'll be there in five minutes," Trudy said. Then the screen went blank.

SELENE

oug Stavenger was getting into bed next to his wife, who was intently studying a handheld reader.

"Must be pretty interesting," he said, sliding a hand along her naked thigh.

Edith gave him a sidelong glance. "Must be six thousand requests from Earthside news bureaus for interviews with Professor Uhlrich."

"Because of the accident?"

"No," Edith said, finally shutting down the reader and placing it carefully on her night table. "Because of New Earth."

Stavenger felt his brows hike with surprise. "You mean that report Uhlrich released yesterday . . . ?"

Edith snuggled down under the sheet as she replied, "Yep. Not only is New Earth just about the same size as Earth, it's also got an Earth-type atmosphere: oxygen and water vapor."

"And the news media are clamoring for interviews with the professor?"

"They surely are. He's a famous man, all of a sudden."

"They're not asking about the accident?"

"Nope. I guess they figure rockets blow up now and then. That's not news. New Earth's atmosphere is news."

Stavenger said, "Just as well, I suppose."

"Got a lot of requests to visit Farside, interview the professor face-to-face."

"Can't do that," Stavenger said. "The facility is under quarantine."

"What? Since when?"

"Since late this afternoon. There's a possibility that the rocket blowup was caused by nanomachines."

"Holy spit! Nanos?"

"It's a remote possibility, but if Farside is infected, we don't want it to spread here."

"Hell no," Edith said with fervor.

"The council's sending an investigating team over there tomorrow."

"Will Kris Cardenas go with them?"

"Kris is already there," Stavenger said. "She just missed being on the lobber that blew up."

"Lord a-mighty on a bicycle," Edith muttered. "What a news story that's going to make."

"No!" Stavenger snapped. "Not a word to the news media."

"I knew you'd say that!"

"We don't want to start a frenzy. Next thing you know the Luddites back Earthside will start trying to tell us how to run Selene again."

"But we've got all these media folks wanting to interview Uhlrich."

"Let them do it electronically. Nobody's going to Farside."

"Except me," said Edith.

"No, no, no!"

"Yes, yes, yes," she countered. Turning toward him, laying a hand on his bare chest, Edith said, "You can tell the Earthside folks that I'll coordinate their requests for interviews. Tell 'em Farside's too small to accommodate them all, so I'll manage things from there and they can all pool their interviews, just like we did during the war."

"I don't want you going to Farside," Stavenger insisted.

But he knew she would go anyway.

Sitting alone in her VIP suite at the Hotel Luna, Anita Halleck debated calling Carter McClintock while she was visiting Selene.

She had sensed subtle vibes from Carter when she'd seen him at Farside. He's interested, she thought. He's curious to know what his father had.

Chuckling to herself, she thought, It would blow Morgan's mind if he knew his son went to bed with me. It might give the old man a heart attack. That would be poetic justice.

And stupid, she decided. That part of your life is over and done with. No regrets, no looking back. The only part of your life you can shape is the future.

Still, she thought, Morgan's thinking of putting money into Professor Uhlrich's operation. And Carter's at Farside to help his father make the decision. Morgan wants to use Farside to kill my program; that would leave Dan Randolph high and dry, after all the money he's already sunk into it.

So she put through a call to Carter McClintock.

McClintock looked decidedly uneasy when his face appeared on the wall screen of Halleck's sitting room.

"You're on the Moon?" he asked, his handsome face wearing a patently forced smile.

"At Selene, yes," she replied. "I came for a conference with Dr. Cardenas, but apparently she's detained at Farside with you."

"Not with me," he blurted. "She . . . she's working with Professor Uhlrich, you know. Building the mirrors for his telescopes."

"Yes. I'm here to see what progress she's made on the mirrors for my array. If any."

"I'm sure she's doing her best," McClintock said.

"Of course."

"Er . . . how long will you be at Selene?"

"Only a day or so." Halleck hesitated, then plunged, "I thought we might have dinner together while I'm here."

He blinked at that. "I won't be able to get away," he said hurriedly.

"That's all right. I'll come over to Farside. Pay my respects to the professor and all that."

McClintock shook his head. "I'm afraid that won't be possible, Anita."

"And why not?"

"Farside is under a lockdown. The accident with the lobber, you know. Selene's sending an investigation team and no one else is allowed to come in here until they've made their report."

"You're quarantined?"

"Lockdown," he quickly corrected. "No one is allowed into the facility . . . for the time being."

Halleck considered that information for a few moments. Then, "Does that mean we won't be able to get together, Carter?"

Squirming, he replied, "I'm afraid it does."

"Too bad," she teased. "One of the reasons I came all this way was to see you again."

Carter McClintock fell speechless. And Anita Halleck thoroughly enjoyed his distress.

Grant stood in the reception area as the four accident investigators filed through the access tunnel from the lobber that had carried them to Farside.

Three men, all of them in unadorned blue-gray coveralls. Engineers, from the look of them, Grant thought. And one tall, willowy black woman who was obviously their boss. Wearing a sea-green long-sleeved blouse over darker slacks, with a necklace and bracelet of jade, she was strikingly good-looking in a lean, long-limbed way, like a professional athlete.

Even Nate Oberman, at the reception desk, seemed awed by her as the other three new arrivals lined up at his desk.

She ignored Oberman and walked straight to Grant.

"You are Grant Simpson, are you not?" she asked, in an accent that Grant recognized as Bantu.

"That's right," he said. "Professor Uhlrich sent me here to see that your accommodations are comfortable for you."

"I am Latisha Luongo," she said. "I am the head of this investigation team. Could you please take me to Professor Uhlrich?"

"Don't you want to go to your quarters first? Unpack? Freshen—"

"Professor Uhlrich, please," said Luongo. "Business before pleasure, Mr. Simpson."

Trudy Yost sat at one of the consoles in the teleoperations center, watching the data rastering across its central screen. The big display screen on the wall showed a blurry sphere, New Earth. The resolution was poor, but it was the best that Trudy could get from the telescope at Mendeleev.

Josie Rivera was working the console next to Trudy, monitoring the construction robots at Korolev crater. Nate Oberman sat beside her. The other two consoles were unoccupied, dark and silent.

Trudy wondered why Oberman was here at the teleoperations center, instead of his regular post at the reception center. Not that there's much of anything to do at the launchpad since the lockdown. Then she realized, Nate's coming on to Josie!

"The accident team from Selene arrived this morning," Josie said to Oberman.

"Yeah, I checked them in," he replied.

Looking up from her screen, Trudy asked, "Do you think the investigators'll poke in here?"

Oberman shook his head. "Probably not. They're outside gathering up the pieces of the lobber. They're not interested in what we're doing."

"Good," said Trudy.

But Josie said, "I'll bet they do come in here, sooner or later. They'll want to stick their noses into everything."

"Let 'em," said Oberman. "I've got nothing to hide."

Josie gave him a knowing grin. "What about those vids you showed me?"

"That's got nothing to do with their investigation!"

"No," Josie agreed, "but it might be the most interesting thing they see while they're here."

Oberman made a mock scowl at her. Trudy turned her attention back to her work.

Grant spent the day outside, tediously searching for pieces of debris from the wrecked lobber. This must be the way archeologists work, he thought as he spotted another twisted chunk of metal. He carefully photographed it before picking it up and labeling it with an indelible marker. He marked its position on the ground from the GPS satellites' signal, and then deposited it in the cart that trundled faithfully behind him.

The ground around the landing pad was strewn with wreckage. Three of the accident investigators were spread out across the area, gathering pieces. The fourth was inside, reviewing the flight monitor's records of the lobber's liftoff.

The lobber that had brought in the investigating team sat on the pad now, a squat dark cone, like some ancient monument. Archeology, Grant thought again. We've gone from astronomy to archeology.

Walking slowly along the sandy, pockmarked ground, Grant realized that he would have to tell the investigators about his nanomachines. Cardenas says they've got nothing to do with the accident, but I can't keep quiet about it, not if there's one chance in a million that I caused the blowup. One chance in a billion.

He did not look forward to making his confession.

After an hour's session with the quartet of investigators in Uhlrich's office, Carter McClintock made it his business to have dinner with their chief. Just the two of them, in McClintock's quarters.

Latisha Luongo was a couple of centimeters taller than McClintock, lean and long-legged with shiny black skin, big deeply brown eyes, and hair cropped down to a fuzzy skullcap. Not a raving beauty, McClintock thought, but her face was remarkably striking, like some sullen fashion model. And she appeared to be somewhat intelligent and rather shapely beneath her open-necked blouse and snug slacks.

She also seemed quite wary once she realized that this dinner would be for just the two of them.

McClintock offered her a glass of fruit juice as he invited her to sit on the sofa. She accepted the drink and perched on the armchair instead.

"I thought you had invited the others of my team," she said, her voice a rich low contralto.

"Perhaps I should have," McClintock answered easily. "But I thought it would be easier to discuss your work one-on-one."

"I see." She sipped minimally at the juice.

"I'm afraid alcoholic beverages are practically nonexistent here at Farside," he said as he sat on the sofa alone. No sense wasting decent wine on a woman who's here to investigate us, he thought.

"Professor Uhlrich disapproves?"

McClintock made a vague gesture. "Let's say he doesn't encourage it."

Luongo almost smiled.

Getting businesslike, McClintock asked, "How does the nanomachine factor affect your investigation?"

"It's too early to tell," she answered.

"If . . . somehow . . . nanomachines caused the explosion, could your team discover it?"

"You don't have the necessary equipment here. We will have to take the wreckage back to Selene for examination."

"The chief of our technical staff believes that nanomachines might have penetrated the ship's oxygen line."

That sparked her interest. "Does he?"

"It's just a wild idea of his."

"I would like to speak to him about it."

"I could arrange that."

"Now," Luongo said. "I would like to speak with him now."

"But dinner—"

"Dinner can wait," she said. "Please order him to come here at once."

SUMMONED

Grant had just placed his dinner tray on the cafeteria table and sat down between Harvey Henderson and Trudy Yost when the cafeteria's overhead speakers blared, "GRANT SIMPSON, PLEASE COME TO MR. McCLINTOCK'S QUARTERS AT ONCE."

Henderson grinned at him. "You're being summoned to the principal's office, buddy."

Grant glanced at Trudy as he got up from the bench. She looked concerned. "There goes dinner," he complained.

"I can reheat it for you," Trudy said.

Grant realized that she meant she would take his dinner to her quarters. We have can dinner there. And then go to bed.

He made a smile for her. "I'd appreciate that, Trudy."

But as he hurried out of the cafeteria he wondered if it was right to carry on his relationship with her. If I'm the reason why these accidents have happened, if I'm responsible . . . Yet he countered his own fears with the memory of making love with Trudy. I didn't hurt her. My nanomachines didn't have any effect on her. We had a great time together.

Conflicted, he made his way to McClintock's quarters and rapped on his door.

McClintock slid it open and ushered him inside. Grant saw a long-legged black woman in bluish gray coveralls sitting on the armchair next to the sofa, eyeing him curiously.

"Grant, this is Dr. Latisha Luongo, head of the investigating team," said McClintock. "Dr. Luongo, this is Grant Simpson, chief of our technical crew."

Luongo got to her feet. She was taller than Grant by several centimeters. Her face was long and serious, but she made a polite smile and held out her hand to Grant.

"Dr. Simpson," she murmured.

"*Mr.* Simpson," McClintock corrected, before Grant could speak. He felt irked by it.

Luongo resumed her seat, and Grant sat on the recliner, facing her. McClintock went to the sofa, between them. Grant noticed that there were two glasses on the coffee table, but McClintock didn't offer Grant anything to drink.

"Mr. McClintock tells me that you suspect nanomachines have been involved in both accidents," Luongo said, with a slight but discernible stress on the *Mister*.

"Three accidents," Grant said. "We had a superconductor coil fail when it lost its coolant due to a pinhole leak in the dewar. A leak caused by nanomachines."

Luongo's brows rose. "I wasn't aware of that."

"Dr. Cardenas has confirmed that the dewar failure and the failure of Winston's suit were both caused by nanomachines," said Grant.

Luongo glanced at McClintock.

"Dr. Cardenas is here," he said, "if you'd like to talk with her."

"Later," said Luongo. Turning back to Grant, she asked, "How did the nanomachines get into these devices?"

"Now wait," McClintock objected. "There's no evidence that the lobber's failure was caused by nanomachines."

"There will be," Grant said.

"The question remains," Luongo insisted, "how did the nanomachines get there? Are they the same type as you have used to construct your telescope mirror?"

"No," said Grant. "But—"

McClintock interrupted, "We really should have Dr. Cardenas in this discussion."

Luongo nodded solemnly. "I suppose so. Can you call her, please?"

"Before you do," Grant said, surprised at how strong and steady his voice was, "I have something to tell you. I have nanomachines in my body. Dr. Cardenas—"

"You *what?*" McClintock yowled.

Almost enjoying the man's consternation, Grant told them, "Dr. Cardenas gave me a dose of therapeutic nanos several weeks ago. They're helping me to work out on the surface without suffering a lot of radiation damage."

"That's illegal!" McClintock barked.

Luongo made a faint smile. "Not on the Moon, sir. Not in the nation of Selene."

Before McClintock could think of anything to say, Grant went on, "Dr. Cardenas has assured me that the nanos in my body are not responsible for the accidents. She says it's impossible."

"But you come back here from Selene filled with nanobugs and we start having accidents," McClintock said darkly.

"There is that," Grant conceded.

Luongo turned to McClintock again. "Please call Dr. Cardenas for me. Now."

McClintock called out, "Phone: get Dr. Cardenas."

For a few tense moments the room was absolutely silent. Then Kris Cardenas's youthful blond face appeared on the wall screen.

"Hello, Carter."

"Could you come over to my quarters, Kris? Right away? The head of the accident investigating team wants to speak with you."

Cardenas's face tightened. "Yes, I imagine she does."

"Could you—"

"I'll be right there," Cardenas said. Then she cut the phone link.

Luongo reached down to the capacious handbag that rested at her feet and pulled out a palm-sized computer.

"If you'll excuse me for a few moments," she murmured.

"Of course," said McClintock.

Grant watched as she tapped on the computer's minuscule keyboard with her long, graceful fingers.

Trudy finished her dinner, left the cafeteria, and headed to Professor Uhlrich's quarters instead of her own.

The poor man must be feeling besieged, she thought. The facility's locked down and even the work out at the telescope sites has been stopped.

But when Uhlrich admitted her to his room, the professor seemed to be in good spirits. He greeted Trudy with a pleasant smile and showed her to the sofa. As Trudy sat she saw that the display screen on the opposite wall was scrolling through messages almost faster than her eye could follow.

"Comments on our note to *IAL*," he said happily. "Our little paper has attracted quite a bit of attention."

"That's good," Trudy said, a trifle uncertainly, as she sat on the sofa.

Uhlrich sat beside her and she noticed that he had a tiny microphone wormed into his ear. He's listening to the comments, she realized. He can't see them, but he's programmed his computer to make them audible for him.

"Have you drafted the full paper yet?" he asked eagerly. "About our spectroscopic results from Sirius C's atmosphere?"

"I'm . . . working on it," Trudy replied.

"Good. Good. We must get it to the journal as quickly as possible. They'll send it out to be refereed, of course, but we can still put it out digitally and get comments from as wide an audience as possible."

Nodding, Trudy said, "Um . . . we can work on it right now, Professor. If you feel up to it."

"Of course!" Uhlrich beamed at her. "By all means!"

So Trudy called up her notes and data and the two of them plunged into writing a full-fledged research report about her work on the atmosphere of Sirius C. Within a few minutes Trudy was caught up in the professor's excitement. It felt good to be working, to be dealing with data and rigorous logic, to forget the accidents and the investigation and personal relationships. Just the work, she thought. That's what really counts. The work. The rest will be forgotten sooner or later, but the work will remain forever.

MÉNAGE À QUATRE

Kris Cardenas looked wary, almost suspicious, as McClintock introduced her to Latisha Luongo.

Perching rigidly on the sofa beside McClintock, she glanced at Grant, still on the recliner, then said, "I don't have to ask why you want to talk to me, do I?"

Luongo reached into her handbag for a pair of stylish dark-framed eyeglasses as she said, "Nanomachines have caused accidents, and Mr. Simpson has just revealed to us that you have put nanomachines into his body."

"Mr. Simpson also drinks water," Cardenas said. "Do you suspect water may have caused the accidents?"

McClintock said, "Come on, now, Kris. Be reasonable."

"I don't like being a suspect."

"Me neither," said Grant, "but we've got to cover all the possibilities, Kris."

"Your nanos didn't cause the accidents," Cardenas insisted, her voice low but firm as concrete. "I've already proved that."

"Have you?" Luongo asked. "I wasn't aware—"

"I can demonstrate it for you again, if you need to see it for yourselves."

"What was your proof?"

"It's very simple," said Cardenas. "I took a sample of Grant's blood. Once outside his body, his nanomachines deactivated themselves in less than five minutes. Without the energy they get from Grant's body heat, they go inert."

"Truly?" Luongo murmured. Her eyeglasses made her look

like an accountant or an office worker, Grant thought, not an investigator.

"Moreover," Cardenas went on, "Grant's nanos aren't capable of gnawing through metal alloys. They're programmed to attack organic molecules that don't bear his own personal genetic markers."

Very gently, McClintock said, "Kris, we all would like to believe you, but all we've got is your word on this."

"I can accept Dr. Cardenas's word," said Luongo. "I see no reason to doubt it."

Looking surprised, Cardenas said, "Why . . . thank you."

"But if the devices in Mr. Simpson's body did not cause the accidents, what did?"

McClintock pointed out, "There's no evidence that nanomachines caused the lobber's crash."

"Not yet," Grant muttered.

"It is a possibility that we must explore," said Luongo.

Turning toward Cardenas, Grant said, "One way or another, the nanos must have come from your lab, Kris."

"No!" she snapped.

Trying to sound reasonable, McClintock said, "But Kris, your lab at Selene is the only place in the solar system that manufactures nanomachines."

For a moment Grant thought that Cardenas was going to erupt in fury. Her face went white, her jaws clenched so hard he could see the muscles in her face tighten. But then she seemed to relax a little. Taking a breath, she said calmly, "My laboratory did not produce lethal nanomachines."

"How can you be certain?" Luongo asked, trying not to be accusative. "After all, you have a staff, don't you? Can you be absolutely certain that none of them produced the gobblers?"

Cardenas flinched visibly at the term, but she responded, "Yes, I am absolutely certain. I have only a dozen people on my staff. I've known most of them for many years. I can vouch for each and every one of them, without hesitation."

"That's carrying loyalty a bit far, don't you think?" McClintock said. "After all, Kris, we're talking about murder here, sabotage and outright murder."

"No one on my staff would produce destructive nanos," Cardenas insisted. "I'd stake my life on that."

Luongo smiled, but asked again, "Then where did the gobblers come from?"

Grant spoke up. "There are rumors of secret nanolabs on Earth. Wealthy people use them for therapeutic reasons."

"And cosmetic," Luongo added. "I've heard such rumors also."

"From Earth?" McClintock sounded totally incredulous. "You mean someone from Earth obtained destructive nanomachines from a secret laboratory and brought them here to Farside to cause these accidents?"

Grant said, "Sherlock Holmes."

"What?"

"In one of the Sherlock Holmes stories, he says that once you've eliminated all the obvious possibilities, then whatever remains—no matter how unlikely it seems—has got to be the answer."

"That's not quite the correct quotation," Luongo said, removing her glasses, "but I understand what you mean."

McClintock still looked unconvinced. "A secret lab on Earth. It's . . . it's . . . melodramatic."

"But it could be a possibility," Luongo said, very seriously.

"Who would carry nanomachines all the way from Earth to cause disaster here at Farside?" McClintock demanded. "And why? What possible reason could he have?"

"Not he," said Grant. "She."

"She?"

"Anita Halleck."

"Anita . . . ?" McClintock's jaw dropped open.

"She's the only visitor from Earthside that we've had for the past few months. And she's placed well enough, high enough, to have access to a rogue nanolab."

"You're forgetting that Swedish fellow," McClintock said. "Palmquist."

"What motive would he have for trying to harm us?" Grant demanded.

"What motive would Anita have?" McClintock countered.

"She's still at Selene, isn't she?" Grant pointed out. "Let's get her here and ask her about this."

"What good would that do?" McClintock groused. "Even if she's the one, she'd just deny it all. And you don't just tell Anita Halleck to haul her butt over here. She'd laugh in your face."

"I would like to talk to her, however," said Luongo.

"Lotsa luck," McClintock said.

"Maybe Doug Stavenger could help us," Cardenas suggested. "He still swings a lot of weight at Selene."

Grant nodded. He saw that McClintock still looked utterly unconvinced.

But Luongo pulled out her pocketphone and said clearly, "Douglas Stavenger, at Selene."

TÊTE-À-TÊTE

his is pretty awkward for me," said Douglas Stavenger.

Sitting beside him on the automated tractor that ran from Armstrong spaceport back to Selene proper, Anita Halleck appraised Stavenger coolly. He really is quite handsome, she thought: his face was youthfully taut, strong bone structure, and just a hint of some African ancestry in his light mocha skin tone.

And his body is filled with nanomachines, she reminded herself.

"It must be quite important for you to take me off the Earthbound shuttle," she replied.

For long moments Stavenger said nothing. Halleck watched the shadows flicker across his face as the tractor trundled along below the tunnel's overhead lights. He looked grim, troubled.

At last Stavenger spoke up. "You know about the accidents at Farside."

"That rocket that blew up," Halleck said.

"And earlier, a man was killed when his space suit failed."

"What does that have to do with me?"

Shifting uncomfortably on the tractor's thinly cushioned seat, Stavenger answered, "The chief of our accident investigation team wants to talk to you about it. At Farside."

A pang of alarm surged through Halleck. "I don't want to go to Farside! I'm due back in my office in Geneva tomorrow."

"I'm afraid that will have to wait. You're going to Farside."

Anger flared. "You can't force me to go to Farside! I have my rights!"

Trying to smile, Stavenger said, "You can go voluntarily or we can obtain an order from the governing council. It's your choice."

"An order?"

"This could turn out to be a homicide investigation, after all. We don't have much of a crime rate here at Selene, but we do have the legal apparatus in place. And security people to enforce the rules."

Halleck bit back the reply she started to snap out at him. For several heartbeats she stared at Stavenger. He's not happy about this, but he's concerned about what's going on at Farside, she realized. He's trying to put it gently, but the government of Selene will arrest me like some common criminal if I don't cooperate.

"I understand," she said at last. "I'll call my office and tell them that I'll be staying here a few days longer than I expected."

Stavenger's relief was palpable. "Thank you, Mrs. Halleck. Thank you for understanding."

Six hours later Anita Halleck approached the same tractor, this time bound outward to the spaceport and a lobber waiting to fly her to Farside. She had chosen to wear a simple jumpsuit of pearl gray. No sense dressing up for Farside, she told herself. None of those techies would appreciate it.

But as she climbed up into the tractor, she remembered that Carter McClintock was at Farside. Carter appreciates the finer things in life, she thought, smiling inwardly.

To her surprise, Edith Elgin was already in the tractor, dressed in a coral pink floral camp shirt and comfortable twill shorts.

"Welcome aboard," said Edith brightly.

"You're going to Farside?" Halleck asked as she sat beside Edith.

"I surely am. I'm going to coordinate the news media interviews with Professor Uhlrich."

"Interviews? About the accidents?"

As the tractor lurched into motion, Edith shook her head negatively. "No, no. About New Earth. Professor Uhlrich's discovered the planet's got an atmosphere like Earth's."

"Has he?"

"News bureaus Earthside are all a-twitter about it. They can't send people to Farside 'cause of the lockdown, so I'm going to coordinate their requests for interviews and background info."

"Really? I thought no one was allowed into Farside while the accident investigation is proceeding."

Edith grinned, strong white teeth gleaming. "*Almost* no one," she said. "But why're you going?"

"Ask your husband," Halleck grumbled.

By the time they landed at Farside, Edith and Halleck had exchanged their life histories. Up to a point.

As they trudged along the springy access tube to Farside's minuscule reception center, Edith was saying, "You mean nobody's ever done a documentary on your life? Cripes, it'd be spectacular!"

Halleck shrugged. "If you think it makes sense to do it . . ."

They stepped through the airlock hatch and into the reception area. Nate Oberman sprang to his feet the instant he recognized Anita Halleck.

"Mrs. Halleck," he said, "I couldn't believe it when I saw your name on the manifest."

"Hello, Mr. Oberman," she said sweetly. Turning to Edith, "Do you know Edie Elgin?"

"I've seen you on the vids a lot, Ms. Elgin," said Oberman. "Welcome to Farside."

"Thanks," Edith said. "Could somebody take me to Professor Uhlrich's office, please?"

"I'll call his assistant, Dr. Yost."

Halleck said, "And I'm supposed to meet a Dr. Luongo."

"That is me," said Latisha Luongo, entering the reception

area from the corridor door. She too was in one-piece coveralls, burnt orange. "Thank you for coming, Mrs. Halleck."

Resisting an urge to complain about being forced to come to Farside, Halleck said, "I'll be happy to assist your investigation in any way I can, naturally."

"I appreciate that. Allow me to show you to your quarters."

With a parting glance at Edith, Halleck followed the tall, leggy Luongo out into the corridor. Edith clutched her travelbag in both hands while Oberman sat back behind his desk and made a phone call.

He looked up at Edith, grinning. "Dr. Yost'll be here in a coupla minutes."

"Thanks."

His grin widening, Oberman explained, "This place is so small it only takes a couple minutes to get anywhere."

"I see."

"Would you like to sit down?" Oberman pointed to the trio of sculpted plastic chairs against the far wall.

"It feels good to stand, actually," said Edith. But she stepped to the chairs and dropped her travelbag on one of them.

Trudy Yost looked the tiniest bit flustered as she entered the room. "I'm Dr. Yost, Professor Uhlrich's assistant."

Edith saw that she was very young; her diminutive size and plain figure making her look almost like a child. She wore a drab pullover blouse and baggy slacks.

Sticking out her hand, "I'm Edie Elgin."

"I'll show you your quarters, and then take you to the professor," Trudy said as they shook hands.

"Fine," said Edith.

FLICKER RATE

Luongo led Anita Halleck down a dismal corridor and into one of the single-room cells that served as living quarters at Farside. Carter McClintock was sitting on the sofa.

Rising to his feet, McClintock forced a smile. "Hello again, Anita. I'm sorry we had to make you return—"

"You don't look sorry, Carter," she snapped.

Grant Simpson was at the desk, fiddling with the computer there. He too stood up. He looked weary, overburdened, his shoulders slumped, his eyes melancholy.

"Mr. Simpson," Anita murmured. He nodded glumly by way of greeting.

This is Carter's living quarters, Halleck recognized as she went to the recliner and sat primly on it. Simpson joined McClintock on the sofa while Luongo took the easy chair at the other end of the coffee table, facing the desktop computer.

"So?" Halleck asked. "Why have you made me come here?"

Luongo slipped on her eyeglasses before replying, "Analysis of the lobber's wreckage shows that its explosion was caused by nanomachines."

"As was the death of one of our technicians," Simpson added.

With raised eyebrows, Halleck asked, "What has that to do with me?"

"You could have access to nanomachines," Simpson said. Flatly. Not accusative. It was simply a statement of fact.

Halleck eyed the man. He looked haunted, she thought. Guilty. As innocently as she could manage, she replied, "How could

I have access to nanomachines? They're banned everywhere on Earth. The only nanolab in existence is at Selene, isn't it?"

McClintock nodded, but said, "The only nanolab that we know of."

"Carter, surely you're not accusing me of causing these accidents."

"Somebody did," Simpson said.

Before Halleck could reply, Luongo asked, "Have you been exposed to nanomachines, Mrs. Halleck? Anywhere, at any time? The exposure might have been accidental."

"I most certainly have not," Halleck said. Firmly.

"You're certain?"

"Positive." Then she added, "Oh . . . Douglas Stavenger. He's filled with nanos, isn't he?"

"Therapeutic nanomachines," said Luongo. "We know about that."

McClintock raised his hands in a gesture of helplessness. "This is getting us nowhere." Turning to Luongo, he went on, "I told you that it was senseless to interrogate her. Anita isn't a saboteur, a murderess."

Luongo removed her glasses and closed her eyes for a moment. Then, "Thank you for your cooperation, Mrs. Halleck."

Surprised, Halleck said, "That's it? You dragged me all the way back here to ask me one question? We could have done this by phone."

"Perhaps," Luongo conceded. "I thought it would be better if we spoke face-to-face."

Getting to her feet, Halleck said, "At least I'll be able to call the lobber that brought me here and tell them to wait long enough to take me back to Selene."

McClintock began to apologize, but Luongo interrupted him with, "I'm sorry if we inconvenienced you."

Anita Halleck decided to be gracious. "I'm happy I was able to be of help to you." If any of them detected the scorn in her tone, none of them showed it.

As she headed for the door, with the three of them watching mutely, Halleck remembered a dictum from some historic figure: If you're going to kill a man it costs you nothing to be polite about it.

Grant watched Mrs. Halleck sweep grandly out of McClintock's sitting room, her pocketphone to her ear.

Turning to Luongo, he asked, "Was that enough?"

"We shall see," said the investigator. She got up from her chair and went to the computer on the desk.

McClintock looked disgusted. "It was a waste of time. We've ticked her off, for nothing."

"Perhaps not," Luongo said, tapping at the computer's touchscreen. "Ahh . . . look here."

Grant got up and went to the desk. Leaning over Luongo's shoulder, he saw that the screen was filled with jagged curves in various colors: bright blue, cool green, bloodred.

Still seated on the sofa, McClintock said, "It looks like a child's drawing of the Alps."

"Hardly that," Luongo murmured. Tracing the sawtoothed red curve with a lacquered fingernail, she said, "She was lying. It's obvious."

"Are you certain?" Grant asked. To him, the curves looked meaningless.

Leaning closer to the screen, Luongo commanded, "Display readout of Dr. Cardenas."

A new set of curves appeared. Grant saw that they were clearly smoother.

"Flicker rate is a very reliable measure of truthfulness, much more reliable than polygraph or syntactical analysis," said Luongo. To the computer she ordered, "Compare Dr. Cardenas's responses to Mrs. Halleck's."

The display split in two. McClintock got up from the sofa and came over to the desk.

"This is from the sensors in those eyeglasses of yours?" he asked.

"Indeed," said Luongo. "The sensors measure eyelid flicker rate, voice tremors, a dozen nonverbal signals that we unconsciously give out when we speak."

"And this can tell you if she's lying?" Grant asked.

Luongo said, "A person may be trained to control his or her breathing, even the pulse rate. But the rate that the eye blinks and the voice quivers is beyond conscious control."

So far, Grant thought.

Frowning at the display, McClintock muttered, "So this shows that Kris Cardenas was telling us the truth?"

"It does," said Luongo.

"And this," Grant said, pointing at the other half of the screen, "tells us that Mrs. Halleck was lying through her teeth when she said she hasn't had access to nanomachines."

"She lied?" McClintock clearly was unconvinced.

"Like a trooper," said Luongo.

"Like a criminal," Grant amended.

BASKING IN THE LIGHT

Jason Uhlrich mopped sweat from his brow with a soggy handkerchief.

"You're doin' fine," said Edie Elgin, smiling brightly at him.

Sagging back in his desk chair, Professor Uhlrich asked, "How many more? I never realized there would be so many—"

"Two more interviews," Elgin said. "Science International and then Selene University's news bureau."

Uhlrich nodded. "Do I look all right?" he asked. He felt limp, exhausted. He had lost count of the reporters who had interviewed him during this long, wearying day. In the morning, when they had started, Uhlrich had felt fresh and eager, happy to explain to his interviewers the importance of the discoveries he had made about Sirius C.

Now, after a whole day of answering the same tired questions, many of them dealing with trivial matters of personality, he wished they would all go away and leave him alone.

Be strong, he told himself. Some of these interviews will be watched by the Nobel committee. Be positive, be charming, be knowledgeable. Let them see you as you would be on the stage in Stockholm, accepting the prize.

Edie Elgin broke into his thoughts. "You'll be talking to Patricia Seery, of Science International. They're the absolutely biggest science-oriented news organization on Earth and she's one of their top interviewers."

Uhlrich nodded again as he brushed his fingers across his tactile screen. In his mind he saw a beefy-faced woman of stern expression. No nonsense. Strictly business.

With a nod, he said, "I am ready."

He had no tactile image of Edie Egin's face, so Uhlrich had to compose her features based on audio input alone. She sounded fresh and vivacious. His visual cortex drew an image of a young flaxen-haired student he had known in his earliest years as a teacher, back when he himself was a young and too-shy lecturer, long before he had lost his eyesight.

"Here's Patricia Seery," Elgin said softly.

Looking into his desktop screen with his sightless eyes, Uhlrich put on a smile and murmured, "Ms. Secry."

"Professor Uhlrich." Seery's voice was girlishly high, a strange divergence from the image he'd already formed of her.

"Before we begin," she said, "I want to tell you how great an honor it is to interview you, sir. I think the work you're doing is very exciting."

"Why, thank you," he replied, breaking into a genuine smile. "It's very kind of you to say so."

"Now then," her tone hardened, "the discoveries you're claiming to have made about New Earth are based on a single observation. Don't you think your announcement was premature, to say the least?"

Stunned by her change of attitude, Uhlrich stammered, "No . . . not at all. I . . . that is, we . . . my assistant and I . . . we decided to release the findings at once because . . . because they were so . . . so . . . important."

"You wanted to claim priority of your discovery, didn't you?"

Straightening in his chair, Uhlrich said, "The discovery of an Earthlike atmosphere on an Earth-sized exoplanet is important enough to warrant immediate disclosure."

"Before anybody else could make the same discovery and cloud your claim to be first," Seery said.

Bristling, Uhlrich snapped, "No other astronomical facility

on Earth—in the entire solar system—could duplicate the results of our hundred-meter telescope!"

"So there's no way that your claim can be independently verified, is there?"

"The data speaks for itself!" Uhlrich insisted. "We are preparing a full report, which will include the details of the telescope's specifications, its capabilities. Detecting oxygen and water vapor on Sirius C is well within our telescope's power."

"But according to the astrophysicists I've talked with, that planet can't have any atmosphere at all, let alone such an Earthlike one. Any atmosphere that New Earth once had would've been boiled away when Sirius B went nova, eons ago."

Sucking in a deep breath, Uhlrich commanded himself to stay calm. Remain tranquil, he reminded himself. Do not let her upset your composure.

Measuredly, he replied, "My dear Ms. Seery, the astrophysicists have their theories. I have actual observations. Sirius C has an atmosphere. An atmosphere very much like our own Earth's. How this can be so is unknown, as yet. But it is so. There is no doubt of it."

"*You* may have no doubt of it, Professor, but—"

"No buts! I have the data. I have published the data for all the world to study and examine. I am in the process of writing a complete report that will allow scientists everywhere to see what I have done and how I have done it. There is no question about it. Sirius C is an Earth-sized planet with an Earthlike atmosphere. When Farside Observatory completes construction of its two additional hundred-meter telescopes, we will be able to obtain imagery of the planet's surface. I have no doubts that we will see oceans of liquid water and green, chlorophyll-based plant life. Sirius C truly is a New Earth."

He sensed the interviewer smiling at him. "Thank you, Professor Uhlrich. That was wonderful."

His brows rising, Uhlrich asked, "That's it? That's all you want to ask?"

"That's plenty," Seery replied. "Great interview. Thank you, sir."

He slumped back in his chair, suddenly drained of all his energy.

"We're clear," Edith Elgin said. "You did fine, Professor. Terrific. I like that spark in your—"

"EMERGENCY," the overhead speakers blared. "AIR PRESSURE DROP IN MIRROR LAB. EVACUATE MIRROR LAB AT ONCE."

MIRROR LAB

Grant was on his way to intercept Anita Halleck before she could get away from Farside on the lobber that had brought her in.

"EMERGENCY. AIR PRESSURE DROP IN MIRROR LAB. EVACUATE MIRROR LAB AT ONCE."

He spun around and sprinted along the corridor toward the mirror lab. Grant could hear the emergency airlock hatches that were located every hundred meters along the corridors slamming shut, like a drumbeat warning of disaster. He had to stop at each one of them, punch out the unlocking code on each keypad, and proceed to the next.

By the time he reached the entrance to the mirror lab, half a dozen technicians were standing in the corridor, looking bewildered, frightened.

"What happened?" Grant demanded.

Phil Rizzo, chief of the mirror lab's crew, shook his head. "I dunno. The emergency alarm went off all of a sudden and we scooted out."

Rizzo was small, wiry, with the narrow face and oversized nose of a rodent. His eyes were wide with fear, edging toward panic.

"Everybody out?" Grant asked.

Rizzo looked around, counting. "Yeah. Everybody."

Yanking out his pocketphone, Grant called the Farside life-support center. "What's going on?" he demanded.

The monitoring technician's dark face looked troubled. "Air

pressure started nosediving, Grant. All of a sudden. There's a leak in the lab someplace, probably the airlock."

More people were coming down the corridor. Just what we need, Grant thought. Half the staff rubbernecking while there's a leak in that damned oversized airlock.

"Get an emergency team down here, quick," he said into the phone.

"They're already on their way. With suits."

"Good. Thanks."

The tech broke into a grim smile. "Just doin' my job, boss."

Grant clicked his pocketphone shut, then raised his voice to the growing crowd: "Go on back to your workstations. Everything's under control here."

The crowd began to break up slowly, reluctantly. Rizzo asked, "What about us, Grant?"

Looking down at the diminutive technician, Grant answered, "You guys can take the rest of the day off."

Rizzo didn't laugh at Grant's weak attempt at humor. He didn't even grin.

"Okay, people," he said to his crew. "You heard the man."

As the lab crew started down the corridor, Grant grasped Rizzo by the shoulder. "Anything special going on in there when the alarm went off?"

Rizzo shook his head. "Naw. Just polishing the mirror, like we have been for the past month."

"Okay," said Grant, releasing his grip. "Take it easy, Phil."

"Yeah, sure."

Rizzo headed down the corridor, passing the emergency crew coming up. An automated cart trundled along behind them, loaded with three space suits. Harvey Henderson was leading them. Grant remembered that Harvey had rotated to the emergency team because usually they had little to do but monitor the station's life-support equipment.

"How's your foot, Harvey?" he asked.

"Still hurts. Dr. Kapstein says it's psychosomatic, but it still hurts."

"Well, you got your gang down here in good time."

"It hurts, but I'm not crippled."

Grant shooed the remaining onlookers out of the section of corridor that ended at the mirror lab entrance.

"We're going to seal this section off," he told them. "When we open the lab door, this area will probably go down to vacuum. You don't want to be here unless you're in a suit."

As they grudgingly headed for the emergency hatch up the corridor, Grant and Henderson started pulling on space suits. The other techs of the emergency team checked them out.

Once they were fully suited up, Grant waved the rest of the team down the corridor, past the emergency airlock hatch. Then he and Harvey went to the lab's door and slid it open.

They stepped out onto the balcony that circled the laboratory, where the monitoring consoles stood unattended but still working, their displays flickering. Below the balcony's railing was the big turntable, still slowly revolving, polishing the mirror that would probably never be used in a telescope. Unless the Ulcer builds a 'scope right here in the Sea of Moscow, Grant thought.

As he and Henderson began to power down the consoles and stop the turntable, Grant called to the life-support monitor, "Give me a reading on the air pressure in here."

"Low, and getting lower," she responded.

"Numbers, kid. I need numbers."

"Six p.s.i. Sinking steadily."

"Not a total blowout," Henderson said.

"Slow leak," said Grant.

"Not all that slow," the life-support monitor corrected. "Just sank past five p.s.i."

Grant clomped over to the central console and pulled drawers open until he found what he wanted: a pad of legal-sized notepaper. Ripping out a handful of sheets, he tossed them over the railing of the balcony.

"What . . . ?" Henderson started to ask, then realized what Grant was up to.

The sheets of paper fluttered slowly downward. As Grant and Henderson watched, they drifted toward the airlock, skittering across the top of the massive turntable and along the concrete floor of the laboratory.

One by one, the sheets of paper plastered themselves against a single spot on the wide airlock, like birds returning to their nest.

"There's the leak," Grant said.

"Yeah," Henderson agreed. "Must be."

"How much you want to bet that it's a pinhole drilled by nano-machines?" asked Grant.

Henderson merely grunted.

UNDER SIEGE

"Where will they strike next?" Professor Uhlrich asked, his voice trembling slightly.

Grant shook his head. "We've sealed the leak in the airlock hatch. The mirror lab is habitable again."

"For how long?"

The Ulcer looked shaken as he sat behind his desk. His face was pale, his hair slightly disheveled. He's scared, Grant realized. He has a right to be.

Carter McClintock, sitting across the table from Grant, seemed more composed. "I imagine we should evacuate the facility."

"Evacuate Farside?" Uhlrich gasped.

"It would seem to be the prudent thing to do," McClintock said. "If there are nanomachines randomly attacking the place, we should get out. We've already had one death—"

"Three," Grant corrected. "The two pilots of the lobber, remember."

"Oh, yes, of course. Three deaths."

"Three murders," Uhlrich muttered.

"Let's get the hell out of here before anyone else is killed," McClintock said, with some fervor.

"And go where?" Grant asked.

"Selene, of course."

With a shake of his head, Grant said, "Do you think Selene will take in a hundred people who might be infected with destructive nanomachines?"

McClintock blinked at him. "They'd have to! They couldn't refuse us."

"They already have," Grant said, feeling weary, alone, with no one to turn to, no one to help him.

"What do you mean?" Uhlrich demanded.

"Selene's flight control people have told our flight control people that they will not accept any flights from Farside until we've solved our nanobug problem. Not Anita Halleck, not even Edie Elgin, and she's Douglas Stavenger's wife, for chrissakes."

"No flights at all?" McClintock whined.

"None," said Grant. "No VIPs, no refugees, nobody. No flights from Farside will be permitted to land at Selene."

"We're trapped here?" McClintock's voice rose a notch higher.

"We're quarantined."

Uhlrich ran a hand through his silvery hair. "Then what are we to do? Simply sit here and let these devices destroy us all?"

The professor's phone buzzed. Tracing his fingertips along his desktop tactile screen, the professor muttered, "Anita Halleck is calling."

Before Grant could say anything, Uhlrich told the phone, "Answer."

Halleck's sculpted face appeared on the wall screen. Grant saw that she looked unhappy, nettled.

"Professor Uhlrich," she said, her voice firm, her tone insistent, "your staff refuses to allow me to return to Selene."

Uhlrich stared blankly at the screen. Grant answered, "All flights have been stopped, Mrs. Halleck."

"Mr. Simpson?"

Uhlrich touched a pad on his phone keyboard and the camera view switched to wide focus, taking in Grant and McClintock as well as himself.

"Right," Grant answered. "With this nanobug problem, Selene's ordered a stand-down on all flights."

Her expression hardening, Halleck challenged, "Do you mean to keep me a prisoner here?"

With a wan smile, Grant replied, "Mrs. Halleck, we're under a quarantine. I'm afraid we're all prisoners here as long as we're under siege from these rogue nanos."

"That's not acceptable, Mr. Simpson."

"Acceptable or not, that's the way it is. Even if we let you take off, Selene wouldn't allow a flight from Farside to land at their spaceport, anyway. Not until we've figured out what's causing this nanobug problem and fixed it."

Just a trace of alarm flashed across Halleck's face. "You can't keep me a prisoner here! Do you have any idea of who you're talking to?"

"It's not me, ma'am. Nobody leaves Farside," Grant said flatly. "You can call Selene if you want to. I'm sure they'll confirm that they won't accept any flights from here."

"That's nonsense! If my rocket takes off from here and approaches Selene, they'd have to allow me to land. They'd be killing me, otherwise!"

"That's why we're not permitting you to leave Farside, ma'am."

"*You're* not permitting me! Since when are you in charge? Professor Uhlrich, I demand that you allow me to leave!"

Uhlrich sat behind his desk, speechless.

"Anita," said McClintock, "I'm afraid that Simpson is correct. It's in your own best interest to remain here, temp—"

"*My* best interest?" Halleck snapped. "Since when have you ever had my best interest at heart, Carter?"

"Now, Anita . . ."

"Professor Uhlrich, I insist that you call Selene. Get to their governing council, to Douglas Stavenger, *somebody*! Make them understand that I'm not to be kept a prisoner here at Farside. I have important work to do!"

Her image suddenly winked out. The wall screen went blank.

"She hung up," McClintock said.

"Or the bugs have hit the comm system," Grant muttered.

FEARS

Doug Stavenger was in the sitting room of his quarters at Selene, talking to his wife at Farside.

"You're okay?" he asked, for the twelfth time in as many minutes.

"I'm fine, honey," said Edith, smiling brightly. "The nanobugs haven't attacked any people."

"Not directly."

"Nope." Edith's normally cheerful expression sobered into a puzzled frown. "It's kinda funny, really. The bugs have hit here and there, sort of at random."

"And killed several people," Stavenger said.

"Yeah, but it's not like the gray goo thing, y'know, where they eat everything in sight."

"But you're all right?" he asked again.

"So far."

"I can't get you out of there," Stavenger said, hating himself for letting her go in the first place. "Farside's quarantined."

"I know. Don't worry about it. It's kinda exciting, y'know. I'm getting to be a news reporter again, digging into the story."

Suddenly alarmed, Stavenger blurted, "No news reports, Edith! This whole thing is under a news blackout."

"Yessir, Mr. Dictator," she said, with a grin and a mock military salute. "But once the blackout is lifted I'll have a firsthand account. I'm interviewing Professor Uhlrich and Kris Cardenas, scientists and ordinary workers—"

The phone screen blinked and the data bar showed an incoming call from Professor Uhlrich.

Stavenger sat up straighter in his chair, a recliner that had been salvaged from a retired Clipper rocket.

"Speak of the devil: it's Professor Uhlrich. Duty calls, darling."

"He's kinda weird," said Edith.

"Yes, but I've got to take his call."

"Sure. I'm goin' to see Kris Cardenas, find out what she can tell me about all this."

"Take care of yourself." Stavenger knew it was lame, but he couldn't think of anything else to say.

"I'll be back soon, Doug honey. With a terrific story!"

He forced a smile and switched to Uhlrich's call.

The professor looked tired, stressed. "Mr. Stavenger," he began, "thank you for taking my call."

"What can I do for you, Professor?"

With an unhappy pout, Uhlrich said, "It's Mrs. Halleck. She's upset about being quarantined here at Farside. She's demanding that we let her fly to Selene."

"That's not possible, Professor. I'm sure you understand why."

"I understand," said Uhlrich. "But she doesn't. She insists that Selene allow her to return there. And from Selene, I suppose, she'll want to transfer back to Earth."

Stavenger shook his head. "If we allowed that, she might contaminate Selene with rogue nanos, and even spread them Earthside. We can't have that."

Uhlrich pleaded, "Will you talk to her, please? She won't pay any attention to me. Perhaps you can make her see the necessity."

Stavenger saw that the professor was close to his wits' end. "Certainly," he said. "I'll call her right away."

"Oh, thank you!"

"Think nothing of it," said Stavenger. To himself he said, I'll call Anita Halleck. But that won't change anything.

·   ·   ·

Edith Elgin saw her husband's image wink off in her phone screen. After a moment's hesitation she told the phone to connect her with Kris Cardenas.

Almost immediately, Cardenas's face appeared on the screen.

"Edith," she said, looking surprised. "You're here at Farside?"

"I surely am," said Edith. "I need to talk to you, get your take on what's goin' on around here."

Cardenas looked suddenly wary. "I'm pretty sure there's a news blackout on what's happening here."

"I know that. But once the blackout is lifted, I want to be able to tell the story and for that I need to interview the world's leading expert on nanotechnology."

For a moment Cardenas hesitated. Then she allowed herself a tired smile and said, "Sure, Edith, why not? I'm on my way to Professor Uhlrich's office. Why don't you meet me there?"

"Great!" said Edith. "See you there."

Anita Halleck was furious. She glared at the image of Douglas Stavenger on the wall screen of her quarters.

"So you see," Stavenger was repeating, "we simply can't allow any flights in here from Farside."

"You mean you *won't* allow any flights," Halleck growled.

Stavenger spread his hands. "Can't, won't, it comes to the same thing, doesn't it? Farside is quarantined until the nanomachine problem is solved."

"But I can't stay here!"

"I know it's scary," Stavenger said, trying to sound reasonable. "My own wife is at Farside, and I'm very nervous about that, believe me."

"But you'll let her die here?"

Stavenger's youthful face went grim. "Mrs. Halleck, let me tell you something. My father chose to let rogue nanomachines kill him rather than infect all of Moonbase, back before this community was called Selene."

"That's got nothing to do with it," she insisted.

"It does to me," Stavenger countered. "I'm very sorry. I know this is frightening. But no one leaves Farside until the nanobug problem is solved. That's it."

Halleck's wall screen went blank. She stared at it for long seconds, desperately rummaging in her mind for some solution to this idiotic problem, some way out, some way to save herself.

The phone chimed again. The data bar said it was Dr. Trudy Yost calling.

Uhlrich's assistant, Halleck thought. What on Earth does she want? Then a new idea dawned in her mind. Of course! Halleck said to herself. This young pup might be my ticket out of here.

COUNTERSTEPS

"We've got to get Dr. Cardenas in on this," Grant said.

"I called her more than half an hour ago," McClintock said from across the table. "She should be here by now. I wonder what's keeping her?"

Professor Uhlrich seemed frozen in his desk chair, immobilized by the enormity of what was happening to his dream.

Grant said, "Professor, perhaps if you called Dr. Cardenas she—"

The office door slid open and Kris Cardenas stepped in. With another woman. Grant recognized the newswoman, Edie Elgin. The two of them look almost like sisters, Grant realized: bright, youthful, blond—like a pair of former cheerleaders.

Cardenas was not in a cheerleading mood, though. "I've been down in the mirror lab," she said, without preamble. "That's why I'm late."

Uhlrich roused himself from his funk enough to introduce, "Gentlemen, this is Edie Elgin, the famous video news star."

Edith smiled prettily for them as Grant got to his feet and pulled out a chair for her. Cardenas went around the table and settled next to McClintock.

"You inspected the mirror lab's airlock?" Uhlrich asked, smoothing his silver hair with an automatic gesture.

Cardenas nodded. "What happened to the airlock looks superficially like what happened to your technician's space suit, but I just don't have the diagnostic tools here to be certain."

McClintock looked across the table at Edith. "Ms. Elgin, you understand that is all off the record, for the time being. If you can't agree to that we'll have to ask you to leave."

"It's okay with me," Edith answered easily. "I'll keep my mouth shut until you've got things under control."

"Good." McClintock turned back to Cardenas.

"If we were in Selene I'd have the equipment for a thorough analysis," Cardenas went on. "But here . . ." She left the thought unfinished.

"What about the equipment in the maintenance center?" Grant asked. "Toshio has that laser probe."

Cardenas almost smiled at him. "Do you want to lug that clunker over to your mirror lab or drag the airlock hatch to the maintenance center?"

Grant understood the problem, but he shook his head as he answered, "We know the spot in the hatch where the leak developed. We take a slice from that region of the hatch and carry it to the maintenance center. That could work."

"And what would it tell us?" Cardenas argued. "That there's a pinhole leak that was caused by nanomachines. We already know that."

"We suspect that," McClintock corrected.

"With about a ninety percent accuracy," said Cardenas.

"So what do we do?" Grant demanded. "Just sit around here while the damned bugs nibble us to death?"

Cardenas said, "If I knew what kind of nanos they are, what they're designed to do, what their limits are—then I could figure out a way to stop them."

"How long would that take?" McClintock asked.

Cardenas shrugged.

"We are all doomed," said Uhlrich, in a deathly whisper. "We are infested with nanomachines and they will kill us all. I should never have allowed nanomachines to enter Farside."

With some heat, Cardenas replied, "Professor, I assure you

that the nanos we've used to build your mirrors have nothing to do with this problem."

"And the nanos in my body?" Grant asked.

"Impossible," she said firmly. "How many times do I have to tell you that?"

"Then where did these destructive nanomachines come from?" Grant wondered.

McClintock said, "According to Luongo, Anita Halleck was lying to us when she said she hadn't been exposed to nanomachines."

"That's pretty thin," said Grant.

"Do you have anything thicker?"

"If we confront her she'll just deny everything," Grant said. Then he murmured, "Unless . . ."

"Unless what?"

Feeling terribly uncertain about the entire matter, Trudy Yost tapped softly on the door to Anita Halleck's quarters.

"Who is it?" came Halleck's muffled voice.

"Trudy Yost," she said. "Professor Uhlrich's assistant."

Halleck slid the door back and stood framed in the doorway for a moment, eyeing Trudy haughtily. Halleck was several centimeters taller than Trudy; she was wearing a one-piece jumpsuit that accentuated her trim figure. Trudy was in her best coveralls, powder blue, but they were rumpled and faded from long use.

"Professor Uhlrich asked me to see if there's anything we can do for you. . . ."

"Yes, you told me that on the phone," said Halleck as she ushered Trudy into her room. "I presume the professor wants to make my captivity here as comfortable as possible."

Trudy blinked at the word *captivity*, but recovered enough to ask, "Is there anything you need?"

"I need to get back to Selene," Halleck snapped. "Actually, I need to get back to Earth, back to my work, instead of being detained in this . . . this . . . outpost."

"I suppose the accommodations here are kind of primitive," Trudy admitted, "compared to what you're used to."

Trudy saw that Halleck's travelbag was on the bed, fully packed and zipped up. She's ready to go, Trudy realized.

"Is there anything I can get for you?" she asked. "Do you want a dinner tray, or—"

A frown etching her fashion-model's face, Halleck said, "Just get me out of here. I want to leave. I want to get back home."

"I understand how you feel," Trudy said, as she stepped hesitantly toward the sofa. "But with the facility under lockdown, there's nothing we can do but wait for them to figure out how to deal with the problem."

"Wait for how long?" Halleck demanded. "Until we're all killed? We've got to get out of here!"

"But there's no place to go," Trudy said, trying to sound reasonable, rational. "Selene won't take any flights from here."

As if the idea had just popped into her head, Halleck said, "What about the sites you've built for your telescopes? They have shelters for people, don't they? Food and water, air recyclers? Don't they?"

Surprised by the idea, Trudy replied, "Yes, they do. But only the Mendeleev site is completed, and there was a nanomachine incident there. One of our technicians was killed."

"But the other two sites," Halleck pressed, "what about them? They haven't been hit by nanos, have they?"

"No," said Trudy. "But there's nothing there except the concrete slabs that will be the foundations for the telescopes to be built at them. And the shelters, of course."

"There's been no nanomachine activity at either of them?"

Trudy slowly shook her head. "No. Neither at Korolev or Gagarin."

"And they both have shelters where we could live for a few days?"

"A week or more."

"Then let's go to one of them!" Halleck said eagerly. "We can stay there until this mess is taken care of."

"I don't think Professor Uhlrich—"

"Damn Uhlrich!" Halleck snapped. "I'll provide you with all the authority you need. If Uhlrich fires you, I'll bring you into my project. I promise you."

Almost dazed by Halleck's insistence, Trudy said, "We'd need a hopper to get out to Korolev, it's too far to go by tractor."

"So? There are hoppers sitting outside, aren't there?"

"Four of them," said Trudy. "But you can't just walk out and take one. You need permission from the flight control director and—"

"I'll take care of that," Halleck answered. With a knowing smile, she added, "Money talks."

"Do you know how to fly a hopper?"

"No, of course not."

"Neither do I," said Trudy, thinking that would put an end to Halleck's wild scheme.

But Halleck said, "That man Oberman can fly a hopper, I'm sure."

"Nate? I . . . I suppose so."

"Get him on the phone," Halleck commanded. "Tell him to come here. Quickly!"

PRISONER

Josie Rivera was watching a comedy video on the main screen of her console. She was taking her assigned turn as flight control monitor, sitting alone in Farside's cramped control center. Just two workstations, and the one next to Josie's was unoccupied and dark.

Nothing coming in and nothing going out, Josie thought, bored almost to tears. We should just shut down the center altogether, there's no reason to keep it manned. The Ulcer would have a fit, though. Everybody's going through the motions, pretending everything's normal, pretending there's no threat, no danger.

The comedy she was watching was inane, a trio of grown men acting like irresponsible idiots. But she tried to concentrate on their dim-witted antics, trying to keep the fear at bay. The facility is infested with nanomachines, she knew. Somewhere, somehow, invisibly small monsters have invaded us, mindless, merciless things the size of viruses are chewing away at us and they won't stop until we're all dead, they'll keep chewing away at us and kill everybody, each and every one of us, they're going to kill me and—

Stop it! she screamed silently, pounding both fists on the console's desktop. Stop it. Nobody's chewing on you. Grant and Dr. Cardenas will find out what's wrong and fix it.

Yeah, she told herself. You hope.

The phone on the console buzzed, making her twitch with surprise.

"Answer," Josie said.

Nate Oberman's lantern-jawed face appeared on the phone screen, a crafty smile on his thin lips.

Without preamble he asked, "How'd you like to make a couple thousand smackers . . . for doing nothing?"

"Unless what?" McClintock repeated.

Grant hunched forward slightly in his chair. "Mrs. Halleck was all stewed up about getting away from Farside."

"Anita Halleck?" Edith asked. "She just came in here on the same flight with me."

"She wasn't happy about coming back here," Grant said, "and she sure worked up a sweat trying to get out."

McClintock nodded slowly. "Anita did seem unusually emotional about it. Not her normal cool self, not at all."

"Because she knows we're being attacked by nanos," Grant said.

"We all know that," Uhlrich snapped.

"But she knows better than any of us," said Grant, "because she's the one who brought the nanos here."

"Anita?" McClintock said.

"Who else?"

Edith asked, "But why would Mrs. Halleck do such a thing?"

"I don't know why," Grant said, "but she's done it."

"How do you get her to admit it?" Cardenas wondered.

With a taut smile, Grant replied, "Simple. Just keep her here. She knows what the nanos are capable of. All we have to do is keep her here with the rest of us. Make her face the same danger she's put us in. Make her sweat it out. Wait 'til she cracks."

McClintock worried, "What if she doesn't crack until it's too late, until this place is collapsing around our ears?"

"It'll be a race," Grant admitted. "A game of chicken."

Uhlrich shook his head. "And if you're wrong, Mr. Simpson? What if she's not responsible?"

"She is," Grant answered firmly. "She's got to be."

Uhlrich looked unconvinced.

Turning to Cardenas, Grant said, "Let's go down to her quarters and brace her. Tell her we know she's the one who brought in the gobblers and she's going to be killed by them along with the rest of us unless she tells us exactly what the nanos are and how we can kill them."

"And what if she doesn't care?" Cardenas argued. "What if she's insane? Suicidal?"

McClintock broke into a mirthless chuckle. "Anita Halleck is not suicidal, I can assure you. Homicidal, perhaps. But definitely not suicidal."

Grant pushed his chair back and got to his feet. "Come on, Kris. Let's put it to her."

"I'm not leaving," Trudy said, sitting tensely on the sofa.

Halleck eyed her coolly. "You'd rather stay here and be killed?"

Oberman was already at the door. Halleck was standing between the desk and the bed, where her travelbag still rested. Trudy had watched, nearly stunned with amazement, as Nate had talked Josie Rivera into turning her back and allowing them to take one of the hoppers without reporting it to Professor Uhlrich or even to Carter McClintock.

"We'd better get going before Josie loses her nerve," Oberman said.

"What you're doing is wrong," said Trudy, her fists clenched on her lap.

"What I'm doing," Halleck said firmly, "is saving our lives. I have no intention of sitting here and letting the nanomachines kill me."

"But—"

"No buts! If you come with me you'll be safe. If you stay here you'll die."

"Along with a hundred others," Trudy said. But she wasn't thinking of the others. Only of Grant.

"There's nothing you can do to save them," Halleck insisted. "If you stay here you'll die with them."

Looking up at Halleck's grimly determined face, Trudy asked, "How can you be so sure we'll be killed? Dr. Cardenas is trying—"

"By the time Cardenas figures out what she's up against, it'll be too late," Halleck said. "The nanos are spreading, just as they were programmed to do."

"Just as . . . ?" Trudy jumped to her feet. "You know about them!"

"I know what they can do," Halleck admitted.

"You've got to tell Dr. Cardenas! Grant and the others. You can't run away and leave them here to die!"

"I can and I will," said Halleck. "And you're coming with me."

"No . . ."

"Oberman," Halleck commanded, "pick her up and carry her."

Looking surprised, Oberman hesitated.

"Now!" Halleck shouted.

Oberman crossed over to the sofa. "C'mon, Dr. Yost," he muttered. "Don't make this tougher than it needs to be."

Trudy could feel her knees trembling. "But why?" she asked Halleck. "Why have you done this? Why do I have to come with you?"

A bleak smile curved Halleck's lips. "As long as you're with us you won't be able to warn Uhlrich or Carter that we're leaving. You won't be able to tell them that the woman in the control center has been bribed to let us go."

Trudy looked from Halleck's coldly determined face to Oberman's flinty expression. I can't fight them both, she thought. What good would it do to try?

Her shoulders slumping, Trudy said, "All right, I'll go with you."

"Wise decision," said Halleck.

But as she stepped out into the corridor, with Halleck in front of her and Oberman behind, Trudy wondered how she might get word to Grant. I've got to warn him! That one thought flashed through her mind over and over, like an old-fashioned neon sign blinking, glaring in her eyes.

FLIGHT

With Kris Cardenas beside him, Grant rapped on the door to Anita Halleck's quarters. No response. He pounded harder.

"She's not there," Cardenas said.

Grant tried the door. It wasn't locked. Sliding it back, he saw that indeed Halleck had gone.

"Where the hell could she be?" he wondered.

"Cafeteria, maybe," said Cardenas.

With a curt nod, Grant headed for the cafeteria, Cardenas half a step behind him. He flicked open his pocketphone, but a brief scan through the surveillance cameras showed no trace of Halleck.

There were nearly a dozen people in the cafeteria, looking halfway between bored and scared. But no Anita Halleck. Grant stepped over to where Harvey Henderson was chatting with a couple of other technicians, his place at the table littered with empty dishes and crumbs.

"Harvey, have you seen Mrs. Halleck in here?"

Henderson shook his head. "Nope."

"How long have you been here?"

With a shrug, Henderson replied, "Nearly an hour. Not much else to do . . . except wait for the nanobugs to eat through all the airlocks."

The woman on Henderson's left grumbled, "You're such an optimist, Harvey."

Turning to Cardenas, Grant asked, "Where the hell could she be?"

Cardenas looked just as puzzled as Grant felt.

"This place is too small for her to hide out for long," Grant said. "Come on, let's get over to the surveillance center. We can run through what the cameras have picked up over the past few hours."

Once they left the cafeteria, Grant broke into a trot, jogging along the corridor toward the surveillance center. Cardenas kept pace with him, puffing slightly.

The surveillance center always reminded Grant of an insect's eye. One lone technician sat in a padded chair, surrounded by screens that displayed all the public spaces in the Farside facility: labs, offices, corridors, the cafeteria, the flight control center. Grant saw Josie Rivera at flight control, idly watching a video.

Grant recognized the man on duty: Sherry Phillips.

"Hi, Grant," Phillips said, looking surprised as he turned in his chair. "What are you doing here? Come to keep me company?"

"Have you seen Mrs. Halleck on any of the screens?"

Phillips smiled amiably. "To tell you the truth, buddy, I haven't been watching that closely. Nothing's going on. Everybody's just moping around, wondering where the damned bugs'll hit next."

"Play back the last half hour on all the corridor cameras," Grant said.

"Why? What's going on?"

"No time to explain, Sherry. Just show me the playbacks. And speed 'em up."

Grumbling a little, Phillips tapped on his central keyboard and a dozen screens showed fast-forward views of Farside's corridors. People scampered along the cheerless passageways like marionettes on amphetamines.

"There!" Cardenas pointed. "That's her."

"Real time," Grant told Phillips. The view slowed to normal and Grant saw Halleck and the two others making their way up the central corridor.

"What's Trudy doing with her?" Grant wondered aloud.

"She doesn't look very happy," said Cardenas.

"And Nate Oberman," Grant added. "Where could they be heading?"

In less than a minute the display screen showed the three of them entering the locker area by the main airlock.

"They're going to suit up!" Grant said.

He glanced at his wristwatch, then checked the time back on the screen. Twenty minutes ago. They went into the lockers twenty minutes ago.

Grabbing Cardenas by the wrist, he said, "Come on! If we hurry we can catch them before they've finished suiting up."

Running alongside him, Cardenas asked, "Why didn't you see them when you scanned the surveillance views in your phone?"

"Because Nate must've disabled the camera in the locker area," Grant replied without breaking stride.

"But why are they getting into suits? Where are they going?"

"Away from here," Grant snapped. "Halleck wants to get away before the nanos wipe out this place."

"But where's she going? Selene won't take her."

"She's got something in mind." Why is she taking Trudy? Grant asked himself. Is Trudy working for Halleck? Is she part of this disaster? No, she couldn't be. Not Trudy. She wouldn't. She wouldn't.

And Grant realized that whether Trudy was helping Halleck or not, he was glad that she was getting away from Farside and the destructive nanomachines.

But he knew that he had to bring her back. And Halleck along with her.

Standing engulfed in a cumbersome space suit, Halleck complained to Oberman, "Can't you go any faster?"

"Gotta check out the suits," Oberman replied as he plugged the life-support backpack into the torso of Trudy's suit. "You don't want to spring any leaks out in the vacuum."

Trudy stood mutely while Oberman finished checking her suit. We're going outside, she said to herself for the hundredth time. Whether I want to or not, we're going outside.

Holding her bubble helmet in her trembling gloved hands, Trudy glanced up at the wrecked surveillance camera dangling from the stone ceiling. Oberman had ripped it loose from its mounting and smashed its lens.

"Nobody'll see us in here," he had assured Halleck.

Trudy hoped that Grant would notice the camera's failure and deduce what Halleck was up to.

Hurry up, Grant, she urged silently. Stop her before she makes me go outside.

As soon as he satisfied himself that Trudy's suit was functional, Oberman began tugging on the leggings of his own suit.

"And who checks you out?" Trudy asked softly.

Sitting on the bench as he pulled on his boots, Oberman grinned at her. "You do, honey. It's not hard to do. Just make sure all the connector lights show green. That's all there is to it."

"Then why does it take so damnably long?" Halleck demanded. Like Trudy, she was fully suited up except for her helmet.

"Don't worry, Mrs. Halleck," said Oberman. "We got plenty time."

"You may think so. I don't."

Getting to his feet, Oberman said, "Didn't you see me reset the lock when we came in here and closed the corridor door? It'll take ten, fifteen minutes for anybody to figure out the new combination." He looked quite pleased with himself.

As he reached for the hard shell of his suit's torso, Oberman went on, "All four hoppers are lined up just outside the airlock. They're all fueled and ready to go: that's standard procedure. The lobber you came in on, Mrs. Aitch, is sitting on the blast pad, so we'll have to take off from where the hopper's sitting."

"Couldn't that be a problem?" Trudy asked.

"Nope. Those little birds can take off from just about anyplace. And land anyplace. Not like the lobbers; they're too big for that. They need a nice smooth pad to sit down on."

Working his arms through the suit's sleeves, Oberman said to Trudy, "Okay, now, Dr. Yost, you pick up my backpack out of my locker and connect it onto the clips on the back of my suit."

Trudy did as she was told, seething inside with a desperate hope that Grant would break down the corridor door and save her before they forced her outside.

ESCAPE

rant skidded to a stop at the closed door to the lockers, with Cardenas a step behind him. He tapped out the entry code, but the keypad flashed red and the door remained shut. Grant tried the code again; still no good.

"That sonofabitch Oberman's changed the code," Grant muttered.

"We can't get in?" Cardenas asked.

"It'll take a few minutes," Grant muttered, flicking open his pocketphone to call up the base's central computer.

"You think they're leaving Farside?"

"What else? The question is, where the hell are they going?"

As Grant queried the central computer for the new entry code, Cardenas fidgeted nervously. "I wish there was something I could do," she said, wringing her hands.

"There is," said Grant, his eyes fixed on his phone's minuscule screen. "Get down to the maintenance center. Toshio Aichi ought to be there with a sample from the mirror lab's airlock hatch. Find out what kind of nanos drilled a hole through the hatch and how to kill them."

Cardenas's jaw dropped open. "You must be joking! How can I do anything without the proper equipment? I'd need an atomic force microscope, to begin with, and—"

"You're going to have to work with what we've got at the maintenance center, Kris. I know it's a tall order, but it's a matter of life or death. Work with Toshio, he's pretty smart."

"Grant, that's like asking a surgeon to operate on a patient blindfolded!"

He looked up from the phone screen and tapped a combination on the wall-mounted keypad. The door slid open.

Turning to Cardenas, Grant said, "You're the world's expert on nanotechnology, Kris. Prove it."

"Thanks a lot," she griped. "And what are you going to do while I'm trying to perform a miracle?"

"I'm going to get Halleck and make her tell us what kind of nanos we're up against."

With that, Grant stepped through the open doorway and into the locker area, leaving Cardenas standing in the corridor, resentful and angry because she knew Grant expected her to do the impossible.

Moving swiftly down the row of lockers, Grant saw that two of the spare space suits were gone, along with Nate Oberman's.

He ran to the end of the row, where the airlock hatch stood. Next to it was the ladder that led up to the flight control center. He grabbed one of the titanium rungs and put his foot on the bottommost. It crumbled under his weight, throwing him off balance.

The bugs are here! he realized.

Cautiously, he climbed up the remaining rungs and through the open hatch into the flight control center. Josie Rivera was still at the only operative console. She jerked with surprise as Grant clambered up beside her.

"Grant! What're you doing—"

"What's going on, Josie?" he asked.

She blinked at him. "What do you mean?"

Reaching across her to the light-dimmer dial on her console, Grant lowered the lights in the cramped chamber.

He pointed through the thick glassteel window that looked out on Farside's spaceport. The lobber from Selene still stood on the sole landing pad, but only three hoppers were lined up between the pad and the airlock's outer hatch.

"Where's the fourth hopper, Jo?"

"It . . . it's gone."

"I can see that. Who took it? What's their flight plan? Where's their manifest?"

Josie shook her head. In a small, frightened voice she answered, "I don't know."

"Josie, you're the flight controller."

"Three people came out and took off on the hopper," she said, trying to avoid Grant's eyes. "I . . . I don't know who they are. They just came out and took off, without permission."

"And you let them go? You didn't try to stop them? You didn't call me or Professor Uhlrich or anybody?"

"What could I do?" Josie wailed. "It all happened so fast. I told them to stop but they wouldn't listen!"

"Where'd they go?"

"I don't know! They wouldn't say!"

Grant saw that Josie was close to panic. She's lying, he told himself. But pressuring her isn't going to change anything. It'd just be a waste of time.

Calmly, almost gently, Grant said, "Josie, I'm going downstairs and suit up. I want you to check with the GPS satellites and get a track on that hopper. Then you come down and check me out."

"Okay, sure," she answered shakily.

"And be careful on the ladder," Grant added, almost maliciously. "The nanobugs are chewing on the rungs."

Josie's dark eyes went wide with terror.

Trudy was trying hard not to look up into the sky. As the hopper soared on its ballistic trajectory across the barren lunar landscape, Trudy looked downward at the dusty, rock-strewn, pockmarked ground. She swallowed bile, trying to keep her stomach in its place while they flew in virtually zero gravity.

It's almost two thousand klicks to Korolev, she reminded herself. It's going to take us close to an hour to get there.

An hour of standing inside this space suit, with Mrs. Halleck beside her, gripping the handrail with both her gloved fists, and Oberman standing at the control podium. I hope he knows what he's doing, Trudy thought.

As if in answer, she heard Oberman's voice in her helmet speakers, "Just checked with the GPS system. We're right on the beam for Korolev."

"Good," said Halleck. Trudy thought her voice sounded anxious, tense.

"Be there in fifty-four minutes," Oberman added.

"Good," Halleck repeated.

And what happens when we get there? Trudy wondered. How long will we have to stay cooped up in that little shelter? What's going to happen to me?

"We should've disabled the other hoppers," Oberman said, almost as if he were discussing the weather.

"There was no time for that," Halleck immediately replied. "Besides, it wasn't really necessary, was it? Who's going to come out after us?"

"Grant Simpson," Oberman said, his tone more serious. "Grant'll come charging out after us."

Trudy hoped he was right.

Cardenas stared at the thin slice of metal resting on the workbench. Toshio Aichi stood a respectful half meter from her side, saying nothing.

"That's the sample you took from the mirror lab airlock hatch," Cardenas said.

"Yes," Aichi replied.

Standing on the other side of the workbench, Delos Zacharias volunteered, "We confirmed that a nanometer-scale hole was drilled through it."

"Using your laser probe?" Cardenas asked.

"Yes," said Aichi. "It has resolution in the nanometer scale." He glanced at moon-faced Zacharias, then added, "Unfortunately, that's not good enough to give us much information about the nanomachines themselves."

Aichi's face looked like a skull with skin stretched over it, Cardenas thought. He was utterly serious, unsmiling, somber.

"Disassemblers drilled a hole all the way through the hatch."

"Pinhole," Zacharias said. "Nanometer-scale in diameter."

"Enough to cause an air leak in the mirror lab," Aichi added.

"What's the composition of this metal?" she asked.

Zacharias started to reply, but Aichi silenced him with an upraised hand. "I will call up the information from the computer files. That will give you a completely accurate report."

He stepped to the end of the workbench and spoke to the computer terminal there.

Zacharias said, "It'll take a few seconds."

Cardenas nodded.

"Here it is," said Aichi, swiveling the display screen so that Cardenas could see it.

As she studied the list, Aichi said, "May I express my pleasure at working with you, Dr. Cardenas. You are most respected."

Cardenas regarded his stiffly somber expression. "Thank you. I hope that together we can solve this problem."

"I have no doubt that you will."

Cardenas had plenty of doubt, but she accepted Aichi's compliment with a mechanical smile.

Scanning through the display screen's list, Cardenas saw that the hatch was made of an alloy of titanium, mixed with aluminum, vanadium, and several smaller components. Most of it obtained from the lunar regolith, she knew, scraped up from the topmost layer of dusty ground and refined in smelters at Selene.

"Was there any residue in the pinhole?" she asked.

"Residue?" Zacharias asked, his round face puckering into a mild frown.

Cardenas told them, "The disassemblers took apart the molecules of the hatch's alloy. They must have been programmed to look for a specific type of atom and remove it from the molecular structure."

"Ah," breathed Aichi. Zacharias nodded.

"So what happened to the atoms they removed?" Cardenas went on. "They must have been deposited inside the hole that the nanos drilled."

Aichi almost smiled. "So we should examine the hole and determine what kind of atoms are contained in the residue."

"Do you have equipment that can accomplish that?" Cardenas asked, feeling eager for the first time.

"The mass spectrograph, maybe," Zacharias suggested.

"Can you do it?"

"We can try," Aichi said. And for the first time he looked eager, too.

.   .   .

Grant stepped from the airlock and plodded toward the nearest of the hoppers.

Josie's voice sounded in his helmet earphones. "Grant, why don't you take the lobber? I can call the two guys who flew it in here and they could fly it to Korolev for you."

She's trying to make up for letting Halleck sneak out of here, Grant thought. Aloud, he replied, "No, Josie, this is our problem, not theirs. Besides, if Oberman has any sense he'll plant his hopper square in the middle of the concrete slab out at Korolev. That'll prevent a lobber from landing there. Lobbers need a pad to sit down on, they can't land on unprepared ground the way hoppers can."

"Oh," said Josie, disappointed. "Yeah."

"You just keep an eye on Korolev, kid. Let me know when they land there."

"Right."

Grant thought, Keep Josie busy. Let her use the surveillance satellites to keep track of Nate's hopper.

As he started to clamber up the ladder to the hopper's platform, Grant realized that he hadn't told Uhlrich what he was doing, what was going on.

The Ulcer would pop a blood vessel, he thought. Be better to tell McClintock. Let him tell the Ulcer.

So, once he checked out the hopper's systems, taking special care to check the propellant supply, he asked Josie to patch him through the communications satellite system to McClintock.

"You don't need the commsats," Josie said. "Your suit radio can—"

"I'm going to be over the horizon in two minutes, Jo," Grant reminded her. "Plug me through the commsats."

No answer for a heartbeat or two. Then Josie asked, her voice low, "Grant, you're not going to tell him that I let Mrs. Halleck get away, are you?"

That's what you did, isn't it? Grant thought. But he said to her, "No, Josie. He won't even think about that. I just want to tell him that Halleck flew the coop and I'm going after her."

And Trudy, he added silently. I'm going out to bring Trudy back here. I don't care if Halleck and Nate break their necks out there. I'm going to find Trudy.

"It's a minuscule sample," said Toshio Aichi.

Zacharias nodded vigorously. "I bet there's not more than a couple milligrams there."

"Will it be enough?" Cardenas wondered.

"I believe so," Aichi replied as he tapped the almost invisible sampling of dust from the filter paper in his hand into the focal point of the mass spectrometer.

Cardenas watched as Zacharias flicked on the spectrometer and the sample in its focus flashed into gas.

"Got it!" Aichi said, pumping a fist in the air.

The bright lines of an emission spectrum showed on the spectrometer's display screen.

"What did we get?" Cardenas asked.

"Hold one," said Zacharias, his chubby fingers working the keyboard. "Yeah! There it is." A comparison spectrum appeared alongside the spectrum of the sample.

"Mostly titanium," Zacharias murmured, studying the spectra. "A little aluminum . . ."

"And some vanadium and minor constituents," said Aichi.

Zacharias looked disappointed. "That's the composition of the titanium alloy that the airlock's made of."

"It doesn't tell us much," Aichi admitted.

"The disassemblers wouldn't be designed to attack all those elements," Cardenas mused, as much to herself as the two men. "They go after specific atoms, one particular element."

"But which one?" Zacharias wondered.

"Unless we know that," said Aichi, "we have no way of protecting the alloy against the nanos."

"The nanos we create at Selene are deactivated by high-energy ultraviolet light," Cardenas said.

"That probably isn't the case here," Aichi countered. "If these devices were produced by a rogue laboratory on Earth they won't have the same safeguards built into them that you would provide."

"They should have a finite lifetime, though."

Shaking his head, Aichi countered, "Only if they were designed so. That does not appear to be the case here. They have been active for several weeks."

"And it looks like they're spreading," Zacharias added.

"How do we stop them?" Aichi asked again.

Cardenas looked into his solemn dark eyes, wondering, when the answer came to her. "Elbow grease," she said, breaking into a grin. "Oil and a lot of elbow grease."

KOROLEV CRATER

tarting descent," Oberman said.

Trudy saw that the hopper was falling toward the hard, hard ground. Abruptly, a feeling of weight buckled her knees. Then it disappeared as suddenly as it came and she was weightless again. In the soundless vacuum, she heard nothing, but she knew that the hopper's braking rockets had fired.

Another jolt, longer this time. Then back to falling like a rock.

"You do know what you're doing," Halleck said, her voice sounding strained in Trudy's helmet speakers.

"It's all automatic," Oberman replied. "Preprogrammed." But he sounded uptight, too, Trudy thought.

The ground was coming up faster than ever. Trudy could see the smooth concrete slab that would one day be the foundation for the hundred-meter telescope, and the little hump of dirt that marked the buried shelter.

Weight returned, and stayed. Trudy gripped the handrail and saw the flare of the rocket engine's exhaust outlining the edge of the hopper's platform.

Then a final jar, and she felt the gentle gravity of the Moon once more. She swallowed burning bile.

"We're down," Oberman said.

"Thank goodness for small mercies," said Halleck.

Trudy saw that Oberman had landed them about fifty meters from the shelter's airlock. The concrete foundation slab sat another fifty or so meters beyond that.

"Very well," Halleck said, "let's get into the shelter and out of these damnable suits."

"Right," said Oberman. Turning to Trudy, he pointed to the ladder leading down to the ground. "Ladies first."

The three of them trudged to the shelter's airlock hatch. Oberman leaned a finger on the green pad of its control panel and the hatch slid silently open.

"Only big enough for two," he said, after a glance inside the airlock.

"Dr. Yost and I will go, then," said Halleck.

"Nope," Oberman said. "You and me, Mrs. Aitch. Trudy can wait out here."

Sudden fear surged through Trudy, close to panic. Stand outside here and wait for them? she thought. What if they don't reopen the airlock? What if something goes wrong?

Halleck was saying, "Very well, then: you and me, Mr. Oberman. Then Dr. Yost."

"Right," said Oberman, gesturing Halleck into the airlock with a gloved hand. Then he turned back to Trudy and said, "Don't go wandering off, kid." She couldn't see his face inside the helmet, but she could hear the smirk in his voice.

"They've gone to Korolev?" Sheer disbelief filled Professor Uhlrich's voice.

"That's what Grant Simpson told me," said McClintock.

The professor's face looked ash gray as he sat behind his desk.

"But why would they do this?" he asked. "How—"

"They stole a hopper and took off, the three of them, Mrs. Halleck, Dr. Yost, and one of the technicians, Oberman. I suppose he's flying the hopper."

"But why? Why?"

"Simpson believes that Mrs. Halleck is the one who brought the nanomachines here, and she wants to get away to safety. Selene won't take any flights from Farside, so she's gone to the shelter at Korolev."

In a ghostly whisper, Uhlrich said, "And she's leaving us to die here."

"That's what Simpson thinks. He's taken a hopper to go after them."

"Or to save himself," Uhlrich muttered.

McClintock said nothing.

The professor sagged back in his chair. "We're going to die. We're all going to die."

"Don't be so pessimistic, Professor," said McClintock. "I'm sure Dr. Cardenas will figure this out."

Despite his words, though, McClintock saw death approaching him.

Grant knew he was breaking just about all of Farside's safety regulations as he flew alone across the Moon's starkly beautiful land. Solo excursions are not allowed: a minimum of two people at all times. The buddy system. Yeah, but we don't have time to follow the rules.

Why did Halleck take Trudy with her? As a hostage? What're they going to do cooped up in the shelter at Korolev? Trudy and Halleck and that jerk Oberman. If Nate lays a hand on her I'll break every bone in his frigging body. Twice.

Over the curve of the horizon he saw the worn, slumped mountains of Korolev's ringwall. Then the floor of the crater came into view. And there was the hopper, parked between the foundation slab and the rounded hump of the shelter.

Dumbass Oberman didn't even have the brains to use the foundation as a landing pad, Grant said to himself.

"Well, this is cozy," Oberman said, once they had taken off their suits and peeled out of their thermal undergarments.

Trudy looked around and saw that the shelter was identical to the one at Mendeleev, strictly utilitarian: a food freezer; a microwave cooker; a table with four flimsy chairs; a desk-type console with a wall screen above it; four bunks built into the wall, two uppers and two lowers.

The tiny chamber smelled of the sharp tang of gunpowder. Their three space suits hung by the airlock hatch, their boots and leggings spattered with gray lunar dust.

"How long will we be here?" Trudy asked.

Mrs. Halleck blinked at her question. "I don't really know. I'll have to call Selene and ask for an emergency rescue flight."

"Do you think they'd come here?"

"They'll have to! They can't leave us here to die. I'm not some anonymous technician. I'll call the chief administrator of the IAA if I have to."

Trudy wished she felt as confident as Mrs. Halleck. But she's an important person, Trudy told herself. She's right. I'm just an anonymous astronomer, as far as the rest of the world is concerned. But she's important. They'll send a flight here to rescue her. And the two of us with her.

Oberman sat on the edge of one of the lower-tier bunks. "Okay, Mrs. Aitch," he said, pointing to the console and its computer. "You start calling." With a leering grin in Trudy's direction, he went on, "I suppose we'll hafta spend a couple of nights here."

Grant landed the hopper squarely in the center of the foundation slab, then climbed down the hopper's ladder and stepped to the edge of the concrete. He hopped down to the ground in dreamy lunar slow motion and strode toward the shelter's airlock, kicking up puffs of dust with each step.

Nobody's going to land a lobber there, he said to himself, with grim satisfaction. If anybody's going to leave here, they're going out with me.

He reached the hopper Oberman had used and ducked beneath its platform. It was awkward work in the space suit, but Grant managed to open the liquid oxygen tank enough to start a thin stream of LOX leaking out of it. The cryogenic fluid flashed into the vacuum immediately. Nodding inside his helmet, Grant said to himself, Nate won't be able to go anywhere with that bird.

CONFRONTATION

Anita Halleck stared at the grainy image in the shelter's phone screen. Her personal assistant, a smooth-faced Vietnamese sitting safe in his office back in Zurich, looked slightly perturbed.

"It's the weekend here, Mrs. Halleck," he explained. "The IAA's chief administrator is at his home in Buenos Aires. That's a five-hour time difference from here, you understand. Most of her staff has gone for the weekend, scattered all across the map."

"You must get to her at once," Halleck demanded, her voice iron hard, "and get her to contact Selene's governing council and arrange a rescue flight here. My life depends on it."

"Yes, ma'am, I'll do my very best," said her assistant.

"Good."

His left eyebrow arching a bare millimeter, the assistant added, "It might take a little time, however."

Halleck's lips compressed into a thin, angry line. Then she replied, "This is an emergency. You stay on the phone until Selene tells you when I can expect a flight to land here and rescue me."

"Of course, Mrs. Halleck."

"And keep me informed every step of the way."

"Certainly, ma'am."

Halleck cut the connection and swiveled the desk chair to face Trudy and Oberman. "Bureaucrats," she muttered.

"But they'll send a lobber here, won't they?" Trudy asked, trying to keep the fear out of her voice.

"Sooner or later," said Halleck.

Still sitting on the lower bunk, Oberman shrugged unconcernedly. "We're going to be here for a couple of days, I bet. Might as well make ourselves comfortable." He patted the mattress and grinned again at Trudy.

Trudy turned away from him, but Halleck said, "I suppose you're right."

"Could be fun, the three of us together," said Oberman.

Halleck glared at him. "Don't be ridiculous."

Before Oberman could reply, Trudy noticed that the light on the control pad on the wall next to the airlock hatch suddenly went from green to amber. Before she could say anything, it flicked to red.

Halleck noticed it, too. "Someone's using the airlock!"

Oberman jumped to his feet. "Grant," he muttered. "Gotta be."

The three of them stared at the control pad as it cycled from red through amber and finally to green once again. The hatch slid open and a space-suited figure stepped into the shelter. It was impossible to make out his face behind the heavily tinted bubble of his helmet but Trudy read the name tag on the chest of his grimy suit: SIMPSON.

"Grant?" Trudy called.

The figure unlocked the helmet and lifted it off his head. Grant Simpson's darkly bearded face looked grim.

"Grant!" Trudy said again, a gust of relief surging through her. She ran to him.

Oberman's eyes flicked around the room.

"Sit down, Nate," Grant commanded. "Just sit down and you won't get hurt."

"Whattaya mean?" Oberman asked. But he sat back on the bunk.

Turning to Trudy, Grant asked, "You okay?"

"Yes," she said.

"Help me out of this suit."

Trudy moved behind him. Oberman remained seated on his

bunk, Halleck stood uncertainly by the console. As Trudy un-latched the life-support backpack, the phone chimed.

"Go ahead and answer it," Grant told Halleck.

She turned and pressed the keypad. A woman's face appeared on the screen: sleek chestnut hair perfectly coiffed, golden tan, wearing an expensive-looking blouse of sky blue. She looked distressed.

"Mrs. Halleck, your assistant said you're in trouble? Some sort of emergency?"

Grant strode to the desk, clomping in his space suit's boots. "There's been a mistake, ma'am. Mrs. Halleck isn't in trouble."

"And who are you?" the woman asked. "What's this—"

Grant cut the connection. Then he smashed the phone screen with a gloved fist. It exploded in shards of plastic.

Halleck shrieked, "What are you doing?"

"Have you ever heard of 'roid rage?" Grant asked, smiling maliciously. "I've been taking steroids for a long time, lady, and I'm getting goddamned furious with you."

Oberman got to his feet. "Hold on, Grant. Take it easy."

Faster than Trudy thought possible for a man wearing a space suit, Grant crossed the tiny shelter in four swift steps and swung his still-gloved right fist into Oberman's face before the man could raise his hands to defend himself. The solid *thunk* of the blow made Trudy wince. Oberman's head snapped back and he toppled backward onto the bunk.

Stomping back toward Halleck, Grant said, "I want to know what your nanobugs are all about. Now!"

Halleck cringed back toward the desk. "You're insane!"

Grant picked up the flimsy desk chair and threw it across the shelter. It banged against the airlock hatch.

"Now, dammit!" he roared. "Start talking."

Halleck's eyes were wide with fright, but she sputtered, "I . . . I don't know what you're talking about."

Grant gripped her shoulder painfully and forced her to sit on the edge of the console.

"You brought the nanomachines to Farside," he said, "and you got that idiot to spread them around for you."

"I . . ." Halleck's voice froze in her throat.

"What do the nanos do? How long do they last? What are they programmed for?"

"You're hurting me!"

"I'll break both your fucking arms," Grant snarled.

Trudy went to him. "Grant, please!"

He pushed her away. Turning back to Halleck, "I want the truth out of you, lady. The truth, or so help me you'll die right here and now."

Anita Halleck fainted.

Grant let Halleck slide slowly to the floor.

Trudy looked from her unconscious body to Oberman, still sprawled across the bunk, and then stared into Grant's darkly frightening face.

"Grant . . . you'll kill her!"

He scowled down at Halleck's body, then said to Trudy, "Help me out of this suit."

He peeled off his gloves and Trudy helped lift the hard shell of the suit's torso over his head. Halleck remained on the floor, her eyes shut. Oberman groaned and tried to sit up. He slid off the bunk and onto the floor.

"Throw some water on her," Grant said to Trudy.

Halleck's eyes snapped open.

With a glance at Oberman, who sat at the foot of the bunk rubbing his bruised jaw, Grant slid his arms under Halleck's shoulders and hauled her to her feet. Trudy rushed to the desk chair, righted it, and rolled it toward them.

Grant pushed Halleck roughly onto the chair. She glared up at him.

"You were going to tell me about the nanomachines," Grant said.

Halleck tried to stare Grant down, but failed. She dropped her chin and muttered, "No one was supposed to get hurt."

"Three people have been killed," Grant said.

Nodding, Halleck said, "That's not my fault. It wasn't supposed to happen that way."

"What kind of nanomachines are they?"

"Gobblers, of a sort. All they're supposed to do is to attack vanadium atoms. They told me that would cause only very minor damage, not enough to hurt anyone."

Grant shook his head wearily. "We're living on the edge of vacuum out here. Don't you realize that *normal* conditions on the Moon are only a centimeter away from sudden death?"

Halleck tried to look defiant, but instead her expression melted into a guilty downcast.

"Why?" Trudy blurted. "Why would you want to hurt us?"

Halleck made a bleak smile. "You don't understand any of this, do you? You don't understand a thing."

"Enlighten us," said Trudy.

Before Halleck could reply, though, Grant interrupted. "I need to know what the nanos are programmed to do, how long they'll remain active, how to deactivate them."

"As I told you, they're programmed to attack vanadium atoms. That's all. The people at the laboratory I used told me that the quantity they gave me could cause pinhole leaks in titanium alloys, produce air leaks. Nothing catastrophic, just enough to cause panic at Farside."

"How long will they be active?"

With an almost careless shrug, Halleck said, "A few weeks, if I remember correctly."

"And they're not deactivated by ultraviolet light, are they?"

"Of course not. There's no built-in way to deactivate them, from what they told me. You have to wait until their programmed lifespan ends."

"That means we'll have to abandon Farside," Grant muttered. "Temporarily, at least."

"I didn't mean for them to cause so much damage," Halleck said, as if apologizing for spilling milk. "I only wanted to slow Professor Uhlrich's work."

"But why?" Trudy repeated.

Halleck answered, "Morgan McClintock humiliated me. I decided that turnabout is fair play."

"Morgan . . . ?"

"Carter's father. He's pouring money into Uhlrich's program so that Farside can be the first to obtain imagery of New Earth. And why? To hurt me. To make me look bad in the eyes of the IAA, of the whole world!"

"That's why McClintock's at Farside?" Grant asked.

"Why else? Carter has no interest in astronomy. He's there to look after his father's interests. Well, I thought it would be poetic justice if Farside failed. Failed miserably."

"For your own personal satisfaction?" Trudy was aghast.

"What better reason could there be?" Halleck replied.

But Grant said, "There's big money tied up in the IAA's program. If Farside can do the job the IAA would drop its program."

"And leave me looking ridiculous," said Halleck.

"And the corporations that're working on your program would have their contracts canceled," Grant added. "They wouldn't like you for that."

Halleck glared at him, but said nothing.

Across the tiny room, Oberman pushed himself to his feet and tottered to the lavatory, still rubbing his jaw.

Grant said, "I have to contact Farside and tell the professor what's going on. They'll have to abandon the site for a couple of weeks."

"And go where?" Trudy asked. "Selene won't take us."

"Yes they will. Now that we know what we're up against, Selene's safety people can screen each one of us to make sure we're not carrying the gobblers."

"Dr. Cardenas is still at Farside," Trudy recalled. "Maybe she can run the screening operation."

"Good," said Grant. "I'll call the Ulcer and tell him that—"

He got no further. Oberman dashed out of the lavatory, a heavy wrench in his hand, and smashed Grant across the back of his head. Grant fell facedown to the floor, unconscious, his scalp bleeding heavily.

FARSIDE

feel stupid," muttered Harvey Henderson as he smeared machine oil across the face of the mirror lab's airlock.

Josie Rivera, working alongside him, said, "You'll feel a lot worse if the airlock springs another leak."

Ten engineers and technicians were industriously covering the airlock's titanium-alloy face with oil. Every man and woman at Farside was coating every titanium surface in the base with oil or margarine or even liquid detergent.

"The Ulcer's gone off the deep end," Henderson complained, "ordering us to do this." Still, he assiduously swept his oil-soaked cloth across the face of the hatch. His hands felt greasy, slimy, and he knew that the coveralls he was wearing were getting stained with oil.

Several of the technicians were on ladders, reaching to the top rim of the hatch, rubbing away and dripping oil down on them.

Rivera reminded him, "Dr. Cardenas says the way to stop the nanobugs from eating holes in the titanium is to coat the metal with oil. The bugs attack bare metal; if the metal's covered with oil the bugs won't bother it."

"That's what she says," Henderson grumbled.

"She's the expert." Rivera turned to the oil dispenser lying on the floor at her feet and bent down to soak the cloth she was using again. Suddenly she broke into a giggle.

"What's funny?" Henderson asked.

"My grandmother," said Rivera, still chuckling. "She worked all her life as a housecleaner. If she could see me now! All my

education, my degree in engineering, getting a job on the Moon—
and here I am, doing the same kind of work she did!"

Henderson didn't find it funny. "I still feel stupid," he groused.

Kris Cardenas stepped into Professor Uhlrich's office, looking intently determined despite her faded, wrinkled coveralls. Her
golden hair was tied up in a no-nonsense upsweep and she carried
a plastic container tucked under her arm.

Carter McClintock, sitting at the table abutting the professor's desk, stared at her.

"Dr. Cardenas?" he asked, looking surprised. "What are you
carrying?"

"Cooking oil from the cafeteria's kitchen," Cardenas replied
with a tight smile.

"Cooking oil?" Uhlrich asked from behind his desk. As usual,
he was wearing a dark jacket over a turtleneck shirt. His silver-
gray hair and beard were combed impeccably.

"For you two gentlemen," said Cardenas, putting the container on the table in front of McClintock. "You can start rubbing
down the emergency airlock hatches along the main corridor."

"I?" Uhlrich blurted. "You expect me—"

"Everyone else is working at it," Cardenas said firmly. "Even
Edie Elgin's out there swabbing away at the exposed metal parts
of the space suits hanging in the lockers."

McClintock slowly rose from his chair. Like Professor Uhlrich, he wore a businessman's jacket and slacks. "I get it." Turning
to Uhlrich, he explained, "This will be good for the staff, Professor, to see us at work alongside them. Shoulder to shoulder, working together. That sort of thing. I'll get this Elgin woman to take
photos of us. Good public relations!"

Cardenas almost laughed. "I hadn't thought of the morale
aspect. I need every hand available in this base. There's a lot of
metal that the nanomachines can attack. I just hope we have
enough oils and greases to cover all the exposed metal around
here."

Uhlrich slowly stood up and came around his desk, the fingers of one hand brushing the desktop. Very reluctantly, he stepped up to Cardenas.

"Very well," he said, like a man forced into a distasteful chore, "tell me where you want us to work."

"Down the main corridor. Cover the emergency airlock hatches and any other exposed metal surfaces you see."

"I'll work with you, Professor," said McClintock. "We'll be a team."

Uhlrich hesitated. He asked Cardenas, "Have you heard anything from Simpson? I thought he'd gone out to Korolev to confront Mrs. Halleck."

Cardenas shook her head. "No. Not a word from Grant. I wonder what's going on out there?"

KOROLEV

Grant came to slowly. His head thundered with pain, his vision was blurred. He squeezed his eyes shut, then opened them again. Trudy's face came into focus, taut and white with anxiety. She was bending over him, holding a towel or something to the back of his head.

"What happened?" he asked thickly.

Trudy replied, "Oberman found a wrench from the tool closet in the lav and hit you with it."

Grant tried to sit up, but the world swam dizzily around him and his guts heaved.

"Stay down, Grant," Trudy urged. "You must have a concussion. Maybe he fractured your skull."

"Where . . . where is he?"

"He ripped up the sleeves on our suits! The emergency suits in the locker, too! We can't go outside! We're stranded here!"

Grant saw that she was trying to control herself, trying to hold down the fear, the panic.

"It figures," he said, his voice weak from the pain. "They don't want . . . any witnesses. Halleck . . . told us too much."

"Then they put on their suits and left," Trudy went on. "They just went into the airlock a second ago."

With an effort, Grant focused his eyes on the airlock control pad. He saw its light flick from green to red.

"They've gone outside," he said.

"Nate was really distressed, kind of wild. He said he's taking Mrs. Halleck to Gagarin, they'll stay in the shelter there until she can get Selene or the IAA or somebody to send a rescue flight to them."

"And they left us here to die," Grant muttered. Yeah, he told himself, that's what Nate would do. Run away and hide. Then he remembered.

"Trudy . . . have you told Cardenas . . . about the gobblers? What Halleck told us?"

"No. There hasn't been time."

"You've got to call her."

"How?" she asked. "The phone's smashed."

"Thanks to me."

"Could we use the radio in one of the space suits?"

Grant started to nod, but the movement sent white-hot streaks of pain through his head. "Maybe," he said weakly, wondering, Is the signal from the suit radio strong enough to get through the shelter's concrete shell and the rubble piled on top of it?

"I don't know what else we can do," Trudy said.

"Pull my suit torso . . . over here and connect . . . the backpack to it. Maybe there's enough juice . . . left in the batteries . . . to get through to the commsats."

Suddenly all the lights in the shelter turned off.

Nate Oberman nodded inside his bubble helmet as he disconnected the power cable leading from the array of solar cells to the shelter.

"That'll do it," he muttered, more to himself than Anita Halleck, standing in her space suit between him and the hopper. "The shelter's batteries'll only last a few hours."

"Let's get out of here," Halleck urged.

"Right." Oberman straightened up and headed for the hopper.

She followed him, thinking, We've taken care of Simpson and Dr. Yost, but now this man is a witness to everything.

Oberman reached the hopper and started up its ladder without a backward glance at her.

On the other hand, Halleck told herself as she put a booted foot on the ladder's first rung, he's a party to the crime. He's helped me from the beginning, and he actually did attack Simpson.

"You may have killed him, you know," Halleck grumbled as they clambered up to the hopper's grillwork platform.

"They're as good as dead, one way or the other. Their electric power'll run out in a couple hours."

And Halleck thought, He'll be able to hold this over me for the rest of my life. I've got to find a way to get rid of him.

"We've got to get over to Gagarin," Oberman was saying. "There's a shelter there just like the one here."

I can accuse him of murdering Simpson and Yost, Halleck told herself. I never told him to do that. I can show myself as the innocent victim of a homicidal madman.

Oberman clomped to the control podium and lifted up its cover.

"What are you doing?" Halleck asked.

"Hot-wiring the ignition. I don't want to turn on the normal controls. Soon as we do, the hopper's beacon will automatically turn on. Then the controller at Farside will know exactly when we left here."

"So what?"

"So they'll be able to figure out that Grant and Yost were still alive when we left, that's what. This way, we can fudge our departure time, tell them they were already dead and we got away from here to save our own lives."

Halleck thought his reasoning was very thin, but Oberman was at least partially right: they had to cover up the two deaths. Two murders, she realized. I'm a murderess! But no, it's not me. He did it, I didn't. I'm going along with him because he might kill me too if I don't do what he wants.

She was still rehearsing the story she would tell the investigators when her suit radio pinged.

"Someone's calling," Halleck said, sounding alarmed.

Oberman heard it, too. "It's gotta be Grant. Ignore it."

But Halleck tapped the radio control on her suit's wrist keypad.

The shelter's lights came on again in a heartbeat, but they seemed dimmer.

"We're on battery power," Grant said weakly. "Nate's disconnected . . . the solar cells."

"How long will the batteries last?" Trudy asked, her voice trembling slightly.

"Five hours, max."

"Then we'll be out of power? The lights, the air recirculator, the heater?"

"Better get the suit radio working," Grant said.

Trudy dragged the suit torso and backpack across the room to where Grant lay on his back, feeling like a helpless invalid, while she connected the backpack.

She looked up from the suit with a little smile. "The lights are all green."

"Okay, good." The pain came in waves, making him almost giddy. "Hand me the . . . the sleeve with the keypad on it."

Trudy grabbed the sleeve and held it over Grant's face. He saw that the sleeve had been methodically ripped to tatters, making the suit useless. Almost useless, he corrected himself. Blinking his eyes, Grant tried to focus on the keypad. Very carefully he tapped out the communications link with Farside. Each movement of his fingers brought a fresh surge of pain washing over him.

"Farside," a voice issued from the speakers in the suit's neck ring.

With an enormous effort, Grant said, "This is . . . Grant Simpson. Patch me through to Dr. Cardenas. Right away. Top emergency priority."

A moment's hesitation. "Dr. Cardenas isn't in her quarters, Grant."

He recognized the man's voice. "Find her, Sherry. Call her pocketphone. Life and death, man."

"Right."

Within moments, Cardenas's voice, high with anticipation, called, "Grant?"

"It's me," he answered weakly.

"What've you found out?"

"They're gobblers. They attack vanadium atoms."

"Vanadium! Of course. Pull the vanadium out of the alloy and the molecules collapse."

"Right," he breathed. "UV doesn't kill them."

"What's their lifespan?"

"Four weeks, maybe a little more." He took a painful breath. "Tell Uhlrich he'll have to . . . get everybody out of the base until—"

"No, no, we won't have to do that." Even in the tiny speakers of the space suit, Cardenas's voice sounded bright, strong. "We're covering every metal surface in the place with oil. That'll protect it from the disassemblers. I've put in a call to Selene for more oil."

"They won't send a flight—"

"Unmanned lobber," Cardenas interrupted. "One-way flight. I talked with Doug Stavenger. He'll get it done."

"Good," Grant said, with the last of his strength.

"We need medical help," Trudy said urgently. "Grant's got a bad concussion. Maybe a skull fracture."

Cardenas immediately replied, "I'll see to it."

"We're running on battery power here," Trudy added. "We've only got a few hours left."

"I'll get help to you right away," Cardenas said.

As she signed off Grant eased his head back on the towel or whatever Trudy had wadded on the back of his head. She'll be okay, he told himself. Farside will send a hopper out to here to pick us up. Trudy'll be okay. He closed his eyes. All Grant wanted was to sleep, to tumble into blessed oblivion, to have the murderous pain go away.

But suddenly he snapped his eyes wide open.

"Nate's taking the hopper?" he asked Trudy. "The one you rode in here on?"

She looked perplexed. "I guess."

"Get him on the radio! Freak two. Now!"

As Trudy obediently picked up the space suit sleeve again she said to Grant, "Lie back. You need to rest."

"Get Nate on freak two," he insisted. "He can't use that hopper. I disabled it."

"Then he'll use the one you came in on," she said.

"If he's smart . . . that's what he'll do. But Nate isn't that—"

Halleck's impatient voice came through the speakers. "What do you want?"

Oberman heard Grant's voice in his suit speakers.

"Don't try to take off . . . in that hopper!"

"So you're awake, huh?" Oberman said. "I always thought you had a thick skull."

"Nate, don't light up . . . that hopper! There isn't enough oxy to—"

"No use begging me, Grant. I'm not taking you or Miss Goody-Goody with us."

"You can't—"

Oberman held his gloved thumb over the control panel's ignition button. "So long, pal," he said to Grant. "Hope I didn't crack your skull."

"Don't!"

To Halleck, Oberman said, "Hang on." And he leaned his thumb against the ignition button.

The hopper lurched off the ground in total silence. The ground fell away.

"We're off!" Oberman said. "Next stop, Gagarin!"

Suddenly the thrust cut off. For a terrifying instant the hopper seemed to hang in space, hovering a few hundred meters above the hard, stony ground.

Then it plunged downward, falling like a stone.

Halleck screamed. Oberman had time to screech "Shit!" before the hopper hit the ground and smashed into pieces.

· · ·

Grant stared at Trudy as he heard Oberman's arrogant, "We're off! Next stop, Gagarin!"

He thought, Maybe there's enough LOX in the pipeline to—

Then he heard Halleck's scream and the radio link abruptly cut off. On the airless Moon, the hopper's crash made no sound at all.

Trudy looked stricken. "Are they . . . ?"

"They're dead," Grant said, miserable with sudden guilt. "I killed them."

The last of his strength seemed to leave him. He faded into unconsciousness.

rant faded in and out of consciousness. Vaguely he was aware of somebody bending over him. Not Trudy.

"Pretty bad," he heard a voice mutter. Dr. Kapstein. Ridiculously, Grant wondered if she'd thrown up again in her space suit on the way over from Farside.

With Trudy helping, Kapstein and whoever else had come to Korolev with her worked Grant into a fresh space suit. He felt them lift his pain-wracked body and carry him to the shelter's airlock. The pain seemed to be easing, but he felt woozy, as if he were muffled in cotton batting. Painkillers, he thought; Kapstein's pumped me full of painkillers.

When he opened his eyes again he saw that he was in the locker area at Farside. Kapstein and Trudy and even Carter McClintock were looking down at him. His nose wrinkled.

"Smells like . . . salad dressing . . ."

Kris Cardenas's youthful face bent over him. "Stopgap defense against the disassemblers," she said. "We used all the salad oil in the kitchen, and lots of other oils."

"Great . . ."

Dr. Kapstein's face looked grim. "We've got to get you to Selene."

"But . . . quarantine . . ."

"The quarantine's lifted," Cardenas said. "Now that we know what we're looking for, Selene's open again."

"Good."

Kapstein said to Cardenas, "Whatever you put into him probably has saved his life."

"Therapeutic nanomachines," Cardenas said.

"They stopped his bleeding and even reduced the subcranial
edema."

With a knowing smile, Cardenas said, "My little nanobugs
have their uses."

Edie Elgin rode back to Selene with Grant. Trudy wanted to go,
too, but Uhlrich insisted there was too much work to be done for
him to allow her to leave Farside.

Grant rode on one of the lobber's passenger compartment
seats, tilted back almost flat. Sitting on the seat next to him, Edith
shook her head mournfully.

"The biggest news story since the war, and I can't say a peep
about it," she complained. "Even my husband has told me to keep
quiet about it."

Feeling light-headed, but free of pain, Grant asked, "How can
you cover up Mrs. Halleck's death?"

"Hopper accident," Edith said with a shrug. "Blame it on the
guy she was with, that Oberman fellow."

It was really my fault, Grant told himself. But he said nothing
to Edie Elgin.

Kris Cardenas stayed at Farside, supervising the cleanup as the
vanadium-gobbling nanomachines ran to the end of their programmed lifespans and went inert. Grant fidgeted in his hospital
bed, wondering how his people were getting along without him.

By the time he was able to walk and exercise normally, Trudy
flew in to see him.

Grant was sitting up in his bed, watching a news broadcast on
the wall-mounted television set when she appeared at the door of
his hospital room, looking bright and fresh and totally happy. He
jumped out of bed as she ran to him. They embraced and kissed
and he reveled in the warmth of her.

Then he realized he was wearing a ridiculous flimsy hospital gown, open at the back.

"I'm not dressed very well," he said, grinning.

"You look great to me," said Trudy.

"My head's okay," he told her as he led her to the only chair in the room. "The medics say the nanomachines inside me accelerated my healing. I ought to be going back to Farside tomorrow."

"I know. I came to see you and go back with you."

"Uhlrich let you go?" Grant asked as he sat on the edge of the bed.

Nodding, she replied, "The professor is just about delirious. Carter's decided that the McClintock Trust will fully fund Farside's operations for the next five years. We won't need to beg money from Selene."

"No wonder he's happy."

"And my paper . . ." She hesitated, then amended, "*Our* paper on the composition of New Earth's atmosphere has been favorably refereed. It'll be in the next issue of the *International Astrophysics Letters!*"

"That's terrific," Grant said. "Your first published paper."

"And it's an important one. The professor's pushing to finish the 'scopes at Korolev and Gagarin. Once we get all three working together, we'll be able to produce detailed imagery of the planet's surface."

"And the Ulcer will get his Nobel Prize after all."

"Looks like," said Trudy.

Grant felt his brows knitting into a scowl. "But it's not fair. You're doing the work. He's just sitting on his butt and taking the credit. What do you get, Trudy?"

She got up from the chair and came smiling to the bed and sat down beside Grant.

"I get you," said Trudy. "The professor can have his Nobel. I get the real prize."

EPILOGUE:
SIX YEARS LATER

The sign on the office door was spanking new:

T. YOST
DIRECTOR
ANGEL OBSERVATORY

Trudy felt weird sitting at the desk that she still thought of as Professor Uhlrich's. As soon as Grant came into the office with their daughter she got up, came around the desk, and sat with her husband and three-year-old Gwen on the side of the long table facing the softly glowing wall screen.

Grant leaned across Gwen to give Trudy a peck on the lips. The little girl fidgeted in the chair between her parents.

"The ceremony will be starting in a few minutes," Trudy said.

Grant glowered at her darkly. "I still think you're the one who ought to get the prize. Or at least he should've told them he'd share it with you."

"We've been over that a zillion times, Grant. Let the professor have his moment of glory."

Before Grant could say anything more, Trudy called out, "Display Sirius C."

The wall screen instantly showed an image of the planet: lush green landforms and deeply blue oceans, decked with streams of white clouds.

"New Earth!" Gwen pointed a chubby finger at the display.

Grant stared at the image, knowing that it was the result of more than a year's worth of painstaking work, taking the interference patterns from Farside's trio of telescopes and meticulously building up a visual image of the exoplanet.

"That's right, dear," Trudy said to her daughter. "That's what Mommy is studying."

Grant said, "I'll take you to Selene, Gwennie, and show you the ship they're building. It's going to take people to New Earth."

"Me too?"

Grant laughed. "Maybe. Not the first ship out, but maybe someday."

Trudy told Gwen, "You can go if you want to, darling. You can go as far as your dreams take you."

Nearly four hundred thousand kilometers from Farside, the Stockholm Symphony Hall was filled to capacity. Standing in his formal white-tie and tails with the eight other Nobel laureates as they waited offstage, Jason Uhlrich could hear the audience's murmurings; he pictured a vast sea of people come from all over the world to witness the ceremony.

The personal aide that the Nobel Foundation had given him was at Uhlrich's side, ready to guide him to the chair waiting for him on the stage. Uhlrich was determined to walk in unassisted.

I did it in the rehearsal this morning, he told himself. *I have the layout of the stage pictured in my mind perfectly.*

"Professor Jason Uhlrich, astrophysics," called the master of ceremonies.

Uhlrich pulled his arm away from the aide's hand and strode out onto the stage, carefully counting his steps. A wave of applause rose from the audience, and he felt tears in his sightless eyes. He smelled the profusion of flowers banked along the rear of the stage but the sensation produced no image in his visual cortex.

He sat and waited while the other laureates came in, one by one, and introductory speeches were made. When it came time to receive the actual award from the king of Sweden, Uhlrich rose to his feet and walked to the podium in measured steps. Behind him, he knew, a giant LCD screen had been lowered to show images of Sirius C. He heard the audience gasp as the images appeared on the screen.

The king congratulated him and handed him the surprisingly heavy portfolio containing the gold memorial medal and a paper-thin flexible display screen that also showed images of the planet produced by the Farside interferometer.

Jason Uhlrich stood before the hushed audience while behind him a picture of an achingly beautiful world of green continents and blue oceans, dotted with white clouds, held the audience, the functionaries of the Nobel Foundation, the king of Sweden, the other Nobel laureates, and the whole world in rapt awe.

New Earth. A world like our own. Unpopulated, no cities, no sign of intelligent life. The Cyclops radio telescope array had scanned the planet thoroughly; it was silent.

But it was a world strikingly similar to our own.

A new world. Beckoning.

TOR

Award-winning authors
Compelling stories

Please join us at the website
below for more information
about this author and other great
Tor selections, and to sign up for
our monthly newsletter!